Titles by Rachel Lynn Solomon

The Ex Talk

Weather Girl

Weather Girl

RACHEL LYNN SOLOMON

PENGUIN BOOKS

PENGUIN BOOKS

UK | USA | Canada | Ireland | Australia
India | New Zealand | South Africa

Penguin Books is part of the Penguin Random House group of companies
whose addresses can be found at global.penguinrandomhouse.com

First published in the United States of America by Berkley,
an imprint of Penguin Random House LLC 2022
Published in Penguin Books 2022
007

Printed and bound in Great Britain by Clays Ltd, Elcograf S.p.A.

The authorized representative in the EEA is Penguin Random House Ireland,
Morrison Chambers, 32 Nassau Street, Dublin D02 YH68

A CIP catalogue record for this book is available from the British Library

ISBN: 978-1-405-95472-3

www.greenpenguin.co.uk

Penguin Random House is committed to a sustainable future for our business, our readers and our planet. This book is made from Forest Stewardship Council® certified paper.

Every time it rains
You're here in my head
Like the sun coming out
I just know that something good is gonna happen

–"Cloudbusting," Kate Bush

For anyone searching for light in the dark,
you deserve every good thing

Dear Reader,

The idea for *Weather Girl* lived in my head for a couple years before I started writing it, and it's been a romantic comedy ever since my first lightning strike of inspiration—one with no shortage of climate-related puns. In the middle of the drafting process, it also became a romantic comedy with a depressed protagonist.

On paper, it sounds like those two things shouldn't mix. Rom-coms are escapist and exciting and often full of hijinks. And yet what I've loved the most about them as we've seen this category evolve is their capacity to balance those wild, escapist plots with the kind of realism I used to avoid in my storytelling. For a while, I've written about Jewish characters whose backgrounds are similar to mine, but it's rarer for me to explore mental health in a way that comes close to my own experience.

In *Weather Girl*, Ari's depression is mostly manageable, and it's taken nearly a decade for her to get to that point. There are also complications with her family and relationship history she works to untangle over the course of the book. I tried to write her depression with care and sensitivity, with the understanding that this illness doesn't have a magic cure. That said, Ari's experience is not every experience, and each mental health journey looks different. Very few, including mine, are a straight line.

More than anything, I wanted this book to highlight a neurodiverse heroine who happens to be on medication and in therapy falling in love and thriving. I wanted to show the messy, heavy parts of her life alongside the moments that sweep her off her feet. And I wanted a hero who'd love her through her dark days, not despite them—because to me, that is the most romantic thing of all.

With so much love,
Rachel

If any of this subject matter is triggering to you, please be gentle with yourself while reading. The following resources are available.

Crisis Text Line: text SHOUT to 85258

National Suicide Prevention Helpline UK: 0800 689 5652

Samaritans Helpline: 116 123

1

FORECAST:

Cloudy with a chance of public humiliation

THERE'S SOMETHING ESPECIALLY lovely about an overcast day. Clouds dipped in ink, the sky ready to crack open. The air turning crisp and sweet. It's magic, the way the world seems to pause for a few moments right before a downpour, and I can never get enough of that heady anticipation—this sense that something extraordinary is about to happen.

Sometimes I think I could live in those moments forever.

"What was that?" my brother asks from the driver's seat. It's possible I've just let out a contented sigh. "Are you getting emotional about rain again?"

I've been staring—well, gazing—out the window as the early morning sky surrenders to a drizzle. "No. That doesn't sound like something I'd do."

Because it's not just that I'm emotional about rain. It's that rain means the thrill of tracking a cold front as it moves in from the Pacific.

It means knee-high boots and cable-knit sweaters, and it's simply a fact that those are the best clothes. I don't make the rules.

For so many people, weather is small talk, the thing you discuss when you've run out of conversation topics at a party or you're on a first date with a guy who lives in his parents' basement and thinks you two could be really happy down there together. *Can you believe the weather we're having?* It's a source of joy or frustration, but rarely anything in the middle.

It's never been small talk for me. Even if we're due for six more months of gloom, I always miss it when summer comes.

"You're lucky I love you so much." Alex rakes a hand through the sleep-mussed red hair we almost share, only his is auburn and mine is a bright shock of ginger. "We'd just gotten past Orion's fear of the dark, but now Cassie's up at five if we're lucky, four-thirty if we're not. No one's getting any sleep in the Abrams-Delgado house."

"I told you she's a little meteorologist in training." I adore my brother's five-year-old twins, and not just because they're named after constellations. "Don't tell her we have to do our own hair and makeup. Ruins the illusion."

"She has to watch you every morning before preschool. Dinosaur-shaped pancakes and Aunt Ari on the TV."

"The way God intended."

"I must not have been paying attention that day in Hebrew school." Alex stifles a yawn as we jigsaw around Green Lake. He lives on the Eastside and works in South Seattle, so he picked me up in my tree-lined Ravenna neighborhood and will drop me off at the station when we're done.

His clock is always six minutes fast because Alex loves the extra motivation in the mornings. Right now it reads 6:08—usually late for me, but thanks to one of Torrance's last-minute schedule changes, I won't be on camera until the afternoon. I might end up staying awake for a full twenty hours, but my body's gotten used to me messing with its internal clock. Mostly.

Still, imagining my tiny perfect niece transfixed by a weather report warms the very center of my heart.

Once upon a time, I did the exact same thing.

"Relax. It's going to be great," Alex says as I fidget with the zipper on my waterproof jacket, and then with the necklace buried in the fuzz of my sweater. I only roped him into this because I didn't want to do it alone, but there's always been a whisper-thin line between excitement and anxiety for me.

Even if my tells weren't so obvious, he'd be able to sense my emotions with his eyes closed. At thirty, Alex is three years older than I am, but people used to think we were fraternal twins because we were inseparable as kids. That morphed into a friendly rivalry as teens, especially since we were in the habit of crushing on the same boys—most notably, this Adonis of a track star named Kellen who had no idea we existed, despite our appearance at every one of his meets to cheer him on. This was made clear on the day of the state championships, when I showed up with flowers and Alex with balloons, and Kellen blinked his gorgeous tide pool eyes at us and said, "Hey, do we go to the same school?"

Reluctantly, I allow the swish of the windshield wipers to lull me into a false sense of calm. We head north up Aurora, past billboards for the Pacific Science Center, for gutter cleaners, for a guy who could be either a personal injury lawyer or a pro wrestler, given the way his face is twisted in a scowl. A cluster of car dealerships, and then—

"Oh my god, there it is. Stop the car. Stop the car!"

"You're not allowed to yell like that when I'm driving," Alex says, even as he stomps the brake, his Prius tossing me against the door. "Christ, I thought I'd hit something."

"Yes. My ego. It's shattered."

He swerves into the parking lot of a twenty-four-hour donut shop, sliding into a spot that gives us an unobstructed view of my very first billboard.

WAKE UP WITH KSEA 6 AT 5! WE'RE ALWAYS HERE 4 YOU, it proclaims in aggressively bold letters. And there's our Colgate-toothed weekday morning team, all of us looking natural and not at all uncomfortably posed: *Chris Torres, news. Russell Barringer, sports. Meg Nishimura, traffic. Ari Abrams, weather.*

And an unmistakable whitish-gray streaked across my smiling face, blotting out my left eye and half my nose and ending in a beautiful bird-shit dimple.

My face *only*.

Chris and Russell and Meg keep on grinning. **WE'RE ALWAYS HERE 4 YOU**, my ass.

"Well. I'm sufficiently humbled," I say after a few moments of stunned silence. "At least my hair looks okay?"

"Am I allowed to laugh?"

A sound that might be a giggle escapes my own mouth. "Please. Someone has to."

My brother cracks up, and I'm not sure whether to be offended or to join him. Eventually, I give in.

"We're taking your picture with it anyway," Alex says when he can breathe again. "It's your first *billboard*. That's a huge fucking deal." He claps a hand on my shoulder. "The first of many."

"If this doesn't haunt the rest of my career." I follow him out of the car, my Hunter boots splashing through a puddle that turns out to be deeper than it looks.

"Say, 'KSEA 6 Northwest News: where we really give a shit,'" he says as I position myself beneath the billboard and mug for the camera. "'KSEA 6: what you watch when the shit hits the fan.'"

"How about, 'Breaking news: Alex Abrams-Delgado is a piece of shit'?" I say it in my best TV voice while giving him the middle finger.

"THANKS FOR DOING this," I say once we've grabbed a table inside the donut shop. I brush damp bangs off my forehead, hoping there's a spare hair dryer in the KSEA dressing room. "I would've gone with Garrison, or with someone from the station, but . . ."

Alex braves a sip of his donut-shop coffee and grimaces. "I get it. I'm your favorite person in the world."

"You are," I say. "But Cassie's a strong second place. Don't take that privilege lightly."

"I could never." He empties a compostable packet of sweetener into his cup. "How are you doing, by the way? With . . . everything?"

Before the *everything* he's talking about, my brother and I saw each other about every month. Now I'm draped across his couch once a week while his chef husband ladles comfort food directly into my mouth.

"There are good days and bad. I'm not sure what today is yet, or if that's a literal sign from the universe that things are about to go to, well, you know." I wave a hand toward the billboard outside before taking a bite of a chocolate old-fashioned. "You're not going to tell me to get back out there, are you?"

That's the worst side effect of a breakup. Let me breathe for a moment before I attach myself to someone else who's only going to end up disappointing me.

I rub the place on my finger where the engagement ring used to be.

I figured its imprint would last longer than a few days, and I wasn't sure how to feel when my skin no longer carried the evidence of our relationship. Truthfully, I never thought I'd be that attached to a ring—until Garrison asked for it back. In his defense, it was a family heirloom. In my defense, he's a human trash can.

A human trash can I've barely been able to stop thinking about since the breakup five weeks ago, when I moved out of our spacious Queen Anne rental and into the studio apartment just big enough for me and my feelings. Our friends felt like they needed to pick sides, which is why these days, my sole confidants are my brother and a precocious preschooler. At least now I can say Garrison's name out loud without wanting to curl up inside one of those nest pillows Instagram is always advertising to me. I think they're meant for dogs, but I can't be the only person who desperately wants one. The algorithm must know I need it.

"Absolutely not. Not until you're ready." Alex reaches for another sweetener packet. "At least you hadn't put any deposits down. Silver linings, right?"

"Mmm," I say noncommittally. Wedding planning was another one of those excitement-anxiety knots for me, though most of the time, anxiety had been winning. Whenever we started talking about it, I'd freeze with indecision. Spring or fall? Band or DJ? How many guests? Even now, it's enough to make me itch inside my cable-knit sweater.

But what Alex said sticks in my brain. Because silver linings—they're kind of my thing. Any time I sense negativity beginning to simmer inside me, I force it away with one of my practiced TV smiles. Leap right over that murky puddle. Keep myself dry before I risk sinking deeper into the darkness.

"We should have these donuts more often," I say, even though it's an entirely unremarkable donut.

Alex must be able to tell I'm not eager to dig up more history because he launches into a story about Orion's determination to lose his first tooth.

"He was trying that old string-and-a-doorknob trick," Alex says. "Only, he completely missed the doorknob part, so I found him sitting in his room with all this string hanging from his mouth, waiting patiently for a tooth to loosen up."

"And why didn't you send me pictures immediately?" I ask, and he remedies this.

Once we've both moved on to our second donuts, my phone lights up with a notification, and I tap it to find an email from Russell Barringer, sports.

If he's emailing me, it can only be about one thing.

> Weather girl,
>
> Seth put up new signs today. Torrance found one on her oat milk and she's livid. Just wanted to let you know you might be walking into a hurricane.

"I should get going," I say to Alex. "Or, we should get going so you can drop me off."

"Something with your boss?"

I do my best to temper my sigh so it doesn't sound as long-suffering as I feel. "Isn't it always?"

We're about to get up when a thirtysomething guy with a soaked umbrella stops in front of our table and stares right at me. "I know you," he says, wagging a finger at me as rain drips onto the linoleum.

"Oh, from the news?" I say. It happens on occasion, strangers recognizing me but for the life of them unable to figure out why. Usually they're disappointed I'm not my boss, and honestly, I'd feel the same way.

He shakes his head. "Are you friends with Mandy?"

"I am not."

My brother waves an arm out the window at the billboard. "Channel six. She does the weather."

"I don't really watch TV," he says with a shrug. "Sorry. I must have been thinking of someone else."

Alex is shaking with silent laughter. I elbow him as we head to sort our trash into its proper bins.

"I'm so glad my pain is hilarious to you."

"Gotta keep you humble somehow." Before we leave, Alex waits in line to grab a few dozen donuts for his fourth-grade class. "Guilt donuts," he explains. "It's state testing week."

"It's a wonder some of us make it out of school with only minor psychological wounds."

He gives me a half smile that doesn't quite touch his eyes, and then he lowers his voice. "You'll text me if you're feeling down or anything this week, right?"

It's so easy to joke around with him that sometimes I forget I can do more than that. "I will." I glance down at the time and tap my phone. "If you can get me to the dressing room in twenty minutes, I'll make Nutella rugelach for Hanukkah next weekend."

"On it," he says, reaching for his keys while I balance his boxes of donuts. "You could really use that extra time."

"Hey, I am very fragile right now!"

With his chin, he gestures outside one more time. "Fine, fine. You look just as good as your billboard."

2

FORECAST:
Showers of shredded paper moving in this afternoon

WHEN I WAS little, I wanted to grow up to be Torrance Hale.

I watched her every night on the evening news, mesmerized by her smooth confidence and the way her face lit up when sun was in the forecast. The way she looked at the camera, looked right at *me*, one corner of her mouth hitched in a quarter-smile as she joked with the anchors—there was something electric about her.

As a baby science nerd, I'd been fascinated by the weather since an April blizzard shut down the city for two weeks when I was in kindergarten. Of course, I'd later learn that this was not normal and in fact a very scary thing, but back then, I wanted to experience as many weather phenomena as I could. Living in Seattle made that tricky, given how mild it is year-round. Still, I saw enough to keep me curious: record-breaking summer heat, a lunar eclipse, a rare tornado that touched down in Port Orchard when my family was on vacation.

Torrance made science, made *weather* seem like it could be glamorous. I didn't have to be stuck in a lab, poring over data and writing reports. I could tell stories with the weather. I could help people understand, even help protect them, when Mother Nature grew brutal.

My mother was unreliable, her dark moods sometimes turning her into a stranger, but Torrance never was. She was a source of comfort and calm, always exactly where she was supposed to be: in front of the green screen at four o'clock and then again at twelve-minute intervals. Friday nights, she hosted a half-hour show called Halestorm that focused on in-depth climate trends, and I'm not ashamed of the party invites I turned down so I could watch it live. I even bleached my red hair blond in eighth grade to look more like her, nearly burning off my scalp in the process.

Even when my own moods dimmed in a way that sometimes matched my mom's, the earliest symptoms of the depression I wouldn't get diagnosed until college, my love never wavered.

A couple years later, after all my red had blessedly grown back out, I won a high school journalism award for a story about the life cycle of a solar panel, and Torrance herself presented it to me at the banquet. I was sure I'd faint—I kept pinching the inside of my wrist to make sure I stayed conscious. When she whispered in my ear how much she'd loved the story, there was zero doubt in my mind: I was going to become a meteorologist.

The reality is that working for Torrance Hale is a very different kind of Halestorm.

"Have you seen this?" Torrance slaps a piece of paper on my desk, her ivory-painted nails trembling with the indignity of it. "It's unacceptable, right? I'm not losing my mind?"

After three years at KSEA, I'm still intimidated by Torrance, especially when she's in full makeup—the kind that looks natural on camera but creepy when you're two feet away from someone's over-blushed, over-eyeshadowed face. As always, her mouth is slicked with her signature lipstick, a shade of cherry red that costs $56 per tube. I used to beg my mother for it every year for my birthday, with no luck. When I finally bought it as an adult, I realized it was garbage with my complexion. Such is life as a pale redhead: keep us out of the sun and away from half the color wheel.

I unzip my jacket and hang it on my cubicle hook. Although technically, we're not supposed to call them cubicles. During orientation, HR stressed to me that this was a "low-partition office," which is . . . basically cubicles, but the walls aren't as high. It was a recent redesign; the staff had been unhappy with cubicles, and an expert had come in and made all these changes designed to increase productivity. I'm not sure if it increased productivity, but it definitely increased people talking about how it's supposed to increase productivity.

It's eight o'clock, meaning the morning show just ended. All over the newsroom in our Belltown station, people are hunched over their desks beneath too-bright fluorescents and a bank of TVs, the one tuned to KSEA currently airing an ad for a carpet cleaner with a too-catchy jingle. On a typical day, I'd be a few hours from the end of my shift, but Torrance is presenting at some gala tonight. As a minor Seattle celebrity, she's always getting invitations like this, and while I've grown out of my obsession with her, the city hasn't.

Without looking at the piece of paper and even without the warning from Russell, I'd know who's behind this unacceptable behavior: Seth Hasegawa Hale, KSEA 6 news director. Torrance's ex-husband.

I chance a peek at it.

Please finish milk before opening new carton to avoid waste. Two containers are already open and more than half full. The environment thanks you. —SHH

Classic Seth. With our general manager a year from retirement and completely checked out, Seth's taken it upon himself to run the station as he sees fit, often in the form of passive-aggressive signs like this one. The irony that his initials are SHH isn't lost on me.

I'm not sure which of Torrance's questions to answer first. "I hadn't seen it yet," I settle on. "Maybe he didn't know it was yours?"

"He knows perfectly well that I've been off dairy for years and soy gives me hives. I'm the only one who drinks the oat milk. This was very clearly directed at me," she says, sparing me from having to take a side in the Great Milk Debate. She leans her hip against my desk, her form-fitting blue dress wrinkle-free even after having been on the air since four in the morning, her blond hair tumbling past her shoulders. At fifty-five, Torrance is, and I say this with a tremendous amount of respect for her as a scientist, smoking hot.

"He can't just do this and expect all of us to fall in line the way he wants," she continues. "If he wants to talk about saving the planet, then he should trade in that SUV he's driving. Or stop wasting all this paper."

I'm fairly certain this isn't about the environment at all, but I won't pretend to understand the intricacies of the Hales' relationship. From what I've heard, they were miserable for a while before they divorced five years ago. I don't love Seth's signs, either—really could have done without the one in the bathroom reminding us that the plumbing is too delicate to handle tampons—but I imagine I'd love them a lot less if I used to be married to him.

I do my best to stay optimistic. Upbeat. "He did say 'please,' at least? And I drink the oat milk sometimes, too . . . maybe it was more of a general note?" I have never had the oat milk.

"Is everything okay over here?"

Seth is striding toward us, hands in the pockets of his navy slacks, hem of his matching jacket swaying as he walks. Posture relaxed, chin tilted upward just slightly. Completely unbothered by his ex-wife's distress. He looks so innocent, he might as well be whistling a tune and wearing a cap at a jaunty angle.

"What do you think?" Torrance asks sweetly, snatching up the sign with her thumb and index finger and dangling it in front of his face. "You realize people might actually do what you want them to if you asked them nicely, right? Instead of this passive-aggressive bullshit?"

"What a shock that I'd want to put it in writing instead of dealing with this," Seth says, monotone. While he's not as imposing as Torrance, he's well past six feet, black hair graying at the temples in that distinguished way only men seem able to pull off, though I'd love to think I could rock a gray streak someday.

Everyone at my old station in Yakima, my first full-time job out of college after I double-majored in atmospheric sciences and communications at the University of Washington, felt like one big family. Maybe the problem here is that the Hales are too much like a dysfunctional one.

As the news director, Seth should be chief meteorologist Torrance's boss, but because of their history and her seniority, she's directly underneath our GM, a man named Fred Wilson whom I have spoken to exactly twice. Given that Wilson's third-floor office stays locked most of the day—when he bothers to show up, which he didn't even do for the seventy-fifth birthday party we threw him last month—this essentially puts Torrance on equal footing with Seth.

The two of them are willing to run this station right into the ground, as long as it means one of them comes out on top.

"I don't need to be micromanaged, Seth," Torrance says. "What I put in and take out of the fridge is my own business."

Seth crosses his arms over his chest, which he probably does in part to show off the way his ridiculous biceps strain against the fabric of his jacket. Sometimes I think Torrance and Seth are locked in a battle to prove who's winning their divorce. I imagine them at gyms on opposite sides of the city, panting on treadmills while personal trainers shout at them to go faster. "Can't say being a team player has ever been your strong suit."

"And not being a massive prick has never been yours."

I bring a hand to my throat and rub my thumb along the tiny lightning bolt at the end of my necklace. The charm is about the size of my pinky nail and hammered gold, a gift from my mother when I graduated from college. A rare day she seemed truly happy. I want to disappear between my low-partition walls, but the whole point of them is that you kind of can't.

"I'm just going to—" I start, but Torrance suddenly stands straighter, something catching her attention across the room, in her office. She marches over there and, in one swift motion, tugs a sheet of paper off her computer monitor. Another sign.

"*Be sure to turn off your office lights to conserve power when you're not using them?* Did you put this in my *office* when I was on the air?"

"I wanted to make sure you'd see it," Seth says with an innocent shrug.

Maybe Seth's requests aren't entirely unreasonable, even if his method is. Yes, they're petty, but Torrance does have a way of forgetting her surroundings when she's at work. On camera, she's poised and professional, but off it, she's a bit of a mess. Too often, I've swept trash off her desk, tidied her makeup in the dressing room, watered the plants in her office. If her ficus is thriving, it's not because of her. It's probably not the best way of getting my boss to pay attention to me, but at the very least, I figure I've prevented a couple Hale v. Hale brawls.

Torrance storms back over to my desk, sign balled in her fist. "That is such a blatant invasion of privacy, I don't even know where to start." She juts her chin toward me. "What do you think, Abrams? Can you imagine if I put up signs in the weather center saying, 'Be sure to check the National Weather Service' or 'Don't forget to smile when you're on the air'? Would you appreciate being treated like a child?"

Again, I get the feeling anything I say is going to be the wrong answer.

"Maybe the weather center would be run much more efficiently if you cleaned it up every once in a while," Seth says. "I don't know how any of you can work like that. That place is a pigsty."

"Because I just finished my shift!"

"Excuse me," I say, backing out of my chair and grabbing my bag, but they're no longer listening to me. If they ever were.

The farther I get from them, the easier I can breathe, but their voices follow me down the hall. I probably could have come in later, since I won't be on camera until three, but I'm an early riser to my core. And I could use some therapeutic alone time with my hair straightener—I've never quite mastered my natural curls and have to iron my shoulder-length hair into submission before each broadcast—and newest eye shadow palette. The people at Sephora adore me. I've been a VIB Rouge since before I could legally drink.

My usual shift may require getting up at 2:30 in the morning, but there's one benefit that wasn't listed in the job description: Torrance and Seth are never there.

On my way to the dressing room, I catch Russell leaving the Dugout, which is what they call the office where the sports team sits. Morning anchor Chris Torres told me—bitterly—they got their own office because one time they were throwing around a football and hit an unsuspecting reporter in the head, but I'm pretty sure that's just a rumor. All I know is that they have their own office, and on days like this, I kind of hate them for it.

I gesture to his empty coffee mug. "Heading back to the scene of the crime?"

Russell's in a charcoal jacket that matches the sky outside, a blue dress shirt underneath. He's a big guy, broad-shouldered and soft-angled, light brown hair usually gelled for the camera, but this morning it's a little unruly. Probably got caught in the rain on his way to the office.

"I warned you," he says, glancing over my shoulder to make sure no one's around to overhear us. "How bad was it?"

"They're children. No, wait, that's not fair to children." I pause next to a flyer reminding us to RSVP for the office holiday party this Friday, which will be at a swanky downtown hotel. Already RSVPed, already dreading going without a plus-one. "I have half a mind to go into the kitchen and dump out the rest of her oat milk."

"She'd just blame Seth." His mouth tips into a grin. "Actually, maybe we should use this to our advantage. We could probably do just about anything, and they'd assume it was the other person."

"You distract them, and I'll take the milk."

"Deal," he says, blue eyes bright behind his rectangular black glasses. He has the longest lashes I've ever seen. If I had lashes like that, I wouldn't be nearly as beloved by my local Sephora. "Well—good luck out there." He motions toward the kitchen, giving me a kind but somewhat muted smile.

"Right. You too."

Russell and I should share a camaraderie of the both-our-bosses-are-assholes variety, but our work friendship hasn't evolved much beyond this. He mostly keeps to himself in the Dugout, friendly with his sports colleagues but surface-level pleasant with everyone else. How was your weekend, polite smile, moving on. He ends conversations too quickly, and I've never been able to get a solid read on him beyond the fact that he might be as miserable as I am.

Except he has a door to shut it all out.

"AS YOU CAN see, we have increasing rain and wind in store for your afternoon commute," I say, moving my hand across the green screen behind me. On the monitor in front of me and in viewers' homes, it's a map of western Washington. "Overnight, we'll be seeing more showers, with temperatures in the low-to-mid-forties."

Most of my weather hits are thirty seconds, but for this longer one, I have two minutes on the clock. I think of it as building a story: I start with a live satellite view of the region to show what's happening right now, and then I explain it through air patterns and pressure systems. I always wrap up by talking about the week ahead.

"We'll be heating up to the mid-fifties tomorrow, thanks to a warm front that's moving in. Behind that, though"—the graphic shifts to a model that shows what's happening off the coast—"we have a stronger cold front that will be marching through western Washington on Wednesday that's going to increase our wind speeds, with gusts of up to sixty miles per hour and possible power outages. We'll continue to keep an eye on that, so be sure to keep checking in with us as we fine-tune our forecast."

The screen switches again, this time to this week's forecast.

"Here's your seven-day forecast, and as you can see, there's not a whole lot of variation. It's going to be wet and windy, with *maybe* a chance of a sunbreak Friday afternoon. It's December in the Pacific Northwest, after all." I bite back a laugh, playing with the audience as I deliver the week's highs and lows. "And it looks like next Monday's system could be another rainy, windy one."

"And you sound positively gleeful about it," says Gia DiAngelo in my earpiece as I walk over to the anchor desk and sit down, the same way I do every morning with Chris Torres.

"I can't help it, Gia. I'm a Seattleite through and through." I hold up my arms, still grinning. "There's rainwater in these veins instead of blood."

It's a running joke that while most meteorologists—most people in general—get excited when sun is in the forecast, I'm the opposite. Contrary to popular belief, it doesn't rain here as much as people think. New Orleans and Miami get more annual precipitation, while the Pacific Northwest tends to get more rainy days on average. Still, there's something about rain in Seattle that's deeply romantic.

Gia chuckles and faces the teleprompter again. "We'll hear more from Ari soon. I'm sure everyone wants to know how all of this will affect their holiday plans. Coming up next: a local woman thought she'd found her dream home—but when she started renovations, the police showed up to tell her the house wasn't actually hers. Kyla Sutherland investigates."

And cut to commercial.

I'm still buzzing with adrenaline when we go off the air. It almost makes me forget the fact that my boss barely notices I exist, unless she needs me to cover a shift. Just once, I'd like her to say, "Ooh, this really meaty climate story would be great for Ari, go ahead and take the lead on it."

"Always nice having you here in the afternoons," Gia says, pulling a compact from her pocket to check that every strand of her glossy black hair is in place. "Even when you're giving us bad news."

"Rain isn't bad news, Gia," I say in a singsong, switching off the mic clipped to my dress and heading for the newsroom to refill my water bottle during this ten-minute break.

Torrance is in her office, gleefully feeding a stack of Seth's signs through a paper shredder.

Instead of allowing it to get to me, I square my shoulders and stop by the cluster of intern desks in the draftiest part of the newsroom, telling them how glad all of us at KSEA are to have them here, and if they ever have questions about broadcasting or about the weather, they can feel free to ask me any time. Their strange looks are worth it for the way the tension eases in my chest, ever so slightly.

"Does anyone know how to fix a paper shredder?" Torrance yells.

They say don't meet your heroes. Don't work for them, either.

3

FORECAST:

Take shelter and brace for Hurricane Torrance

"WELL . . . THEY TRIED," I say.

"Did they, though?" asks traffic reporter Hannah Stern, pushing aside a tree branch.

We lean closer to inspect the Christmas tree in the hotel ballroom—more specifically, the single menorah ornament, dangling in all its blue-and-silver glory behind a surfing Santa carrying a red bag. Seems like an inefficient way to deliver gifts, but okay.

"It's one more Jewish decoration than last year," I say, searching for a positive. And because beaming out a compliment always seems to help, I gesture to Hannah's gold T-strap heels. "And I'm obsessed with your shoes."

This Jew is not backing down from a Christmas party, especially since it took me three hours to get ready. I straightened my hair before worrying it looked like I was trying too hard, so I spritzed it with water and scrunched to bring back the waves. Then I took out my flat iron to add more curl to the ends, burning my palm in the process and rushing to the kitchen for an ice pack. All I found was an overpriced Amy's ravioli I'd been saving for a special occasion. It's quite sad, how much I've been looking forward to that ravioli, which I bought during my first post-Garrison grocery trip. My life may not be on the right track if the sole bright spot is a box of frozen pasta.

Maybe that billboard really was an omen.

The hotel ballroom is decked with garlands, snowflakes, and multicolor lights, a band onstage playing "Jingle Bell Rock." Our holiday party is Seattle black tie, which means you can get away with wearing jeans. I tried on no fewer than four outfits before settling on the black lace dress I wore for my engagement party. I'm giving it new life, freeing it of its association with my ex. To further sell that to myself, I swapped my usual lightning bolt necklace for a vintage pin Alex found at an antique shop and gave as a birthday gift one year, a little gemstone-dotted cloud. It was missing half the jewels, so I scoured Etsy and Seattle bead shops to fix it and strung on a few blue crystals for rain. I am nothing if not tragically predictable. That repair mission grew into a full-fledged hobby, one that takes up half my kitchen table, complete with an entire drawer unit and all kinds of tools I wouldn't have known the names of a year ago, and relaxes me when the world is too much.

I'm doing great! is what this outfit says, only I'm not exactly sure who it's declaring it to. Maybe I'm trying to prove it to myself.

Hannah and I are the only two Jews at KSEA, though because Hannah works afternoons, we don't often cross paths. As a result, we haven't broached the gap between work friends and outside-of-work friends, which is starting to feel like a pattern with me. Maybe I'm the common denominator, which would require a whole lot of self-reflection I'm not sure I'm ready for.

I follow her back to a table with her boyfriend Nate and a few other reporters, at which point it becomes clear that I'm one of the only people at this party who didn't bring their partner. Despite my comfort on camera, I've never been naturally outgoing, able to strike up a conversation with strangers. I don't have my forecasts and graphics as a safety net.

"Any chance of snow this year?" Gia DiAngelo's husband asks me, in that good-natured way you ask someone you know precisely one thing about. I imagine it's similar to asking a doctor acquaintance whether they'll take a look at a mole on your inner thigh.

"All my models are predicting warmer weather than usual," I say. "If we get snow this winter, I don't think it's going to be in December."

He lets out a long sigh, like rising global temperatures are my fault. "My kids'll be disappointed. Just once, I'd like to have a white Christmas." He waves a hand at the fake snow that's part of the table's centerpiece. "Wouldn't that be something? Get everyone on the air wearing Santa hats, too—I bet viewers love that."

"They absolutely do," I say with a false smile. Hannah's on my other side, talking animatedly to our weekend meteorologist, AJ Benavidez. I stand to head for the buffet. "Excuse me." The line is already long because there are few things that get a roomful of adults excited like free food. To be fair, I am one of those adults.

I realize I live in a city with a Jewish population of less than two percent, but the assumption that everyone celebrates Christmas has never not rubbed at me like the softest sweater's sharp-edged tag. This time of year, it's nearly constant. I've been the only person ever not wearing a Santa hat during a broadcast, and our social media blew up with accusations that I hated America.

"Weather girl," someone says from behind me in line, and I feel myself relax when I turn to find Russell, wearing black jeans and a burgundy tweed jacket over a black button-up. His jackets are always a little more colorful than any of our coworkers. Tonight he's more dressed down than he is on camera: no tie, the top button of his shirt undone. A shadow of stubble along his jaw that I don't recall seeing earlier in the week.

"Sports dude," I say, and then wrinkle my nose. "It doesn't quite have the same effect, does it?"

He cracks a smile. "Not really, I'm afraid."

The first few times Russell used the nickname, I worried he was trivializing what I do. Demeaning it. But he's only ever said it in a good-natured way, and that's part of the problem: everything about Russell is so good-natured that I'm not sure how to get to know him beyond that.

"The game today was, uh, pretty intense?" I ask, realizing too late that I'm doing what Gia's husband was doing to me.

"You don't follow sports, do you?"

I give him a grimace. "It's the timing. If games were at three in the morning, I'd be all over them."

The smile gives way to a laugh. "I'll see what I can do. I'm sure you'll be thrilled to know that the game I covered was college football, and the final score was 66-60."

"I may not know much about football, but those numbers seem . . . high?"

"Oh, they were. I'd never seen anything like it. Great offense, embarrassing defense."

The buffet line inches forward, and I'm a split second too slow to react, the few sips of wine I had at the table going to my head. The wind must have had its way with Russell's hair during the game, and there's something about men with messy hair that just does it for me. Now that I'm no longer in a relationship, my brain has run wild checking guys out. My crushes are unstoppable.

Guy whose apartment mailbox is next to mine and subscribes almost exclusively to cannabis magazines: cute.

Guy who smiled at me on the bus last week and who upon closer inspection was hiding not one but two ferrets inside his coat: so cute.

Guy in the employee cafeteria who somehow manages to make a beard hairnet look alluring: against all odds, *extremely* cute.

That's all they are, though—fleeting *oh, he's cute*s. Given how disastrously it ended with Garrison, they have to stay that way, which means giving up on my dream of becoming Mrs. Beard Hairnet.

"I always feel a little weird at these things," Russell says, tugging at the collar of his jacket. "If anyone's talking to me, it's usually because they want to know what their favorite player is like off the field, and if so-and-so is as much of a dick as everyone says he is."

"Same, except they want to complain about the weather. At least the food is good. It's possibly the only thing that makes all of this worth it."

He nods toward a display in one corner. "Not a fan of baby Jesus riding Rudolph?"

"Oh—I'm Jewish," I say, wishing I hadn't brought it up in the first place. "Not exactly the most inclusive holiday party."

He goes quiet as he glances around, and my regret quadruples. Russell and I aren't close. All the complaining we do about our bosses—it's lighthearted. I'd never want him to think I'm the complete opposite of the sunshine girl I am on camera. I do my best to make sure no one does. "It's certainly festive," he says in this strange flat way.

Still, there's prime rib and honey-lemon asparagus and caramelized-onion mac and cheese. Our station may be dysfunctional, but we're not hurting for cash. Russell and I fill our plates in relative silence, save for a moment when he tells me an asparagus spear is dangerously close to tumbling off my plate, and return to our respective tables: Russell with the rest of the sports desk, me as a ninth wheel.

Once the buffet has been demolished, the overhead lights dim, leaving just the twinkling lights hanging from the ceiling and wrapped around Christmas trees. Torrance and Seth take the ballroom stage, Torrance looking like a fierce snow goddess in a silver jumpsuit, Seth in a slate-gray tux and candy cane-printed tie, dark hair slicked back in this way that makes him look like a movie star from the 1940s.

Our gorgeous, terrible overlords.

"Good evening, everyone," Torrance says into the microphone, the lighting turning her curls golden. "We want to thank you for another amazing year."

"We're able to tell important stories and maintain high ratings because of each and every one of you. From news, to sports, to weather." Seth's eyes land on Torrance, mouth curving upward. "And a big congratulations to Torrance for being named Seattle's favorite meteorologist for the seventh year in a row by *Northwest Magazine*!"

Ample applause. Almost three decades after she started here, Torrance still nails it every night.

A rack next to them displays a collection of awards, something they also like to do every year. It's nice, I have to admit, to see this clear measure of success in the form of winged statuettes.

"And congratulations, too, to our station for sixteen regional Emmy nominations and five wins!" Torrance says. "Including Seth's stellar piece about the revitalization of Seattle's waterfront."

She claps him on the shoulder, and he gives her this aw-shucks grin. There's a moment—or at least, I think there's a moment—when their eyes lock and they retract their claws and they look like two people who used to love each other. Used to respect each other. Torrance's icy exterior seems to melt, and Seth even touches her hand, giving it a few pats. It's a great performance; I can almost believe they don't despise each other.

Torrance and Seth getting along: maybe this really is the most wonderful time of the year.

She's clearly in a good mood tonight. I'd love to catch her alone, have a real conversation. I vow to do it as soon as she's free.

"With dinner winding down—yes, let's give it up for the Hilton catering staff!" Seth breaks for applause. "With dinner winding down, we wanted to get started on what's always been our favorite KSEA tradition. You know what that means . . . it's time for our annual white elephant gift exchange!"

Our tables are arranged in a semicircle around the ballroom's largest tree, and with more than sixty people in attendance, there's a significant stack of boxes beneath it. I brought a cheese board shaped like Washington state I found at a boutique near my apartment.

"Please don't bring home anything embarrassing," Hannah says to Nate.

"I'm offended. You know you've used last year's Ove Glove as much as I have, if not more."

Our places at the table had numbers when we arrived that designated our order in the game. Hannah winds up going first, unwrapping a trio of scented candles. Reporter Bethany Choi goes next, picking an oddly shaped package that turns out to be a tiny USB-powered vacuum.

Then it's Seth's turn. He bypasses Hannah's and Bethany's gifts for something new, and I have never seen a grown man's face light up the way his does when he pulls out a breakfast sandwich maker. "No way," he says, holding it like I imagine a parent holds their newborn baby for the first time. "This can do an English muffin, egg, and ham all at the same time?"

"And cheese," offers up Chris Torres. "I have one of those. It's a game changer."

"I do love breakfast sandwiches." Seth tucks it under his arm and heads back to his seat. "If anyone comes for this, I hope they're ready to forgo their next raise. Kidding, of course."

"I don't think he's kidding," I whisper to Hannah.

"Funny you're so enamored with that," Torrance says in a tone that suggests it isn't funny at all. "Because as I recall, I bought you something very similar—some might even say identical—for Christmas one year."

"Yeah. You did. And you took it in the divorce," Seth says calmly.

From a table away, I catch Russell's eye, and I don't miss the twitch to his jaw.

We make it through the next few players without incident, and then it's my turn. I pick a craft cocktail kit that gets stolen in the next round. That makes it my turn again, and that's when I see the opportunity.

Torrance is still sulking while Seth reads the sandwich maker box, making a big show of it. The game had a fifty-dollar limit, so it's not as if it's something he couldn't have bought for himself, but I can tell it's the principle of the thing. And if I want Torrance to like me, or at the very least to respect me—I'm a realist, I know I can't have both—I have to do something to earn it. Clearly, that something hasn't happened during work hours yet. At the station, I either disappear or distract, though it usually ends up being the former. Tonight, maybe I can smooth some of the friction between them.

"I'll take the breakfast sandwich maker?" I say. It comes out like a question.

Both Seth's and Torrance's heads whip toward me. There's this unspoken rule in white elephant: you don't steal from your boss.

"You don't want this, Ari," Seth says. "It's a piece of junk. It'll probably break the first time I use it."

"She can make up her own damn mind, Seth." Torrance is not doing a great job suppressing her glee. She might be seconds away from leaping across the circle to yank the gift from Seth's grasp. "If she wants the breakfast sandwich maker, she should take it. It looks like it can make mini pizzas, too?"

"Yeah." Seth crosses his arms, biceps straining against the suit fabric. "It can."

Suddenly I'm no longer sure if I want to get in the middle of some Torrance-and-Seth pettiness. I glance around the circle, most people averting their eyes. I didn't know a party game could be this fraught. But of course, this is what the Hales do. The Hales are why we can't have nice things. They turn anything, even a simple game at a holiday party that is a Christmas party with one sad menorah ornament, into a standoff.

"I—I can take something else," I say. "I'll steal something, or I'll pick a new gift, or—"

But Seth's already stepping forward and handing it over, and that is how I learn it's possible to feel both triumphant and like a total piece of shit at the same time.

He picks another gift, one with penguin-patterned wrapping paper. "A set of reusable straws. Cool," he says, with all the excitement of a kid who's gotten socks for their birthday.

"Great!" Torrance's smile gleams brighter than it does on TV. "Who's next?"

• • •

THE PARTY DRAGS on, dessert and dancing and people laughing over their white elephant gifts. Fleetingly, I wonder why Garrison couldn't have waited to dump me until after New Year's. Then at least we wouldn't have had to suffer through these parties alone. Though he's probably having a blast at his investment firm's annual yacht party.

I'm picking at a plate of "holiday" cookies—a Santa, a tree, a sleigh—and debating giving up on the whole thing when Torrance drops into the chair next to me. "Hey there, Ari Abrams," she says, the words running into one another. Drunk. And still, her lipstick hasn't budged. If we ever become close, which would require one of us developing incurable amnesia, I'll beg her to teach me her tricks. "Ari Abrams. It's a good name for TV, isn't it?"

"I hope so, given that I'm already on TV." I inch a glass of water her way, hoping she'll take the hint. I like Sloppy Torrance even less than Hurricane Torrance.

"I'm sorry about all of that," Torrance says, waving her wine toward the mess of wrapping paper and empty boxes, the liquid forming a merlot tsunami inside her glass.

"It's okay," I say quickly, because I'm so used to being steamrolled when it comes to Torrance that I can even do it to myself. And then, because I hope I didn't sound too dismissive, I add: "Congratulations again on the awards. There's no one who deserves favorite meteorologist more than you." Positivity. There.

But she ignores the compliment, giving me this look I'm not sure I've seen on her before. Apologetic? A few mascara crumbs dot her cheekbones, and her face is flushed a warm pink, and those cracks in her façade make me soften a little. "It's not okay, Abrams. And you don't have to say it is just because I'm your boss."

Some of the tension I've held onto all night, or maybe even for the past three years, loosens. Not a lot, but it's a start.

"I wish it weren't so rocky between Seth and me," she continues. If their relationship is rocky, Mount Everest is a speed bump. "It's always been intense. When we were in love, we had so much passion that sometimes we couldn't even be in the same room without wanting to rip each other's clothes off. And then, when we fell out of it . . . that intensity was still there. It just morphed."

Not sure if I needed to hear about my boss and this particular kind of passion in the same sentence, but more power to her. I hope someone still wants to rip my clothes off when I'm in my fifties.

"What happened?" I ask.

"Oh, a lot of little things that probably seemed about as petty as our arguments these days. I'm not sure either of us could pinpoint a single event that caused it." She says this breezily, but she's not making eye contact. Instead she's watching Seth across the room, laughing with a trio of anchors and their spouses. "I figured one of us would leave KSEA, give the other some breathing room. But either we're both too committed to the station or we're playing the world's longest game of chicken."

I think about that for a long moment as the band starts playing a jazzy version of "Winter Wonderland" and couples head to the dance floor. I get the distinct sense there's more to the story, but I'm not about to push.

"Plus," she continues, "our son Patrick—his wife's pregnant. Due in May. I never thought I'd feel this way, but I can't wait to be a grandmother." At that, her face changes, smile turning genuine. "I wasn't close with my grandparents, and I always wish I'd been. I love the idea of being able to babysit whenever they need it, being there for every birthday and holiday. I don't think I could leave Seattle. And I'm guessing Seth feels the same way."

"That's really great," I say, meaning it. Of all the things I didn't expect from Torrance tonight, a confession that she can't wait to be a grandmother is near the top of the list. That gooey center of my heart—it's fully activated. "My brother has five-year-old twins, and they're pretty fantastic."

"You should bring them by the station sometime. Give them a tour." Torrance covers my hand with hers. Her nails are painted silver with tiny white snowflakes. "And Ari, we should really talk more." I don't point out that she's been the one doing most of the talking, and I don't care if she's drunk—this is too nice. I want to enjoy it as long as I can.

Buoyed, I turn back to my cookies, biting off Santa's ruby-cheeked face. It tastes a whole lot sweeter than it did a few minutes ago.

Seth waltzes up to us. "Excuse me, ladies," he says in this faux debonair tone that makes me cringe. "I've come with a peace offering. How about a dance, Tor? For old times' sake?"

"You remember," she says, eyes lighting up.

"Of course. How many people's favorite Christmas song is 'Run Rudolph Run'?"

"*Plenty,*" she insists, like this is something they've joked about for years.

"I feel like I owe it to you after the white elephant debacle." Seth gives me a half-hearted shrug, as though that's all he needs to do to be forgiven. "Sorry about that, Ari."

"I guess I can't say no to that." Torrance throws a look over her shoulder at me as she takes Seth's hand, as though to say, *this is what I meant.*

And to my utter shock, the two of them start swing dancing, Torrance laughing as Seth twirls her around the floor. We've slipped back in time. They're *good*, and I have to assume they danced all the time when they were together. I can't help wondering when it turned sour, if it was five years ago exactly or whether it built to a crescendo, and if it happened the way Torrance said: a lot of little things that eventually became impossible to ignore. With my parents, it was one big thing—I'm certain of it, even if I haven't heard from my dad for about fifteen years. And then with Garrison, it was a little thing that he turned into a big thing, though I realize it didn't feel little to him at all.

As the song changes to something I haven't heard before, I'm starting to think that maybe this is okay. Maybe Torrance and Seth have realized they're making all of us miserable. Maybe this really was a peace offering.

Of course, that's when I hear it.

"You never appreciated anything I gave you," Torrance is saying from the middle of the dance floor, dropping her arms from around his neck.

"Is this still about the fucking sandwich maker?"

"The sandwich maker is a fucking metaphor!" she shouts back. "You never appreciated the sacrifices I made, or the kind of effort that it takes to do my job well. And now you can't even appreciate the hard work that went into this party?"

Silver lining, silver lining . . . there has to be one. It's what keeps me from falling apart: focusing on something brighter, something joyful.

But I'm alone at the table, and everyone is fixated on the Hales.

A few hotel staffers dressed all in black have started to approach, ready to intervene if necessary. I get to my feet on instinct, unsure what to do but whatever it is, I can't be sitting down for it. I'm furious and disappointed and *embarrassed*, most of all. These are my adult coworkers, adult *bosses*, and they're making a scene in public.

"Hey, man, let's take a walk," morning anchor Chris Torres says, reaching for Seth's sleeve, but Seth shrugs him off.

"We can handle this," he says through gritted teeth.

Torrance storms over to the rack of awards. "Maybe you didn't care about that story, but it was important to me." She runs her snowflake manicure along Seth's Emmy. "Just like this is important to you."

Before anyone can stop her, Torrance grabs the statuette, draws her arm back, and pitches it through the ballroom window.

4

FORECAST:

A full night of wallowing gives way to a little light scheming in the early morning hours

THE HOTEL STAFF swoops in to clean up the broken glass. A tarp is draped across the window. The sugar cookies rebel inside my stomach.

For a brief moment when the glass shattered, I was awed by Torrance's strength. Then again, maybe I should have expected as much from the woman who once ate a ghost pepper on live TV.

Torrance and Seth are asked to leave immediately, and with all my remaining optimism, I do my best to salvage what's left of the party. Most of that optimism went out the window with Seth's Emmy, but there's the slightest glimmer left.

"We have the band for another hour," I tell news producer Avery Mitchell and her wife as they're shrugging into their coats. Yes, I was dreading this party, but this can't be how it ends.

"Babysitter," Avery explains. "Sorry. They really went overboard this time, huh?"

Hannah gives me a sympathetic look as she swipes one last cookie. "I think we've more than overstayed our welcome. I doubt the Hilton will be having us back anytime soon." She places a hand on my arm and squeezes. "You don't have to try and fix it, Ari. I'm not sure anyone could."

"It's not all bad," I say in a quiet voice, not fully believing myself. There were moments Torrance and Seth didn't entirely hate each other. Too fleeting, sure, but they were there.

When it becomes clear the rest of my coworkers would rather head home to sleep off this fiasco than take more selfies with baby Jesus and Rudolph, I find myself wandering toward the bar. Now all I want is a strong drink and a wretched hangover—because I'm no longer sure I can find a silver lining.

There's only one other person at the bar, a figure in a burgundy jacket hunched over a glass.

"Drinking your feelings?" I say as I slide onto the stool next to Russell, rearranging my skirt so I don't flash him. The bar is all warm lighting and mahogany furniture. Cozy. Not lavish enough for me to feel too out of place, given I'm not in the habit of haunting hotel bars.

"Something like that." He takes another sip of his drink before setting it down on a black napkin. "Nice of you to join me. I'm guessing you're here to drink your feelings, too? Possibly for the same reason?"

"Unfortunately. What is that, by the way?"

"Whiskey sour," he says, and I signal to the bartender and order one for myself.

"Cheers to feelings," I say when it arrives, clinking my glass with his. He watches me as I down three-fourths of the glass at once. And—oh god. That was a mistake. It goes down like a bag of Sour Patch Kids. I'm grateful when the bartender places a glass of water on the counter next to it. "How much of a nightmare is work going to be on Monday?"

"Category seventy. At least."

Russell's collar is unbuttoned, his light brown hair a little mussed, nothing like the expertly combed way he looks on TV. It's interesting, talking to someone in real life when you know their TV persona, too. Both people are *them*, but one version lets you see their blemishes, and the other doesn't.

"That was the most aggressive game of white elephant I've ever played," he says. "And then—well, you know." He gestures toward the bar's exit. *The window. Seth's Emmy. Any semblance of dignity KSEA had left.*

"Ughhhhh." I drop my head dramatically to the counter. "Let's talk about something else." There's a silence, and suddenly I'm worried Russell and I don't have "something else" to talk about. We've only ever talked at work, about work.

But then he asks, "You were flying solo tonight?" and I've never been so relieved to bring up my broken engagement.

I tip my drink to him. "That's what happens when your fiancé dumps you on Halloween. While dressed as one of those flailing tube things they have at car dealerships." I'd painted a couple cardboard boxes red to turn myself into a used Toyota Camry. We would have killed at his firm's couples costume contest, had we managed to make it out of the apartment. When Russell stares at me, I say, "It's okay. You can laugh. It's almost funny."

Even as I say it, there's a tug at my heart that feels a little like longing. I don't want to be thinking about Garrison—not now, not after tonight. I was so convinced we'd be spending the rest of our lives together: marriage, kids, a house in the suburbs, though I joked to Garrison a couple times that he'd have to drag me kicking and screaming out of the city.

When you spend so long imagining your life with someone, after they leave, you don't just lament the loss of that person. You have to grieve every piece of your life they touched that they don't anymore. Every image of your future that you planned together.

"I wasn't going to laugh," he says. "I'm so sorry to hear that." He sounds genuinely sympathetic.

I shrug, staring down at the ice cubes in my drink. "It's a good thing, because at least he didn't have to witness this shit show." I almost ask him the same question, but it's clear he was flying solo, too. Otherwise, we wouldn't be drinking at a hotel bar together.

"What happened to talking about something else?"

"There is nothing else!" I must say it too dramatically, punctuate it with a too-hard bang of my fist on the bar, because Russell's eyes widen. "Do you know that Torrance hasn't done an actual performance evaluation with me for the past three years? She's my *boss*, and she doesn't care about her employees getting better at their jobs." I glance around the bar, worried about speaking about them this candidly, even after they were kicked out. "Most people probably want less attention from their bosses, not more. I realize that. But Torrance is the whole reason I wanted to work here. I grew up watching her, and I was so excited to get this job—to have a chance to learn from the best. And she completely ignores me. Sometimes I feel like if she were happier, if there weren't all this drama at work . . . she'd be more available.

"Maybe one day I'd like to be in a top ten market or go national, but I won't have a shot if I don't have better training or mentorship. For now, I love this job and I want to be good at it. I want her to tell me I'm not fucking up my forecasts. Or even better, give me advice on how to improve. That's it. Sure, I'd love for her to bring in a talent coach for us, and I'd love to be a guest on Halestorm or do some field reporting, but god, I'm not even on her radar. I've given up hope of any kind of promotion at this point. The most I ever get is a pat on the shoulder and 'keep it up, Abrams.'" My face has grown warm, and when I reach for my glass of water, I nearly knock it over.

Russell isn't blinking, and I realize this is more than I've ever said to him at once. And . . . oh my god. It was too much. Way too much.

The alcohol is clearly already doing its job, mucking up my brain-to-mouth filter and letting out all this negativity. It's the only explanation. This isn't me. Not around anyone who isn't my brother, at least. Every time Russell and I have bitched about our bosses, it's accompanied with a *well, what can you do?* shrug. This was so far from the Ari Abrams I am on TV, and even further from my real self. I'm convinced he'll signal for the check and disappear into an Uber, leaving me to continue drinking my feelings on my own.

"She's not bad at her job," I say, backtracking. "I still admire the hell out of her. She's just . . ."

"Distracted," Russell fills in. "Yeah. Seth too."

"Things must be going okay for us if our worst problem is that our bosses aren't paying attention to us." I force a laugh, silently willing Russell to say more than three words. "Or—well, I don't know Seth, but . . ."

Russell is quiet for a moment, staring out at the shelves of liquor behind the bar before swiveling his head back toward me, a new determination in his eyes. "When I was hired . . . it must have been pretty soon after they got divorced. I was in a meeting with him and Wilson, who didn't want me on camera at first. Said it wouldn't look good to have a sports reporter who was a fat guy. And since he's the GM, I worried he might have the final say."

I've never heard anyone speak so brazenly about their size like this, and I'm not entirely sure how to react. After a brief pause, I decide to go with honesty. "That's really fucked up."

"All throughout the interview process, Seth had been so excited to have me on board, and he didn't say a thing. The worst meeting of my life. It wasn't that I expected him to defend me, necessarily—I mean, he barely knew me. But I thought he'd at least say *something*. He kind of checked out after that, like he thought he'd made a mistake by hiring me. But when my ratings are great, because I'm good at my job, he's been all over it. Happy to claim that for himself." He doesn't say any of this arrogantly—he's stating a fact. Russell's ratings *are* great. "The most frustrating part is that I've been here for four years, and I'm still covering college sports."

I don't know much about the KSEA sports hierarchy. "Instead of pro?" I ask, and he nods. It makes sense that a happier Seth might lead to a promotion for Russell, too. "Torrance scheduled me to work every night of Hanukkah last year because she didn't realize it isn't on the same days every year and didn't think to ask."

"One time, Seth cut a story of mine after a fight with Torrance because his favorite team had lost."

"Torrance only cares about my opinion when she's using me as a pawn to get me to take sides."

"Seth never cares about my opinion."

It's like we're trying to prove who has the worse boss, and it's a game that, much like white elephant, no one wins.

"It's a real shame they divorced," I say. "They deserve each other."

"It's hard to imagine them being more miserable than they are now." He nods toward my empty glass. "Need another?"

I'm already flagging down the bartender.

• • •

"I SWEAR, ONE of these days my hand is going to slip and I'll dump dish soap into Seth's coffee," Russell is saying, waving his arm for emphasis, as though to illustrate how easy this would be.

A half dozen empty glasses cover the bar in front of us, and we are a *mess*. Russell's burgundy jacket is draped across the stool on his other side, the sleeves of his black shirt unbuttoned at the wrists and rolled up. He keeps jostling his glasses when he gestures too wildly with his hands, the way he's doing right now. Every time, I have to fight the urge to reach over and stop him from flinging his glasses off his face.

I tied my hair into a topknot with an elastic I found in my purse, and I'm too far gone to care that it's probably sticking out in every direction. Holding myself upright on the stool: another skill I can't quite master.

"Don't tell me that!" I say, but I'm laughing. "I don't want to be an accomplice. I don't need this on my conscience."

"Listen. I have to tell you, so you can be my alibi."

It's kind of great to complain about work with someone who's gotten just as shitty a hand as I have. Garrison's analyst job was so stressful that I tried to stay quiet about work around him, except on rare occasions I couldn't keep it in anymore. Still, I'd always worry when I let something slip that he'd react by pushing me away.

I feel like I don't even know who you are anymore, Garrison told me during our last fight, which was also one of our first fights. Halloween. *You've never been real with me, have you?*

It was the worst kind of insult because I didn't know how to make myself more real, more authentically Ari Abrams. I felt pretty human;

I wasn't some otherworldly monster parading around in a human costume. But Garrison thought I never took off the sunshine mask I wear on camera, the one that helps me smile even when things are falling apart.

The only things I kept from him were for his own good. Although lately, I've been wondering how happy I really was with him if I hid that much of myself.

"Have you thought of quitting?" I ask Russell, trying to smooth out my topknot in a way I hope looks casual.

"Sometimes?" he says, phrasing it as a question. "I got pretty far in the interview process at a station in Tacoma a couple years ago, but ultimately I didn't get the gig. And any of the smaller stations don't pay nearly as well, even if the pay here isn't that incredible to begin with. I need the stability."

"Ah. Student loans?"

"Something like that." His cheeks glow bright pink. Drunk looks cute on him.

I lift my eyebrows at him, but he just reaches for his glass. Secret agent mode activated. He could tell me he's financially supporting a family of woodland elves that have taken up residence in his basement and subsist on glitter and marshmallows, and I'd believe him.

"For me it's that this was supposed to be my dream job," I say. "Going from Yakima to Seattle, getting to work where I grew up . . . that was a huge. And I mean, I finally got a billboard."

"*We* finally got a billboard," he says.

"That was your first one, too?"

"Up on Aurora, near the donut place?" Then, clearly realizing what happened to the billboard, his grin slips into a grimace.

"Oh no. The bird shit's still there, isn't it?"

Russell holds a solemn hand to his heart, like he's vowing to avenge me. "How dare that bird deface an image of one of KSEA's finest."

My face heats up again. I should stop. I should have stopped a couple drinks ago, if only because my meager salary cannot support drinks in hotel bars, no matter how desperately they're needed.

"God, I can't remember the last time I drank this much." I bring my hands to my cheeks, wanting to signal to him that this is why I'm so flushed, not for any other reason. Definitely not because with the two of us sitting this close, I can tell that beneath his single opened shirt button is a patch of chest hair, and I've always been drawn to a man with chest hair. Not like, to the point where I seek them out, but I've felt a little thrill when undressing someone for the first time. Mountain men and beard hairnets? Whatever, I'm owning it.

"Hell of a Christmas party," he agrees.

"Holiday party," I correct.

At that, he gives me this sheepish look. "I probably should have mentioned this earlier, but I guess I've gotten into the habit of not talking about religion at work. I'm Jewish, too. And this was definitely a Christmas party."

"Wait, *what*?" I knock his arm with mine, an action that sends electricity across my skin. It may be the first time I've touched Russell Barringer, and he immediately glances down to where my arm met his, as though he's realizing it, too. "I thought there were only two of us! We should start a club! You, me, and Hannah Stern."

He scratches at his stubble, pretending to look pensive. "What would we do during club meetings?"

"I don't know, learn how to make hamantaschen? I've always wanted to." With my glass, I gesture between us. "Look at us, two Jews, the last people to leave a Christmas party."

"Hey, we keep Hanukkah going for eight nights. We don't skimp on celebration."

"I feel like most Jewish holidays are observance and reflection as opposed to celebration."

"Fair point," he says, nudging his glass against mine with a soft clink. The way alcohol has unstitched him, turned my ever-pleasant coworker into someone honest and fun—I don't hate it.

I still can't get over this fact about him. It shouldn't be groundbreaking, but there it is: Russell Barringer is Jewish and drunk and kind of adorable, and his leg is five inches from mine. If I slipped off my stool, which is a distinct possibility, I'd fall into his lap.

His eyes lower before flicking back up to mine with an intensity that wasn't there a few minutes ago. Is he checking me out? I'm so out of practice.

"I like your pin," he says, his voice a quarter of the volume it is when he's reporting a story from down on a football field.

So, not checking me out, despite the pin's close proximity to my breasts. "Oh. Thank you. I'm not sure when we as a society stopped wearing brooches, but I'm determined to bring them back." I make to touch the pin, but I've lost so much coordination that I overshoot it and wind up cupping my own boob. Classy. "What good is being a meteorologist if I can't use it as an excuse to make these very extra accessories?" I tuck a loose strand of hair back into my topknot, revealing a matching pair of sun-and-moon earrings.

Not flirting. I'm not flirting with him, because he's not flirting with me. It's the whiskey convincing me his gaze lingers a moment too long.

"You made those?" he asks, sounding genuinely surprised.

"They weren't that hard. I found the charms and then added the earring backs. I added these raindrops to the brooch, too. *Brooch.*

That's a fun word, and I am very not sober." And there I go, cupping my boob again. "Something I do with all the free time that isn't spent agonizing over my future."

"That's really impressive. They're beautiful."

It's such a sweet compliment that I feel myself flush even hotter. "You're telling me you don't have basketball cufflinks or something? Spoons in the shape of golf clubs?"

"Hockey's more my thing," he says. "Used to play, actually. In high school." Then he clears his throat, changes the subject. "Here's what I don't get. If what broke them up was so bad that they're still at each other's throats, why are they still working together? Why subject themselves to seeing the other person every day?"

"It's impossible to know what really goes on in a relationship." I think back to Garrison again. Back to my parents, when my dad was still around. I barely remember him, but I used to wonder how long he'd been plotting his escape. "The worst part is, this is their normal, and no one can say a thing because they're the ones in charge. Our GM sure doesn't give a shit. HR is scared of them. They make work hell for us, and we can't do a damn thing about it."

Russell stops drawing a finger through the condensation on his glass, looks up at me through his thick lashes. "What if we could?"

"Is this about putting something in their coffee again? Because I don't think I'd do well in prison. Redheads look terrible in orange."

He leans in closer, the woodsy scent of his soap mingling with the tang of alcohol and a hint of sweat. "What if we figured out a way to get them back together?"

I blink at him before I burst out laughing. "Get them back together? Russell, they *hate* each other."

"Hate and love are two sides of the same coin. As the saying goes."

"That's ridiculous." I take another sip of whiskey, but it doesn't taste sour anymore. I've probably burned off all my taste buds.

"Is it, though? They're miserable, and they're making work miserable. And not just for us. What if there was a way we could figure out what went wrong for them? A way we could fix it?"

I think back to what Torrance said at the party, about the intense passion they had. The look they shared onstage. How she lit up when Seth asked her to dance.

There's still a spark there.

"If I'm humoring you," I say, "which I am, because I am not at all taking this seriously, how would we even go about it? Are we taking cues from 1998 classic *The Parent Trap*, starring Lindsay Lohan and Lindsay Lohan? Because yes, it's a perfect film, but I'm not sure it was intended to be a how-to." Though I definitely spent summers wishing I'd meet a long-lost twin at camp. "And if so, in this scenario, are you the snobby rich Lindsay Lohan or the badass poker-playing Lindsay Lohan?"

"That's the one where one of the Lindsays gets her ears pierced with the apple, right?" He pantomimes this with his hands, knocking his glasses askew again. "That freaked me out as a kid."

"Yep. Iconic. God, Dennis Quaid was hot in that movie. He was my first crush, actually. And my first—" I break off because Russell does not need to know that Dennis Quaid as a rugged Napa Valley winemaker was so formative for my burgeoning sexuality that he was the first guy I pictured when I discovered another use for a high-pressure showerhead. "He was peak DILF," I finish awkwardly.

"DILF?"

"Dad I'd like to—"

"Oh." There's something strange in Russell's expression, which

I've gathered is his go-to expression. "I think we're getting off track. What I'm trying to say is, I really think we could do this. We work more closely with them than anyone at the station, right?"

Maybe we do, but I still barely know Torrance. The first year I worked with her, I was reconciling the real version of her with the idol I'd grown up with. It was sobering, to have that vision of her erased. Now I just try to stay out of her way. I don't know what she does for fun. I don't know what ended her marriage or what it would take to get her to give Seth another chance.

It's still laughable, but I can play along.

"So we'd, what, write steamy love letters and sign their names?" I say.

"Or trap them in a stalled elevator and get them to remember all the good times they had together."

"Light candles in one of their offices and play some Marvin Gaye."

He taps the bridge of his glasses. "See? We'd be unstoppable if we tag-teamed this."

I allow myself to picture a Torrance who sets biweekly meetings with me and watches my clips to give me advice. Without all their ex-marital strife, I want to think it would be a possibility.

"Fine, fine," I say. I'm still joking—at least, I'm pretty sure I am. "I'm in."

He raises his fifth or sixth drink to mine. "To peace and harmony at KSEA 6."

"That, I'll cheers to."

Russell sets down his glass and checks the time. "Holy shit, it's almost two in the morning."

"This is usually the time I wake up."

He shakes his head. "I don't know how you early morning people do it."

"I like it," I say. "There's a different kind of energy in the mornings. It's exciting to know you're the first person someone's hearing from that day." I've had some coworkers who mainline caffeine pills to make it through the morning, but I've only ever needed a bit of coffee and the joy of weather forecasting models. "Tomorrow's gonna be brutal, though."

We pay our tabs—yikes—and when we get to our feet, he reaches out to prevent me from toppling over with a firm hand.

I'm going to regret all of this tomorrow. It'll be something we laugh about in the break room—*can you believe we wanted to get Torrance and Seth back together?*

At least it gave me a flicker of hope for a few minutes.

"Good night, sports dude." I give him this salute that's meant to be cute but probably looks unhinged, given my current state of inebriation. I'm not sure I've ever saluted someone before, but it suddenly seems like the right way to say goodbye.

He returns the salute. On him, it really is cute. "And you have a good morning, weather girl."

5

FORECAST:

Some unwelcome introspection with a glimmer of hope on the horizon

A GOOD MORNING, it is not. Sunlight streams in through the window across from my bed, my blackout curtains shoved to the side. My head is pounding and my tongue is too large for my mouth and my throat feels like I swallowed a vacuum cleaner filter and washed it down with straight vinegar. It's the most expensive hangover I've ever had.

I almost faint when I check the time on my phone. One o'clock in the afternoon on a Saturday, which means I slept through the equivalent of an entire morning shift. When I started this job, I relied on Tylenol PM to help me fall asleep and energy drinks to keep me awake. Now I maintain the same schedule on weekends, or at least very close to it.

Garrison never loved my semi-backward schedule, even if I did. I do miss the way he'd cuddle me when I woke up when it was still dark out, his warmth almost enough to keep me in bed. I haven't cried about it for a couple weeks, and that feels like progress. The last time was when I was watching Netflix and *The Crown* popped up as "something you might be interested in," and I started bawling because yes, not only was I interested in it, but we'd watched the entire series on his account. The idea that my own Netflix account didn't know about my love of royal melodrama and therefore didn't care about my breakup was, in that moment, unfathomably inconsiderate.

What I kept from him, the subject of our final fight, wasn't a big thing—in fact, it was quite small. Thirty pills about the size of my pinky nail, my prescription refilled each month at the nearby Bartell Drugs. The bottle had fallen out of my purse in our rush to get our Halloween costumes ready. My depression was under control, manageable, the way it had been for years with the exception of a couple medication changes when side effects wouldn't go away and a new therapist when I moved back to Seattle from Yakima. I take those pills every morning, just as I'm doing now, plodding over to the bathroom and opening up the medicine cabinet.

It was easier if he didn't know. I didn't want him drawing a connection between my mother and me, asking more questions about why my dad left and who my mother was dating this month.

What I needed to do was simple: prevent what happened with my parents. None of my exes had Garrison's problem. They seemed perfectly content not knowing everything. They loved how upbeat, how positive I was, how I let them get out their anger while never airing any of mine. I was the cool girl, the easygoing girl, and I loved her. If I was upset about something, I journaled or rage-texted Alex. If they forgot an anniversary, I bought myself flowers. I was—*am*—bright sides and silver linings, and it's always worked for me before.

If I insisted on being difficult, if I let any of the darkness out—well, then I'd end up like my mother.

"You can't be sunshine all the time, Ari," Garrison said during that fight, when his inflatable tube man costume had lost all its humor and lay flattened on a couch cushion. He didn't understand. I lived in two realities, and he could only be in one of them with me. If I've learned anything from my mother, it's that sunshine is the only way to make someone stay. "No one can."

Funny, really, since I don't like sunshine at all.

Determined to get myself back on schedule, I go to a yoga class and the farmers market, keeping myself busy by cooking an elaborate, too-expensive meal for one person. At the very least, I've discovered one great thing about living alone: I don't have to hide from anyone.

By Sunday afternoon, my goal is to tire myself out so I can get to sleep as close to my regular bedtime of eight-thirty as possible. I ride for an hour on the cheap exercise bike I nearly broke my back hauling up the stairs. Then I hunch over my kitchen table, bending wire and stringing beads for a pair of chandelier earrings. It's soothing, losing myself in this work for a couple hours. Once I've finished them, I light candles around my apartment, pull up some of my favorite videos in an incognito browser, and give myself two orgasms before my vibrator runs out of batteries and I can't find any new ones, even after I turn my apartment upside-down and open every device. Apparently, nothing else uses triple–A.

Except when I crawl into bed, knowing I have to be up in six hours, I can't sleep. Back when I was training my body for this, the more anxious I'd get about needing to go to sleep, the tougher it would be to fall asleep. I wasn't lying to Russell—I really do love mornings, but I love them a little less when it's nine o'clock, ten o'clock, ten thirty, and I have to be up in three and a half hours.

Eventually, I grab my laptop, pay $3.99 to rent an HD version of

The Parent Trap, and drift off right around the time the British Lindsay Lohan flies to Napa Valley to meet Dennis Quaid for the first time.

MY ALARM GOES off at 2:30 and again at 2:40 and finally at 2:47, I force myself out of bed, force myself to be content with the couple hours of sleep I got, even if remembering the Emmy incident makes me want to hibernate for the rest of winter.

I throw my makeup into a bag and stumble out to my car, bleary-eyed. Sometimes I do my makeup at home and sometimes at work and sometimes while stopped at traffic lights, and today is a traffic light kind of day. I picked one of my favorite dresses to combat my exhaustion, a three-quarter-sleeve mulberry sheath paired with brown suede calf boots. I have five of this dress because the camera prefers rich colors and solids. No green, or I'd disappear into the weather map. Patterns can wobble and shake, which is bad news for the frightening amount of weather-themed clothing I've accumulated over the years.

I was never fully prepared for viewer comments about my clothes. It was shocking at first, people not just judging my appearance but outright rating my hotness. They usually score me the lowest when I wear pants. I hate that I've gotten used to it, but it's a hazard of the job. My first couple years working full-time, I thought about what kinds of comments I'd get when I got dressed, but I haven't since I started working in Seattle. If the trolls want to waste energy talking about it, that's their choice. And it's our choice to hit delete. There probably isn't a piece of clothing I could wear that wouldn't draw either scrutiny or a string of fire and/or eggplant emojis. It's not worth it to dress for anyone but myself and, more importantly, the map.

After I drop my bag off at my desk, I make my way to the weather center, a cluster of computers in the studio we use mainly for forecasting, though sometimes we shoot in there, too. I check all my usual models and data, starting with the National Weather Service and the University of Washington, taking notes and crunching numbers before putting my own daily and seven-day forecasts together on one of our forecast sheets. This worksheet might seem basic, but it's how meteorologists have been doing this job for years, and many of us still do it by hand. After I finish, I'll start building the graphics viewers will see during the broadcast.

I yelp when I feel a hand on the back of my chair.

"Sorry," Torrance says, and prior to Friday, I wouldn't have been sure I'd ever heard her utter that word. "Can I talk to you?"

I set down my pen in the middle of a Wednesday sunbreak and turn in my chair to face her. "Of course." This is far too early for her to be at the station. Something's up.

The coffee I drank too fast churns in my stomach. There's no way she could have overheard Russell and me. And yet there we were, so openly shitting on our bosses in a semipublic place. It's not impossible that it got back to her.

She slides into the chair next to me, looking a little softer than usual in jeans and a white sweater. No camera makeup, just a touch of eye shadow and mascara. "I was hoping to catch you without too many people here," she says. "I wanted to personally apologize for what happened on Friday. Sober, this time. What we did—what *I* did—was unacceptable, and at a party, no less."

Torrance Hale is apologizing to me. *Again*.

It's almost as out of character as this meme of her that went viral before I started at KSEA. She was covering a heat wave and getting some man-on-the-street footage at Hempfest, Seattle's annual marijuana festival, when a guy offered her a joint on camera. She declined it with a laugh and a "maybe later," and I've never known whether she meant it or whether she was joking. Regardless, the internet turned it into a GIF that still makes me double-take whenever I see it. Some people swear they can see her winking as she responds, while others have argued that it's just a blink.

"Oh . . . okay?" I manage, my thumb brushing the lightning bolt at the base of my throat.

Torrance straightens some papers, and I wonder if she's thinking about what Seth said about the weather center being a disaster zone. "Seth and I shouldn't have dragged you into it, with that game. We were acting immature. It was personal, and we should have stopped ourselves before we went that far. I absolutely should have stopped myself before what happened with the Emmy."

I want to tell Torrance that it wasn't just what happened at the party. It's been a hundred different things—this is just the one with the most visible wreckage.

"I—I appreciate that." In spite of everything, my optimism takes over. I want to believe her. And maybe this makes me naive, but part of me does. I believe the Torrance who was on my TV as a kid, who was there for me when my mother was sunk in her own deep depression.

I'm just not sure how much of that Torrance is the one sitting next to me right now.

She grins like she's about to tell several thousand viewers that there's no rush-hour traffic today. "Let me take you out to lunch today to make it up to you? You pick the place."

A lunch invitation, like maybe it really is that easy for the two of us to be something more than employee and distracted boss. Like maybe there's more of my childhood idol in her than I thought.

"You really don't have to," I say.

"I insist." Torrance cups my shoulder with one hand, gives me that upper-seventies smile again. "Thanks, Ari. I look forward to it."

I glow the rest of the morning, the conversation waking me up more than any amount of caffeine. My first forecast, I'm all smiles, despite my three hours of sleep. I'm half tempted to edit emojis into my cloud graphics. Maybe Torrance and I will talk about Halestorm, about the bigger stories I want to be doing. Maybe I'll bring up my annual eval, and while I won't say how disappointed I was last year when she simply said "You're doing great, Abrams" and gave me the union-mandated 1.5 percent raise, I'll make sure she knows how eager I am to learn. To improve.

By eleven o'clock, I'm scanning menus of the Belltown lunch spots I haven't tried yet and posting viewer photos of last week's storm on social media when I hear Seth's voice booming from Torrance's office.

"I told you we can't air this," he's saying. The office door is open a crack.

Avery Mitchell catches my eye from a couple desks away. "Torrance's story about Dungeness crabs and climate change," she says by way of explanation. "About how the rising acidity in the ocean is damaging their shells. We were working on it all last month, talked to a ton of scientists. It was supposed to air this afternoon as part of a series on marine life, and I'm guessing Seth just watched it."

"What was wrong with it?" I ask, just as Torrance yells, "It's not biased, it's science!"

Avery shrugs as though to say, *that*.

"You know that and I know that," Seth says, "but the advertisers don't, and I'd rather not field a dozen angry phone calls about it."

"We get angry phone calls whenever we talk about climate change. I report the weather. I can't not talk about it."

"I'm aware of that! But we have to be careful about how we do it. This is about *all* our viewers, not just the ones who agree with you."

"Well, the ones who don't are wrong."

I'm firmly on Torrance's side. It's something we have to contend with every so often on social media, though not nearly as much as the comments we get about showing both too much and not enough skin. It's disheartening how many more people care about our bodies than rising ocean levels.

Seth goes quiet, too quiet to hear. And then: "What if you cut out this part at the end, or–"

A sharp laugh from Torrance cuts him off. "I know what's going on here. You're trying to get back at me for Friday. Your Emmy."

"That is blatantly untrue. I'm just doing my *job*, Tor."

"I don't think you are. I think you're trying to silence me to make yourself look like the big man here. So you can feel better about your pathetic little–"

And I'm done.

With shaking hands, I push out my chair, making more noise than I intend as I shove to my feet and stalk out of the newsroom. My ears are ringing, my lungs tight. No one can see me like this, and if I stay in this room a second longer, I'm going to scream.

When the door to the Dugout opens and someone says, "In here," I'm in such a state that it takes me a moment to register the voice as Russell's. He opens the door wider, beckoning me inside. The Dugout isn't super high-tech or anything, but it's quiet. There's Russell's desk, and those belonging to our other sports reporters and anchors, most of them strewn with sports equipment and memorabilia, the walls covered with jerseys and pennants and posters of athletes. Maybe there was something to Chris Torres's football theory.

It's stunningly, blessedly empty.

"Thought maybe you needed to hide as much as I did." He gestures to a free chair at the empty desk next to his before leaning back in his own chair. He looks so casual here, so *right*. The kind of comfort I've never managed to grasp at the station. "Everyone's out to lunch, but I had a story to finish up."

I finally let out a breath, collapsing into the chair he rolls over to me. Out there, my emotions were on the verge of taking over. In here, I'm safe. "Thanks."

"Hey," he says, leaning forward, a little worry-divot appearing between his brows, right above his glasses. "Are you okay?"

"I'm not sure yet."

He reaches for a candy jar on his desk and holds it out to me.

"You guys really do have privacy in here," I say as I grab a handful. The sugar helps. A bit. "All we have out there are our low-partition workspaces. And those do approximately nothing to shield us from the Hales."

"Somehow, I get the feeling you didn't come in here to talk feng shui."

I crunch down on a mini Snickers. "I am so fucking naive."

At first, I'm surprised I say it out loud. I don't make a habit of swearing at work, and I don't do anything nearly as aggressive as the way my teeth are tearing apart this Snickers. It must be last week's drunken gripe fest that's made me okay talking to Russell like this. Letting him see a less polished version of Ari Abrams.

Russell's brows crease again, his eyes growing concerned. They really are a brilliant shade of blue. "What do you mean?"

"Torrance apologized to me this morning. She got here early, told me how embarrassed she was about what happened at the party. She even said she'd take me to lunch, like we're friends, when we've never gone out to lunch together before." I shake my head and unwrap a 3 Musketeers. "I really let myself believe her."

"I get it. Even in here, sometimes I feel completely . . ." He motions to the walls around us. "Trapped."

Trapped. That's exactly the right word for it.

"What we talked about on Friday," I start slowly. "Are you still—is that still something you might be open to?"

"We were both pretty plastered. I had the headache all weekend to prove it." He drapes his hand over a baseball on his desk, rolls it in a circle. "But . . . I'm serious about it if you are, Ari."

I'm not used to hearing my name from him. It's always been *weather girl*, and there's something about my name that snags my attention. Something that turns me serious, if I wasn't already.

"I just want to not dread going to work," I say plainly. "Yes, I'd love to be valued a little more. I'd love to take on some bigger weather stories. But I used to look forward to work all the time, which is maybe a weird thing to say when it requires getting up at what most people would consider an ungodly hour. But it's true. I love my job. I don't love the way Torrance and Seth run this station, and it's clear neither of them has plans to leave. Even if this means we spend more time around them and quite possibly lose our minds in the process . . . I want to at least try."

"I know you're not into sports," Russell says as he tosses the baseball once in the air before catching it. "But that kind of sounded like you were a coach giving a halftime pep talk to a losing team."

"Hopefully it wasn't prophetic, then."

He holds up a finger, one corner of his mouth quirking into a smile. "Ah, but that's the great thing about sports. We love an underdog story."

6

FORECAST:

It's raining gelt (and chardonnay)

THERE'S A LIMIT to the number of times one can hear the dreidel song without losing one's mind. I hit that limit about a dozen *I have a little dreidel*s ago, and yet I paste on my sunshine smile for my niece and nephew, who could probably keep playing until midnight without getting bored.

"I have a little dreidel, I made it out of . . ." Cassie says from where she's sitting on the living room rug, a heap of gelt and pennies spread between her and her brother. We're all wearing matching menorah light-up sweaters Alex got us for Hanukkah last year, and she keeps scratching at the collar of hers.

"Pizzadillas!" Orion shouts, showing off his adorable jack-o'-lantern smile. He finally lost his first tooth over the weekend, and I can't remember ever being that proud of something. Oh, to be five again.

"What's a pizzadilla?" I ask from the couch, where Javier and I have been both playing and refereeing the game.

"A quesadilla with a pizza on top!" Orion gets so excited, he flings the dreidel across the room. "I thought you were *smart*, Aunt Ari."

"I'm sorry, I'm sorry. I should have known. My pizza knowledge is sorely lacking," I say as he scurries to collect the dreidel. "You'll have to make them for me next time."

"Let's make them now!" Cassie bounds up to me, her curly dark hair springing in all directions. The oversize menorah sweater hangs to the knees of her blue-and-white striped leggings. "I'm going to make you the best one, but Papa will have to put it in the oven."

"Kiddo, we're not making anything. We just ate," Javier says, running a hand through Cassie's wild hair that matches his. "And I think that's enough dreidel. Why don't we save some for the remaining seven nights? Aunt Ari has to be up early in the morning."

"And that is entirely because the station doesn't respect Jewish holidays." I consider that for a moment. "Although frankly, sometimes neither do I. It's a fine line to walk."

"One more round." Cassie gives her dad these pleading eyes that are impossible to resist. "Please?"

"They don't teach you how to say no to that face in parenting classes," Alex tells me as he heads into the room, drying his hands on his jeans.

With glee, the twins grab the dreidel again. *I have a little dreidel, I made it out of Aunt Ari's existential angst.*

Until Alex had kids, I was convinced I didn't want them, certain my genes would make me a terrible parent. But spending time with them has changed my mind completely. I'm not sure how many and I'm not sure when, but all I know is that I want this kind of family. I want this joy we didn't always have growing up.

"You look beat," Alex says to me as he settles into an armchair, stretching out his long legs. The shammash light on his sweater keeps flickering on and off, though he changed the batteries before dinner. "Dreidel too intense for you?"

"I'm fine," I insist. It's been my mantra lately. *Fine* that Garrison dumped me. *Fine* that Torrance would rather resurrect petty arguments than be a real boss. Again I summon that *here's your weekend forecast* smile. But even *fine* sounds forced when you have to insist that's what you are. So I amend it. "I'm great. Really."

And I'll be even better once I meet up with Russell tomorrow evening to discuss our plans. A couple hours before my usual bedtime, but it's definitely worth staying awake for.

"You lose," Orion informs us as the dreidel lands on gimel and he takes all my gelt and Cassie's. "You all lose!"

I pretend to pout. "Oh no, again? You're a real high roller!"

Both Orion and Cassie burst into giggles, their little-kid laughter soothing my soul just a fraction. It's always been a toss-up whether a holiday or birthday or other celebration would include my mother, depending on her mood that week. I assume Alex invited her, and it's almost a relief that she didn't show up.

"That's game." Javier collects the dreidel and transfers Orion's winnings to the coffee table. Cassie must be too hopped-up on sugar—I brought a *lot* of gelt—to contest Orion's victory. "I'll take them upstairs if you two want to keep talking."

"That would be great, thanks," Alex says.

The twins throw their arms around my neck, and I pretend they're hugging me too hard. "You're too strong! I'm not sure how long I can last!" I groan as if I'm in pain. This of course makes them laugh harder, hug tighter, and eventually I give in and squeeze them back. "Happy Hanukkah," I say, ruffling their hair and dropping the kind of too-loud kisses they pretend to hate on top of their heads.

"Make sure Cassiopeia has her water in the purple cup," Alex calls, and Javier holds it up, grinning.

"How do you even bring yourself to discipline them?" I ask as the trio clomps upstairs, Cassie already telling Orion how she's going to get him back at dreidel tomorrow night.

"Oh, somehow we manage."

I'm pushing my own bedtime again, but I think I needed this. Alex disappears into the kitchen and returns with two glasses of wine, watching as I gulp down half of one.

"Should I get you the whole bottle?"

"I'm cutting myself off," I say as I pour his glass into mine. "After this one."

"I was about to ask if it's been a long week, but it's only Monday."

I wave my hand. "Long week, long month, long year."

"Anything you want to talk about?"

"My boss. As usual. When isn't it my boss? And thank you, but . . . I'm dealing with it." Or I will be, with the ever-polite but still mysterious Russell Barringer. Tomorrow.

"Well then," Alex says, sliding onto the couch next to me, "I wanted to talk to you about something." He plays with a frayed edge of a blanket, and—oh. Javier must have taken Cassie and Orion upstairs to give us some time alone. "It's about Mom."

I wish I could undo the visceral reaction this sparks in me. I hate that those three words conjure up the kind of anxiety that makes me want to sprint upstairs and hide in a child-sized bed. "Okay."

Alex takes a deep breath. "She's at a psychiatric treatment center."

A cold front rushes in, filling my brain with static. "She—*what*? Is she okay?"

His expression softens, but his words remain serious. "Ari. It's a good thing. Or—it's going to be, at least. She went to the ER yesterday after calling 911. The guy she was seeing, Ted? He broke up with her last week. And it brought all her emotions to the surface in a really extreme way. They told me she was having a panic attack when she called, and she was convinced she was going to die, and that—that she was going to die alone." He pauses to collect himself, running a hand down his freckled face. "It sounded like she didn't think she could take care of herself. But she's safe now. That's the most important thing."

Okay. She's okay. She's safe.

I can barely process the rest of it because I can't quantify the number of times I've wanted my mother to get help. I can't visualize her in the kind of hospital I've only ever seen in medical dramas.

It wasn't until I was an adult that I really understood something was wrong, and then it became so crystal clear. Hindsight: that precise and painful thing that made all the fragments of "that's just Mom" click into place. In high school, when she was teaching me to drive and she broke down sobbing in the middle of the freeway because her boyfriend had dumped her via text. In middle school, when she shut herself in her room and refused to leave for three days, and I begged Alex to help me pick the lock because I didn't know if she was still alive. In elementary school, when our dad told her he couldn't be around her anymore, that she was bringing him down, and couldn't she just be happy for once in her goddamn life? For a few years after he left, he sent cards on our birthdays. The last one was for my bat mitzvah, and I didn't bother keeping it.

When my mother was deep in one of those moods, it seemed like nothing brought her joy—not her job, not family outings, not working in the garden, which she loved on her good days. If Alex and I were excited about something, she couldn't muster even a tenth of the enthusiasm. She used so many sick days, I was shocked she was able to keep her job, and she'd make snide remarks about my appearance I told myself she didn't really mean.

Then there was the revolving door of boyfriends who ranged from scumbag to fixer, calling her "hysterical" or "batshit" or "crazy." Alex and I learned how to be independent, how to cook if we needed to, how to use public transportation if she wasn't up to driving us somewhere. It wasn't all the time, which made it easier for us to pretend nothing was wrong. Sometimes she'd go weeks or months without an episode. She'd go back to gardening and we'd pile on the couch to watch a movie together and I'd think, *This is okay. Everything's okay now.* But then she'd swing right back.

In high school, I started feeling off. Withdrawn. An acute sadness crept in that I could only occasionally attach to something specific. At first, it was easy to ignore because I was usually too worried about my mother. So I didn't tell anyone, just let it live alongside me and turn my world grayer.

I went to therapy for the first time in college, the heaviness I'd lived with for a few years making it impossible to concentrate, despite how much I loved what I was studying. It scared me, how similar it looked to what my mother was going through, that for a while I assumed it had to be normal. I slept too much and had trouble making friends. I didn't know when it took root, only that I was having fewer and fewer good days in between bouts of hopelessness and lethargy. I didn't know if anyone in the campus clinic could help me, but at the very least, I figured I couldn't feel any worse than I already did.

"I just feel . . . off," I told the therapist. I learned there was probably a name for what my mother was struggling with, even though she'd never been diagnosed, never talked to anyone, never taken medication. I learned that all the reasons I was furious with Amelia Abrams and found her emotionally draining to the point where I'd need twelve hours of sleep the next day to recover from a visit home—they were beyond her control, to a certain extent. She was suffering, too. But she wouldn't help herself.

And then I learned that the thing weighing me down wasn't just an adjective, but a noun. Depression. I was clinically depressed, and I wasn't going to let it control me. My mother had always been against medication. She said it was because of the side effects, but she wouldn't even take Advil when she had a headache. But I wanted a life on the opposite end of the spectrum from my mother's, so I filled my prescription.

It had been such a relief to have a name for it—until I came home for winter break and tried to explain it to her. Some part of me hoped she'd see herself in my diagnosis, that it might spark her to get help. "We're all depressed," she said instead, brushing it off. "The world is fucking awful. We just have to learn how to deal with it."

I wouldn't let her pull me back under. For almost ten years, I've been on meds and in therapy, and they've changed my life.

"It's a great place. I checked it out online, and it has solid reviews," Alex is saying, and I briefly imagine a Yelp for psychiatric hospitals. "She wants to change, Ari."

"And you believe her."

"She's always wanted to. It's just . . . taken her a while to get there."

She's always wanted to. Those words send me into another spiral. When my first boyfriend dumped me after a homecoming dance because he thought I wasn't fun enough, and she asked what I'd done to drive him away. "We're too much for them," she told me, and I believed her. When my college boyfriend, a guy named Michael I'd only been dating for a few weeks, dumped me because I spilled everything to him—my mother, therapy, my new antidepressants—and he said he wasn't ready to be in a serious relationship with me.

From that point on, I vowed to keep it all hidden, to be the shiny happy person I became on TV.

"How do you know all of this?" I ask, tugging a crocheted blanket around my legs. "You've been talking about it with her?"

"I'm, uh, her emergency contact."

"Right." I stiffen, trying to tell myself I shouldn't feel hurt by this. He's the older sibling, after all.

It's been gradual, letting her calls go to voice mail and leaving her texts unanswered for days at a time. She doesn't even know about my breakup yet. My current therapist, Joanna, advised making space so I can focus on myself, since she's so good at dragging me down. Even if sometimes I wish we had a relationship that enabled us to get margaritas or go to brunch together, it's not unusual for months to go by without hearing from her, and when she reappears, for it to only be with bad news.

"I want to support her," I say quietly. "I want her to get better. I do. I just . . . I'm sorry, I'm having a hard time believing it. Why now, after all these years?"

What I don't say: *we weren't enough for her.*

He nudges my foot with his latke-patterned sock. "The best we can do right now is be there for her, and be ready to keep supporting her when she comes home. She's taking personal leave from work." She's been at Boeing for decades, working her way up to a job as an executive assistant. "This place has regular visitor hours, and I was thinking of going soon. I know it would mean a lot to her if you came, too. She still watches you," he continues. "Almost every day."

This is a lot to process. I pull the blanket tighter around myself, the emotion I've been fighting off for the past week threatening to surface. "I'm not sure I can decide right now. I get that she's dealing with something huge, but she's been dealing with it for *years*, Alex. And we didn't matter enough to her for her to get help when we were kids, or when we were teens, or when we finally moved out of the house. So I'm sorry if I'm a little low on sympathy for her at the moment."

"I get it." He throws an arm around my shoulders and gives me a gentle hug. He's a good caretaker. A good dad. "I get it, and it's shitty. Whatever you decide to do, I support you. One hundred percent."

"I appreciate that," I say, meaning it. "I'll let you know."

After a few more minutes, Javier appears at the foot of the stairs. "Cassie's demanding a bedtime story from her favorite aunt. You up for it?"

"Of course," I say, and even though I hope it'll feel natural once I see my niece, I turn on the smile before I head upstairs.

7

FORECAST:

A gentle breeze of an evening interrupted by a sharp gust of reality

"SO WE'RE REALLY going to Parent Trap our bosses," I say, hoping it'll sound more believable once it's out of my mouth. Nope. Still absurd.

"We really are." Russell leans across the table at the Ballard taqueria we picked because it's always busy and we didn't want anyone to overhear us. "Look at this," he says, showing me his phone. It's an article from when Torrance was hired at KSEA, a fluff piece about the Hales' plans to revitalize the station. "Proof that they were happy once."

She and Seth are sitting at the anchor desk, looking not at the camera but at each other. It's not tough to fake a smile for the camera, but the joy in their eyes? The way Seth is gazing at her, all pride and adoration? That's real.

Russell swipes to another photo.

"Is that a picture of them . . . swing dancing?" Maybe it shouldn't be too much of a surprise, given the moves they busted out at the holiday party. In this photo, they look like they're from another era: Torrance's blond hair in pin curls and Seth in a fedora. He's holding her in a dramatic dip, her back arched at what should be an impossible angle.

The thought *Are we really doing this?* has been running through my head on a near-constant loop. Every time I wonder whether this is too manipulative, I remember what Torrance said the night of the party. Somewhere beneath the barbs and bravado are two people who used to be in love with each other. We're just going to give them a push.

And if it's also a way to distract myself from what's happening with my mother, well, that's just a bonus.

I crunch down on a tortilla chip and slide the phone back to Russell, who's in a green sweater beneath a deep caramel corduroy jacket with elbow patches. Combined with his rectangular glasses and stubble along his jaw, he looks like a professor who stays long past his office hours to make sure every one of his students understands the material because that's just how much he cares.

"We'll keep digging." After work, I took off my camera makeup and changed into jeans and a striped cardigan. It makes this feel less like a work meeting and more like—well, I'm not sure what to call it. A plot-a-thon? A scheme sesh? "But I think we need to lay out what we know about them, so we can get a better sense of who they are."

Russell opens up a notes app on his phone, motions for me to continue.

"I've worked for Torrance for three years," I say. "She's good at what she does. Obviously. And she's passionate about weather and science. She loves doing charity work, mostly environmental causes. She likes flowers but prefers succulents. She only drinks oat milk because she doesn't do dairy and she's allergic to soy. On occasion, she will tolerate hemp milk. Her lipstick never budges or transfers, and before I die, I swear to god I will find out how she does it." I allow myself space to take a breath and keep racking my brain. "She and Seth have one son, Patrick. I think he works in tech? His wife Roxanne is about to have a baby."

"That's a good start," Russell says as he types.

"What do we know about Seth?"

"He likes to have a hand in everything going on in the newsroom, but sometimes he goes a little overboard. Gets too involved. Everything has to be *just so,* or he loses it." He dunks a chip in salsa. "Uh . . . let's see. He gets takeout from that Greek place on Vine at least once a week. Oh, and he loves Garamond—that's what all his signs are typed in. Like he thinks it'll make them less aggressive because Garamond is such an innocuous font."

"I do like Garamond. It's professional, but in a friendly way." I reach for another chip. "So this is what we've got. Fonts and milk."

A woman at the counter calls out our order number, and Russell hops up to grab our taco plates, with sides of black beans topped with cotija. For a few minutes, we eat in silence, save for the occasional sound of approval. That push we're going to give Torrance and Seth—we're going to have to use heavy machinery.

"Did you always want to cover sports?" I ask once I've demolished my first taco, carne asada with a verde sauce so spicy it nearly makes me weep. Sure, this dinner isn't strictly for socializing, but this is the first time Russell and I have been out alone, not counting that night at the hotel bar, and I've been curious about him. This is my chance to learn what's beneath that modest professorial exterior.

"Actually, no," he says. "I've always loved them, but I didn't think you could do something like this as a career. Like, getting paid to go to games? Sounds fake. But I liked writing, and I liked sports, and it wasn't until college that I took a sports journalism class and realized I might want to do it professionally."

"And you didn't start out in broadcasting, either."

He shakes his head. "I was covering sports for a paper in Grand Rapids, where I grew up. I wrote about high school sports at first—that's where most people start."

I have to hold in a laugh. "I'm sorry," I say. "I'm imagining you at a high school football game, taking very serious notes while the homecoming king and queen ride out onto the field in a convertible."

"You laugh, but . . ." The single light bulb above our table glints off his glasses as he leans forward. "My first season there, I did a story about the homecoming queen. Who was also the starting quarterback. She took them to the state championships for the first time in the school's history. Sports—it's not just about the numbers. It's not just wins and losses, like weather isn't just about the little suns and clouds that pop up on-screen. There are entire personalities and stories behind the players, and that's what I've always loved. It's about the people, more than anything."

"I'm not sure if I've ever thought about it that way," I say. "But I like that. I didn't go to any football games in high school or college. The whole school-spirit thing kind of missed me."

"It doesn't have to be solely motivated by school spirit. When you go as an adult, I'm guessing it's not because you're all rah-rah Seattle. Most people go for the atmosphere."

I give him my guiltiest cringe.

"Holy shit." He pauses with a chip halfway to his mouth. "You've never been to a sporting event."

"It's not that I don't like sports," I say quickly, not wanting to offend him. "I didn't play any growing up and neither did my brother, and no one in our family watched anything. It wasn't part of the Abrams culture, I guess."

Russell leans closer to place a sympathetic hand on my shoulder. "Ari Abrams. This is an absolute tragedy." His hand is warm through the fabric of my shirt, and when he pulls back, I find myself wishing he'd lingered a few moments longer. We broke the touch barrier the night of the party, but something about this feels different. "So you're telling me you've never been to a Sounders game? They're as un-sports as sports can be. Most people don't even go because they love soccer; they're just there to drink or eat garlic fries."

"Wait, wait, what? Garlic fries? No one ever told me about garlic fries."

"The best eight twenty-five you'll ever spend." When I gasp at this, he winces a little. "Okay, yeah, they're way too expensive for fries, but the overpriced food is part of the whole experience. There's this infectious energy in a stadium I've never found anywhere else, all these people coming together for the same thing."

"You've convinced me. I'll go to a sports."

He just shakes his head at me, his eyes crinkling at the edges when he grins. I'm not sure I've noticed that about him before. "What about you? How'd you get into weather?"

"It's mostly those little suns and clouds," I say, and this deepens his smile. "I was one of those kids who was obsessed with storms. Any severe weather, really. I used to track it in a notebook, week by week, and try to make predictions. As I got older, I got more curious about the science behind it. The news can be so dark. So grim. And then I get to come on-screen and be goofy and give people good news. News that might help them make immediate decisions. Like I told you during the party, I grew up watching Torrance, and what she did felt so powerful. I'm still awed by the elements, and all of us, no matter who we are—we have to obey."

"It can be terrifying," Russell agrees. "We were used to snow in the Midwest, but one winter, we got two and a half feet, and they still only shut down school for a few days."

"We're lucky in the Northwest. Ten-year-old Ari would have been so jealous of you in Michigan. Our sprinkling of snow every other year was never enough for her." Honestly, it's not enough for adult Ari, either. I force myself to take a breath. Typical Ari Abrams: waxing poetic about weather. "Sorry. Am I talking too much about the weather?"

Russell lifts an eyebrow. "I literally asked you about the weather."

"I know, I know. Just—some people think it's small talk, that it's not, like, intelligent conversation or whatever. Or at least, I've been told that before." Any time I was at a party with Garrison and someone said *some weather we're having*, I'd rush in with an explanation. I learned quickly that people didn't usually want the science behind it.

"And then some people think you're making a political statement about the earth getting warmer, about the extreme weather we're experiencing more frequently than we ever have. Even though there's nothing about climate change that should be political, in my opinion."

I'm relieved when he meets this with a firm nod. Not that I'd expect anything else, but I'd have some strong feelings about scheming with a climate change denier.

"One hundred percent," he says. "And hey, sometimes games get delayed or canceled because of the weather. What you do directly affects what I do. It affects everyone, really."

"Right!" I say, waving a tortilla chip for emphasis and accidentally flinging salsa onto my sleeve. "I've heard people say it takes zero effort to do the weather, that the station could put anyone up there to deliver a forecast, and the implication is that it's unimportant. But nothing could be further from the truth."

A grin starts in one corner of his mouth and slowly spreads across his face. I realize my cheeks are warm, a side effect of getting so animated about this topic.

"You're giving me a look. I *am* talking too much about the weather. I knew it. I'll stop. My brother says I have a tendency to get emotional about rain." With a fingertip, I graze the lightning bolt at my collar. "And he's not wrong."

"Ari," Russell says, laughing. There's this lovely openness on his face when he does it, and it makes me wonder whether he's been holding himself back every other time he's laughed with me. "No. Please don't. It's just—your expression completely changes when you talk about it. I can tell it's more than just a job to you. It's not just that you're excited about it. It's your passion."

Now I feel my chest bloom with a different kind of heat. However I must look right now, I want to tell him he looked the same when he was talking about sports.

"Is Ari short for anything?" he asks.

"Arielle."

"Why are you making that face?"

I sigh, unscrunching my nose. "Because even though it's Ahr-i-elle, everyone thought it was Ariel. Like *The Little Mermaid.*" I hold up a strand of my red hair, which has rejected the straightening I subjected it to for the camera. "You would not believe how many kids in elementary school asked me where my fins were, or started singing 'Under the Sea' when they saw me. It was easier to go by Ari."

"I like both," he says. "And you're safe, because I can guarantee you don't want to hear me sing."

This is *fun*, plotting to get our bosses back together, even if we haven't mentioned either of them in the past twenty minutes. Aside from Hannah, I don't really have work friends at KSEA, and I've missed this kind of conversation with the friends Garrison took with him after the breakup.

But Russell Barringer and I—we could be friends.

We talk more about Torrance and Seth, making some plans for low-level espionage. Most of it will have to wait until after the new year.

"We're going to have to get them together outside of work," Russell says. "You just moved into a new place, right? What about a housewarming party?"

"In my studio apartment? I respect my possessions too much." I consider it for a moment. "But you're right. We need to force proximity the shit out of them. It's just too bad we don't have a camping trip or anything like they do in the movie, though I guess that was more to scare away their potential new stepmom."

"No," he says. "But we do have the KSEA retreat next month. You're going on that, right?" I nod. It's a mix of people every year, since the station can't exactly function with all of us gone. "It'll almost be like being on vacation, and who doesn't want to fall in love on vacation?"

In a way, all this scheming makes me feel a little powerful. Garrison thought I was too sunshine? Not real enough? Well, here's my edge. That TV version of myself, the one he thought I never turned off, wouldn't be going behind her boss's back like this, even if it were for the greater good.

We're down to only chip crumbs when his phone rings. It's been on the table between us, but we've barely glanced at our phones, let alone reached for them. When he sees who's calling, though, he picks it up.

"Sorry, I've got to take this," he says, his mouth set in a firm line.

A server swings by the table and swaps our empty basket for a new one, the chips fresh from the fryer and glistening with salt. I mouth *thank you* to him, trying not to overhear Russell's conversation, even though it's happening two feet in front of me.

"Of course. I can be there in twenty. Hang tight." He hangs up, smoothing out the collar of his jacket with his free hand. "That was my daughter. She has play practice after school, and I guess she's not feeling well, and . . ."

The rest of his sentence is lost as my mind tries to make sense of this new information.

"Your . . . daughter?"

"Elodie. She's twelve." He signals to the server for the check.

I just stare at him. He barely looks older than I am. How can Russell Barringer, KSEA sports reporter, have a twelve-year-old kid? Named Elodie?

When I'm quiet for a beat too long, he says, "Oh. Oh no. I hope you don't think I'm like, the worst father ever, getting drunk with you at the holiday party. She was at her mom's that weekend, and I don't usually go out even when she's not there. I never drink that much, and never in front of her, and—"

"No, no, I wasn't thinking that at all. I swear. That's awesome! Wow. Um . . . congratulations!" I sputter out. Because congratulating someone on their twelve-year-old child is super normal. Hallmark definitely sells cards for that. *Congrats on keeping a human alive for a decade!*

"Thank you?"

I clap a hand over my mouth. "Oh my god. That thing I said. About DILFs. I'm so sorry, I hope that didn't offend you or anything—" I need to stop talking. A bolt of lightning can strike me down any time, even though the odds of that happening to someone in any given year are about one in a million, according to the National Weather Service.

"No—not at all. I mean, you had to tell me what it meant, so . . ." He trails off, rubs the back of his neck as crimson attacks his cheeks. "We'll continue this soon?"

"Right. Yeah," I say, still reeling. "I hope your daughter is okay."

He gives me a tight smile, and then he's gone.

8

FORECAST:

Clear skies and attempted optimism to kick off the new year

LAST YEAR, I spent Christmas with Garrison's family in a postcard-perfect cabin on the Washington coast. We'd just gotten engaged, a moonlit walk through our neighborhood when he stopped to tie his shoe and then produced the box with that heirloom ring inside, and we were drunk on each other, drunk on the idea of our futures intertwined.

Most guys I'd dated weren't Jewish, and even though I'd spent two Christmases with the Burkes, the rock on my finger turned me newly awkward around them. Eggnog lattes and Santa-shaped pancakes with his nieces and nephews and his parents asking "How's your mother?" and my pinched answers. Hounding us about when they were going to get more grandchildren—"But really, whenever you're ready! As long as it's soon!"—which made me feel more like a pair of ovaries than an actual human woman. They even gave us a teeny stocking for our future mini Burke, though when I told his parents I was planning to keep my last name, they pretended they hadn't heard me.

I looked for bright sides all along the coast, forcing a smile so wide it made my jaw ache. *They'll be different once we're married.* Probably not. *Maybe next year they'll care that I'm Jewish.* Unlikely. *At least the pancakes were good.* Okay, I could cling to that one.

Whenever Garrison asked me if anything was wrong, I told him no and kept right on grinning.

This year, at least I don't have to pretend I like eggnog. Hanukkah is over, and I take advantage of the holiday pay to work both Christmas Eve and Christmas. When you're Jewish in the media industry, everyone assumes you'll work on December 25, which is maybe not a great assumption to make, but I don't hate the extra money in my bank account.

Even with my depression at manageable levels, every so often, I have a dark day. A day where everything feels heavy, the smallest tasks become impossible, and my brain can only conjure worst-case scenarios.

I'll be miserable at this station forever.

Or Torrance will find out what Russell and I are planning and make sure I never work in this industry again.

My mom will reject all the help she's getting.

I'll never have a meaningful connection with another person.

As obvious as it sounds, I just feel really fucking *sad*, and while I can try to distract myself or reach out to my therapist, sometimes I have to let the fog run its course, the logical part of my brain knowing I won't feel this way forever. In past relationships, I did my best to hide my dark days. I'd make a spa appointment I couldn't afford, or I'd say I had errands to run and get in my car and just drive. Even if sometimes "just driving" meant grabbing Taco Bell and sitting in a parking lot for hours trying not to cry because I couldn't summon the energy to turn the car back on. Most of the time, I don't want to be around anyone, because forcing a smile on a dark day is a little like trying to turn concrete into gold.

Unfortunately, this dark day coincides with a text from Garrison. Two days after a Christmas I spend at a Chinese restaurant with my brother's family, my ex asks me to come over and collect some stuff. I'm tempted to reply with Torrance's "maybe later" gif, but instead I trudge from Ravenna to upper Queen Anne, intent on getting in and out as fast as possible. But looking for parking on my old street feels inexplicably heartbreaking. Sometimes it took half an hour to find a spot, and we'd circle and circle because no way were we paying $200/month to park in the building's garage. I never thought I'd reminisce over struggling to find parking, but here I am.

As soon as he opens the door and lets me inside, I want to melt into the plush carpet, use the macramé rug as a blanket, splay my body on top of the walnut credenza. The idea of having enough space for a credenza suddenly seems revolutionary. God, I loved this apartment. So many of my touches are still here, and it hits me that we haven't been broken up for that long. Of course the wall hanging I found at the Fremont flea market is still up, the arched brass floor lamp not yet replaced.

Garrison kept this place because he could afford a two-bedroom and I couldn't. We talked about buying a house after we were married, but we were reluctant to potentially leave this place behind. I might miss our apartment more than I miss him, which is at the very least a sign I'm moving on.

Garrison is tall and white, with floppy dark hair and dark eyes that make him look like Standard-Issue Attractive Male, Aged 25-34. A small mole beneath his left cheekbone, a cleft in his chin I used to poke my thumb into because it made him laugh.

"Hey," he says, sounding much softer than he did over text. "You look . . . really great."

He's lying. I just spent fifteen minutes walking up a hill after finding parking. My hair is a windblown mess and my breasts feel superglued to my bra. The nostalgia evaporated in about ten seconds, annoyance taking its place. I'd love one of those overpriced spa days right about now.

"I'm parked in a loading zone. I can't stay long."

"Parking around here is still shit, sorry." The sheepishness in his voice tugs at my heart.

There were good times, too, though it's harder to remember them the further I am from the breakup. We'd load the car with snacks and go to drive-in movies during the summer, making out in the backseat until someone forced us to leave, and then we'd giggle at being caught like lovesick teens. He'd pop an allergy pill and we'd go to a cat café, sipping lattes with kittens in our laps. Wherever we were, if anyone recognized me from TV, he'd glow with pride. *It's so cool that people know you*, he'd say.

"Is that it?" I ask when he hands me a box with some kitchen supplies and other knickknacks inside. The remainder of my dark day agenda is waiting for me at home: weighted blanket, reality TV, Kraft macaroni with two cheese packets instead of one. Thinking about it makes me somehow feel better and worse at the same time.

"Yep. Wait—you don't have to go just yet, do you?" He looks so forlorn as he says it that my shoulders sag, and I place the box on the floor. "I was hoping we could talk a little."

Nothing about that sounds like a good idea. Nothing at all sounds like a good idea except for processed cheddar. But because apparently being back here has cut out my spine, I follow him over to the couch.

He asks if I want anything to drink and I tell him no, though I regret not requesting hard alcohol as soon as he picks up my hand and says, "I've missed you, Ari." His thumb rubs a gentle circle on my palm, and I let him. "How have you been? Really."

"Not bad," I croak out. The sensation of his skin on mine is too distracting. I've missed being touched like this. I've missed being *touched*, period, and depression brain tells me I haven't deserved to be.

"Not gonna lie, part of me was hoping you'd tell me you've been completely miserable for the past couple months," he says. "But I guess that's how you've always been. Determined to look on the bright side."

"There's nothing wrong with that." Although I've been wondering lately just how much of that brightness the Hales block out.

He's quiet for a moment, and then reaches over to sift his other hand through my hair, naturally wavy today. "Maybe you're right. Maybe . . . we could all use a little more bright side."

It happens so quickly, I'm not sure how to process it. One moment, there's a good couple feet between us. The next, his hands are cupping the sides of my face and I'm clutching at his collar and he's on top of me, pressing me down into the couch that we have done this on too many times to count. His mouth is hot on mine, too eager, just like the bulge in his pants. It's immensely gratifying, knowing how instantly turned-on he is, and it dials my self-esteem all the way up to eleven.

No one else will want you, depression brain says. *At least he already knows about all your issues.*

And he didn't want me, either.

"You feel so good," he says beneath my ear, and thank god, the sound of his voice wakes me up. My spine grows back.

Seeing Garrison again has tangled my emotions so thoroughly that I can't stick to a single decision. My trains of thought are on a hundred different tracks racing toward a hundred different stations. But this can't happen, not after he made me feel so terrible about myself, forced me to question the one thing that's protected me all these years. This would only make my dark day worse, and I'd wake up tomorrow unable to leave my bed.

My lungs are tight as I place a hand on his chest and push. When gentle doesn't work, I use more force. "I can't. I can't do this."

Garrison draws back onto his heels, face twisted in frustration. "Are you serious?"

"Yes." Breathing hard, I get to my feet, smoothing out my sweater and combing a hand through my hair. "You're the one who broke up with *me*, remember? Because I wasn't 'real' enough for you."

"Whoa, whoa, whoa," he says. "This wasn't me trying to get back together with you. This was just—it was just physical."

I scoff at that, because I'd love for it to be just physical. I'd love nothing more than to text him every Friday night to come over and go down on me for a solid fifteen minutes, zero emotional attachment. But if I have any hope of moving on, I can't do that.

"It doesn't matter. Even 'just physical' is going to be a mistake. Is that real enough for you?"

I grab my box of things, leaving him on the couch with mussed hair and a raging hard-on.

"Happy New Year," I say from the hallway before I shut the door.

When I get back to my car, there's a parking ticket wedged between the windshield wipers.

• • •

I TURN THE remaining days of the year into an exorcism. I try on my entire closet and donate anything that reminds me of him, a dress he loved or an accessory he bought me. The only exception is a pair of jeans he said made my ass look incredible because, well, they do.

I'm leaving him in December because I can't leave him back at Halloween, and I can't carry him with me into January.

This year, I'm going to be good to myself. I'm going to do things differently. I'll go on a date and *Get back out there, queen!* the way every millennial lifestyle website is telling me to. Maybe I'll learn how to do this casually and I'll be okay with Friday nights alone, the way my mother so rarely was.

If I'm casually dating, I don't have to tell anyone about my family or my prescription or my dark days. Because even if Garrison threw all of that into question, I still have no idea how to talk about it with someone. On the third date? The seventh? Right before you sleep with someone? It's never felt right, never felt natural, and that makes me think it's never going to.

So I reinstall the app Garrison and I matched on, the one I deleted a few weeks into our relationship. And when Alex texts me asking if I'm free to see our mother after the KSEA retreat next week, it must be the newer version of myself who responds, Okay.

I decline a New Year's Eve invitation from him in favor of self-care. I've never eaten in a restaurant by myself that wasn't fast-casual, but I make a reservation at my favorite Italian place and simply shake my head when the server asks, "Are we waiting for one more?"

"No," I say. "Just me."

I force myself to leave my phone in my bag to savor the atmosphere and the independence. And . . . it's kind of great, no pressure to talk as I listen to a string quartet play Sinatra.

Only once, in between courses, do I pull out my phone and find a Happy New Year text from Russell. I parrot it back and add a few emojis, but I hesitate before I hit send.

The revelation about his daughter threw me. I'm ashamed to admit I scoured social media afterward, but I couldn't find any of his profiles. Smart of him, frustrating for me. Still, he's not married, I'm pretty certain of that. No ring, no mention of a spouse. Then again, this was the first I'd heard of his daughter.

I push him out of my mind. This could be the year of casual dating, learning how to be single, having dinner by myself.

So I order a double chocolate torte for dessert, and I scrape the plate clean.

THE FIRST DAY of the new year, I sign up for a Costco membership and buy a sixty-four-pack of triple-A batteries.

9

FORECAST:

Freezing temperatures and warm gooey feelings

WE START SMALL.

At our GM's seventy-fifth birthday, the one he declined to attend, I learned that Torrance and Seth happen to be the only people at the station with a deep and abiding love for carrot cake. I even wondered if Torrance, who planned the party, ordered it just because she knew no one else would eat it.

Our first day back in the office, Russell orders one from a downtown bakery, propping it up in the kitchen with a note that reads HAPPY *NEWS* YEAR! beneath a doodle of a TV wearing a party hat.

"There's carrot cake in the kitchen," I tell Torrance with a knock on her half-open door, while Russell does the same thing with Seth down the hall. Bonding over their favorite food—it's got to put them in a good mood.

Later that week, I spend an afternoon at a greenhouse picking out the most attractive and least fussy succulent I can find. The woman loves plants, but the less she has to water them, the better. It's not cheap, but it'll be worth it. I schedule a delivery and don't include a card.

"That's a nice succulent," Seth says the next day when it shows up, leaning against the wall outside Torrance's office. It's exactly what someone who anonymously sent a plant to her would do, and I send him a thousand mental thank-yous.

"It is." Torrance rearranges some of her pots to find a place for it on her desk. I can tell it's taking every ounce of restraint not to ask him whether he sent it.

The problem, though, is that we're not close enough to either of them to know how they're really reacting. Whether any of this is making an impact.

At the end of the week, after a near-constant exchange of ideas over text and email, we get lucky.

I loop a scarf tighter around my neck, shivering inside my puffy coat as I scan the rows of seats in the arena. Russell waves me over, and I mutter, "Sorry, sorry," as I climb over legs and bags and foamy cups of beer to get to him.

"You made it," he says with a grin. His hair spills out of his knit hat, curling over the top of his glasses. He's not quite as bundled up as I am, probably because he's more used to the cold. "I was worried for a moment that you'd changed your mind. Or that you'd gotten lost."

"I took my niece and nephew to see *Frozen on Ice* here." I take the seat next to him and rub my mittened hands together. "Which in retrospect was a little redundant?"

I didn't think my first foray into sports would happen so quickly, but the game presented itself as a golden opportunity to get to know one half of the Hales—the half I know less about. Seth has two pairs of season tickets he's in the habit of sharing with the sports desk, and Russell jumped at his latest offer.

I assumed it wouldn't be very busy the week of New Year's, but the arena is packed. The whole place buzzes with restless energy, tinged with the salt of stadium food and the brine of beer, and I can't deny it's contagious.

"Just know that if you call it 'sportsball,' you have to go sit in the nosebleeds," Russell says.

"I wouldn't dare. But what about 'iceball'?"

"While you're at it, you should yell, 'GO EDMONTON!' Especially when Seth gets back."

I tap my nose. "Got it."

Seth returns to our section with a buddy of his, a guy named Walt whom he introduced as "my oldest friend," after which Walt ran a hand through his thinning gray hair and pretended to be wounded.

"What do you think, Ari?" Seth says, nestling his beer into a cup holder on Russell's other side. "Russ said it was your first hockey game?"

"It's cold," I admit, which gets a couple *well, duh* laughs. "Really, though, I'm excited. Thanks so much for bringing us."

"I'll be right back," Russell says, and I stand to give him an easier exit.

With an empty seat between us, Seth tips his beer at me and gives me an awkward nod. A tight smile. "Everything going all right for you at the station?" he asks. The go-to conversation topic for coworkers who've had no reason to spend time together outside of work until now.

"Yep. It's great."

"Good," he says. "And you're on that billboard up on Aurora? Exciting stuff."

I nod so vigorously I worry my hat will fly off. I don't know why people think weather is the worst small talk. Coworkers with nothing in common so they by default talk about work—that's the worst.

Russell reappears with two spiked hot chocolates and an order of garlic fries, steam rising from the basket and smelling fantastic. I'm not sure who's more relieved, Seth or me. Probably Seth, who draws Walt into a debate about one of the players.

"They definitely didn't have these at *Frozen on Ice*," I say, marveling at the basket of golden, garlic-flecked goodness. "You are amazing. Thank you."

"I just . . . really wanted you to have a good time. This is like, a big deal, being part of your first game. This might sound corny, but I'm kind of honored?" There's a little self-consciousness in the way he says it, and it endears him to me in a way I wasn't expecting.

I tug off one of my mittens and reach for an overpriced fry, brushing his gloved hand in the process.

A gloved hand should not send a shock of electricity up my spine.

He has a kid, I remind myself. A twelve-year-old named Elodie. If I hadn't been such a disaster that evening at the taqueria, I'd have told him it's a beautiful name.

"My first sports," I say, dipping the fry into ketchup. "And we don't even have to worry about the weather."

Russell, bless him, tries his best to explain the game to me as the players take the ice and an announcer calls their names.

"Those two at the red line are the centers," he says. "And what they're doing now, that's called a face-off. It's how they start every period and every time someone scores."

The puck is dropped directly between the two centers, and after a brief clashing of sticks, Seattle takes control and bats it back toward another one of their players, the crowd erupting into cheers.

It's a raucous, fast-paced game, almost dizzying. More than a few times, I lose my eye on the puck.

"What position did you play?" I ask Russell.

"Goalie." He points at Seattle's goal. "That shaded blue area in front of the goal—that's called a crease. The goalie is allowed to do their job there without interference from any opposing players. A lot of goalies are bigger guys. You have to be quick and flexible, too." He trails off as one of our players takes a shot on Edmonton's goal and misses, which is met with a collective *awwww* from the arena. "You have no idea how excited I was when we finally got a hockey team in Seattle. I'd resigned myself to it never happening and needing to go up to Vancouver to catch games, so this . . . this is really incredible."

It's very cute, how nerdy he gets about hockey, the way he can recite not just stats but all these details about the players, like how Seattle center Dmitri Akentyev always sleeps in a jersey from the opposing team the night before a game and Edmonton goalie Bo Madigan eats exactly two snickerdoodle cookies before taking the ice. Plenty of people love sports—I'm aware of that. But I'm not sure how many watch a game the way Russell does, like he's holding his breath, quietly urging his team forward. He's not rowdy or belligerent, but calm. Focused.

Still, I'm aware that as much as we're getting to know each other, there's a huge piece of his life I know nothing about. A few times, I come close to asking about Elodie, but I don't want him to think I'm prying or judgy. I'm just curious, eager to know more about this guy I've committed to matchmaking our bosses with.

If Russell and I are friends, it's perfectly fine that he happens to be cute. A harmless newsroom crush.

• • •

"IS TORRANCE A hockey fan?" Russell asks at the intermission between the first and second periods. Edmonton is up 1–0. All around us, people are stretching their legs, heading to get more food.

Seth's just returned from grabbing a hot dog, but Walt isn't back yet. "Loves it," Seth says. "We used to go all out, painting our faces, getting dressed up." He takes a bite of his hot dog, and I'm impressed he manages to do this without getting mustard in his mustache.

I try to imagine the two of them at a game together, and I can't help it—a laugh slips out. Seth pauses between bites of his hot dog.

"Sorry. I'm picturing Torrance dressed like that guy." I point to a fan a few rows down, face painted green, batting his wild blue wig out of the way as he goes to town on a pretzel. "It's just—I've worked with her for three years, and I still feel like I barely know her. Except for, well . . ." *Everything that goes on between the two of you.* And even that is a mystery.

I do my best to sound as casual as I can. None of what I've said is a lie, which makes me feel slightly less Machiavellian. Still, I'm not in the habit of grilling people for information, especially about their personal lives. Any time I'm reporting a man-on-the-street weather story, the questions are all softballs. *What do you think about all this rain? How does this affect your weekend plans?*

"All the fighting?" Seth says. I nod slowly, bracing myself for him to shut down this conversation. Instead, his dark eyes soften. "You don't have to tiptoe around it. I know what we're like." He polishes off his hot dog and reaches for his beer. "Is it pretty bad?"

He winces, waiting for our verdict. Everything in me is crying out to tell him that no, it's not that bad. Avoid conflict at all costs.

"Well—" Russell starts, and I can see the indecision march across his features. Seth is his boss. He's not about to insult him to his face.

His silence, however, seems to speak loud enough for Seth.

Seth drags a hand down his face, the sharp angles of his jaw and graying stubble. At work, he's so polished that I can't quite believe this is the same person. That version of Seth would never admit fault. The arena beers are doing some heavy lifting. "Shit," he mutters. "I guess it's possible we've been too much lately. We—we'll tone it down. Sometimes it's easy to pretend we're in our own little world, huh? I think I'm a bit"—he laughs, as though unable to believe he's saying this—"a bit embarrassed."

"You shouldn't be—" I start, before I can catch myself.

"You don't have to sugarcoat it, Ari." Seth gazes out at the rink, and maybe it's really dawning on him how rough it's been for the rest of us. "I want our employees to like coming to work. To feel at ease in the office. Can you honestly tell me that's true?"

"I love what I do." I say it emphatically, no forced sunshine necessary.

Russell immediately backs me up. "Absolutely. But sometimes, the station itself . . . well, it's not always the most welcoming atmosphere."

"Jesus. It must all seem so childish. Sometimes I wonder, if we'd worked things out . . ." He cranes his neck to look beyond our row, as though silently willing Walt to return and save him from this conversation. "Look. I've probably already said too much. We all work together, and I don't want to make you uncomfortable with her."

"You're not," I say as gently as I can. His expression has changed, and I think I might recognize it. So I take a leap. "I know what it's like when something ends and it isn't your choice. When you're still invested, but the other person is just . . . done."

"That happen to you, too?"

"I was engaged. Until three months ago. I can see now that maybe it should have ended earlier, but when we broke up, it was a complete surprise."

"I'm sorry." Seth really does look it. "Relationships are fucking complicated," he says in this way that manages to sound profound.

"I'll drink to that." Russell raises his cup of beer, and we all take a sip.

My confession buoys Seth, seems to make him more comfortable. "Tor was the one who wanted the divorce," he says. "I wanted to work things out. To try harder. But I had no fucking idea how."

It takes everything in my power not to flick my gaze over to Russell. Torrance wanted the divorce. This is huge. I'm painfully curious what *things* needed to be worked out, but we're making progress, and I don't want to ruin it by pressing too hard on a bruise.

"Did you?" I ask. "Try?"

A guilty look from Seth. "Barely. I wanted to, sure, but I didn't have the right tools. About six months after the divorce was finalized, I got my ass to therapy. It's the toughest and most rewarding thing I've ever done. And I think I had to do it for myself first." His fist clenches around a napkin, then loosens. "I sure as hell didn't make things easy for her back then, but I've changed. I'm not the same man I was five years ago."

This conversation is starting to prove that. He can speak openly about therapy, while I'd never been able to. Maybe it's the alcohol loosening him up, but this version of Seth is different. Aware.

Heartbroken.

That realization must make me brave. "And you want her to know that you've changed?" I say. "Because . . . the signs probably aren't helping."

"Yeah. You're not wrong," he says with a sigh. "But we've gotten into this pattern. One of us provokes the other, and the other reacts.

It isn't that I don't know the signs are bullshit. Trust me, I feel like a dick every time I put one up. But there's something about knowing just how to get underneath someone else's skin."

"So it's a way to talk to her," Russell says.

"Probably not the best way, but at least she's talking. Even if most of the time, she's yelling. At least if she's reacting . . . well, part of me thinks it's because she still cares. It's a relief, almost, that we still have that."

"What exactly are you saying?" Russell asks slowly, and my heart lifts. It's very possible our mighty news director is telling us he wants to get back together with his ex.

Seth takes another sip of beer. "It's not easy," he says, "to keep loving someone who's given up on you."

"Maybe she hasn't." I fill my words with hope. It's not a lie if I believe it's true. "If you wanted to change things—if that's something you wanted to do, I mean—what if you aired Torrance's crab story? Isn't it worth it, making viewers a bit mad, if it'll make Torrance happy? If you're meant to be with her, isn't it worth bending a little?"

"I'll think about it," Seth relents, and it feels like a tiny victory. I had no idea this sensitive man was buried beneath those Garamond-font signs. "It could be a start, at least."

Walt returns from concessions with a pretzel and another cup of beer. "Hell of a line back there," he says.

When the second period starts, I try my best to focus because I really do like the game, but all I can think about is this revelation from Seth. He wants her back. He wants her back, and he's been trying to change.

Soon the score is tied, and when Seattle sinks another goal to bring us up to 2–1, Russell's hand drops to my knee. It's a soft, victorious gesture, one that communicates *yesssss our team scored*, and maybe I can barely feel it through the fleece-lined tights I'm wearing beneath my jeans, but every cell in my body focuses on those few inches of denim.

I swallow hard, wondering how it's possible that a hand on my knee is enough to make me warmer beneath all these layers than I've been the whole game.

It's so loud that he has to lean in, putting his mouth right next to my ear. "You having a good time?" he asks.

"Absolutely," I say in a strained voice I don't recognize as my own.

Finally, he seems to notice the placement of his hand, because he glances down and moves it away. A flush spreads across his cheeks. Maybe he thought it was his own knee. Maybe the warmth I felt was simply that I overdressed.

Seattle wins, 3–1, and I allow myself to get swept up in the chaos as we weave through the arena, everyone yelling and whooping, strangers hugging and high-fiving.

"I can see why you love it so much," I tell Russell when we step outside, his glasses immediately fogging up. The city has turned dark, the nearby bars filling up with fans. "I feel kind of victorious? Even though I had no impact on the game."

"Yeah?" Russell pulls off his glasses to swipe the lenses with the fringed end of his scarf, and it is maybe the cutest thing I have seen an adult man do. "You really liked it?"

"I really did."

A sloppy Seth stumbles toward us and throws an arm around each of our shoulders. "My hockey crew!" he yells, and I don't know whether to laugh or to cower from embarrassment. "You guys are the best. We have to do this again."

"Definitely," I say, struggling to keep my balance. "Now let's get you home."

10

FORECAST:

Rock step-triple step and a lightning-strike attraction

". . . AND WOULD you look at that—I think he's smiling!"

"Well, I think we can all agree that Bobo the primate pianist really gives new meaning to the phrase 'monkeying around.'" David Wong and Gia DiAngelo share the kind of laugh perfected by news anchors who have reported on too many heartwarming, slightly ridiculous animal stories to count.

"Up next, one of the fastest growing sports in the United States might be the one with the silliest name," Gia says. "That sport? Pickleball."

It's been a while since I watched a show in the studio, but on Friday, I make an exception. KSEA isn't big enough to have a studio audience, so I'm standing behind the cameras, doing my best to stay out of everyone's way.

"I remember playing that as a kid in gym class," David says, pretending to bat away an imaginary ball. "And I don't think I was very good. Unlike most of these folks we're going to be hearing from next. Professional pickleball has been picking up steam, especially here in the Northwest, where we're always looking for indoor sports during those wet winter months. Russell Barringer has more."

The story opens with a few thwacks of the pickleball on an indoor court. And then Russell's voiceover: "You may not see it in the Olympics yet, but pickleball is a rapidly growing sport with legions of devoted players."

The sound of his voice makes me bite back a smile. After we got Seth safely into an Uber, Russell mentioned this story would be airing today, and how excited he'd been about the chance to do some field reporting that wasn't a college game.

Russell explains that pickleball is local to Washington state, invented on Bainbridge Island in 1965. He interviews a few players and the manager of a pickleball league, interspersed with B-roll of people playing.

"They even let me take a turn on the court," he says, and the camera cuts to Russell in athletic shorts and a T-shirt, two things I've never seen him in at work. I force my gaze away from his calf muscles, as though everyone in the studio can tell exactly where I'm looking.

"Okay, so you're going to want to hold it like this," the league manager is telling him.

A ball sails Russell's way, and he misses, laughing good-naturedly. "Guess there's a bit of a learning curve."

It's endearing, the way he isn't instantly perfect at it, that he was okay committing this to film. It would have been so easy to write this off as a fluff story, and maybe that's what people in their living rooms are doing right now—scoffing, changing the channel, switching to one of our competitors.

But it would be wrong to pass that kind of judgment. Watching him, I see what he was saying about the personalities behind the players. The league manager who met her husband playing pickleball, and after he passed away, established this league in his honor, which she runs with the help of her kids. Every year on his birthday, they throw a massive pickleball tournament that draws players from all over the world. It's a testament to the power of recreation to create community, just as Russell says at the end of the piece.

After a commercial break, it's time for Halestorm, which is the reason I'm here: Torrance is in the best mood after it airs, and armed with what we know about Seth, I'm going to need her in a good spirits.

It's got to help that Seth hasn't posted any signs this week.

There's her too-catchy intro music I find myself humming every so often, playing over an animation of a cartoon Torrance caught in a storm, umbrella turning inside out and nearly getting whisked away before the sun appears. Halestorm, which is Torrance's platform to analyze climate trends and bring on meteorology experts as guests, is a thirty-minute segment, which seemed short to me when I was a kid and always wanted more.

Today she's talking about the long-term effects of wildfires on our region. They've been growing worse each year, to the point where during the summer, the smoke is so thick that we're advised not to go outside for sometimes an entire week—or longer. With her usual magnetism, she manages to communicate how terrifying this is, interviewing a woman who lost two houses to wildfires a year apart and wrapping up with how viewers can volunteer to help.

"That was really powerful," I say to Torrance as she walks off the stage.

"I hope it makes people care about the fires year-round, and not just during the summer," she says. "Haven't you been here since three a.m.? Aren't you exhausted? You can go home, Abrams."

"I know." Like I rehearsed, I hide a yawn with the back of my hand, though I stole a nap before the afternoon show. "I'm trying to tweak my sleep schedule so I can go swing dancing tomorrow night."

Torrance pauses as we reach the newsroom. "Swing dancing? I didn't know you swing danced."

"I love swing dancing. I've only been doing it for a few months, so I'm not amazing, but I'm obsessed. Over at Century Ballroom in Capitol Hill."

"Huh." Her eyebrows knit together. "East Coast swing, right? Not West Coast?"

"East Coast and Lindy Hop," I say, like I didn't just look up the differences between them last night after studying that old photo of Torrance and Seth on the dance floor. The one they looked so happy in.

"I used to go all the time, but it's been a while," she says. "I'm surprised we've never discussed it." Maybe because we never discuss anything.

I follow Torrance into her office, trying to disguise the joy I feel when I spot the succulent on her desk. "That's really gorgeous."

With a fingertip, she grazes one of its violet-green leaves. "It's the strangest thing. Showed up without a card. No idea who it's from." She drops her hand and takes a seat. "Seth used to send me succulents all the time. Never flowers—they didn't last long, and I could never keep up with the watering." Then she laughs this off, like the thought is absurd. "But I doubt it's from him. Probably one of the interns, trying to butter me up so I'll write them a recommendation. What were we saying about swing dancing?"

"Right. You should come tonight," I say. "We could make a whole thing of it, even. Get the whole station involved."

"Plenty of us will be on the retreat next week."

"There's no such thing as too much team bonding." It's a miracle, how I'm able to fight a cringe as I'm saying it. Years of smiling on TV have prepared me for this moment.

"Okay then," she says, cherry lips curving into a grin. "Go ahead. Send out an all-staff email."

"I DON'T THINK they're coming," Russell says, rubbing his hands together to keep warm.

We're standing outside Century Ballroom in Capitol Hill, next to an ice cream shop with lines down the block even on cold winter nights. It's been in the low-to-mid-forties all week, dropping into the upper thirties in the evening.

"Torrance seemed . . . moderately excited," I say, trying to sound more confident than I feel. "She'll show up any minute. And if Seth is as in love with her as he said he was, hopefully he will, too."

"Ari!" someone calls, and while I brighten at the sight of Hannah and Nate, I'm also disappointed it's not either Hale. A few other people from the station are already inside. "Thanks so much for organizing this. We've always wanted to try this place, and this was exactly the nudge we needed."

"Hannah's going to make us all look bad, though," Nate says. "She danced for twelve years as a kid." He turns to Russell, holds out his hand. "I don't think we've met. I'm Nate, Hannah's less talented half."

"Russell."

Hannah lifts her brows at me regarding Russell, and I give her a swift shake of my head. No need to fuel the office rumor mill, especially when there's nothing going on.

"We'll see you inside," I say with a wave.

A few minutes later, a petite woman in a polka dot dress appears at the door. "We're about to start," she says. "If you're waiting for someone, I'm afraid they'll have to join us during the social dance afterward."

Glumly, I follow Russell inside, hand over ten dollars, and check my coat. The first hour of the dance is a lesson. Since Torrance and Seth already know how to dance, they're probably skipping it. That has to be it.

I tuck my necklace into the T-shirt I've paired with a flared skirt and blue Keds, along with tiny sun studs I picked so they wouldn't get in the way while dancing. With a little more pep in my step, I take my place in the group of a couple dozen that's gathered around our instructors, the woman in the polka dot dress, who can't be more than five feet tall, and a beanpole of a guy in shiny Oxfords and a newsboy cap. They've kicked off the class by dancing to a Ray Charles song with so much energy it looks as though the guy is tossing the girl around. She never loses control, swiveling her legs, throwing out her arms, and at one point stealing the guy's cap and putting it on her own head.

When the song ends, everyone claps.

"Good evening, everyone!" the girl says in a bright and booming voice. "Welcome to Lindy Hop 101. I'm Zara, and this is Theo. We'll be your instructors."

"We're pretty fond of swing dancing, so we're jazzed you're all here to learn." At his pun, Theo gives us an impish grin. "The amazing thing about swing dancing is that it's all improvised. None of it is choreographed. So if you were watching us just now—all of that, I was making it up as I went along."

"And I was following based on the cues he was giving me," Zara says. "The first thing we're going to do is split you into two groups: people who want to lead, and people who want to follow. The lead has been the more traditionally male role, but that's super outdated and I kind of hate it. I actually prefer leading to following. So for now, if you're a more experienced dancer, whatever that experience happens to be, I'd recommend leading. But you can also feel free to pick whichever one speaks to you, and we'll even them out if we have to!"

"I don't have any rhythm," I whisper to Russell as I pick the follow group with Nate, and he and Hannah, the experienced dancer, head to the lead side.

Zara and Theo talk us through the most basic step, the one that will be the foundation of everything we do: the rock step, where weight is transferred from one foot and then to the other. Then we add on two triple steps—"Quick, quick, slow," Zara chants as we do it with her—and string the whole thing together.

"Perfect," Theo says once we've danced it a few times with music. "Now it's time to pair up! Find someone on the opposite side, and once you're partnered up, let's form a circle."

Somehow, it isn't until that moment that it hits me: I'm not just in a dance class. I'm in a dance class with *Russell*, and that means I'm going to be dancing with him.

That realization temporarily freezes me in place, so when Russell reaches me, I've barely moved. He's in a gray striped button-up and dark jeans, paired with Adidas. Casual Russell.

"Do you want to be my partner?" he asks with this shy half smile.

"Yes. Save me from the traumatic middle school flashbacks."

"I refuse to believe that Ari Abrams was ever picked last for anything."

My brain runs wild with that sentence—I can't tell if it's a compliment or not. "I'm fairly certain it's a rite of passage," I say, which sounds safe enough.

We find a place in the circle next to Hannah and Nate, David

Wong and morning producer Deandra Fuller on our opposite side. Zara and Theo demonstrate how to hold hands, elbows loose and at our waists, Russell's hands open, palms up, my fingers curled gently over the tops of his.

"This okay? Not too tight?"

"Perfect," I say quietly, too focused on how perfect it is. Every slight movement feels like breaking news. *RUSSELL BARRINGER JUST RAN A THUMB ALONG MY KNUCKLES; WHERE WILL HE STRIKE NEXT? MORE AT ELEVEN.* His hands make mine seem tiny, and I'm more aware of his scent, cedar and citrus, than I've ever been. It goes straight to whatever part of my brain is responsible for crafting daydreams.

Somehow that night in the hotel bar was only a few weeks ago, and now he's in my life and lighting up my thoughts.

It could be three minutes or thirty that we practice the rock step-triple step-triple step together, the hypnotic, repetitive rhythm lulling me into a trance. I'm desperate to learn a new step, something that will either push me closer or farther from Russell. I'm not sure which one I'd prefer.

Then Zara and Theo call for us to switch partners, which we do every five minutes. My head clears, giving me a chance to keep watching the door, which also means I keep apologizing for stepping on my partners' feet. Not everyone has such a natural grip or comfortable presence. There's an older guy who clenches my fingers so tightly they turn white, and a woman who is focused so intently on the dance that she doesn't utter a word. We go through several other moves, including one called "the cuddle," which Russell comes right back around the circle for. His cheeks are flushed from exertion now, which gives that daydreamy sector of my brain more material.

"So I think it goes like this, and then—" He leads me through it, his arm sliding around me. "We did it!"

The enthusiasm in his voice is too endearing, his citrus scent too overwhelming. In his excitement, he lets go of my hands, grinning down at me, and this time, I'm less thrilled to switch partners.

Torrance shows up first, with about five minutes left in the lesson, and I might squeeze Russell's arm a bit too tightly when I spot her. She's all elegance, her lips bright red and her hair curling from a high ponytail. She's in the kind of skirt that must twirl when she dances, and she checks her coat and bag like she's done this a hundred times before catching my eye and giving me a half wave.

When Zara and Theo let us loose for the social dance, which begins with a bouncy Ella Fitzgerald song, Seth appears in the venue doorway. He's in a starched white shirt and suspenders that somehow make him look more buff than usual, hair gelled back the way it was the night of the holiday party. He might even be carrying a fedora.

"They're here," I say on an exhale. "Oh my god. They're really here. And they're both dressed up. This is too cute for words."

"Let's not get too excited yet," Russell says. "They might not be glad to see each other."

Seth actually *tips his hat* to us, and I feel we've time-traveled a solid seventy years into the past.

I'm so caught up in the thrill of seeing them both here that it takes me a split second to notice Russell holding out his hand to me. "What do you think? Ready for the big leagues?"

"Of course you would make a sports reference." I give him my hand, and he leads me to a corner of the dance floor. A man extended a hand to Torrance right away, but Seth remains seated.

All around us, much more experienced couples fly across the

floor, skirts swishing and shoes squeaking. The sight of Torrance and Seth has made me jittery, and it's not long before I fail to pick up on one of Russell's cues and stumble into him, brushing against his stomach, where he's the roundest.

"Sorry," he says quickly, recovering and sending me into an overhead turn.

"No, I'm sorry—I'm the one who bumped into you."

"Oh. It's okay." He shakes this off, but I don't miss that he puts a little more space between us, as though anxious about his size—or how he thinks *I* might feel about his size. I can't help wondering whether a thinner guy would have apologized, and it makes me want to reassure him in some way. Tell him it didn't bother me. Except I have no idea how, so I just keep following the bends and twists of his arms.

The song ends, and while most dancers switch partners, neither of us lets go.

"Your story today was fantastic," I say. Torrance is now dancing with Zara, the two of them talking like old friends who haven't seen each other in a while, and maybe they are. "The pickleball one."

"You know you're doing something right in life when you're getting paid to be shit at pickleball."

"I love that about your stories. That they're not just about sports—they're about people."

At that, he meets my gaze and grins, eyes crinkling at the corners. Up close, his long lashes might be deadly. If my limbs turn to goo, at least he'll be here to hold me up. "That's exactly what sports are about."

It's after the next song, while Russell and I take seats on the sidelines, marveling at the ballroom's grand architecture, that an out-of-breath Torrance makes her way toward the water fountain and Seth removes his hat, tapping her shoulder with the brim. She whirls around, and I'm expecting her to admonish him, but instead she swipes the hat and playfully smacks his chest with it.

And when Seth extends a cupped hand, Torrance raises an eyebrow at him—before turning his hand over and leading him out onto the dance floor. In their bygone-era clothing, they match.

We're not the only ones mesmerized by the sight of them. Torrance is a skilled lead, while also giving Seth a chance to shine. Beat by beat, they push and pull against each other, rarely breaking eye contact. It's as though this place has transformed them both, and I'm a little out of breath just watching.

I know it may not last, that we might show up at work on Monday and nothing will have changed. But for now, it feels almost magical.

"I can't believe it," Russell says, his elbow bumping mine and scattering sparks across my skin. "Well done, weather girl." After another half hour of dancing, Zara walks to the middle of the floor and takes the mic.

"Good evening, everyone," she says. "If you've been here before, you know what time it is . . . it's time for the birthday dance!"

Everyone who knows what this means erupts into cheers, including Torrance and Seth. I glance at Russell, but he just shrugs. The dancers have started to form a circle around Zara.

"Can I get anyone who had a birthday this week to raise their hands?" No hands go up, and everyone glances around the room to see if there really are no birthdays. "Really? No one?"

Slowly, Russell raises his hand.

"It was your birthday?" I whisper. "When?"

"Uh . . . today." He looks so adorably sheepish as he tries to hide a smile.

I'd be mortified, but he walks right up to the middle of the circle when Zara beckons him.

"Since this is your first time, I'll explain," she says. "The birthday dance is a swing dance tradition. You and I will kick it off, and anyone can take my place at any time to dance with you. You ready?"

"As I'll ever be," he says.

They start dancing as the circle claps to the beat, and though he's a beginner, Zara has this way of making him look much more experienced. Other dancers cut in, usually for a few bars at a time, and Russell does his best to lead them all, grinning the entire time like the good sport he is. Some of them have flashier moves than others, but none of them are beginners. Even Torrance takes a turn.

When someone switches her out, she sidles up next to me and nudges my shoulder. "Go," she urges, and it's all the encouragement I need.

There's a bit of fumbling as he reaches for my hand, but eventually, he grasps it, and we rock step-triple step-triple step together.

"I can't believe you didn't tell anyone it was your birthday," I say as he spins me.

"I've never been that into birthdays," he says. "I didn't want to make it a big deal."

"Like, dancing with a dozen strangers kind of a big deal?"

"Exactly."

The song is in its last chorus, and while I expect someone to interrupt us, no one does.

I shake my head, laughing. "Happy birthday," I say into his ear as he pulls me into the cuddle.

It's the best night I've had in a long, long time.

11

FORECAST:

Cold air moving in alongside an avalanche of awkward

THE ANNUAL KSEA retreat is more corporate team-building than vacation, but this year, I have an extra reason to look forward to it. Torrance, head of the planning committee, booked a lodge-slash-spa outside of Vancouver, BC, and Russell and I make plans to drive together to prolong our scheming time. "I'm not sure my car will make it to Canada," he said, so the next Friday morning, I pull up in front of his house on a quaint Phinney Ridge street shaded by tall evergreens.

Nothing wrong with sharing a three-hour drive, plus border wait time, with an attractive coworker I now know how to swing dance with.

As soon as I stop my car, I notice a girl sitting on the front steps, a book in her lap.

A girl who looks about twelve years old.

When she spots my car, she leaps to her feet, long dark ponytail swinging behind her. "Dad!" she yells into the house. "Your ride's here!"

I freeze with my car door open, unsure what to do. Fortunately, Russell appears in the doorway, asking his daughter something I can't hear, and she shrugs in return. I give him an awkward wave as he beckons me forward.

"Hey," he says, tugging on his collar in this way he tends to do when he's nervous. Today's jacket is more casual, a KSEA 6 zip-up. "This is Elodie. Elodie, this is Ari."

Elodie surveys me, blue eyes behind thin oval glasses, and I've never before wondered if my fashion sense is preteen-approved. She's wearing high-waisted jeans and an oversize striped sweater and looks two hundred percent cooler than I do in my suitable-for-a-long-drive leggings and UW atmospheric sciences department sweatshirt.

"Nice to meet you," she says.

"You too." I busy my hands fidgeting with the strap of my bag. "Your dad said you're in the school play?"

"*Musical*," she corrects, with all the confidence of a theater kid, but I can tell she's pleased he mentioned her. She holds up the book she was reading, which I now see is a script. "It's *Alice in Wonderland*. I'm the Queen of Hearts."

"Ooh, the villains always get the best songs."

Her eyes widen. "You know musicals?"

"I know zero about sports, but musicals, I'm all over," I say. "My brother and I used to save up money to catch the Broadway tours when they came through Seattle. We saw *Dear Evan Hansen* last year and it was transformative."

Elodie lets out a shriek. "I've been wanting that one to come back here forever! It was amazing, wasn't it? Did you cry?"

"So much," I tell her, and just like that, her hesitation turns to a combination of jealousy and awe.

Russell clears his throat. I hope I haven't said too much to her, though I'm nothing to Russell but a coworker. A co-schemer. "Her mom was about to pick her up, but she just texted that she's running late," he says. "Do you mind if we stick around a few minutes?"

"Oh—sure. That's completely fine."

Except he looks deeply uncomfortable, focusing on plucking a stray thread from his jacket and not quite making eye contact. It's clear this wasn't planned, that Elodie's mother was supposed to be here before I pulled up. I'm not sure how many people at work have met his kid, but I'm going to guess not many. Again, I wonder how old he is. After the birthday dance, I had to hold myself back from asking because I worried he'd be able to tell I was doing mental math. For all I know, she could be adopted, though there's a clear physical resemblance in the blue of their eyes, the shape of their faces.

"Do you want me to wait in the car?" I ask.

Russell's brow furrows. "No, of course not. You can come inside."

A bit gingerly, I step over the threshold, like maybe Russell's hiding even more secrets inside. The house is cozy, warm tones and plush rugs, bright-colored vintage artwork on the walls along with framed photos of Elodie as a baby, as a kid, as the preteen she is now. And of course, some sports memorabilia: a black-and-white team photo, a framed jersey with the name of a player I don't recognize.

"It's a great house," I say as I spot a wood fireplace in the living room.

"It was a bit of a fixer-upper." He leans against the wall next to a photo of toddler Elodie clutching a stuffed cow and grinning at the camera. "But the fixing is all wrapped up, at least for now. There are a few more things I'd like to do to it, but it's tough to find the time. No one told me that when you get a house, your weekends are spent primarily fixing up the house."

"Do not get him started on the house," Elodie warns. "He'll never stop."

"If I recall, you were a pretty big fan of the loft we built in your room."

Elodie mimes zipping her lips. "What? I love the house? Say anything you want about the house?"

My mind is working overtime to process this. This is Russell Barringer, father. Homeowner. Wearer of excellent jackets. Maybe I wasn't getting to know him that well after all.

When Russell's phone lights up in his hand, he doesn't even let it complete its first ring. "She's here," he says to Elodie. "You have everything you need?"

"Let's see, hair dye, DIY tattoo kit, fake ID . . . check, check, and check." If I didn't already know she was a theater kid, her killer straight face confirms it. "Don't have too much fun."

"That's my line." He pulls her in for a hug, and oh—oh no. Something terrible is happening to my heart.

The wind chimes sing, and a white woman with a brunette pixie cut and long wool coat appears, pushing open the door.

"Elodie?" she says, stepping inside. "You ready?" Then her gaze lands on me, her face splitting into a grin. "Hi! You must be Ari Abrams." She extends her hand. "I feel like I know you already! I watch you every morning."

"Oh—thank you?" I phrase it like a question because this scene feels straight out of a sitcom. This is Elodie's mother. And she's . . . excited to meet me? I'm getting too many mystery pieces of Russell all at once.

"Sorry, I'm Liv. Ahhh, I'm a little starstruck!" She laughs, running a hand through her short hair. "I know, I know, Russ is on TV, too, but we've known each other forever. So this is like . . . meeting a local celebrity."

"I definitely don't feel like a celebrity when I'm microwaving frozen ravioli in my 450-square-foot studio apartment," I say, and it's meant to be a way to break the tension, but it only comes out sounding pathetic.

Either oblivious to the awkwardness or all too aware of it, Elodie says, "I forgot my retainer!" and turns to rush upstairs.

Russell has become a statue next to me. "Liv, Ari. Ari, Liv. Though, uh, I guess you two kind of already covered that."

Liv touches his arm in this familiar way that reminds me she's not just Elodie's mother: she's Russell's ex, from who knows how long ago.

Someone's knocking at the door. Again. And again, they don't wait for anyone to answer it.

"What's taking so long?" asks a tall, trim guy with salt-and-pepper hair and one of those down vests all men over the age of thirty in Seattle own. I think I got Alex the same one for his birthday. "Let's get this show on the road."

Russell's gaze flicks from me to this new stranger. He looks as though he might self-destruct. "This is Perry," he says, seizing the opportunity to preempt the introductions this time around. "Liv's husband and Elodie's stepdad." He glances behind Perry. "And is that Clementine I see back there?"

Perry grins. "She just dozed off. I couldn't bring myself to wake her." He holds out his hand for me to shake before turning back to Russell. I take it Clementine is a baby. "The Kraken is looking solid this year. Think they have a chance at the playoffs?"

"Hope so." Russell scrapes a hand across his chin, no longer making eye contact with any of us. "Well. Since I didn't intend on hosting a party today . . ."

Liv gazes around at our motley crew. "Oh my. I fear we've overwhelmed poor Ari. I'm so sorry. We're a bit overly friendly in this family."

"As long as a Saint Bernard doesn't barge in here next or anything," I joke.

"Don't worry, we left him in the car!" she says, and I'm not sure whether she's kidding.

"Found it!" Elodie calls, bounding down the steps. When she lands with a soft thump, she surveys us like we're a mildly interesting TV show Netflix has asked if she's still watching. "Why are you all just standing here?"

"Great question." Russell ruffles a hand through her hair and slides up one strap of her backpack that's fallen down. "We're on a schedule, too. Enjoy your weekend, I love you, don't forget to actually *wear* that retainer."

Elodie pats the front of her backpack. "I'm sure you'll barely have time to miss me."

THE FIRST FIFTEEN minutes of our drive are silent, except for a few seconds when the audiobook I was listening to starts up, and I have to smack the power button because I'm fairly certain my romance novel was heading toward a sex scene.

"So, um. That was a little . . ." I fiddle with the wrapper of one of three strawberry fruit leathers I brought on the trip, none of which sound appetizing.

"Awkward?" he supplies, then forces a laugh. "Just a bit."

"Liv is your ex-wife?"

"We were never married, actually." He stares out the window. "I wasn't trying to keep them a secret or anything. It's . . . complicated."

But he doesn't elaborate on precisely how it's complicated, and I'm not about to probe him for answers. I'm not sure where I would start. So . . . okay then. That's that.

It's only when we hit Everett traffic that he turns to me, as though we've left all that weirdness in Seattle.

"I booked a massage for Seth this evening, only he won't know it's really a couple's massage," Russell says. "He's always complaining about his back, and especially after a long drive, it seemed like just the thing."

"Perfect. And I signed all of us up for zip-lining tomorrow." If reality TV has taught me anything, there's nothing like an adrenaline rush to bring two people together. "Aside from that, I'm going to try to get closer to Torrance. Get to know her better. We know Seth's side of the story, but we won't have the full picture until we hear hers."

"Are we—do you think we're still doing the right thing here?"

The car inches forward. "What do you mean?"

"What if it was something really terrible that split them up?" he asks. "What if one of them cheated?"

"Hopefully we'll know more after this weekend." Again, I think back to what Torrance said at the holiday party. "And we'd draw a line if it got to that point. We can't make anyone fall in love. All we're doing is creating an opportunity. I definitely wouldn't want to push Torrance into something she's not comfortable with—that's why it's so crucial I make progress with her," I say. "Maybe it's naive to believe that Seth's changed, but I want to be naive, damn it. Has he been different with you at work?"

"Different?"

"More attention? Any pro sports?"

"Oh. Yeah. I'm covering a few basketball games next week."

I brighten. "Russell! That's great."

He gives me a half smile, and I feel half better.

"All I want is for them to ride off into the sunset and be together forever," I continue. "I want to throw them a fiftieth anniversary party. That's gold, right? I'll have to sell off an internal organ to get them a massive gold sculpture of themselves, but it'll be worth it."

"I'll chip in," he says. "I don't need both kidneys."

And then we fall into silence again.

Things with Russell don't return to normal, not when we stop for burritos in Bellingham, not when we wait in border traffic, not when we make it into Canada. The energy around us is charged, not light and easygoing like it usually is. I miss it. We've become something close to friends over the past month, and I'm not ready to go back to what we were before, despite this inconvenient crush I have on him.

That's all it is—a crush, and it will pass. Just like my crush on the guy in the employee cafeteria, who recently shaved his beard. Is there a direct correlation between the end of my crush and the disappearance of the beard? Who's to say?

Of course, I know the real reason for this strained drive. I met Elodie, and his ex, and his ex's husband. Even if everyone seemed to get along, I can't shake the feeling we've crossed some line he didn't want me to cross.

If that's true, I'm not sure how to uncross it.

12

FORECAST:

An unexpectedly balmy afternoon, clothing optional

AS IT TURNS out, Russell didn't just book a couple's massage for Torrance and Seth.

Somehow, he booked a couple's massage for all four of us.

"It did seem a little pricey when I talked to them on the phone," Russell mutters as we're ushered back into changing rooms in the lodge's spa, after they've told us they don't do refunds. We've already checked into our rooms, which are wooden floored and rustic, with sweeping views of the surrounding forest. "Even with the retreat discount."

"Come on, Abrams." Torrance is already unbuttoning her coat. "Don't tell me a massage doesn't sound incredible after four hours in the car."

That's how I end up facedown on a massage table, underneath a too-thin white sheet and naked except for my underwear, sandwiched between Russell and my boss. Both of whom are also naked, to unknown extents.

I love this. I have never been more relaxed in my life.

"You can take off your underwear if you want," my masseuse says as she adjusts the sheet.

"Oh, I'm okay," I say in this squeaky voice that's even higher-pitched than my niece's. The table is heated, at least, and the lavender essential oils are doing their best to soothe my chaotic brain. I try to focus on the soft piano melody playing in the background.

Still, our tables are so close together that I can hear every sigh, groan, and grunt of satisfaction as a masseuse works on Torrance.

And on Russell.

"Let me know how the pressure is," his masseuse is saying. "If you need it to be more or less firm, just tell me."

"That's good." Russell lets out a low moan—quiet, like he doesn't want anyone to hear him but just can't help himself. "*Perfect*."

I will myself to get swept away by the music. It doesn't work. Because of course I can only think about Russell's sounds in other contexts. My death is simply unavoidable. It'll be tragic, perishing almost naked in the middle of a massage, but my brother won't make too many jokes about it at my funeral. Probably.

"You're very tight."

"What?" I say, maybe a little too sharply.

My masseuse, a woman named Sage, chuckles. "Your shoulder muscles. I haven't felt shoulders like yours in a while." *Oh*. Obviously that's what she was talking about. I immediately want to apologize, like my body has done something wrong by holding on to all this anxiety.

She beckons over another masseuse. "Anita, come see this. Feel how tight she is."

Another pair of hands joins Sage's. "*Wow*. A lot of stress?"

I nod miserably into the face hole. I hear the sound of Torrance's muffled laugh.

"Sorry," she says. "That might be my fault."

"No," I rush to say as my masseuse attacks a knot beneath my left shoulder blade. "Work's been fine. It's just . . . been a rough couple months outside of it."

"Too much talking," Seth murmurs from Torrance's other side.

"If you fall asleep, you won't be able to enjoy it," Torrance says in this mocking singsong, but she's wrong. I'd give anything to fall asleep right now, especially as Russell's masseuse hits a spot that he seems to really, really enjoy.

When I think I'm finally about to relax, my masseuse pats my back. "All done."

Oh. Okay then.

There's some awkwardness as we navigate how to leave in our varying states of undress, and I decide to keep my head down as long as possible. The masseuses encourage us to use the sauna so the heat can melt away the toxins in our systems. There's one in the women's locker room and one in the men's, so we split up. Here it is, my chance to talk to Torrance one-on-one.

I wrap myself in a towel, not relaxed enough to show my boss my boobs. And yet there's Torrance, letting it all hang loose. Actually, loose is the wrong word because Torrance Hale has a phenomenal body. If I looked like that at fifty-five, I'd be prancing around in the nude, too. She must notice my comfort level isn't quite where hers is, though, so she grabs a towel and cinches it around herself before we make our way to the sauna.

I sink down onto the wooden bench, idly wondering if my crush on Russell is a toxin the sauna can whisk away.

"Breakup, right?" Torrance says. Her blond hair is piled on top of her head, and this might be the first time I've seen her without makeup.

"Sorry, what?"

"The source of your stress. I'm guessing part of it was your breakup?"

Torrance knows only the basics, not the ugly details. If I open up to her, like with Seth, maybe she'll be more likely to open up to me. So even though Garrison isn't a source of stress for me, not right now, I make a feast of ugly details for her.

I nod. "My fiancé ended things in October. It wasn't the most cordial breakup." Not entirely a lie.

"I remember when you got engaged," she says. "That was a beautiful rock."

That's surprising—not that she remembered, but that she isn't quick to denounce marriage, tell me I dodged a bullet.

"It was a surprise, but in retrospect, it was for the best." I'm nowhere near ready to tell my boss the real reasons for the breakup, so I go with a vague, "We weren't a good fit."

"Better to know as soon as possible," Torrance says. "Reminds me of my first husband."

I have to fight to keep my jaw from dropping. "You were married? Before Seth?"

"Only for a short time. We got it annulled after three months. It was a Vegas wedding—we'd gone there for some friends' joint bachelor-bachelorette party and drank a bit too much. This was back when I was still an intern. Anyway, when we got back, we thought, 'why not try to make it work?' But he didn't like that I was so buried in the station." A wicked smile. "Sometimes I think of him seeing my face all around the city and on TV as my revenge. He can't get away from me."

I have to laugh at that. "I had no idea."

"I don't talk about it because, well, there's not much to talk about." She curls and uncurls the edge of her towel, staring down at her French-pedicured toes. "Seth and I were friends when I was with my ex. Nothing happened between us, but we were close, and it wasn't long after my annulment that Seth and I started seeing each other."

There's something in her tone that I'm stunned to realize might be nostalgia. This love for Seth, this thing I've been told used to exist but I haven't been able to wrap my mind around.

Summoning all my journalism instincts, I stay quiet, letting her speak. What someone says after a long pause is often the juiciest information. That probably goes double when the person's just had an aromatherapy massage, loose limbed and hopefully loose-lipped. I focus on the heat in the sauna, trying to relax as much as my brain will allow.

Sure enough, Torrance keeps talking. "Seth was my favorite thing about work, and after a while, I realized I was looking forward more to coming in to work and seeing him than going home to my ex. But. You know. Then that ended too, and I realized the only person I could ever truly rely on is myself. Other people only let me down."

"How did he let you down?"

She snorts, a very un-Torrance-like sound. "Oh god, how didn't he? You don't really want all my dirty laundry, do you?" She doesn't even wait for a response, clearly eager now to spill. "We were interns at a medium-sized station in Olympia. We were both interested in the weather, and we had similar backgrounds. And, well, I got called up to fill in first when their regular meteorologist was sick. I've never been so fucking nervous in my life."

I can't imagine Torrance Hale being nervous. Even though it happened years ago, it humanizes her—a little.

"I had this natural talent that people really responded to," she continues. It's not bragging—she's simply stating a fact. "We didn't want to compete against each other. Seth wanted to be on the air, but he was also drawn to the managerial path. So that's what we did. He went that route, and I stayed on camera. He followed me around for jobs when I got promoted to bigger and bigger stations. Eventually, I landed this job in Seattle, and we settled down and started a family.

"He got jealous of the fame. I was earning more than he was, even when he became a manager, and he felt frustrated that he couldn't provide for me. For our family. No matter how many times I told him that he didn't have to be the one providing, that maybe that was how it was for our parents, but it didn't have to be that way for us," she says. "First, he was passive-aggressive about it, little barbs here and there. Once he even said, 'I'm not saying you're famous because you're a hot blonde, but I'm not *not* saying it.' And I'd remind him that I was a *scientist*, first and foremost, until I realized, fuck that, I didn't need his toxic masculinity. Jealousy has this way of simmering beneath the surface. When you don't talk about it, it builds and builds until you think it might even be part of your DNA. We could be fighting about unloading the dishwasher, but it was never about unloading the dishwasher. It was about how Seth felt inferior, and he couldn't handle it."

I don't have any tolerance for that kind of toxic bullshit, but there's no hope for humanity if we can't grow and evolve, become better versions of ourselves. Bad choices and bad behavior don't doom someone to a lifetime as a bad person. I want to believe people can change, and while I don't want to redeem murderers or anything like that, how Seth acted—that's fixable. It has to be.

It's not naivete—it's *hope*.

"I don't want to cross a line or anything, but . . ." It kills me to say that, knowing how wrong it is. But we're getting somewhere.

"Ari. We were just lying naked a few feet from each other. I don't think lines exist anymore."

"Fair point," I say, laughing. "Did you ever try therapy?"

Torrance doesn't seem at all bothered by the question. "I wanted to. For a couple years, I insisted we should talk to someone, but Seth was too proud. He didn't think we needed someone else knowing our private business. He thought we could figure it out on our own. And obviously, we didn't."

"I've always thought people can change." I want to tell her Seth went to therapy, but that's not my story to tell. "The signs have stopped, right? And I saw you two dancing at Century Ballroom."

"Before we get much deeper, I should make sure you take my insurance. Do you charge by the hour?"

I wince. "Sorry, sorry. We can talk about something else."

"I'm messing with you. You're making it way too easy for me." Torrance becomes pensive, stretching out her legs that remain golden-tan even in the winter. "When we worked, we *really* worked," she says, sounding wistful. "I'd give anything to get those moments back. Maybe we were both too busy, or maybe it was something that happened naturally after being married almost twenty years. I don't know." A long sigh, and I wonder if she really means it: that she'd give anything to get those moments back. "The people who love us the most have the power to hurt us the most, too."

The sauna timer goes off, which is probably a good thing, since I'm beginning to feel light-headed.

"We should get going before this thing burns us to a crisp." Torrance gets to her feet, pulling the towel tighter across her chest. "What do you think, facials next?"

• • •

AFTER I'VE BEEN plucked, tweezed, buffed, and exfoliated within an inch of my life, I change for our all-staff welcome dinner. I'm starting to think this retreat is more R & R than work, but I guess I can't blame Torrance for wanting a break from it all. An escape.

It's possible I spend a little longer than usual deciding what to wear. Russell's room is right next door to mine, as luck would have it, and once I've slipped into my favorite dark jeans and a burgundy sweater over a cloud-printed button-up, I knock on his door, assuming we'll go down together. When there's no answer, I knock again. Nothing.

I'm on my way to the elevator at the end of the third floor hallway when I spot Torrance and Seth sitting together on a sectional in an alcove next to a fireplace. Their faces are bent close, their knees touching.

It's definitely not a casual pose.

For a few moments, I'm frozen. I could head back to my room, wait until they're gone. I could walk by, risk interrupting them.

Or . . . I could stay here, next to this column, in case I can overhear anything they're saying.

They look so cozy that I can't help wondering if whatever's going on here is a result of the conversation Torrance and I had in the sauna. And that's what draws me closer, until I'm pressed up against a second column, trying to breathe as quietly as I can.

If there's a line I haven't already crossed, I am aware that this, hiding behind a column and kind-of sort-of spying on my bosses, might be it. But it's not that I'm curious in some voyeuristic way. It's that I genuinely want to know if they're getting along. The way they're seated, the way they were dancing last week—all of it makes me think they might be able to get back the good parts of what they used to have.

Maybe after all my talk about wanting to improve the station, what I really want is to see the two of them happy.

"... sure it's a good idea?" Torrance is saying.

"It's worth a try," Seth says.

And then something terrible happens.

I shift positions to stretch out some lingering tension in my back, and my boot lets out a high-pitched squeak on the polished wood floor.

Their heads whip my direction as I spin and bolt down the darkened hallway, cursing these new rain boots, furious a favorite article of clothing betrayed me like this. Shit, shit, *shit*.

They'll think I was spying on them. And—okay, I was, but for a good reason. They'll know why Russell and I have been asking so many questions, and they'll report us to HR and realize they really do hate each other after all. With a single uncontrollable action, I may have ruined our entire plan.

I've spiraled so deep in my head that I miss the sign at the end of the hall that says **WET FLOOR**.

And then I miss the staircase.

13

FORECAST:
A torrent of secrets and at least one questionable decision

"CAN YOU BEND your wrist a little more?" asks the X-ray technician.

"This is about as far as I can go," I say, grimacing as a sharp pain shoots from my wrist to my elbow. "Am I bending it at all?"

"Nope. Here, let me help you."

He tries to bend it for the X-ray, and *holy fucking shit,* it hurts more than my IUD insertion. I hiss out a string of colorful curse words, followed by an apology.

"Not to worry," he says. "I've heard worse. I'm told to go to hell a few times a week at least."

He tells me to hold it there for five seconds, during which time I learn that when you are in this much pain, five seconds can feel like an eon, until the machine clicks. The way my body is contorted must be undoing every bit of the massage.

The actual fall is blurred from my memory. All I remember is my foot catching air at the top of the staircase and then how hard I landed, the surge of fear when I couldn't move my left arm. The way Torrance and Seth and eventually Russell appeared in front of me and sat with me, helped me to my feet, asked the lodge staff for some ice. I remember holding the melting ice pack to my left arm as Russell helped me into an Uber, grateful when he slid in next to me, silently freaking out because I couldn't move any of my fingers.

I've never broken a bone, never twisted an ankle or sprained a finger or chipped a tooth. So of course, at the age of twenty-seven, I manage to topple down a flight of stairs and likely fracture my elbow.

Bright sides: I know I was lucky. I know it could have been so much worse.

But it's also really fucking painful.

The tech takes me back to the exam room, where Russell's sitting in a hard plastic chair, one leg bouncing up and down. His hair is mussed, like maybe he's been raking a hand through it. Earlier, when a nurse first brought me back and asked if I was currently taking any medications, I stammered out an, "Oh. Um," and he said, "I'll wait outside until you need me, okay?" If I ever had doubts about him being a certified Good Person, that would have confirmed it.

I gestured for him to go back in when I went for X-rays, and now he jumps to his feet as soon as I reenter, the tech letting us know that the doctor will be in shortly.

"Hey," Russell says softly. "Everything go okay?"

I nod, swallowing hard to keep the emotions at bay. My makeup is probably smudged all down my face. The exam room is too cold, my sweater too thin. I have to pee but I'm afraid I won't be able to manage it by myself. I can't even hold my left arm up without using my right.

"I'm so sorry about all of this." It's at least the tenth time he's said it. "Are you shivering?"

"Maybe a little."

He takes off his corduroy jacket and drapes it across my shoulders, and it's much too big for me but it smells like his citrus-cedar soap, a welcome contrast to the clinical hospital smell.

"Thank you." I grab it with my right hand, tugging it tighter around me. Even the slightest movement bumps my left arm and makes me wince.

The doctor comes back in, her name stitched above the pocket of her white coat. Dr. Jacobs. "It's just as I thought," she says, sliding onto a stool next to her computer and pulling up my X-rays. "Your elbow is fractured."

"How long until it heals?"

"Could be six weeks, could be twelve. We don't have a good way of knowing the time frame." She swipes over to another image. They all look like the blurry bones of a ghost to me. "It looks like you also bruised a rib, which we unfortunately can't do much for—just painkillers, rest, and ice."

"That would explain why it hurts to breathe," I say with a forced laugh. "And to laugh, though I guess I haven't been doing much of that in the past hour."

She tells me to see an orthopedic doctor when I get back to Seattle, that it doesn't look like I'll need surgery but they'll probably want me in weekly physical therapy. She unwraps a navy sling from a plastic package and helps me secure my arm, indicating my hand and forearm should be resting above my elbow. Then she gives me a prescription for pain relievers, my X-ray on a CD, and a whole bunch of paperwork.

MY FIRST THOUGHT when we make it back to my hotel room is that I wish I'd done a better job cleaning up. I'm amazed by how much mess I've created in half a day from items packed solely for a long weekend, but I can't bring myself to care about the bra hanging off the back of a chair.

"I can't believe I did something so careless. So stupid." I kick off my boots and collapse on the bed, draping my uninjured hand across my face.

Russell gestures to the bed next to me, as though asking if it's okay for him to sit down. I give him a nod. "You're not stupid. It was an accident. It could have happened to anyone." Gently, he grazes the arm I have across my face with a few fingertips, and I feel my skin prick with goose bumps.

"I know, I just . . . didn't exactly imagine this weekend playing out this way."

"At least now you know carrot cake M&M's exist." He reaches for a bag at his feet and empties it onto the bed next to us. Needless to say, we missed the team dinner, though Torrance and Seth are about the furthest thing from my mind at this point. The lodge's kitchen is closed, and I told him I wasn't hungry enough to order food, but he stopped at the vending machine while we waited for the elevator. And now my grumbling stomach is grateful he did. "Personally, I'm not sure how much longer I could have gone on without that knowledge."

"Ugh, don't make me laugh. It's too painful. I need Serious Russell."

He schools his face into a serious expression, eyes unblinking behind his glasses. "There are four major golf championships in the world that take place between April and July. The most prestigious is the Masters Tournament, which is hosted by the Augusta National Golf Club in Georgia."

"Yes. More of that. That's perfect." I scoot higher on the bed, trying to find a comfortable position with my arm in a sling. Spoiler:

there is none. "Do you mind grabbing my phone for me? It's all the way over there." I gesture to where I set my bag on the desk, which right now feels very far away.

He retrieves it, handing it to me without so much as glancing at the screen. God, he's just so *polite*, and maybe my standards are way down in the gutter, but still. It makes me wonder what it would take to unstitch him. To mess up his hair and rumple his jacket.

I thank him and unlock my phone. A text from Torrance, asking how I am. I fumble with the keyboard for a while before giving up and sending a voice text, filling her in on the past couple hours.

"Is there anything else I can get you or do for you? Really, just say the word."

"I'm okay for now. Thank you." I drop the phone to the bed next to me and let out a laugh I immediately regret, given the way it makes my chest ache. "I feel like I'm going to run out of different ways to thank you. You really don't have to do any of this. I'll be okay for the rest of the night if you want to go meet up with everyone else."

He must hear the longing in my voice, the truth that I don't want him to go meet up with everyone else at all.

"I'm happy to stay," he says. "I broke my arm playing hockey when I was in middle school. I was such a baby—my mom had to cut up my food and help me wrap my arm in plastic every time I took a shower."

"That sounds adorable, your mom fawning over you."

His mouth kicks into a grin. "I was a little shit about it. Definitely not adorable." He shifts on the bed, his shirt stretching across the curve of his belly. "Seriously, though. Whatever you need."

"Maybe you could just talk to me?" I don't want to talk about Torrance or Seth or work. I just want to relax, which I guess is what we came all the way up here to do.

"I can do that."

About five seconds of silence follow, and I burst out laughing, in spite of the pain.

"You put me on the spot! That was a lot of pressure!" he says, but he's laughing, too.

"Can you . . . tell me about Elodie?" I say, worried for a moment that he'll shut down, the way he did on the drive. I reach for a pack of Skittles, using my teeth to tear it open.

"Well . . ." He draws out the word, busies himself with opening the aforementioned carrot cake M&M's. I'm convinced he's going to change the subject, tiptoe around it. But he doesn't. "She's in drama, as you know. Ever since she was little, she's loved the spotlight. She loves show tunes, and she can really sing. For her ninth birthday a few years ago, we went to New York and spent the whole week seeing shows."

"She seems awesome. I haven't spent much time around twelve-year-olds lately, but damn, she's *sharp*. Are they all like that?"

"She and her friends definitely keep me on my toes. She's a good kid, though. A great kid. Her bat mitzvah is coming up, too, and I thought she'd complain about having to get up early every Saturday, but she hasn't, not even once."

"How's that going?"

"I've had only a few painful flashbacks to my own," he says. "I'm excited for her. Liv isn't Jewish, and we wanted Elodie to be able to decide for herself what she wanted to do, and she's been focused on this for a while. I'm really proud of her for committing."

I knew Russell had this whole other life as a father, but it's not until this moment that it hits me how different his set of priorities is. He's not just responsible for another human—he has this whole range of emotions reserved for only her, pride and awe and comfort. It's staggering, really, to imagine what these past twelve years have been like for him.

A silence passes between us, during which I unearth a purple Skittle from the bag and chew it slowly.

"It felt like maybe you were upset with me," I say. "In the car."

"Ah. It may have seemed that way because . . . well, I'm not sure if I was upset, exactly. There's just . . ." He becomes inordinately fascinated by the floral pattern of the bedspread, knotting his fingers with the tassels on the duvet. "It's complicated."

"We have all night. Or until these meds make me pass out. If you want to talk about it, that is." I don't want to force him, but I can't explain how badly I want to know this side of him. How it feels like if I don't, he'll go back to being a work acquaintance, when I want him to be so much more than that. This has to be the first step—I'm certain of it.

His blue eyes flick up to mine, and then back down to the bed. "Elodie was born when I was seventeen."

Oh.

"You just turned twenty-nine?" It's not the first question on my list, but it's the only one that comes out.

He nods, still not making eye contact. "Liv and I had been dating since freshman year of high school, and we'd known each other since we were kids. Our parents were best friends, and we even hid our relationship for the first few months we were dating because we didn't want them to get too involved. Obviously the pregnancy wasn't anything we were planning," he says with a rough laugh. "We talked about it, and we weighed all the options, and ultimately it was her choice. She wanted to have the baby, and I wanted to be there for her any way I could."

I'm still trying to process this, searching for the right thing to say. "I can't imagine how hard that was," I settle on.

"An understatement. The year she was born was the hardest of my life. We were teen parents. We had no fucking clue what we were doing. We were lucky that our parents supported her choice, and I know now that we both had a tremendous amount of privilege. Don't get me wrong, they were *furious*, and they were disappointed. But they helped us out, both financially and as babysitters. Kids at school were considerably less understanding. Some of them tried, and some teachers, too, but there was so much judgment. Liv got the worst of it, and I felt terrible.

"And I did it, too, for a while," he continues, and at this, he finally meets my gaze again. It's not pain in his eyes, I don't think—it might be weariness. "I judged myself so harshly. How could I have made this mistake that would irrevocably alter the course of my life? I'd wanted to go to college, maybe on a hockey scholarship, but I quit—I had to. It was expensive, something I'd been fortunate enough not to think about very much when my parents were footing the bill, but suddenly *everything* was expensive, and of course, there wasn't enough time."

"And you and Liv stayed together, at least for a while?"

"Until sophomore year of college, yeah. It took us a couple extra semesters to make it through, but we managed. Liv studied engineering, and she got a job offer in Seattle almost right after she graduated. She didn't want to take Elodie away from me, and I didn't want to be away from either of them, so moving was an easy decision to make."

"And then you wound up at KSEA."

"Not right away," he says. "I networked a ton, freelanced a ton. Became friends with the guy who used to have my job, who put in a good word when he moved to ESPN. I don't think Edible Arrangements makes a big enough basket to thank him for what he did for me."

A pause as he reaches out to help me with the stubborn wrapper of a Twix. "I still have a lot of residual anxiety from all of it, I guess. I don't talk about Elodie much at work because I don't want to have to explain how old I was when she was born. I don't want anyone leaping to the conclusion that because I was a teen dad, that must make me a fuckup."

"You are absolutely not a fuckup." I place my right hand on his arm. "Russell. You're not."

"I wasn't trying to hide her. And I love being a father. I love Elodie—she's the most important person in my life. So when you met Elodie, and then Liv showed up, I just . . . shut down."

"I get it. I mean, I haven't been through it, but I understand why, and I'm not judging you. I wouldn't." As if of its own accord, my hand strokes up and down along his arm. The meds must be making me loopy, giving me this freedom to touch him in ways I may not have been brave enough to do otherwise. "Thank you. For telling me."

"I wanted you to meet her," he says. "And that was before I knew you were as into show tunes as she is."

I try not to linger on what it might mean that he wanted me to meet her. "She's got great taste." Slowly, I move my hand away, dropping it back to the bed. "You and Liv are still close? That's pretty impressive."

"It took a while to get there, but yes, I guess so. I never wanted to be the kind of parents who made things hell for their kid by not being together, so it's been a huge relief. There were a couple years where it was awkward with the two of us, but maybe because we'd been friends for so long before Elodie, we eventually found our way back to that. We alternate custody every other week, and so far we haven't had any problems with it," he says. "Liv got married a few years ago, and they had a baby last year, Clementine, who Elodie absolutely *adores*. We're a complicated family, maybe, but it works."

"They all seem wonderful. Truly."

He gives me this half smile, and I want so badly to make this equal, to let him in the way I softly knocked and asked for his secrets. It's different from how I've felt with guys before, and sure, that could be the meds, too, or maybe it's that I feel this distinct sense of *calm* around him. But the way I'm lying down, my shirt is twisted behind my back, and I can't move without jostling my arm.

I must make some kind of noise because Russell's face turns serious again, that cute furrow appearing between his brows. It's a good thing he wears glasses—without that barrier, the lovely blue of his eyes would be far too powerful.

"You okay, weather girl?"

God, that nickname. Why does it sound even sexier at night in a hotel room? "Yeah, I just—I might be more comfortable in pajamas?"

"I could help you change," he says, and then quickly adds: "Only if you want me to."

My burgundy sweater is across the room, but I'm still in a button-up. Jeans. A belt.

It's a lot of clothing to need help with.

"Don't sound *too* eager to get me undressed," I tease.

A flush creeps onto his cheeks. "I swear to god, that's not where my mind was going."

I snicker as I lift myself off the bed and stumble toward my suitcase, digging through it one-handed before producing my pajamas, a short-sleeved Henley and a pair of shorts that I know for a fact are see-through. When I catch my reflection in the mirror above the desk, all my bravado vanishes. I should put the hotel room ice bucket over my head—I'd look cuter. "I'm a mess right now, I'm sorry."

"You're not," he says, and even if he's just being nice, I don't hate hearing it. "I don't think you could look like a mess even if you tried."

He moves closer, until there's only a foot and a half of space between us, and reaches for my belt buckle. My most innocent clothing item. He undoes it as delicately as if it were made of glass, and instead of letting it thump to the floor, drapes it on the armchair next to my suitcase. Then he carefully un-Velcros my sling, placing it next to the belt so neatly, I have to wonder if this is how he does his laundry, too.

"What next?"

"Shirt," I say, because my arm is begging to be free.

"Cute pattern," he says about the tiny clouds. "Very on-brand."

He gets to work unbuttoning, starting at the top, his face close to mine. Long lashes and citrus and body heat. He pauses after each button, the briefest hesitation, and I realize it must be because he doesn't want to hurt me. He's maybe six inches taller than I am, so he has to duck his head, but every couple buttons, he flicks his gaze to mine, as though checking in with me. Each time, I give him what I hope is a reassuring half smile. *This is okay*, that smile says. *I am not at all aroused by this.*

When he reaches the last one, I let out a long, slow breath. It takes some wincing and maneuvering to extricate my arms from the sleeves, and then he folds the shirt next to my belt and sling. A split-second too late, I fling out my right hand to cover my bra.

I'm in a hotel room with Russell Barringer, wearing jeans and a pink lace push-up.

"Do you, uh . . ." He swallows hard, staring at my tiny pile of clothes. "Do you want your bra off, too?"

With the three brain cells I have left, I consider this. Do I want Russell to take off my bra? It's a rhetorical question—obviously I do. And undoubtedly I'd be more comfortable sleeping without it.

I pause for too long, imagining his fingertips running along the straps, sweeping up to the nape of my neck and then back down my spine.

"If you could just unhook it in the back, then I should be able to get off on my own." Freudian slip. "Get *it* off on my own."

"I can do that."

The warmth of his hands on my skin is too good. Like everything he does. Again, he takes his time. Logically, I realize he can't notice my nipples tightening to almost painful peaks, and if he hears the hitch in my breath, he probably assumes it's because of my injury. I melt into his touch as he unhooks me with deft fingers, wondering what he'd do if I turned around. If he'd take me in for a few moments, admiring every curve and dip and freckle, or if he'd be so overcome with want that he'd need his mouth on me right away. Under different circumstances, I'd want him to push. To pull. To grip me hard and sear my skin.

Unfortunately, the meds swimming through my bloodstream are stronger than my libido.

"And the necklace?" His fingers ghost over the chain, and I wonder if he can sense my shiver. When I nod, it takes him a few seconds to unclasp it. He places it on the bureau while I grab my pajama shirt with my right hand, attempting to cover my breasts with my bad arm.

An image from this afternoon pops into my head, unbidden. A laugh bubbles up my throat—I can't stop it.

"What is it?" he asks, looking pointedly at the window curtains.

"I almost got into the sauna with Torrance completely nude earlier," I say, and this makes him laugh, too. "I swear I'm not a prude, I just . . . did not expect to see my boss naked today?"

"You really have had a rough day."

"So trust me. This is a lot less awkward than disrobing in front of Seattle's favorite meteorologist."

Except then I have to move the hand on my breasts to get it into the shirtsleeve.

"I'm not looking." His voice is a low scrape, sounding somehow across the room and right up against my ear all at once. I am no longer laughing. "I swear."

If I told him he could look all he wanted, I'm not sure I'd want him to admire me first. His fingers could do all the appreciating I needed.

I press my thighs together, let out a shaky breath. Maybe my libido is perfectly fine.

Finally, only my jeans are left. As he unbuttons them, a thumb whispers across the skin just below my navel, that soft touch nearly making me gasp.

"Sorry!" he say, pulling back. "I wasn't—I didn't mean—"

"No, no, it's okay," I say, trying to reassure him. "You can keep going. I'm just—ticklish, I guess."

"I can be gentler." He hooks his thumbs through the belt loops and guides my jeans down my legs, his palms tracing my hips. Gentler, it turns out, is fucking torture.

Then we're done, and I find myself wishing I'd dressed for an expedition to Antarctica.

"Thank you." My first instinct is to hug him, but I haven't figured out how to do that with one arm. So I inch forward, dropping my forehead to rest lightly in the space just above his heart.

As though realizing what I'm attempting to do, he puts his arms around me, uncertain at first. Then he pulls me closer, tucking me against him, and I'm half certain I could fall asleep in this position if I weren't so wildly turned on. A few fingers skim up my spine, back and forth in a hypnotic motion. My eyes fall shut. With each stroke, I imagine he's touching me somewhere else. My lower lip. The inside of my wrist. A birthmark on my left hipbone.

I inhale, drawing in his citrus-cedar scent and pure Russell sweetness. "Thank you," I repeat, stumbling back on unsteady legs.

"Of course." His face has gone red again, and he's not making eye contact. "Do you, uh—want your shorts?"

I glance down at my bare legs.

Oh my god. I hugged him in a shirt and panties. Why was abject horniness not listed as a side effect on this medication?

"Excellent idea," I croak.

That ice bucket is looking more and more appealing. I shimmy into shorts and move back to the bed, trying to control my breathing as he perches on the edge again. So goddamn gingerly.

"Russell. You just took off my clothes. You can lie down on the bed if you want."

He gives me a half smile before sliding onto the bed next to me and stretching out his legs. He lets out this long breath, like we've done something far more aerobic than putting on pajamas. Somebody kill me, because it's the sexiest sound I've heard in months.

I'm exhausted, too, but he's given me so much tonight. The least I can do is reciprocate.

"My love life has been kind of a mess, too," I say. "I thought I'd be getting married this year. I'd be deep in wedding planning right now, picking a caterer and a band and a font for our invitations."

"I get the impression that maybe you're glad not to be?"

"I really am. We'd barely started planning, and his parents were already putting pressure on us to start having kids." Of course, not the reason it ended, but it didn't make anything better.

"Do you think you want them?" he asks. "Kids?"

Normally, it would be such a personal question, one I've rolled my eyes at and complained about in the past. Most people don't even ask—they just assume that of course you will procreate, so they don't care about the *if*. Only the *when*. But I don't mind him asking at all.

"I do," I say. "Someday. I spend a lot of time with my brother's kids, and I love them. But it wasn't so much about that as it was that I couldn't picture the wedding itself. I couldn't make any decisions about it, and I'm pretty sure that's because it wasn't right. Not that something being right makes it easy, but . . ."

"It makes those hard parts a lot more manageable."

I turn to him, propping my head up with my right arm. "Right. Exactly. My ex isn't a bad guy. He just thought I wasn't 'real enough.' " I say the words like I'm putting them in air quotes, and the ease with which I'm able to share this with Russell catches me off guard. "He told me I was too sunshine. Which, rude, using my own job against me."

"What does that even mean, too sunshine?"

"That I'm—that I'm pretending with everyone. That I'm hiding real shit because—" I break off, shaking my head. I can't get into the tidal wave that is my mother. Not when I'm going to see her the day after tomorrow.

We're too much, I can hear her saying. Usually when my mother crosses my mind, I force a smile and send out a positive affirmation. But not right now. Not when I'm trying to explain to Russell that this was the reason Garrison wanted out.

I've locked all this darkness in a room at the end of the hallway and haven't let anyone inside.

But for him, I crack the door. Just a little. Just for tonight.

"Because it's harder to deal with," I finish. A partial truth. It's all I can give him for now.

"I don't think you're like that at all," Russell says. "You're the kind of person who makes other people feel good to be around. That's a great thing."

"You feel good being around me?" I ask in this paper-thin voice.

His gaze is heavy on mine, and it's more intimate than when he had his hands on my bra. "All the time."

It might be the loveliest thing someone's said about me.

"I—thank you." I swallow hard, allowing those words to sink in. *All the time.* I want to ask if he really means it, if he's talking about the times I've let the mask slip around him, too. The times I complained about our bosses and acted like it was all hopeless. But he hasn't seen me at my worst, on my darkest days.

And he never can.

As badly as I want to linger in his compliment, I have to change the subject. "Maybe I'll try the whole casual-dating thing TV shows about hot twentysomethings living in the big city make look so easy."

The spell broken, Russell readjusts on the bed, crossing his legs at the ankles. "I wish I had some great advice to give. But—" He breaks off with a grimace, runs a hand down his face. "Don't judge me."

"I won't!"

"Okay." A long exhale, and then: "I haven't been on a date in five years."

I just stare. "Five . . . years?"

When he laughs, it's a disbelieving, self-conscious kind of laugh. Like even he is shocked by it. "I know. At first, it was because Liv and I had broken up, and Elodie was still a child. And then moving to a new city . . . it was all so much. Eventually, I fell into my routines, and they didn't end up including dating. The more time passed, the scarier it seemed to start trying again."

My brain practically short-circuits with this information. Five years. Five years since he sat across from someone in a swanky restaurant and drank overpriced cocktails, since he saw a movie with a

65 percent on Rotten Tomatoes, hoped it would at least be decent, and was frustrated by how aggressively mediocre it was.

Five years since he kissed someone goodnight at the end of an evening, blood spiked with adrenaline, pulse hammering in his throat.

"Well, that's it," I say, trying to erase that mental image. "We'll get Torrance and Seth back together, and then we'll find you your first date in five years."

He lifts an eyebrow, like this is a ludicrous proposition. "I'm so out of practice. I wouldn't even know what to do."

"That's easy. You just say, 'Hi, Ari Abrams, you look absolutely stunning in that sling. It really brings out your eyes. Do you want to have dinner with me?' "

I might have a fever, and this time I'm certain it's not a side effect of the medication. I hope he knows I'm joking. That I'm not actually encouraging him to ask me out.

At least, I think I hope so. Despite my New Year's Eve resolution to start dating again, I'm unsure how to navigate a relationship post-Garrison, especially a relationship with a single dad.

"Good to know," he says in this light, joking tone I've come to like quite a bit. "All the broken-armed women of Seattle aren't ready for me to sweep them off their feet."

We talk about Elodie, about his childhood in Michigan, about my brother, about my jewelry-making. Almost never about work, and it's such a relief. Until the day takes its toll on me and I feel my eyes start to close.

Still, I don't ask him to leave.

"You're really good," I say before I drift off. "You know that? I know any decent human wouldn't have made me go to the hospital by myself, and maybe they would have made sure I had something to eat, but you're just . . . a really good person."

I'm not sure what it sounds like to hear someone smile in the dark, but that must be what he's doing when I feel his hand on my shoulder, thumb rubbing back and forth against my thin T-shirt as he tells me thank you in a soft, sleepy voice.

Yes, he's good, it's true—and yet when we're close like this, when there's only a fraction of space between my hips and his, I want to make him very, very bad.

14

FORECAST:

A treacherous morning commute leads to gloomy winter doldrums as the week wears on

THE FIRST THING Torrance wants to know is when I'll be out of the sling.

The second is whether I'm okay.

"Fine," I grit out as I reach for the basket of English muffins on the breakfast bar in the lodge's dining room. If anything, the pain is sharper, more persistent than yesterday. The initial shock has worn off. I try to force my usual smile, but that must have fractured on my way down that fateful flight of stairs, too. "The doctor said a few weeks, but I'll have a better idea once I see someone in Seattle."

Torrance at least has the decency to realize she said something wrong, her features rearranging into what might be compassion. "I'm so sorry. I should have asked how you were doing first. I was just so shocked to see you like this!"

I had to sleep upright, my arm in its sling elevated on a pillow next to me, and when the pain jolted me awake around five a.m.—RIP my sleep schedule—I was even more shocked to discover Russell sleeping next to me. On top of the comforter, clothes still on, looking adorably rumpled. His glasses were on the bedside table next to him, and something about seeing them perched there made my heart twist.

It must have been uncomfortable, sleeping in his clothes, but he didn't say anything, just ran a palm along his stubbled face, his other hand tripping along the bedside table until he found his glasses. Then he asked if I needed any help, and I told him I should be able to manage, mainly because I didn't know if I could handle him undressing me again. I could barely handle the warmth of him in bed next to me.

I probably could have used the help, given that I nearly fell and broke my other arm in the shower. It took me ten minutes to put on a shirt and pants, after which I immediately needed to pee, and it took me another full minute to wiggle my jeans down my legs.

Torrance grabs my plate of food, and I mutter a thank-you as she helps me to a table. Then she and Seth return to a table by themselves, seemingly of their own volition, where Seth cracks a Canadian newspaper and Torrance scrolls through her tablet, leaving me wondering what the hell went on between the two of them last night.

It's decided that it's for the best if I head home early. Because I can't drive myself, Russell volunteers to drive my car back with me, his hair shower-damp, wearing the same corduroy jacket he draped over my shoulders in the hospital yesterday.

"I hate to take you away from all of this," I say. He just gives me this look, and I struggle to hold in a laugh.

Something changed between us last night, and whether we're simply closer friends or poised on the verge of something more, it fills me with a buzzing energy I haven't felt in a long time.

As he rolls his suitcase from the lobby to the car, Torrance gives me a subtle lift of her eyebrows. I glance away quickly.

The only hint at last night's tension during the drive home is when the audiobook I narrowly avoided on the way up starts playing as soon as I plug my phone in to charge.

"He bent down to worship at the altar of her thighs. God help him, he was going to pleasure her tonight until both of them saw stars—"

"Please kill me," I say, scrambling one-handed for my phone.

"Oh, uh—did you want to listen to an audiobook?"

I shut it off. "Nope. I do not."

Though he laughs, I don't miss the pink tint to his cheeks.

The trip home is pleasant enough, and here's the Russell I've grown accustomed to over the past few weeks. Sure, we talk a little about Elodie, and about other topics we wouldn't have been as open about during our first few meetings. But I want the Russell from last night, the one I can no longer pretend I don't have feelings for, even if that still terrifies me.

I've never dated someone with a kid, and while of course he's an independent person, capable of making his own decisions, Elodie changes things. After all, he said she's the reason he hasn't dated for a while.

Five years. Of course, that doesn't necessarily mean it's been five years since he last had sex with someone. But it could . . . and I can't say I wouldn't love to be the person who ends that dry spell. Every so often, I glance at his hands on the steering wheel and remember them on my skin last night. If we slept together, I'd want to see him completely give in. Surrender. The opposite of the measured way he unbuttoned my shirt, unhooked my bra.

An out-of-control Russell, one with his glasses askew and mouth swollen and fingers making imprints above my hips. Jacket tossed in a heap on the floor. A Russell who asks permission with a whispered plea in my ear. Begging me to undo him. To wreck him.

Once he leaves after helping me bring my bags inside, I take a cold, cold shower.

When that doesn't work, I become very grateful I can move all the fingers on my dominant hand.

I TAKE THE next day off work to see a doctor, who confirms the elbow fracture with another X-ray. I sign up for physical therapy and grocery deliveries and a credit card with rideshare rewards points, since it'll be about a month before I can safely drive again.

And then I spend far too much time picking out what to wear to see my mother.

"You didn't have to throw yourself down a staircase to get out of this," Alex says when he picks me up.

"Shut it, you." I readjust my sling, and he reaches over to help me with the seatbelt. "I want to see her."

It's half true, at least, and I'm hoping for the other half on the drive to the hospital.

It would take a whole fleet of masseuses to work out the anxiety coiled tight in my body. I'm not sure what I'm expecting her to look like after nearly six months apart, if she'll be exactly as I remember her, or if I'll be able to tell, just by looking at her, that something's different.

I know this isn't going to be easy. My mom could drag me down better than Garrison, better than any of the guys I tried to project a positive front for. And she was the reason I did it. The reason I pretended to be sunshine, the reason I said everything was okay when nothing was.

Because our father couldn't handle her darkness, and I couldn't let that happen to me.

I won't let her comment on my appearance or my career or my relationship status. I told Alex he could let her know Garrison and I broke up, but she doesn't know the reason why, and I won't let her needle me about it.

By the time we arrive, I've stuck and unstuck the Velcro on my sling so many times that it's no longer tacky in certain places.

The hospital is a newer building downtown. After we check in at the front desk and go through a metal detector, a nurse leads us to a bright, cheery room filled with paintings donated by a local artist, all the tables empty except for the one Amelia Abrams is sitting at.

She cut her hair. That's the first thing I notice. Alex, our dad, and I were a trio of redheads, our blond mom the odd one out. She took such pride in it—it was damaged beyond belief and she was always dyeing out the grays, but it was long and mostly blond and that was what mattered to her. She never wanted to look old, she told us, as though looking your age was some kind of punishment. When I got haircuts, she'd always say, "Not too short!" Like if I lost my hair or had too little of it, I'd be losing some of my value.

Now my mother's light hair is trimmed to just above her shoulders, shorter than mine, in a style that's not completely modern yet not outdated. It's cute—that's what it is. And her grays have grown out a bit, but she doesn't look old. Not the way she was always fearful of, at least. What she looks is tired.

"Hey there, Alex. Arielle," she says as we join her at the table. My full name, used so infrequently these days, yanks me back in time.

Those memories aren't all bad. There were the Shabbat dinners she tried to make special, the prayers she taught us. The year we went as rock, paper, scissors for Halloween, won an elementary school costume contest, and collected more candy than I could ever hope to eat.

Until she made us sell it to the dentist the next day because candy caused breakouts and god forbid her preteen daughter have a zit.

Her boyfriends are only in those memories occasionally, the ones who made an effort to get to know Alex and me, the decent ones who gently encouraged her to talk to someone. "You want to medicate me? Turn me into someone different?" she yelled at one of them, a well-meaning accountant named Charlie. I was eleven and wholly unsure what being medicated meant.

I sit up straighter and summon a smile, as though the force of it can banish the grayest parts of the past.

It's not until we've exchanged pleasantries and I shuck off my jacket that she notices my arm. "Ari!" she gasps. "What happened?"

"A couple of viewers disagreed with my forecasts," I say, then relent and tell her the almost-truth.

Her mouth forms a small O. "I'm so relieved you're okay."

Alex catches her up on the kids and his job, getting out his phone to show her a video of the twins dancing to Starship's "We Built This City," which he says is, inexplicably and unfortunately, their favorite song. I catch her up on KSEA, and she nods and laughs when she's supposed to, even if the laughs sound a little foreign. It's not that she seems happy, exactly—content is maybe closer to the right word.

Still, I can't help thinking of all the years she refused treatment. Every time Alex and I worried about her, only for her to wake up the next day, pretending nothing was wrong. This hospital is an extreme—she's only here because her brain took her to the darkest of places. Because she was afraid, and she didn't know what else to do.

My adult life would be different, I'm sure of it, if she'd gotten help sooner. There are too many what-ifs down that road, and yet I can't seem to redirect myself.

She tells us about the hospital's recreational activities, the doctors, the group therapy, leaving out the more personal details. "The food is actually amazing here," she says.

What I want to know is *why* this time is different. Why she changed her mind about medication, or if she's only taking it so they'll discharge her. If she'll fall back on her old habits once she goes home.

And she can't stop staring at my sling. "They're going to let you on camera with that?" she asks.

"I sure hope so, given it's my job."

"It doesn't reflect poorly on the station?"

"Why would it do that? It doesn't affect my ability to forecast the weather."

Dial it back, Alex's expression says. *She's trying. Give her a chance.*

"We're all really glad you're here." Alex touches her arm, ever the peacemaker. "We want to support you however we can."

She gives him a tight smile, and I try my best not to read into it. I've never known what's going through my mother's head—I can't imagine that changing now.

Eventually, the conversation moves to my breakup, just as I feared it would.

"We weren't right for each other," I say with a shrug, because I can't bear to tell her the real reason. "It just took us a while to realize it."

I'm fully prepared for her to say something shitty, even though she doesn't know the details. *You were too much. He couldn't handle it.*

Instead, she reaches across the table and places a hand on mine, her skin weathered and dotted with freckles. "I'm sorry," she says, and if I close my eyes, I can pretend she's apologizing for so much more.

15

FORECAST:

Rough seas ahead, both literal and metaphorical

"DID YOU HEAR about the meteorologist who broke her arms and legs?" one of the camera guys calls to me as I position myself in front of the green screen. "She had to wear four casts."

"That's hilarious, Glenn. Top-notch humor." I wince as morning producer Deandra Fuller helps me adjust my mic over one of my five-of-the-same-dresses in navy today. Zipping it up was hell. "Are you sure this is going to be okay?"

"Absolutely," Deandra says. "Remember when Gia broke her wrist playing rec volleyball last year? She showed that video of people helping her get made up in the dressing room that everyone *loved*. And hey, maybe you can make a joke about it when you're on the air. You know, make the viewers feel less awkward about it by showing that *you* don't feel awkward about it."

What that turns out to be is this: "A lot of snow in the mountains this week, which is good news for skiers and snowboarders," I say, lifting my left arm. "Though I won't be doing any of that for a while!"

I can barely keep my eyes open during the show. It's gotten easier to sleep upright, but I'm going to have to take a break before Russell and I launch the next phase of our plan tonight. I'm a pro power-napper, but I tossed and turned between the hours of eleven and two, and when I forced myself out of bed at two fifteen, my head was pounding and my stomach was unhappy with me. Once again, I regret not buying that dog pillow from Instagram.

It's not just lack of sleep, though. I recognize the signs of my depression creeping in, probably a mix of my injury and my mom and, as always, my brain chemistry. The littlest things make me overly emotional, like the feel-good story that wrapped up our morning show about a golden retriever who traversed three states to catch up with her family when they went on vacation. The thought of sweet Beatrice missing her people so desperately that she couldn't bear to be separated from them for a few days . . . *damn it,* I might be on the verge of tearing up again. I'll be okay—I'll just have to work harder to force the smiles on and off camera.

Force them enough, and they start to feel real.

I'm on my way to my desk when a conversation stops me in my tracks.

"He's been different lately," investigative reporter Kyla Sutherland says to Meg Nishimura in the hall between the studio and the newsroom. "I saw him go into her office this morning. I thought it was going to be another one of those signs, but he left a latte on her desk."

"Oat milk?"

"Probably."

"Maybe they finally called a truce."

"Or banged out all the tension."

The two of them laugh, and despite the layer of mental fog, I let this knowledge buoy me as I head into the newsroom.

Unfortunately, it's short-lived. I'm trying to update our social media with my forecasts, but there's something wrong with my internet. I disconnect and reconnect. Restart my computer. Nothing. And Torrance is in the weather center now, working on her own forecasts. I know from experience that it's a solitary task for her.

I glance around the newsroom, finding exactly zero open computers.

"Is your internet working?" I ask Meg as she takes her desk on the other side of the low-partition from me.

"Seems to be," she says before slipping on headphones.

Doing my best to suppress a grumble, I get to my feet. Russell's covering a game this afternoon, so maybe his computer will be free. Before I knock on the half-open door, I rearrange my features to smooth out my RBF. He's already seen me in ways I'd never allow someone else to, drunk and bitching about our bosses, drugged up and spilling my history with Garrison. I can't do any of that at work.

"Hey," I call out when I spot Russell behind his computer, trying to sound casual. "Could I talk to you for a moment?"

He's not the only one in the office. Sports anchors Shawn Bennett and Lauren Nguyen are at the desks across from him, watching our interaction very closely.

"We'll leave you two alone," Shawn says.

"Oh—no—you don't have to," I say, but he and Lauren are already snickering as they leave the office. There's no way Russell and I can be fodder for office gossip yet, unless they're really starved for it. And I can't imagine Russell's said anything to them about me. Then again, what would he say? That he platonically removed my clothes while I was high on prescription painkillers? That I hugged him in my panties?

The memory ups the temperature in the Dugout a good fifteen degrees.

They close the door behind them and god, I hope they don't think Russell and I are going to suddenly start making out against it. Still, I'm grateful for the privacy, though it's very possible my face matches my hair.

"Sorry about them," Russell says, more to his computer than to me. Maybe he's equally embarrassed—and maybe it's because he doesn't have the same feelings for me. It's very possible my face matches my hair.

"It's okay. You're on your way out, right? I, uh, wanted to see if I could use your computer? Mine's on the fritz."

"Oh—sure." He types a few sentences, tells me he'll just be ten more minutes.

I lean against the wall beneath a vintage Ken Griffey Jr. Mariners jersey. "I saw that all-staff email Seth sent around this morning. They hired someone for the college football beat?"

Russell's hands pause on the keyboard. "Yep, new guy fresh out of school. Shawn's going to be on paternity leave soon, so I'm going to be covering some pro games."

"Russell, that's amazing!" I don't even have to try to brighten my voice with enthusiasm. I really am thrilled for him. Even if it's not a direct result of our plotting, it's *progress*. Though . . . we have something big planned for tomorrow night that we arranged on our drive back to the US. "You're sure you still want to do this? With the Hales?"

"Why wouldn't I be?"

"Well, work seems to be improving for you. This was what you wanted, right? Covering pro sports?"

His brow furrows. "It's not just about me. You haven't gotten that attention from Torrance yet, have you?" My silence speaks for itself. "And the office might be a *little* better, but I don't think we can call it quits yet. Are *you* sure, with your arm? This whole thing has already been . . . a bit more destructive than either of us anticipated. We can stop anytime, you know."

"I think we're close. They seemed so *peaceful* at the lodge." Or I'm so used to seeing them at each other's throats that anything else is groundbreaking. "And I overheard something earlier about Seth leaving coffee on her desk. Other people at the station are starting to notice."

"Okay," he agrees, pushing out his chair. "I'm just. Uh. Going to open that door before anyone gets the wrong idea."

And that settles it. Whatever I thought he might have felt in my hotel room—there's no trace of it today.

"Right." Now I can't look at him, either. "I'd hate for that to happen."

THE GOAL IS to re-create Torrance and Seth's first date. Apparently, Russell and Seth had as much of a heart-to-heart in the sauna as Torrance and I did. About twenty years ago, when they were still working in Olympia, Seth drove her down to Seattle one July evening for a dinner cruise around Lake Washington. There was a specially curated menu, one that combined his Japanese heritage with her Scottish, and even though the captain told them it was unlikely to spot a whale on one of these cruises, they did—a majestic orca lifting a fin out of the water as if to say hello.

We lucked out with a Groupon and booked a dinner cruise for the four of us, telling them it was a thank-you for the retreat, and that I'd felt especially bad I hadn't been able to stay. The whale is, unfortunately, beyond our control. Before the boat takes off, one of us will fake an excuse, thus leaving them alone in a deeply romantic setting, if the photos on the website are to be believed.

For the most part, yesterday's heaviness has lifted, and I'm relieved seeing my mom didn't sink me deeper. It's impossible to know how long those moods are going to last or whether they require moving up a therapy appointment.

"I'm getting déjà vu," Russell says as we wait on a dock downtown. In the summer, this area is so packed with tourists, I avoid it completely, but it's empty in February. The water is choppy, the wind toying with the ends of his hair. Russell in a knitted scarf: a sight I could get used to.

"They're going to show up this time." It's a free dinner cruise. Who could say no to that?"

I readjust my coat, because one thing I've learned lately is that wearing a coat and a sling is a complicated endeavor. You can either wear the sling over your shirt and drape the coat across one shoulder, or you can get dressed like normal and do up the sling over your coat. I've gone for option number one, which means I have to keep tugging up my coat so it doesn't fall down. It's very fashion forward. Very chic.

A man who appears to be in his early thirties approaches us, wearing a vest that indicates he works for the cruise company. "Hi there, I'm the captain," he says. "You two are on our Moonlit Magic cruise this evening? Mr. and Mrs. Hale?"

I hold in a laugh. "They're our bosses. They should be here any minute."

His smile reveals a rather lovely dimple. "Great. We're thrilled to have you here. This is going to be a really special night for all of you." He motions to my sling, smile drooping. "What happened there?"

"Fought a pigeon when it tried to steal my lunch."

"Ouch."

"You should see the pigeon."

He pauses for a moment, scrutinizing me. "I swear this isn't a line," he says, "but I'm pretty sure I've seen you before."

"I'm a meteorologist for KSEA 6. I'm usually on weekday mornings."

"Yes! That's it," he says with a snap of his fingers. "I don't always watch very religiously, but I usually have it on in the background. And now I'm regretting saying anything, because it makes it sound like I don't value what you do at all. Ari Abrams, right?"

"I'm flattered. Really," I say.

"Craig," he says, holding out his hand.

"Nice to meet a passive fan."

He's still grinning at me, and I'm not at all used to this. Russell checks something on his phone, then cranes his neck to see if the Hales are headed our way.

"Ari Abrams of KSEA 6," Craig continues, "do you think I could get your number? Assuming, of course, that I get all of you back to land in one piece?"

"Oh—okay?" I'm so thrown by this whole interaction that it comes out like a question. I'm not used to men being this forward. I dig for a more positive answer. "Sure. Of course."

Russell is determinedly not looking at either of us right now, and maybe it's my imagination that his shoulders stiffen.

This doesn't have to be awkward. I force myself to look on that bright side everyone assumes I live on. I keep telling myself that maybe I'll figure out how to date this year. This could be how it starts.

Craig types out a text as I recite my number, and then my phone buzzes with a message containing a waving hand and a boat emoji.

I'm so struck by this unexpected boost to my self-esteem that I'm startled when Russell calls out, "Seth!"

"Sorry I'm a little late. Thanks again for doing this." He's holding a succulent, one in a cute patterned pot that looks like it was expensive, based on what I know from my greenhouse trip last month.

Torrance shows up a few minutes later, looking elegant as always in an ankle-length black coat with a faux fur collar, and when Seth presents the succulent to her, she turns nearly the shade of her signature lipstick.

I can't help wondering if both of them being late is some sign they're meant to be together or if it's as simple as neither of them wanting to be the first one here.

Craig guides all of us toward the ramp that will take us to the boat, a small but sleek white yacht with the name *Seas the Day*. Russell and I fall in step behind the Hales, but halfway up the ramp, he comes to a dramatic stop.

"You okay?" I ask him.

"Yeah, I—I'm sorry. I just get . . . a little seasick sometimes."

Torrance whirls around, a breeze sifting through her glossy curls. "Seasick?"

Russell holds up a hand. "It's really no big deal. I'm sure I'll be fine." With that, he doubles over, clutching his stomach.

It's such a performance that I have to bite the inside of my cheek to keep from laughing.

"Look, Russ, if you need to sit this one out, that's okay," Seth says. "We'd hate for you to be stuck if you're not feeling well."

"And the wind speeds are the highest they've been all week. It's supposed to reach thirty miles per hour tonight," Torrance adds. "Water might be rocky."

Russell continues to milk it with a long, shaky breath, and when he glances at me, I half expect to catch him wink. "Yeah, maybe you're right. That's probably for the best."

"I'd hate for you to miss out," I say, stepping into my role: convincing them we don't want to leave before making the assessment that Russell's too sick to take himself home.

"He's looking a little pale." Torrance sounds concerned. "Do you want to make sure he gets home okay, Abrams?"

It's a miracle I don't bite through my lower lip entirely—because I was going to suggest the exact same thing. Either Torrance cares deeply about Russell, or she's realized this means an opportunity to soak up all that Moonlit Magic with Seth. Alone.

"I can do that." I pretend to give *Seas the Day* a longing glance. "I'm so sorry. We were really looking forward to this."

"Well—" Torrance breaks off, glancing between Seth and the two of us. "We should still go, right, Seth? It would be a shame to waste it . . ."

She wants to spend time with him.

Or she wants a free boat ride and dinner, but still, they're going to be on that yacht for three whole hours. Either they'll emerge with a newfound affection for each other or one of them will toss the other overboard.

"I'm game if you are," Seth says. I can tell he's trying to sound as though he has a tremendous amount of chill about this alone time with Torrance when he probably has about zero. "Thanks again, you two. It's too bad you won't be able to enjoy it."

I wave my hand. "Don't mention it. Have a great night."

I link my right arm through Russell's, and he lets out another moan for good measure. Once my back is turned, I can't help it—I start laughing, and Russell's shoulders start shaking, and we rush off the ramp as quickly as possible.

"Oh my god," I hear Torrance say. "Remember this? It's the same bottle of wine from our first date."

When we're safely back on land, Russell meets my gaze, moonlight glinting off his glasses, and I know we're thinking the same thing: It's working.

16

FORECAST:

An inevitable collision of two high-pressure systems; beware falling objects

A NEWSROOM NEVER really sleeps. While I'm used to getting to the station when it's still dark out, nine o'clock is a different kind of dark. Almost eerie.

Russell had some coverage to wrap up for the website, and since he's the one driving, I wasn't about to complain. Sure, I could have taken an Uber home, but I must have been a matchmaker—or more specifically, a shadchan—in a previous life, because imagining Torrance and Seth on that yacht together has filled me with too much adrenaline. I'm not ready for the night to end.

"You really sold the seasick thing," I say as we head into the empty Dugout. "You looked truly miserable."

Russell flicks on one set of overhead lights, casting the room in a soft, warm glow. "I do get seasick. I was sparing all of you."

I flop down onto the couch between Russell's and Shawn Bennett's desks. "I can't believe you guys get a couch. This is discrimination. Against people who don't work in sports."

Russell makes a low sound in his throat as he sits down at his computer, but he doesn't make a move to open up any of his files.

"Sorry, sorry. I'll let you work. I'm just so amped right now." I slap the couch's armrest for emphasis. "I feel like I could lift a motherfucking truck."

"It was pretty great, seeing them like that," he says in this flat voice. All his giddiness from when we raced off the ramp—gone.

"It was a *victory*. They're on a romantic cruise around Lake Washington right now with Captain Craig, and it's because of *us*." I can't stop grinning. "We're doing it. We're really doing it."

I'm rambling. But Russell is acting odd, and I'm not sure how to get back what we usually have, or if we still have a "usually" after the weekend. My hotel room. His sharp intake of breath when he unhooked my bra.

If I sleep with a hundred more people, I'm fairly certain it'll remain the sexiest moment of my life.

"We're lucky that Craig was so helpful," I add.

It's an obnoxious thing to say, I realize that. I'm following a hunch, testing whether this is the reason he's upset. And it works.

"Right. Craig was so thrilled to help you." The weight he places on the last word is slight, but I catch it.

I sit up straight, aiming my newfound frustration right between his shoulder blades. "Okay. Can you explain what's going on?"

He spins in his seat, blue eyes flashing. "Really, Ari? Give me some credit." I've never seen him this visibly riled. He takes a deep breath, like he's trying to calm himself down. When he speaks again, his voice is more level. "He asked you out right in front of me, and you couldn't have been more eager to say yes."

"What does it matter that it was right in front of you?" I say. "And so what if I was eager? I'm single."

If he's jealous, he's going to have to spell it out for me. If he feels for me any fraction of the way I do for him, I don't want to keep wondering.

"Because he was all . . . I don't know. Chiseled. Fit. Like a Ken doll. And I thought if that was your type . . ." He trails off, scraping his hand along his stubbled jaw in a way I wish weren't impossibly sexy.

The way he's sitting there, with his glasses and his scruff and his jacket with the elbow patches—the idea of him not being my type is about as ridiculous as saying I don't really care about clouds.

"If that was my type . . . ?" I prompt, as gently as I can.

"It's not important. I don't want to be the jealous asshole here."

"Why would you be jealous of Captain Craig?"

At that, he rises from his chair, sending it spiraling back against his desk with a muted thwack. "Because I find you so incredibly charming! I have for a while, and you saying yes to this guy you just met when you were standing right in front of me made me jealous. I'm not proud of it, but there it is. I'm extremely out of practice, and nothing could make that clearer than what happened tonight. And I wanted Torrance and Seth to have a great night, I did—but that's why I'm not all gung ho about what happened out there."

The look in his eyes has grown so intense, unblinking as he waits for my next move, and all I can focus on is the quick rise and fall of his chest. In and out and in and out. There might not be enough air in this room.

We've always been so cordial to each other, and now that we're this-close to confessing how we feel, the claws are coming out.

On shaking legs, I push to my feet. "Russell," I say. "Russ." I try out the nickname, loving the way his face softens when I say it. "He's not my type."

"No?" There's a glimmer of hope in his voice.

I shake my head as I inch closer, stretching out my right hand to graze his arm. He wants this as much as I do, and that makes me brave. Now my breathing is as labored as his, anticipation filling my lungs until I think I might collapse before I reach him.

Luckily, he's there to hold me up, his mouth meeting mine right as his hands grasp my hips.

It's a hard, fast kiss, and I open for him right away. This is Russell, who took me to my first hockey game and waited with me in the hospital and undressed me without looking. Sweet, ever-polite Russell, losing all pretense of pleasant as he catches my lower lip with his teeth while his hands dive into my hair. I thought he'd be shy, reserved, but there's a desperation even in the way his thumb sweeps along my ear. The scrape of stubble against my chin and cheeks.

And I can't get enough.

A rumble in his throat makes me kiss him deeper, grabbing the lapel of his jacket tighter with my good hand. Now I'm certain there isn't enough air in here, but I can't bring myself to care. All I want is for him to make that sound again and again.

I forget for a moment that I don't have use of both my arms when I attempt to pull him closer, breaking away with a sharp inhale.

"Shit," he says, features pinched with alarm even as he's breathing hard. "Did I—?"

"No, no, that was my fault." I readjust, tightening my sling. With a sheepish half smile, I say, "I was just trying to get more of you."

When he reaches for me again, he spins us around, backing me up against his desk. He gives me the lift I need to slide on top of it, and I wrap my legs around his hips and—*yes*. He's warm and soft against me, except for where he isn't, and that sends a jolt of satisfaction to all the most sensitive parts of my body. This time, he doesn't say anything when I brush against his round stomach—only tugs me closer.

"I don't want to mess up anything on your desk," I say as his mouth trails down my jaw.

"I can tell you with complete honesty that I really, really don't care if you do."

Still, I'm reluctant at first as I push things to the side—a stapler, I think, and then a notebook. It's not until he starts sucking at the spot where my neck meets my shoulder that I throw caution to the wind and start shoving. Papers, pens, a pair of headphones. I can feel the heels of my shoes digging into his back, but if it's bothering him, he's sure as hell not saying anything.

I've had the occasional office fantasy, but *god*, the reality is even better. He's solid heat, lips dipping lower, dropping kisses along my collarbone and down my neck. His hands are at my waist, fingertips skimming along my ribcage, and I can sense he's uncertain about going higher.

If I can't do everything I want to with an arm in a sling, the least I can do is help him.

So I drape my hand along his, inching it upward, until his thumb is stroking one breast through the fabric of my sweater.

"This is okay?" he asks, and it's absurd, how okay it is. He's not even touching my skin, and my nipples are already aching.

"God. Yes." My mouth falls open against his, and he swallows my moan, tongue swirling as I move my hand from his to clutch at the back of his neck.

He bunches up my skirt and pulls me to the edge of the desk until we're lined up in the most torturous way, the rough friction of his jeans driving me wild. My struggle to put on these tights this morning was thoroughly not worth it. I'd have risked being cold all day if it meant I could feel him exactly where I want to right now, hard against my center while he groans into my ear. I roll my hips against his, turning that groan feral and drawing out a gasp of my own. I want to unbuckle him, unzip him, have him lay me bare in his office so he remembers this every morning when he gets to work.

When something falls off his desk with the loudest thump so far, Russell breaks our kiss, panting. I stifle a laugh as he walks around to check what it was, coming back with a baseball player Funko Pop still in its plastic box.

"Cute," I say.

"King Félix Hernández is not cute. He's a collector's edition." He places it back on his desk, then seems to think better of it and stows it in a drawer.

Still, it seems to shock us back to reality, which is maybe a good thing. I'm not sure how far we might have gone. I have to squeeze my legs together, bite down on the inside of my cheek. I've always struggled to let go with new people, and I've never had an orgasm with someone on a first encounter. But I'm so keyed up that a few more minutes and I might have fallen apart, and I would have made certain I dragged him down with me.

"This was . . ." he says as he plays with a wavy strand of my hair. ". . . not how I imagined the night would turn out."

"I've imagined this two or three times." Heart still racing, I hop off his desk, doing my best to tidy it up. "Only there's usually a blizzard, and we're trapped here for days with nothing but each other's bodies for warmth."

"I'm sorry I was jealous." He cages me in, interrupting my tidying to press a kiss to the shell of my ear. "I just hadn't figured out how to be brave with you yet."

"You've always seemed brave to me," I say. "Even before this."

His whole face shifts, eyes crinkling at the corners in that way I like so much. It's incredible, watching this confidence change him. "Have I told you," he says, "that you look absolutely stunning in that sling, Ari Abrams?"

I bite my lip to keep from grinning. "Yeah?"

"Oh yeah." His hand comes up to my face, his thumb skimming my cheekbone. "Really brings out your eyes."

17

FORECAST:

A hazy few days of uncomfortable truths

MY THERAPIST'S OFFICE has a view of Lake Union and a couch that contours to my body so perfectly I'm scared to ask her where she got it, because I know it'll be out of my price range. I've been in a handful of therapists' offices, and none of them have made me quite as calm as Joanna's.

Today's a therapy doubleheader. I'm still a little sore from physical therapy after a woman named Ingrid stretched and bent my elbow, wrist, and fingers for thirty minutes, and now this. I've been seeing Joanna for almost three years, since I moved back to Seattle and my former therapist retired and recommended her to me. Seeing someone new is daunting—starting from the beginning, unpacking all your baggage for a stranger, knowing they won't think less of you for your irrationalities but being terrified nonetheless—but it was worth it to find her. I go every few weeks, sometimes less frequently if I feel like I'm managing okay.

"How's work been?" Joanna asks, taking a sip of tea from her mug with a watercolor Seattle skyline on it. She drinks it every time I'm here, and the soothing lemon scent must have a way of untangling my messy brain as well as her questions. With her long dark hair and straight-across bangs that always make me consider cutting mine, I've never been able to guess how old she is. She looks like she could pass for twenty-five, but she carries herself with the wisdom of someone who has helped a lot of people wage war against their demons.

"Not too bad." Almost ten years I've been in therapy, and every time I'm here, I'm all brief answers at first. *How are you? Okay. What have you been up to since last time? Not much.* I have to ease into it, a duckling learning to swim again and again. Joanna must be used to it because she lets her questions breathe. Therapy and journalism have that in common. "A little challenging with my arm, but I'm getting used to it."

"I'm so sorry that happened to you," she says in her ever-warm way. "Has Torrance been understanding?"

"She's been much better than usual, actually." And this is where I debate how much of the plan I want to share with her.

Logically, I know it's the job of a therapist not to judge you. While I know Joanna wouldn't outright express disappointment, I'm still reluctant to tell her I've kind-of sort-of been manipulating my bosses to fall back in love with each other.

I opt for a half-truth. "She and her ex-husband seem to be getting along, which is good for the rest of us."

"Her ex-husband, the news director? Seth?" Joanna's memory astounds me. I'm not sure if she just takes meticulous notes or what, but she's able to recall names even of people I've mentioned offhand.

"No passive-aggressive signs, no blowups in the newsroom for the past couple weeks. I'd forgotten what that kind of harmony felt like."

"Ari, that's *great.*" A kind smile, another sip of her tea. "You've been wanting more attention from her for a while. Is that something that feels a little more attainable now?"

"It might be. With her in a good mood, though . . ." I've been biding my time, waiting for Torrance to take an interest in my career. "Maybe I could even bring it up to her directly. Not anytime soon, but at some point."

"We can definitely talk about strategies for that when you're ready," Joanna says. "Is there anything else you wanted to discuss today?"

"I've been spending a lot of time with, um, one of the sports reporters," I say, figuring I've got nothing to lose by telling Joanna about Russell. "In a romantic way?"

"Oh?"

"It's still really new." *Really* new. That kiss in the newsroom was Wednesday, and today's Friday. "So I haven't talked to him about . . . all of this yet." I wave my hand around the room.

After we rearranged his desk to make it look less like he'd been mauling me on top of it, I started yawning, and he gave me a ride home, saying his work could wait. "There's no way I'm going to be able to concentrate now," he said with a rough laugh, one I felt down to the tips of my toes.

He has Elodie this week, meaning our schedules won't match up again until next weekend. We've been texting, though, and the next night we both have off, I'm taking him on his first date in five years.

"That wasn't going to be my next question," Joanna says.

"Okay, fine, but I could tell it was coming. Eventually."

We discussed this when I was with Garrison: why I felt I couldn't tell him about my every-three-weeks visits to this office or the pills in my purse. "Do you think," Joanna had said, "that maybe he isn't getting all of you? He loves you, Ari. He might understand what you're going through more than you're giving him credit for. Might even support you."

"I just don't want to lose him if I do," I'd say.

As open as I've been with Russell, he has only a fraction of my history. I want to think it would be different with him, but I'm not sure yet if it's worth taking the risk. I have no way of knowing what would happen if I gave him every broken piece of me—and it's the uncertainty that keeps those pieces stashed away.

"Let's talk about something else," I say quickly. "Let's talk about my mom."

Joanna's eyebrows climb so high they disappear beneath her bangs. "Voluntarily bringing up your mother? I can roll with that."

She has a point—I don't do it very often. In therapy, even when I don't have to be that sunshine version of myself, I'm always on edge when we discuss my mother. "I saw her last week. She's going home in a couple days."

"How did that go?"

"Not terrible. She seemed . . . good. From what I could tell, at least."

"Have you thought about what you want that relationship to look like? I know she's your mother, but you have every right to make whatever decision is best for *you*."

I let the question hang in the air. Weighing it. "I have. And I want a close relationship with her, or however close we can get. I know it's not going to look how I imagined it would when I was younger, and I'm okay with that. I want to get to know this different version of her." Once the words leave my mouth, I'm surprised to realize they're true.

"You know she isn't going to be instantly cured," Joanna says. "That this is a process, and she'll have to keep up with her therapy and medication." It's maybe a reference to the joke I made after our third session. "I'm cured!" I crowed, and she shook her head, smiling. One of my past therapists didn't have a sense of humor at all. It was important to me to find someone who could laugh about things. "And that she may not entirely be the version you're expecting her to be."

"I—I know that. I still want to see her. To try."

Joanna sips her tea, nodding slowly. "Should we talk through some of those strategies to handle the things she might say to you?"

"Okay," I say quietly, and that's what we do for the rest of the session.

THAT SUNDAY, I meet up with Alex and Javier for boozy brunch at an upscale diner Javier is trying to poach a chef from.

"This kimchi hash is to die for," he says between bites. "Imagine what she could do in our kitchen." Javier's place, a Cuban fusion restaurant called Honeybee Lounge, is consistently getting rave reviews, but he has his heart set on a Michelin star.

"Isn't poaching a chef kind of morally questionable?" I drag my fork through my stack of pancakes. He's not wrong; everything here is amazing. And I probably shouldn't be the judge of anyone's morals.

"Happens all the time in the industry. Especially if you have a rock star chef who's not getting the attention they want, which I suspect is the case with Shirley Pak, given the very casual, not at all morally questionable conversation we had over drinks last week."

"I guess that happens in TV, too." I tilt my head toward the ceiling, pretending I'm calling up to the universe. "If the *Today* show wants me, feel free to let me know any time!"

"Don't worry, I've already sent them the photos of your billboard." Alex takes a sip of his mimosa, his freckled cheeks already prosecco-flushed. "God, it's weird being out without the twins. It's almost too quiet, isn't it? Shouldn't someone be screaming?"

Javier nudges him. "Quiet can be a good thing."

This would be the perfect time to tell my brother and brother-in-law about Russell, but especially after confiding in Joanna, I'm not sure how much vulnerability I have left in me.

All around us, groups of friends are toasting one another and laughing and stealing food off each other's plates. For the past couple months, I've been thinking I lost all these friends to Garrison. Sure, they were all his friends first, but I'm struggling to remember who I had before that. Later in college, I had a few close classmates, but we all split for different cities after graduation. There were a couple people in Yakima, including their chief meteorologist, whose goal was to keep that job for the rest of his career. He wanted to be *the* Yakima weatherman, and while my dreams were different, I could respect that.

When I got back to Seattle, I had Alex again. My hope of hopes was that eventually I'd have Torrance, too. I'm friendly with meteorologists at other stations, to the point where we chat if we see each other at industry events, and while we always promise to grab coffee sometime, it never happens.

I excuse myself to use the bathroom, dreading the feat of engineering that is unbuttoning my jeans with one arm in a sling. On my way there, I spy a familiar blond head at a two-top across the diner.

My first instinct is to swing by and say hello. But when her tablemate comes into view, I'm so startled I have to rush into the bathroom for fear of letting out an audible gasp. I don't trust my eyes or my brain until I reenter the dining room, slowly, slowly. Because that is Torrance Hale, and the man she's sitting across from, her hand on his forearm, is not Seth.

I stumble my way back to our table, where the view is more obscured but feels about a thousand times safer. The guy looks about Torrance's age, maybe a bit younger, with overly styled brown hair and a silver hoop in one ear. They're dressed casually, which of course for Torrance still means flawless lipstick and a sweater that probably cost more than a month of my rent. Sure, he could be a relative . . . but the way she's leaning forward, giggling at something he's saying is decidedly date-like.

"You all right?" Javier asks. "You look a little spooked."

"Fine," I choke out, spilling water down the front of my shirt.

It seemed like Torrance and Seth were getting along. I don't think I imagined that. And not just getting along—actually enjoying each other's company. The conversation on the retreat, that lack of passive-aggressive signs in the newsroom, the yacht . . .

Maybe the truth is that we've never had control over them at all.

18

FORECAST:

Look to the sky for a dazzling natural phenomenon; temperatures reach all-time highs toward the evening

"FAIR WARNING," I say when Russell picks me up for our first official date the following Saturday in an aging Subaru, "this is going to be extremely nerdy."

"Good." He leans over to kiss me, and I'm thinking it will be a peck hello, but it's deeper, longer than I imagine, one hand sliding into my hair. It's midmorning, and I can still smell the clean citrus of his soap. "I feel like I need to ease back into this. We can't go rock climbing or ax throwing right away."

"You did a lot of ax throwing five years ago?"

His mouth pulls into a crooked smile I want to bite right off his face. "Guess you'll never know." When he starts the car, the *Hadestown* soundtrack starts playing. "Elodie was messing around with my phone. My Spotify is show tunes and only show tunes."

"A hero."

I put our destination into Google Maps but I won't let him see where we're going. This week, we've stolen kisses in the Dugout or in the kitchen when no one else is there, but they always end too soon. We're not hiding it, necessarily, but I think we're reluctant to go public before we've had the chance to discuss what it means. And now that we're finally on a date, I'm determined to make it the best first date I can.

"Technically," Russell says as we head toward I-5 from my Ravenna neighborhood, "we've already been on a date. It was just Torrance and Seth's."

I groan. "Let's leave them at work today."

Fifteen minutes later, Google Maps lets us know we've reached Discovery Park.

"Wait," Russell says as he pulls into one of the last parking spots. I picked this place because I was hoping it wouldn't be as crowded as some of the other parks, but perhaps I've underestimated the general public's interest in weather phenomena. Which does make the meteorologist in me happy, so I can't be too upset about it. "Is this the solar eclipse?"

"You got me."

We've been reporting on it all week, including the best spots to watch. It's always one of the coolest things to see people get excited about. While solar eclipses happen a few times a year, the path of totality can be pretty limited. Total eclipses themselves are quite rare, and this one is only a partial eclipse.

With my right arm, I reach into my bag and produce two pairs of solar eclipse glasses I ordered online. "We're going to want these. Since you're not supposed to look directly at the sun, which I usually think is a given, but based on what I've seen on KSEA's social media, apparently it isn't."

We head toward the park, the sky already beginning to darken. It won't get as dark as it would during a total eclipse, since the moon is passing between the sun and the earth but will only cover part of the sun. Sun, moon, and earth won't be perfectly aligned. Even so, eye protection is a must.

"The wild thing about an eclipse," I say, twirling the end of my eclipse glasses, "is that it lasts for such a short time. So people will sometimes trek all this way, even camp out for a couple days, just for two minutes." I pause and flash him a grin. "And it's totally worth it."

"Have you ever done it, camped out somewhere for an eclipse?"

"Nope, but I've always wanted to. There's a lunar eclipse next year when Portland will be in the path of totality. Also, you can tell me to shut up if you just want to enjoy it. I'll understand."

"Are you kidding? You let me ramble plenty about hockey." He drapes an arm over my shoulders, careful not to jostle my sling. I'm a little chilly in a floral midi dress and jean jacket, complete with a bumblebee brooch, but I wasn't about to bother with tights again. Not with Russell involved. "Besides, eclipses are fascinating. I'm ashamed to admit I don't know very much about them."

People are standing in clusters and in larger groups, some with snacks and almost all with their cameras ready, pointed at the sky. There's a palpable energy here. An electricity. They all know what's about to happen is special. Russell and I find a spot in the grass, near the edge of Puget Sound.

"Are you nervous?" he asks. "You're so quiet."

I shake my head. My heart is pounding, but it's all giddy anticipation, not nerves. All we have to do is watch and let the universe do its thing.

As 1:02 approaches, the park falls silent. The sky is a grayish green now, this haunting loveliness in the middle of the day. Russell and I slip on our glasses, his fitting a little awkwardly over his regular ones. He slides his hand into mine and squeezes, and then—

Magic.

The whole sky seems to shimmer as the sun becomes a brilliant yellow crescent.

For those two minutes, everything is perfect.

THE DATE ISN'T over yet. Our next stop is an aging mall on the Eastside, one Alex and I used to go to all the time growing up, before millennials like us started killing malls the way we killed bar soap and napkins. I am sure there are still nice malls, the kinds of places with luxury stores and five-star restaurants and fountains that have been cleaned at some point this century. This mall, with its neon-patterned black carpet and food court full of bizarre knockoffs like Pizza House and Wowzaburger (which actually isn't that bad), is not one of them.

"Oh my god," Russell says once we've navigated through body jewelry kiosks and packs of sullen teenagers, arriving at a section of the mall with ARCADE spelled in glowing letters. "I haven't been to a place like this in forever."

The empty arcade is about as decrepit as the mall itself, with games that probably haven't been updated since the early nineties. But there's a nostalgia to the way they're all beeping and buzzing and enticing us to play.

And most importantly, it has an air hockey table.

I feed a five-dollar bill into the machine, and as I'm waiting for my quarters, a warm body presses behind me.

"This is really great," Russell says with his mouth next to my ear, breath rushing over my skin. I shiver against him, distantly aware we're in public and wondering how it's possible to be this turned on in a mall that still has a Sears. "Thank you."

"I had to bring my A-game to welcome Russell Barringer back to the world of dating." The air hockey table turns on and lights up with a low whooshing sound. I hold up my sling as I grip the scratched-up red paddle with my right hand. "I'm just going to point out that you have a distinct advantage here." This distracts him, as I hoped it might, and I slam the puck right into his goal. "Ha! I thought you played goalie."

"You tricked me!" He blows on the puck as if for good luck before dropping it back on the table. "Well then. It's war now, weather girl. I'm not going easy on you."

"Don't you dare."

We're somewhat evenly matched during the first game, but with my arm, I grow tired easily, and he handily wins the second and third.

Eventually, we grab a pretzel from the nearby food court and slide into a secluded vinyl booth in one corner of the arcade, as a group of kids takes over the air hockey table.

"Tell me more about playing hockey in Michigan," I say, tearing off a sugary hunk of pretzel.

"As a kid, I'd play out in the streets with friends over the summer. I didn't hate school or anything, but that was the reason I always looked forward to summer. It wasn't until middle school that I started playing on a team." He takes a bite of the pretzel. "What did you do as a kid in Seattle?"

"I came here a lot with my brother." I wave a hand around the arcade. "We've always been pretty close. Most of what I remember from childhood, Alex is there. You don't have any siblings?"

"Only child. Which I think means I'm supposed to be antisocial and bossy?"

"That tracks."

He snorts. "What about your parents? Do they still live in the area?"

I hope he doesn't notice the way my body stiffens. "My mom does. My dad left when I was in elementary school."

An ordinary day—that's what I remember most. It was an ordinary day in an unseasonably warm October, school and afternoon snacks at a neighbor friend's house before Alex and I came home to find our mother sprawled on the couch. Our dad had raised his voice at her the night before. "I can't be around you when you're like this," he'd said, and I wasn't sure what *like this* meant. "Can't you just be happy for once in your goddamn life?" Naive kid that I was, his words hadn't struck me as final. They argued from time to time, and I'd gotten used to it.

The TV was on, but she wasn't watching it, and there was a box of pizza sweating on the coffee table in front of her. I'd wanted a slice so badly, but it looked like it had been sitting out for a while.

Dad's spending some time with his parents for a while, she told us. Alex asked if they were sick, and she said no. Her rage must have been stronger than her sadness, because she suddenly got up, took the pizza box into the kitchen, and asked if we wanted to go to the movies, something we never would have done on a school night.

An ordinary day, until it wasn't. Until she ran out of excuses for him and it slowly dawned on me that he wasn't coming back.

"I'm so sorry," Russell says.

"Thanks. It's okay," I say, trying to brush it off, trying to force my usual smile. For some reason, my mouth doesn't cooperate. "We don't have to talk about it. I don't want to bring down the mood."

He has plenty to deal with. He doesn't need my issues on top of that, though I don't miss the furrow of his brow.

From the other side of the arcade, the kids let out a chorus of groans as one of them smacks the air hockey table. It brings me back to reality only slightly.

"I realize this is partially breaking our rule," Russell says, "but part of me was worried we wouldn't have anything to talk about if we weren't talking about Torrance and Seth."

"Ah, so you're relieved that I'm a halfway decent conversationalist?"

"Yes. But I'm not surprised." He offers me the last piece of pretzel. "I have to confess something. About Torrance and Seth. And then we won't talk about them the rest of the day."

"Okay . . ."

"It's not bad. I promise." He glances out at the arcade and the very contentious air hockey game going on before returning his gaze to me. "When we first started talking about doing this—"

"—which was *your* idea," I remind him.

"Right. Right. So, of course, I wanted things at the station to get better. But I also saw the way the fighting was impacting you. And, well, you've noticed my beat has changed, and I don't know if it's a direct result of what we've been doing, or just that someone new was hired and someone else was going on leave. Part of the reason I was so on board with it . . . was that you were so earnest about wanting to get closer to Torrance. You grew up watching her, and the reality was so different from what you'd imagined. I didn't want to see you so miserable. So I thought we could make work better for both of us, and you'd be able to get what you wanted, too."

His admission steals the words from my throat. All that time I tried to hide how unhappy I was, turning it into a joke or waving it off. He saw through it.

"Russell . . ."

"Oh no. Are you completely furious at me?" He pretends to get up, but I place a hand on his arm.

"No! I just . . . don't know what to say. I'm touched that you wanted to do this to help me." It's the truth. Russell Barringer is sweeter than I ever thought, and I could fill a month's worth of forecasts with how much I've thought about him.

He lets out an exaggerated sigh of relief. "For a second there, I thought this was going to be our first and our last date."

"Definitely not." I turn his hand over, running my fingers along his palm. His hand twitches, as though he's ticklish, but he doesn't move away.

"Because I'm so out of practice, I'm curious: what would you usually talk about on a first date?"

"I'm no expert," I say, since it's technically been a couple years for me too. I follow the lines on his palm, charting a path from his wrist to his thumb. "Our jobs, our families, what we like to do for fun. Which we've already covered a lot of. There'd probably be something like, oh, you look so much better than your profile picture, even if that's not actually true."

"Of course."

"Maybe one of us would ask why the other was still single, and it would really hit a nerve, but we'd try our hardest not to let that show. There'd be the arguing over who pays the bill." I nod toward the pretzel wrapper. "I'm glad you didn't chivalrously insist on paying the four dollars for this."

"Only because I promise to get the pretzel the next time we come here."

He fights a smile nestled in one corner of his mouth as I doodle a rain cloud on his skin, fingers shaking before he closes his hand around mine. In one swift motion, he flips it over so he can have his way with it. With his middle finger, he traces what I think is my heart line, back and forth and back and forth in these slow, searing arcs.

I bite down on the inside of my cheek, struggling to focus on the conversation as I imagine that finger sliding down my stomach. Parting my thighs. Making me gasp. "And then at the end of the night . . . I'd probably be stressing about whether we were going to kiss."

"Who would be making the first move? You or me?"

"Depends," I say, my voice strained. Now he's etching circles into my palm, varying the pressure with each revolution. *Fucking hell*. "I don't mind making the first move, but if the guy does it, he should be sure it's what I want, too. And I don't want it to feel like an obligation. I want him to kiss me because he's been thinking all night about how much he wants to."

"So . . . kind of like this?" He drops my hand, burning with the memory of his fingertips, and stretches forward. He skates his thumb along my jaw, draws my face closer so he can kiss me across the table.

Except—he doesn't. Not right away. For a few seconds, he simply lingers there, lips a whisper from mine. Waiting. Finally, when I'm a moment away from leaping across the booth and crushing myself into his lap, he brushes his lips against mine so slowly. Sweetly, though he has to know how evil he is right now.

Before he pulls away, he teases his teeth along my bottom lip.

There. Evil.

"Yes," I breathe, already missing the press of his mouth as he settles back into the booth. "And if the date is going *really* well, I might invite him over. It also depends."

"On?"

"How badly I want him to touch me."

His eyes are laser-focused on me, the silence between us electrically charged. Every ounce of my attention is focused on the hardening of his jaw and the bob of his Adam's apple as he swallows. I lied—it isn't that I want him to touch me. I need him to.

"Well. What's the verdict?" His voice is a low, lovely scrape.

"Russ," I say, placing my hand on his knee beneath the table. "Do you want to come over?"

We can't get out of there fast enough.

19

FORECAST:

Record-breaking heat gives way to a satisfying downpour, putting an end to a five-year drought

BY THE TIME we get to my apartment, it's dusk, the Seattle sunshine lingering only at the edge of the horizon.

"It's very you." Russell motions to a framed piece of art on my wall, a star-dotted black background with SWEATER WEATHER scrawled in white cursive.

I shrug out of my jean jacket, careful not to let the brooch's sharp edges catch my dress as I hang it up. "A college graduation gift from my brother. You must have seen it before when you dropped me off."

"True," he says. "But I was too focused on making sure you were okay and trying my best not to let on that I was extremely attracted to you. It was a tricky balance."

I bite back a grin. "Good to know you were suffering, too."

He unlaces his shoes without asking if he needs to, setting them neatly at my door. Then he moves into the living room, eyes landing on my table of jewelry projects.

"This is where you make those earrings and necklaces?" he asks. "And brooches that you're determined to bring back into style?"

"Yep," I say, trying not to think about how long ago it was I mentioned the brooches, and whether it means he simply has a memory to rival Joanna's or something else entirely. It was probably just that I was wearing one today. I lift my sling. "Though not a ton is happening right now."

I head into the tiny kitchen, wondering what says *I asked you here to get you into bed and the beverage is merely a formality at this point.*

"Can I get you anything to drink?" I ask. "I have beer, wine, some hard cider."

He lets out a rough laugh. "Honestly? No."

"Oh, thank god. Because I really just want to skip to the part where we make out again."

This seems to flip a switch in him. He strides forward, pinning me in the entrance of the kitchen, tilting my head upward so he can capture my mouth with his. I sink into the kiss, so eager to get my fingerprints on every inch of him that I'm not sure where to put my one good hand first. His chest, where his heart hammers against it. The back of his neck, where it's easiest to pull myself closer. Into his hair, soft and lush and perfect.

When he parts my lips, he still tastes like cinnamon sugar.

I tug him out of his light spring jacket and drape it on the back of a chair, leading him the three steps from the kitchen to my room. Studio apartments have their advantages. A few more seconds and I've got him on my bed, my legs at his hips as I press my need against his, inhaling his exhales and swallowing every hungry sound he makes. He gives it all right back, trailing kisses along my jaw and down my neck, gripping my waist before his hands move up my sides, skimming my breasts. Just like in the Dugout, I'm stunned by how it can feel this good with most of our clothes still on.

And that fact makes me draw back for a moment, unable to catch my breath.

"I have to tell you something," I say. He secures his hands at the base of my spine. "I—I'm nervous."

He gives me a very serious look, compounded by the fact that he's still wearing his glasses. "You should be. I haven't done this in five years."

When he cracks a smile, it breaks some of the tension between us, though my heart still drums a frantic beat against my ribcage. Because somehow *I haven't done this in five years* turns me on even more.

There's something undeniably hot about being the one to break his dry spell. In this moment, it feels like a privilege, and I'm honored he's giving it to me.

"If you're not comfortable," he says, fingers stroking up my spine, "we can stop. We don't have to do anything."

"I want to."

The nerves aren't gone as I grab for him again—first for his glasses, which I place on the nightstand next to us—but the desire is stronger. Wilder. Still, I don't have as much range of motion as I'd like.

"Have you ever seen anything sexier?" I ask as I slowly, dramatically remove my sling, dropping it onto the pale blue comforter with a flourish of my uninjured arm.

"How did you figure out my exact kink?"

I feel like I never stop laughing when I'm with him. It's a little concerning, given my reluctance to jump into anything serious, but god, I want this. We've been on the edge of a cliff, and I might actually die if we don't tumble off together tonight.

Gently, he tugs off my dress, his mouth exploring each new piece of me. A kiss to my navel. A bite at my hip. A stroke of his tongue in between my breasts and along the lace of my bra.

One-handed, I fumble with his belt, my hand skimming the curve of his stomach.

He recoils. "Sorry."

"No—it's okay," I say, even as he's reaching down to help me with the buckle. I want to tell him he has nothing to apologize for, but he seems ready to blaze past this, lips meeting mine again in desperate, open-mouthed kisses.

If I'm the one ending his drought, I want this to be the best fucking sex he's ever had.

My hand is too impatient as it dives inside his jeans, finding him warm and stiff and already straining against his boxer briefs. *God.* He reacts instantly—a sharp intake of breath. A low moan that sets my nerve endings on fire. Slowly, I rub back and forth as his head drops to my neck.

"That night on the retreat. In your room," he murmurs, pressing kisses along my collarbone. His cock pulses in his boxers against my hand. I'm dying to see what he looks like without all this cotton and denim in the way. "I was hiding the most painful hard-on of my life. When you hugged me, I thought I was going to pass out."

"You were such a gentleman, though."

"On the outside, yes. You'd just fractured your elbow. No way in hell was I going to initiate anything. But my mind . . . was fucking filthy."

His words send red-hot electricity up my spine. I can't help wondering what *fucking filthy* things we were doing in his imagination.

"Russ," I say, and I like the way his eyes flutter shut at that nickname. "You don't have to close your eyes this time."

That elicits a lovely groan from him, and I remove my hand so he can shuck off his jeans, sending up a quick thanks to the Patron Saint of Boxer Briefs.

I can't marvel for long, though, because he's turning his attention to my bra, tracing a finger along the black lacy straps. "This is beautiful. But unfortunately, it has to come off." It only takes a twitch of his thumb for the front clasp to fall open. Then I'm just in matching black lace panties and my lightning bolt necklace, Russ in a gray T-shirt and boxers.

"Christ. So gorgeous." His mouth parts as he looks me up and down. "Can you just . . . I want to look at you a second."

It's not until he says it that I realize my body is slightly scrunched, the way I usually am with new partners, not ready to completely expose myself yet. But the pure want in his voice is enough to ease that shyness. I relax my muscles, stretch out my legs, letting him drink me in.

It's a raw, heady feeling, being able to see someone's attraction like this. Russell wears it plainly—a dark intensity in his eyes, an exhale of breath, a curve of his lips that gives way to a wicked smile as he lowers himself over me. He's careful to avoid my left arm, I realize, his hands cupping my breasts as he kisses my neck, his erection grazing my thighs. Crushing his mouth against the charm on my necklace, the cold metal pressing into my skin. It's not that his touch is sloppy or inexperienced—it's reverent, almost. Experimental, the way he rolls a nipple between his thumb and forefinger, listening to the way my breath hitches, finding out what I like.

With Russell, I'm beginning to think I like just about everything.

When I reach for his shirt, though, he freezes up again.

"What is it?" I ask, my hand pausing at the hem. I will my breaths to slow down. I want to give him space to tell me how he feels—if that's something he's ready for.

He pulls back on his heels, gesturing to his stomach. Not quite meeting my gaze. "I, uh—I don't want my stomach to be in the way, or for you to feel disgusted by it or anything. I know I'm fat."

"You're not—" I start, ready to defend him, but he holds up a hand.

"It's not a bad word. It's just an adjective. It's just the way I am." He waits a few beats before speaking again, as though deciding how much he wants to tell me. A soft sigh. A hard swallow. Maybe that is the sound of letting someone in. "I've been fat since I was a kid. And most of the time, it doesn't bother me. It used to, and some people sure as hell think it should and go out of their way to make sure I'm aware of that. They're sneaky about it sometimes, too—it's all under the guise of caring about my health, even though I'm perfectly healthy." He brings his eyes back up to mine. "So if it bothers you . . . I could maybe leave my shirt on? If that's what you want?"

Hearing him say all of this breaks my heart. "No, no, no," I say quickly, placing my hand on his arm. "Honestly? That's the furthest thing from my mind right now."

"Are you sure?"

I push to a sitting position so I can cup his face, have him look at me. "Yes. You're *hot*, Russell, and I really fucking want you. All of you." And then, to prove it, I take his hand and guide it between my legs, where I'm wet and needy for him.

He slips a finger inside my underwear and groans. Slowly, slowly, his finger brushes my center, achingly close to my clit. An excruciating circle, and then he finds it again. My hips buck, begging him to move faster.

"*Fuck*," he says under his breath. I love the way he lets himself enjoy this, bit by bit. "Fuck, Ari. You are . . . incredible."

I can't take it anymore, not feeling skin against skin. Greedy, I lunge forward, eager to rid him of his shirt. And—he's absolutely beautiful. I force myself to slow down, to take him in the way he did to me. I run my hands along the pink stretch marks on his belly, on the sides of his stomach, along the chest hair I've been wondering about since that night at the hotel bar. I kiss as much of his skin as I can, until he reaches for my panties and I'm all too happy to help him take them off.

Without the fabric in the way, he trails his hand up my thigh, parting my legs before sliding a finger where I need him most. *Jesus.* There's that experimental touch again as he learns my shape, up and down and up, a second finger, *up, yes,* and I lean my head back against the pillow, arching my back.

All while his fingers are circling.

And circling.

And circling.

Every time I think I might be close, shutting my eyes and focusing on that building sensation, it slips away. He's encouraged by my breaths, the way I grip his shoulder, but after a while, his hand slows, like he's too tired or I'm not giving him what he wants. Or both.

Fuck. I was hoping this wouldn't happen. Not with him.

"I'm sorry," I say, positive he can hear the frustration in my voice.

"Hey. You have nothing to apologize for." He sits back and looks at me, his other hand perched on my hip. "Is there anything I can be doing differently?"

I lift up onto my elbows, my face heated with both arousal and embarrassment. I was worried this might happen. I thought the excitement of doing this with Russell might get me there quicker . . . but no such luck.

"It's not you." I hope he knows I'm not just saying that. "I'm self-conscious with new people. I've always been that way. Like I can't turn off my brain or can't fully relax. Sometimes . . . sometimes it takes a few times. I've never been able to—the first time."

I've been with guys who take this as a challenge, declaring that no woman has ever had trouble achieving orgasm with them, which feels *great* when you're already naked with someone, imagining them pleasuring another partner. I'd love to be the type of girl who collapses into ecstasy the instant her partner touches her, but I'm just . . . not. And my antidepressants, as wonderful as they are, dim my libido a bit.

He's quiet for a moment. I almost wonder if he's going to say we should stop, that it's not worth it. Or that we should full-steam ahead right into intercourse, which, sure, is plenty fun, but I've never had an orgasm that way either, even if I've faked it a good dozen times. I don't want to do that with him.

When he speaks, it's not at all what I was expecting. "So the thing is," he says, his voice low. "I really want you to come. Tonight." He might get me halfway there if he keeps talking like that. "I have an idea. And you can absolutely say no." He presses a kiss to my cheek, thumb lingering on my cheekbone as he pulls away. "What if you made yourself come? Here. With me." I must make some kind of expression, because he continues, "If you think it might be easier?"

His hands on me are so gentle. He's not demanding an orgasm from me. He's not frustrated—he wants me to enjoy this.

"I don't know," I admit. "I've never done it in front of someone else." This wasn't exactly what I pictured when I imagined our first time. When I thought about what I'd do to him as my "welcome back to sex" gift.

But . . . there's no reason it can't still be mind-blowing.

"So you want me to—touch myself while you watch?"

He laughs darkly. "As appealing as that sounds, I could do it, too. If it would relax you."

It conjures an odd mental image at first, but his face is so open, so earnest.

I really want you to come. Tonight.

"Okay," I say, my heart pounding. "Let's try it."

As much as I can, I help him out of his boxer briefs, rubbing my hand along his cock as he sucks in a ragged breath. Russell is naked in my bed and waiting for me to pleasure myself. And . . . I'm deeply, breathlessly turned on.

My hand only starts shaking when I sit back up, palming one of my breasts, pinching at my nipple as I stare down the length of my body. "Should I just . . . start?"

"Whatever makes you the most comfortable," he says, brushing his fingers across my waist. He's very clearly ready, but he waits.

So I scoot to the top of the bed and lie down, with him stretched out next to me. It's not until I let my hand drift between my legs as I've done so many times before, only never with an audience, that he wraps a hand around himself. And it's no longer strange—far from it. I don't dare break eye contact as he strokes downward, then up to the bead of moisture forming at the tip.

"How is that?" He's already breathing hard, his question rough like gravel.

"Good," I manage as I find a rhythm. I'm lying. It's fucking amazing, and watching him while he's watching me might be the most intensely sexual thing I've ever experienced. I didn't anticipate the sight of him touching himself being so erotic, but *fuck,* it is. The image of him with his hand around his dick, the tensing of his jaw and the shuddering of his breaths and the way he grips my ankle like an anchor with his free hand . . . yeah, that's going to be burned into my brain for a while.

Then he turns his body so he can kiss me, and *god*, it's too much, too good. All of my senses are lit the brightest neon. Now that an orgasm feels not only possible but imminent, I let myself loosen up even more, moving my fingers faster. Out of the corner of my eye, I spy a scrap of black lace, and before I can think twice, I reach for it and pass it to him.

He just looks at me as his hand moves up and down, one side of his mouth twitching. But then he takes my lead. First he brings my panties up to his face. Inhales. Then he moves them lower, lower, until he's thrusting into them, and just watching him is enough to take me over the edge.

"These," he says, "are so—goddamn—hot. *You* are so goddamn hot."

"*Russ.*" I bite it out on a gasp as I rub my clit with two fingers. The truth is that I've never felt this sexy. This powerful.

I get there first, a sweet rush of pleasure, my legs quaking before my body collapses. Then he's kissing my breasts, my neck, my lips, my eyelids. His cock is firm, solid heat between us, and I realize he's held back so that I can finish. That knowledge makes me slide my hand between us, desperate to undo him.

"I don't want you to get messy if you don't want to," he pants. I can tell it's taking all the self-control he has not to let himself go.

"I want to."

And it only takes a few more pumps of my fist before he groans, hips rocking forward as he paints my breasts with his release, warm and slick.

"God," he says, still trying to catch his breath. "You are—that was—"

I laugh, dragging my fingers up his back. "Same. Unexpected, but . . . really fucking fantastic."

He disappears for a moment to clean up, coming back to sweep a damp towel over my skin first and then his.

"The benefits of a studio," I say as he pulls my body to his. "The bathroom's only ten feet from the bed. And we have a great view of the kitchen from here."

He nuzzles his face into my neck. "And yet somehow, I want to stay exactly where we are. Unless it's already morning."

I motion to my blackout curtains. "I think it's nighttime, but you can never be too sure with those."

"Ah. I was going to ask about those, but my mind was elsewhere."

I don't want to forget the way he looks right now, flushed and content, his hair sticking out in a hundred directions. Wrecked in the best possible way.

I realize we have to talk about the difficult things: what we're going to do at work, what this relationship means. If a relationship is something we both want.

Elodie.

But right now, I just want to savor this.

"Ari," he says into my hair, his hand resting on my hip. "I really like you."

"Me too," I say quietly, and I wish it didn't feel so terrifying.

20

FORECAST:

Mild discomfort leads to a long-awaited heart-to-heart

WHEN I USED to picture Torrance's house, I imagined the kind of place in furniture showrooms, sophisticated and spotless. The reality isn't too far off. Her Dutch Colonial in Madison Park is painted robin's-egg blue, and everything inside is done in shades of white and cream with warm wood accents. I'm so worried about tracking dirt onto the rugs she tells me she custom-ordered from a Seattle artist that I half wonder if I should have taken off my shoes outside. At least I washed my sling last night.

"Make yourself at home." Torrance hangs up my coat and gestures to a cream sectional topped with no fewer than a dozen decorative pillows. Next to it is a towering shelf full of succulents. Making myself at home might require becoming a different person entirely. "I'll be right out with the wine and cashew cheese. Trust me, it's better than it sounds."

When she invited me over for a "girls' night" and told us we would be the only two girls in attendance, I was skeptical. In three years of working for her, Torrance has never expressed a desire to see me outside of work. But then I thought back to the massage, and how she opened up. And how great it felt, even just for a while, that she was listening to me. This whole time, that's been the goal. I'm just not sure I can accept that it's happening.

I debate where to rehome the pillows on Torrance's couch, settling for stacking them in the matching armchair, before sitting down, and—*oh*. This is a phenomenal couch. Between my therapist's, my brother's, and Torrance's couches, I'm starting to think I need to go furniture shopping. I remove my sling so I can stretch my arm a bit—after physical therapy this afternoon, my elbow's a little sore.

The arrival of a gorgeous wood charcuterie board snaps me out of my sofa envy, with five kinds of vegan cheese and a marble-handled cheese knife. Cured meats and wedges of grilled bread, green olives and fig jam. It's a Williams-Sonoma catalog come to life.

"This looks incredible," I say. "Even the vegan cheese."

Torrance waves a freshly French-manicured hand. "I love entertaining. Seth and I used to do it all the time, but I don't do nearly enough of it on my own these days."

It's been almost three weeks since the yacht, and I hope it's a good sign that she brought up Seth without my prompting.

She pours herself a glass of white wine and lifts it to mine for a toast. "We're going to have the best time!" she says, and I'm not sure if she's trying to convince me, herself, or both of us.

After we get the pleasantries out of the way—*how's your arm, how was your day, how's work been*—she settles back onto the couch. I expected weekend Torrance would be casual Torrance, and she is—a little. Jeans, a loose top, hair naturally straight instead of the barrel curls she wears on camera.

She spreads some fig jam on a piece of bread, which she then tops with a single olive. "It's good. You should try it," she says when I give her a horrified look.

"I'll take your word for it," I say as I help myself to a hunk of imitation cheddar.

I'm reminded of that moment at the holiday party, when she and Seth joked about her favorite song. There's a true goofball stuck in Torrance's body, and I want to draw her out as much as I can.

"We've talked far too much about me lately," Torrance says after another fig-olive monstrosity. "Are you still single?"

I cough, trying to dislodge the olive caught in my throat. "I'm . . . I don't know what I am right now, honestly."

"Is it someone I know? Someone from work?" She leans in and drapes a conspiratorial hand over her mouth. "Is it *Russell*?"

My blush must completely give me away.

She reaches out to gently slap my knee. "You and Russell," she says, a lipsticked grin spreading across her face. "I'm not sure I'd have predicted it, but I can see it. He's very cute. Nice, too."

"He is," I say, my mind drifting back to just how nice Russell was in my bed last weekend. How eager I am to get him back there.

Except for Joanna, Torrance is the first to hear about him. With my brother, anything I tell him gets passed to Javier, which I don't mind, but I'm not quite ready for that. It's tough not to envy what they have, this assumption that you can trust someone with a secret as much as the person telling it could trust you.

I'm not sure I've ever felt that with someone. Not even with the man I thought I was going to marry.

If I can trust Torrance with this secret, though, maybe she'll trust me with hers.

"You are hard-core blushing." Torrance lets out a giggle I've never heard from her, this sound that has nothing in common with her TV laugh. I realize I haven't talked like this with anyone in a while, and it feels *good.* "Did it happen on the retreat? When he took you to the hospital?"

"I was way too zonked on Vicodin for anything to happen," I say. "We just talked. A lot. Our first date was only last weekend."

"I love this so much. I love this for both of you."

"We still haven't defined it or anything. And he has a kid, and . . . I've never dated anyone with a kid."

"You two are smart," she says, sounding encouraging. "You'll figure it out."

With a jolt, I realize this is the kind of reaction I'd want from my mother. In an alternate universe where my mother is the first person I tell about a new relationship, this is how I'd want to her reply.

And it makes me pull out one of my sunshine grins and immediately change the subject.

"This is a gorgeous house," I say, because if there's one thing people with nice houses like, it's showing off how nice their house is. "When did you say it was built?"

But Torrance doesn't take the bait. "You're always doing that."

"Doing what?"

"Giving out compliments like that. Completely out of nowhere." She backtracks, as though worried she's offended me, which might be a Torrance first. "It's not that they aren't nice, they're just . . . a bit random, I guess."

"I—I'm sorry." It isn't that I don't mean them, but of course, I can't tell her the real reason. "I guess I just . . . get too deep in my head sometimes." I drain my glass of wine, hoping this works as a brush-off. "I'm serious, though. I'd love to see more of the house."

And maybe Torrance realizes that's all she's going to get from me, so she leaps up—still elegant, still poised, though probably not for long, if the amount of wine in her glass is any indication—and starts the tour.

She leads me through the kitchen, an exercise room, gestures toward a hot tub in her backyard. The hallway is lined with photos, a tribute to Torrance and Seth and questionable fashion choices. Seth with a mullet, Torrance in the mid-nineties with the Rachel haircut.

"That's me the first year I was on TV," she says, tapping her hair in the photo. "That didn't work for my face at all. Somewhere, a hairdresser should lose their license." She lets out a half laugh, her gaze lingering on the next picture, one of a surprisingly scrawny Seth in a too-big suit jacket. "But Seth looks cute here."

Then there's Patrick, her son, growing up, getting braces, graduating high school. Patrick and his wife, Roxanne.

We end the tour back in the all-white kitchen, where I spot the succulent Seth gave her, sitting on the marble counter all by itself. "Seth knew how much I loved this house," she says. "He wanted me to keep it."

"It seems like you two have been getting cozy lately?" I say.

"That night on the yacht was . . . well, it was amazing, to be honest," she says, running her knuckles along the leaves of the succulent. And—she's blushing.

Torrance Hale is *blushing*.

"Amazing, huh?"

"Against all odds, yes. Even if part of me is waiting for the other shoe to drop."

"And . . . you haven't been seeing anyone else?" I ask, thinking back to when I saw her at brunch. If we're intruding on some other relationship, I have to know.

"A couple dates here and there," she says, dismissing this with a wave of her hand, and the relief is immediate. "Nothing serious."

"Seth has seemed . . . less antagonistic lately. Maybe it's because you two have been spending so much time together."

"Huh. I didn't know you two were close." She lets go of the plant and reaches for another bottle of wine. "Anyway. I don't want to get too sappy because it doesn't go with my brand, but this is fun. Thank you. Even if it's the least wild girls' night in the history of girls' nights."

Against all odds, Torrance Hale and I might be becoming something I never anticipated.

We might be something like *friends*.

"I WANT TO tell you a secret," Torrance says from the armchair, legs dangling off one side of it. From where I'm sprawled across her couch, decorative pillows in a heap on the floor, I can't see her face. I thought drunk Torrance was weird, but happy-drunk Torrance is even weirder. "Did you know"—hiccup—"my last name isn't really Hale?"

"What? What is it?"

Her head pops up as she repositions herself in the chair, regarding me with a serious look. "Dalrymple. It's Scottish. For the first twenty-five years of my life, I was Torrance Dalrymple. No one could spell it, let alone pronounce it. Then when I was going into broadcasting, I thought it would be easier, and maybe even catchy, if my name matched the job. There were so many meteorologists who had gimmicky names, like Storm Field or Johnny Mountain. I didn't want it to be too obvious, like Torrance Tornado or something."

"Torrance Barometric Pressure really rolls off the tongue."

"I wanted it to be believable. So . . . Torrance Hale. And then Seth added Hale to his last name when we got married, though I didn't ask him to. It was his idea, to make my fake name feel more legitimate, I guess. Like I could have really been born Torrance Hale and grown up to be a meteorologist." She pauses for a moment. "Sometimes it all feels fake," she continues, and suddenly, that happy-drunk sheen is gone. "The faces we wear on TV. All the smiling. Even my name is fake."

"Nothing you do has ever felt fake to me."

"I'm sure there are plenty of people online who'd say otherwise."

"Don't tell me you read our Facebook comments after all this time." It's the darkest hellhole of our social media, reserved for older people who haven't quite grasped the concept of social media and/or assholes who are more honest and vile than on any other platform.

"Not often, unless I'm tagged in something that's impossible to avoid. People call me a slut because I have the audacity to have breasts. Because I'm blond. Because my skirt stopped above my knees. Because I wore red. Because I laughed with a male anchor."

I lift my glass to that. "To casual misogyny. May it kindly fuck off forever." Some of the comments I got when I started at KSEA, mostly from men, still live rent free in my head, and I hate it. *Wonder if the carpet matches the drapes. Jump to 2:36 to see her cleavage. There's a chance of showers in my pants.* It's endless, even if you stop looking. No matter how many people you block, they always have a way of finding you, through tags or emails or DMs. "We could wear a burlap sack, and people would still be talking about whether it's too tight."

"That shade of burlap is all wrong for your skin tone."

"How could you have picked such a sexy sack?"

After we stop laughing, Torrance turns protective. "Are you doing okay, though? Have you gotten anything really bad? You don't need me to put a hit on anyone, do you?"

I'm not sure she's kidding. "No, no, just the usual. I can handle it now, but it was rough at first."

That hangs between us for a few moments. I wish Torrance and I could have talked about this back when I started. When I wondered whether I'd made the right career choice after all, because as much as I loved the weather, there were always going to be people out there who assumed I was only there to smile and point.

I wonder if this silence means she wishes the same thing.

"The best revenge," she says, "is just being really fucking good at your job."

I reach for a wedge of bread, chewing it thoughtfully. Torrance was right—this *is* fun. Maybe we've only grown close because of some gentle manipulation, but I want to believe it would have happened regardless.

"If I'm being honest," I say, and at this point it's only half the Chateau Ste. Michelle chardonnay talking, "I felt a little adrift when I started at KSEA. You were one of the reasons I wanted to work there. I watched you all the time growing up—I know I mentioned that in my interview." At the time, I'd been embarrassed, worried I'd made her feel old. But she just brushed it off, and it made me like her even more. Until, of course, I started working with her. "I'm not sure if you remember this, but you actually gave me an award. For high school journalists, about ten years ago."

Her face falls. "Ari. I'm so sorry. I wish I remembered, but—I did a lot of those things back then."

"It's okay," I say quickly, because it is. I don't expect her to have attached some sentimental value to it the way I did. "But when I started out, I guess . . . I guess I had kind of hoped for some mentorship or something."

My whole body stiffens as I wait for her response, preparing for the worst.

But she surprises me, as she's done a number of times over the past couple months. "I . . . think I would have really liked that, too," she says softly. Then she clears her throat and says more loudly, "Do you think anyone else feels that way?"

"Maybe? I thought for a while that we might get a chance to bond at the retreat, but . . ." I lift up my arm.

"That impromptu couple's massage was the highlight."

"Those masseuses deserve a raise." Then I turn serious again. "I guess it's because sometimes whatever was going on with Seth felt more important. Like the fact that we haven't done a real performance evaluation in three years."

She sits up straighter, something a little like shock pulling her mouth into a tight line. "I didn't realize you felt that way. I thought . . . well, part of me thought it would be nice not to have to go through all that red tape, but maybe that was my way of making myself feel better about not doing it."

I become braver. "A lot of other stations bring in talent coaches regularly. And I can do bigger stories, too. I could even be on Halestorm. I love this job, and I'm grateful to have it. I just want to feel like I'm going somewhere. Like I'm growing."

"Absolutely." She stretches forward to graze my shoulder with her hand, her once-icy gaze honest and insistent. "We'll talk this week, okay?"

"I'm looking forward to it," I say, believing her. Torrance blots her mouth, her lipstick still flawless after hours of drinking and eating and soul-searching. Frankly, it's unfair.

"I just have one more question. *How* do you manage to get your lipstick to last that long?"

She grins, showing off that perfect cherry shade. "It's a multistep process. Primer, lip liner, lipstick, and then finishing it with a translucent setting powder. That's what really does the trick. And you have to make sure you exfoliate your lips first, too." A glance between me and the now-empty bottle. "I'll go get more wine."

While she's in the kitchen, her phone lights up on the coffee table. Patrick Hale, it says.

"Torrance?" I call. "Your phone's ringing. I think it's your son?"

She races into the living room, bottle of wine and stopper still in hand, grabbing the phone on what sounds like its last ring. I don't want to eavesdrop in case it's personal, but she doesn't make any move to switch rooms. "Oh my god," she says. "It's happening? Right now? I'll be there as soon as I can."

She turns to me, phone hanging limply in her hand. "My daughter-in-law is going into labor. We have to get to the hospital." Then she presses her fingertips to her temples and groans. "I need water. And food. Jesus, I can't believe I'm going to be *drunk* when I meet my grandkid."

"It's going to be okay," I say, trying to sound soothing, but I have no idea what to do in this situation, either. When Alex and Javier's surrogate was pregnant, they were already in the same place: her water broke when they were having lunch at Javier's restaurant. "I'm sure you'll have sobered up by the time the baby's born. I'd offer to drive you, but, uh—" I hold up my arm.

"Right. Right. We'll call Seth." Her phone lights up with another incoming call. "Wait. That's him. How does he know we were talking about him? Is this one of those things where your phone is listening to you?" She's really losing it.

"Patrick must have told him Roxanne was going into labor, too," I say to her, as calmly as I can.

"Seth? Hi. I'm a little tipsy." At this, she knocks over the charcuterie board, sending crumbs and crusts of bread to the floor. "If you could come get me . . . yeah. Okay. Thank you." She hangs up. "He'll be here in twenty."

Fifteen minutes later, once we've cleaned up the living room and the wine Torrance spills on the couch, a KSEA 6 van screeches to a halt in her driveway, Seth waving an arm out the window.

"I got here as fast as I could while still obeying the speed limit," he says, popping the driver's side door.

"Thank you so much." And Torrance nearly falls into his arms in an attempt to do . . . well, I'm not quite sure what, but she lets out a squeal while doing it. "We're going to be grandparents."

He grins as he steadies her. "I can't wait."

"I can call an Uber," I say, not wanting to intrude on this private moment.

"No, Ari, it's okay. You can come with us!" Torrance says. I don't know if it's the alcohol or the excitement talking, but she's so *giddy*, it's impossible to say no.

So I hoist myself inside and buckle up.

21

FORECAST:
A midnight truce (or two)

IT'S CERTAINLY AN experience, racing through downtown Seattle in the KSEA 6 van with my boss and her ex-husband. The contrast between the two of them is even more pronounced. For all her panic at the house, Torrance has become calm, while a frantic Seth white-knuckles the steering wheel, missing the exit for the hospital once before having to double back. When we get to the maternity ward, he dashes toward the front desk, Torrance and me trailing behind him.

"Roxanne Hale," he says, nearly out of breath. "Where's Roxanne Hale?"

"Dad?" A man who looks to be in his late twenties approaches, holding a bottle of water. "Hey, thanks so much for being here. They're only letting me go back there right now. Her contractions are still about ten minutes apart."

Patrick got his parents' best features; it's no shock that he's as gorgeous as they are. Dark hair, trimmed beard, cheekbones so sharp they should come with a warning label.

Seth wraps an arm around his shoulders. "How are you holding up?"

"Oh, I'm doing okay. A bit frazzled, but overall okay. Roxanne's the one who's going through it." His gaze lands on me, and I give him an awkward wave.

"Hi, um—congratulations! Or, almost congratulations. I was with your mom when she got the call, so . . ."

He grins, the same megawatt smile Torrance has honed for the cameras. "The more the merrier!" he says, and he exchanges a few more hugs with both his parents before he heads down the hall.

Seth only gets more antsy, pacing back and forth until watching him makes me dizzy. He buys exactly five things from the vending machine before it jams and then he spends a solid fifteen minutes tracking down someone who can fix it.

"Seth?" Torrance says sweetly, from where she's sitting next to me. "Why don't you go downstairs to the gift shop?"

"Excellent." Seth bites into a Twizzler before tossing the wrapper in the trash. He already offered some to Torrance and me. "Great idea. I'll be right back!"

"Take your time!" she calls after him, and once he disappears, she starts laughing. "He was like this when Patrick was born, too. More on edge than I was."

I put down the *Highlights* magazine I've been paging through, having finished the Goofus and Gallant comic. Goofus is just as much of a little asshole as he always was. "I've never seen him like this, not even when we have breaking news. He's always so composed at work."

"It's endearing, really." Torrance pauses for a few moments, silently examining her manicure. "Patrick was a bit of a preemie, by four weeks, so I was in the hospital a little longer than expected. Everything was okay, and the doctors were amazing, but I was so ready to start nesting. When we brought Patrick home, I found that Seth been spending all the time he wasn't at the hospital in our kitchen making dinners. He'd had to buy an extra freezer because we didn't have enough space—that's how much he cooked so neither of us would have to worry about it." She smiles at the memory, and maybe that version of Seth isn't too different from the one I've gotten to know over the past couple months. "And he was a great dad. *Is* a great dad, I should say. I've always loved watching him as a father."

It's impossible not to think of Russell when she says that. I haven't had a chance to process the longer-term implications of our relationship, if that is in fact what this is becoming. I've never dated a parent, and even though I want kids, I'm not sure I'm ready *now*. I'm probably overanalyzing, since I've only met her once, but the longer this goes on, the more I'll have to reckon with what I am to Elodie—if I'm anything at all.

Then again, maybe he doesn't want her to be involved. Even though he said back in Canada that he'd wanted me to meet her, that doesn't mean the three of us are going to suddenly start spending time together.

Torrance's phone buzzes again. "That's my sister. Seems like this has made its way through the family grapevine. You don't mind if I take this, do you?"

"Go ahead," I say, and she leaves the maternity ward to answer the call.

Left alone, I consider the absurdity of the situation. I have no personal investment in this, aside from wanting the kid to be born healthy. And yet the fact that Torrance wanted me here compels me to stay.

You'll never believe where I am, I text Russell.

Back at the mall to challenge
those kids at air hockey?

I send back the GIF of Torrance declining a joint at Hempfest and saying, "Maybe later."

At the hospital with the Hales. Their
daughter-in-law just went into labor.

And they're . . . getting along?

You're right. I don't believe it.

I snap a photo of *Highlights* and send it to him. In response, he sends me a photo of a paused TV screen, and I have to bite my lip to keep from grinning. *The Parent Trap*.

Movie night with E. It's intermission
right now because she insisted on
making caramel popcorn. I'm waiting
here until the smoke alarm goes off.

Does she love it?

So far, the verdict is there isn't
enough singing or dancing.

I'll give her that. There isn't.

And we've stopped it several times so she can learn the handshake. Honestly, I'm lucky she's still at an age where watching movies with her dad isn't deeply uncool yet. Not sure how much of that I have left.

The visual sounds so cozy, and I'm fairly certain it's not just the movie they're watching. It scares me a little, how appealing it is.

Weather girl?

Yeah?

I can't wait to see you again.

Those seven words do something to my heart.

Torrance comes back with two cups of coffee, her hair pulled into a ponytail. "Figured this would help me finish sobering up," she says, passing me a cup.

It's ridiculous to be this touched by a cup of coffee. The maternity ward must be making me overly emotional.

Torrance and I spend the next twenty minutes on a crossword puzzle in a parenting magazine, until Seth reappears with not one but seven balloons.

"I, uh, couldn't decide," he says, a flush touching his cheeks. "Though I'm partial to this one." And he hands her the one that says PROUD GRANDPARENTS.

• • •

WE PASS THE time with more crossword puzzles, work emails, and questionable sandwiches from the hospital's cafeteria. After a couple hours go by, I stop asking Torrance whether she wants me to go home. Even when she and Seth are getting along, it's clear she likes having me here as some kind of buffer. Or maybe it's to make up for not being there in the past. Whatever it is, I'm glad to stay.

It's just past eleven o'clock when Patrick rushes back in wearing scrubs, a wild grin on his face. "We have a baby girl," he says. "Penelope Rose. Penny. They're both doing fantastic."

Torrance and Seth leap to their feet, crushing him into a hug.

"We have a granddaughter," Torrance says, tears in her eyes. "I'm a grandma."

"The hottest grandma I've ever seen," Seth says before he releases Patrick to pull her into an embrace.

It happens so quickly, it takes me a few extra moments to process: Torrance flinging her arms around his shoulders and Seth's hands settling against her lower back, her lips landing on his with all the longing of five years spent apart.

And . . . I can't believe it.

Honestly, I might start crying, too.

"Congratulations," I tell Patrick before I excuse myself to give them all some privacy.

"You sure you don't want to come see her?" Torrance asks, still wrapped up in Seth. He's toying with the end of her ponytail.

"No, no," I say. "I've intruded enough. Go. Enjoy."

Gently, she extricates herself from him to give me a wine-and-coffee-scented hug, and of all the surreal things that have happened tonight, that might be the strangest.

I grab my purse and head for the elevator, hitting the down button.

Maybe I'm too sensitive. There's so much going on in this place—not just the Hales, but all the families going in and out all night. I hate that it makes me wistful about my own family, wishing the bad moments had been better, and that the good moments had lasted longer.

My memory snags on what Torrance said about Seth being a good father. *He was a great dad.* Is *a great dad*, she corrected. Because it doesn't end when your kid hits eighteen and moves out. It doesn't end when they take a job on the other side of the state or when they get engaged or when that engagement falls apart.

Maybe it's Torrance acting so motherly that makes me realize it, or maybe it's been tapping away inside my brain, waiting for the right moment to make me aware. But I miss my mother. With all her flaws and all our painful history, I miss her. I missed her before she went to the hospital, even if I wouldn't admit it to myself.

When I get down to the lobby, I head right outside without requesting an Uber yet, letting the crisp, low-forties air nip at my exposed skin. It's been a week without rain, and while typically I'd lament that, today the clear sky seems right.

Before I can give it a second thought, I call my mother.

"Ari?" she says when she picks up on the second ring. "Everything okay? It's almost midnight."

Oh. Whoops.

I am but a simple millennial: phone calls are terrifying and for emergencies only. Calling someone out of the blue and so late at night is supremely out of character for me.

"Fine, Mom." I swallow, trying to keep the emotion out of my voice. "I just . . . wanted to say hi." I don't want to admit to her everything that made me emotional, don't want to expose that soft part of myself. Not right now.

"Hi," she repeats, sounding puzzled. And I don't blame her—I can't remember the last time I called her. "Did you see the eclipse last weekend?"

My heart swells at that. "Of course I did. It was incredible."

"It really was," she says. "It looked like someone had taken a bite right out of the sun."

If anything could confirm that weather isn't small talk, it's this. Weather connects us. A shared experience, even when we aren't in the same place.

We talk about the eclipse for a while, with me probably giving many more details than she'd like, but still, she listens. I ask her how work is going, and she tells me about the new paper shredder her boss got that plays the sound of someone shredding on the guitar when you feed paper through it. And I don't have to force myself to laugh—it comes naturally.

I want to ask about therapy. I want to make sure she's taking her medication.

But if there's anything I've learned about depression, it's that it is an intensely personal journey, one that never really ends.

"Do you think I could come over sometime soon?" I ask when the conversation starts winding down, the static warping the sound of my mother's yawn.

"Ari." There's an odd tone to her voice, and I worry for a moment that I've ruined the conversation. "You don't have to ask."

22

FORECAST:

A new front promises severe weather and severe anxiety

TORRANCE AND SETH aren't exactly back together—not yet, she tells me at lunch on Monday.

"It's still complicated," she says between spoonfuls of green curry at a Thai restaurant a block from the station. "We're taking it slowly, and we have a lot to talk about. Isn't that completely bizarre, though? I'm dating my ex-husband."

I don't miss the new expression on her face when she talks about him, calm with a hint of a smirk. Or an old expression, rediscovered. The station has become considerably more peaceful, too, to the point where my coworkers have started asking me if I know what's going on with Torrance.

"I can't believe he changed his mind about that," Avery Mitchell said to me this morning, when Seth aired Torrance's crab story.

"Did I just see Torrance and Seth holding hands on their way in to work?" Hannah Stern said last week.

And I just shrugged, biting back a smile. Trying *not* to smile—that's a new one.

I'm not sure what to expect when Torrance calls a spontaneous meeting the next afternoon, and even people who don't directly report to her are curious enough to show up.

"I have something exciting to announce," she says, standing at the head of the small conference room table. She's in one of her power dresses, a form-fitting deep red with three-quarter sleeves paired with knee-high black boots.

"I've been talking to a lot of people at the station over the course of this week," Torrance continues, "and it's come to my attention that some newer staff feel like they aren't getting the support they need. I've discussed this with Seth and with Fred, and we've decided to launch a mentorship program."

A wave of chatter spreads around the room, as though the words *Torrance Hale* and *mentorship program* used in the same context do not compute.

She goes on to explain that it'll be a three-tiered program: a senior staff member matched with someone who's been here for a few years, who's then matched with an intern or a student. The whole time she's explaining it, I just stare. I *love* this idea, and the fact that she came up with it as a result of what I told her during our girls' night . . . I'm incredibly touched.

Her boots click across the floor as she walks over to my chair, dropping a hand on my shoulder. "And Ari, who helped give me the idea for this program, is going to be my first protégé."

The rest of the staff looks like they're not quite sure how to react, but eventually Hannah starts clapping and everyone else join in. Torrance gestures to me, as though wanting me to say something.

I clear my throat, completely unprepared. "Thank you. I—I'm really excited about this, and I'm honored to be mentored by Torrance."

When the meeting's over, Torrance catches me before I leave, promising she has one more thing she wants to discuss with me in her office. Despite having worked here for three years, I've mainly been in Torrance's office to turn off her lights and tidy up. Times I've been invited? Not even in the double digits.

"There's no easy way to say this," she says once she drops into her chair, pushing aside a couple empty coffee mugs, maybe in an attempt to make her desk look like less of a hellscape. "But if I'm going to be your mentor, which I'm really looking forward to, then I can't be your boss, too."

"Are you . . . firing me?"

"Firing my first mentee? No, definitely not. I just want to reorganize the weather team a bit. Make us feel more like a team instead of a hierarchy. Your new boss would be Caroline." Caroline Zielinski: our assistant news director.

"I like Caroline."

"Great," she says. "We'll start the transition Monday."

It's almost too much good news to process in so little time. At least, until I leave her office and notice the sign on the inside of her door. Garamond font.

Your smile is my favorite thing in the world. Especially when I get to see it first thing in the morning. —SHH

"USUALLY IT'S A little . . . stormier." My interview subject gives me a pointed look, as though it's my fault the weather isn't cooperating.

It's a calm, almost windless Thursday at a beach in Lake Stevens, about thirty-five miles north of Seattle. My forecast yesterday called for the opposite.

"You know what they say about meteorologists," I say, trying to lighten the mood. "We're never right."

"Patience is an important quality for a storm chaser to have," says Pacific Northwest Weather Chasers president Tyler "Typhoon" Watts—really. He insisted that be on his chyron. He strikes me a bit like someone preparing for an apocalypse, and he's one of the more oddball characters I've interviewed: a thirtysomething dressed all in black, shaggy dark hair and shaggier beard, equipped with a tool belt and a massive backpack that isn't doing his posture any favors. Getting him mic'd up was a Process. "It's a lot of hours spent in the car driving. Sometimes you can't even take a bathroom break—you can't give the storm a chance to chase *you*."

A few weeks ago, Seth suggested sports and weather collaborate on this story. I leaped at the chance to do some field reporting, especially with Russell. He's both my field producer and camera operator today, because when you major in journalism, you have to learn how to do everything, and he's just as easygoing and encouraging as he is the rest of the time. Maybe we trade a few more smiles than usual, but aside from that, he's a true professional.

"And it's worth it?" I ask Tyler.

"I probably don't have to convince you of that," he says, wincing as he adjusts the front strap on his backpack. When we arrived, I told him he could take it off, but he wanted to make sure we shot him in his full getup. "It absolutely is. Every time." In his tool belt, his phone rings. "Hold up. I think I'm getting a lead on a storm out east. Do you mind if I make a call?"

"Go ahead," I say.

Russell takes some B-roll of the lake and beach while Tyler speaks forcefully into the phone ten yards away.

"He seems like he might be a while." Russell stops shooting and gives me a hopeful, hesitant look. "I hate to ask this, but I'm covering a hockey game tomorrow, kind of last minute, and Elodie's mom is away on business. She's usually fine without a babysitter, but I've always been a little nervous, leaving her alone at home for too long. So I was wondering . . . if maybe you'd be able to stop by and grab dinner with her? I can leave some money."

When I'm quiet a beat too long, he seems to interpret it as disinterest. "You don't have to stay long. Just dinner, just to check on her. And you're, like, one of the only responsible people I know," he continues, "and you have your niece and nephew, so I figured you probably aren't too terrible with kids."

"I think I'm flattered?" I say with a laugh, which serves to mask whatever else I'm feeling. Fear, maybe. Affection, definitely. "I'd love to. Really."

"She'll probably just want to run lines, maybe practice her Torah portion. She's a super easy kid." As though that's the reason I wouldn't want to do it, the only thing stopping me from giving him an immediate yes. "I don't want it to mess with your sleep schedule or anything."

I wave this off. "I'll nap beforehand. We can watch bootleg Broadway tapings all night."

A soft exhale. Relief. "Good. Thank you." He steps closer, grazing my wrist with a few fingertips, and I savor this brief at-work physical contact.

Tyler/Typhoon hangs up and heads back toward us, backpack swaying.

"Okay," he says, shoving the phone back into his belt. "So it looks like I'm going to be heading out to Darrington. Wanna tag along?"

As we pack up, my mind wanders away from storms and wind patterns and air pressure. Spending time with Russell's daughter is a huge step, and the fact that he asked me to fills me with a mix of warmth and anxiety.

I just have to hope I don't screw it up.

23

FORECAST:

One hundred percent chance of show tunes

"YOU HAVE TO agree that Janis is the real star of the show," Elodie says, tucking a strand of dark hair back into her haphazard bun before reaching for a bottle of glittery gold nail polish. "Her *voice.* The way she brings that character to life."

"I'll give you that. But don't you think part of it is that she's given the better songs?"

Elodie considers this. "Maybe," she relents.

We're in her living room, sprawled out with a dozen bottles of nail polish on the coffee table, listening to the *Mean Girls* musical soundtrack.

"You just do musicals, not plays?" I can grasp the nail polish with my left hand at this point, but I don't quite have the stability needed to paint my nails, so I've told her she can paint my right hand any way she wants. She's taken this under careful consideration, testing a few shades on a sheet of paper before deciding on a blue base with little suns on top.

Elodie leans over my hand, dotting the sun on my thumb with two eyes and a black dash of a mouth. "If there aren't songs, what's the point?" she says. "Sorry, this one looks kind of angry."

"It's okay. She's still cute." I peer down to admire her handiwork. "And you're right. I get so bored during plays."

Elodie gives me this long-suffering look. "*Thank you.* My dad dragged me to Shakespeare in the Park last year, and I fell asleep at the beginning of the second act. He said he was exposing me to 'culture,' but honestly what is more cultured than *Hadestown*?"

I'm laughing, imagining Russell doing this. The *Mean Girls* soundtrack ends, and Elodie leaps up to find a new one on her phone. She knows all the words even to shows she hasn't seen. It's impressive.

"You don't have to sing so quietly," I say, and she blushes. "You have a great voice."

"Sorry. I get a little shy singing in front of new people sometimes. It's different when you're onstage, in a costume. Did you ever do theater?"

"Does Tree #2 in my middle school's production of *The Wizard of Oz* count?"

"But you're on TV."

"It's a very different kind of acting," I say. "Our goal isn't solely to entertain people. Well, we hope we're entertaining, but we're delivering information, first and foremost, and we want to make sure we're doing that in a clear and non-biased way." I consider that for a moment. "Except when I'm going on about how much I love the rain, but that's not exactly a hot-button issue."

"I always ask my dad if it would really kill him to cover the arts every once in a while so we could get free theater tickets. When we do see musicals, he tries to sing along sometimes. But here's the thing you need to know about him if you're going to date him." She lowers her voice conspiratorially. "He is a *terrible* singer."

"Oh—we're not—" I say, stumbling over the weirdness of explaining your relationship to a twelve-year-old when you don't even know what that relationship is.

"O-kaaay," she says in this singsong, and once our nails dry, she runs upstairs to grab her script.

While she's gone, something catches my eye: a large bright yellow book on a side table next to the couch, so thick it's nearly bursting.

"What's that?" I ask when she gets back, script in hand.

Elodie groans. "My baby album. It's the most embarrassing thing."

"I don't think I've ever seen one of these in real life."

"Your parents didn't do one?" she asks, and I tamp down every emotion that wants to escape as I tell her no. "I swear it's like, a national emergency if I have a milestone they don't get a chance to put in the book. They even pass it back and forth. For a while I had to take it with me from house to house, but I had to put my foot down because it was too much, even for them." She shakes her head, more hair escaping her messy bun. "They're obsessed with me."

"You're their first kid. I think that warrants a little obsession."

She rolls her eyes, but I can tell there's some pride there. "I need to show you how ridiculous it is." She snatches up the book. On the cover is a photo of Elodie as a baby, faded with age. "The ticket my dad got when my mom was in labor because he didn't know where to park. My first hat. My first pair of socks."

My eyes snag on a picture of Russell at seventeen, a blanket-bundled Elodie in his arms. His hair is a little too long, and he's in what looks like a hockey jersey over a long-sleeve shirt. Even though he's wearing glasses, I can tell he's gazing at his baby with pure awe.

There aren't enough words to describe what happens to my heart at that point. Whatever it is, it's not something I knew my heart was capable of doing.

"I know. He was really young. I think the book was a way for them to process everything? Which makes me feel a little bad about making fun of it, but"—she flips a few pages—"the receipt for my potty chair?"

I laugh along with her, but I don't think it hit me until now, looking at the pictures, how young seventeen really was. I can't imagine everything he had to take on at that age, the things he put off and those he gave up completely.

And of course, all the things he's denied himself since then so he can be a good father, which he so clearly is. The evidence is all over this house, in Elodie's love for theater, in the way they joke with each other.

Elodie turns the page, and there's Russell and Liv with a toddler Elodie. Again and there they are on Halloween, Elodie dressed as a tiny Bob Ross, Russell as a palette and Liv as a canvas.

What I don't tell her: I kind of love this scrapbook.

"I might throw up," she says as she stabs a glittery nail at a small stapled bag. "That's my first toenail clipping."

RUSSELL LEFT SOME money for dinner, and since it's what most people would call a "nice evening"—meaning, no rain—we decide to walk five blocks to Elodie's favorite Mexican restaurant to pick up some takeout.

After we put in our burrito orders, Elodie uses the bathroom while I reply to a text from Russell asking how it's going. All good, I write. She's a freaking delight. I'm scrolling through social media when I hear a frantic hiss from the dark, graffitied hallway.

"Ari?"

I slide my phone into my pocket and step closer to the bathroom. "Everything okay?"

The door opens a crack, and there's Elodie's head, her face pinched with concern. "Do you have any . . . you know? Period stuff?"

"Oh!" *Shit*. With my IUD, I don't get periods. I haven't carried around a spare tampon or pad in years. "I don't. I'm so sorry."

"I didn't think it would come for another week." There's this panic in her voice so unlike the way she's chattered on all night.

"Number sixty-two!"

"That's us," I say. "Let me grab it and we'll head right home. Do you want me to call an Uber?"

Another pause. "I don't actually have anything at home, either?" She phrases it as a question. "I just . . . it was supposed to come next week, so I didn't get anything from Nina or Sasha, even though I probably should have."

She's lost me. I assume Nina and Sasha are her friends, but I'm not sure whether they're running some kind of underground menstrual products ring or what. "That's okay. We can get some." I take out my phone again, searching the map. "There's a Walgreens about ten minutes away."

"Number sixty-two?" calls the cook again, and I want to yell that I have a twelve-year-old in crisis and to just give me a goddamn minute.

"Can you just get the food?" Elodie's voice breaks, and the door inches shut. "I'll use toilet paper for now."

So I do, and after I've paid, I find Elodie waiting for me on the sidewalk outside, her Eleanor Roosevelt Middle School drama sweatshirt tied around her waist. She's toying with the arm of it, flapping it back and forth while she stares at the ground.

"Hey," I say, trying my best to show that I'm someone she can confide in. Not a friend, not a parent, but somewhere in between. "Do you want to tell me what's going on?"

Elodie sinks down onto a bench next to a bus stop. "It's really not a big deal," she mumbles, toeing the ground with one of her striped Keds.

The way Elodie and I have cracked jokes and talked about Broadway, it almost felt like hanging out with a friend. And while she's plenty independent, now she feels very, very twelve.

"I don't like talking to my parents about any of this," she says.

"You don't have to be ashamed of your—"

Her eyes flash to mine. "I know I don't have to be ashamed of my body," she says quickly. "I'm not! Really. I'm more than happy to let it do its monthly thing. But I don't want my parents to know about it."

I urge myself to stay calm. "You don't want your parents to know when you need more pads?"

"I don't want them to know I started my period."

Oh.

Again, I arrange my face into something I hope looks neutral instead of alarmed. "How long has it been?"

"Um . . . four months? I've been tracking it in my bullet journal. It was supposed to get here next week, like I said, but I know sometimes they're not super reliable when you're just starting, and . . ." She starts playing with the arm of her sweatshirt again. "Should we go eat? I'm hungry. Are you hungry?"

I don't move from the bench. She's had her period for four months and hasn't said anything to her parents. "Can I ask why?"

A long sigh. "They treat everything that happens to me as the Best Thing Ever. Elodie ate a slice of apple for the first time? Better take a photo. She scraped her knee? Put her Band-Aid in the book." She drums on the bench with one hand, tapping out a melody I don't recognize. "I didn't want the wrapper of my first pad in the album," she says. "With a giant caption that says ELODIE'S FIRST KOTEX."

I try my best not to laugh at the imagery. "I'm sorry. You do realize it's a lot of work to hide something like this. They're going to find out eventually."

"Yeah, but I hadn't thought that far ahead." At that, she gives me a half smile.

"If you want to talk about period trauma," I say, not quite believing I'm discussing menstruation with a twelve-year-old in front of a neighborhood Mexican restaurant. "Mine happened in the middle of gym class. While I was wearing white shorts. Needless to say, I was not picked first for dodgeball."

Elodie holds her sweatshirt sleeve to her mouth, trapping a gasp. "You win."

"I have to grab a couple things from Walgreens anyway," I say, gathering the takeout bag as I get to my feet. "So if we happened to get a box of pads while we're there . . ."

"Then I guess that would be okay." She gives me a pained look, and I know the discomfort of translucent public bathroom toilet paper all too well. "Do you mind if we take an Uber?"

By the time we get home, we have to reheat the burritos, which a much-brighter-spirited Elodie asserts makes them taste even better.

"So," she says when we finish, helping me sort everything into compost, recycling, and trash. "You're probably going to tell my parents?"

I consider this. I want her to be safe, but I don't want to break her trust. They have to know, but I'm not sure I should be the one to tell them. "Honestly? I don't know. But I think you should."

"I know, I know. I just—" She breaks off, twisting her mouth to one side. "If they reach for the book, I am running away and changing my name. To something really basic, like Amy or Janet, so they can never find me."

"Fair."

Though Russell only wanted me to come for dinner, I can't resist when Elodie asks me to run lines with her. And when Russell gets home at a quarter to nine, almost Elodie's bedtime, he and I are both shocked to see each other.

He looks both lovely and exhausted, blue eyes warm and hair windblown. Especially now that I've seen the scrapbook photos, I can tell where age hangs on him: in the soft creases at the corners of his eyes, the few threads of gray woven into his hair. The slump to his shoulders, like he carried too much weight too soon, but he's doing his best.

And there's that tug in my chest again, the one that seems entirely unique to Russell Barringer.

"You're still here?" The question is incredulous, but not cruel.

I scramble to a seated position from where I've been lounging on the couch, suddenly self-conscious. Maybe I've overstayed my welcome. He only asked about dinner, after all. "I had no idea this much time had passed. I'm sorry—I can go."

"No, no, I'm glad you two have been hanging out." He places his gear bag in the hall before hanging his coat. "And hey, the house is still standing. That has to be a good sign."

"The dad jokes. They hurt me." Elodie tosses her script on the sofa cushion between us. "Did sports win?"

"By a landslide." He turns to me with a gleam in his eye. "Do you see how she belittles what I do for work? The thing that puts slightly charred caramel popcorn on the table?"

This way they joke around with each other does something to my heart, too. There's a layer of nostalgia there—a pang, really. If I ever had this with my mother, I don't remember it.

"You just about ready for bed?" Russell asks.

Elodie gives the staircase a prolonged glance, her shoulders drooping. "There's actually something I wanted to talk to you about first."

I get to my feet, fiddling with the strap on my bag. "I should go."

"No, you don't have to!" Elodie must realize she says this a little too quickly, a little too loudly. "I mean. I'm the one who dragged you into this scheme."

Russell stares between the two of us, looking deeply confused. "Scheme?"

"I'll just, um, wait down here," I say, settling back on the couch.

"Night, Ari." Elodie gives me a quick squeeze. "Thank you," she says into my ear.

She and Russell disappear upstairs while I sit awkwardly in the living room, answering a few work emails.

About fifteen minutes later, Russell comes back down, looking even more exhausted.

"So that was . . . a lot." He sinks down into the armchair opposite the couch, runs a hand over his stubbled face. "I can't believe she felt she needed to hide her period from us. We've always encouraged her to come to us about anything, and we've tried to be as open as we can with her. Our parents were so old-fashioned that we were terrified to go to them when Liv got pregnant. I never had a sex talk—I think they were shocked I even knew what sex was."

"My mom was like that, too. I had to rely on Google for most of the finer details."

"I guess the best we can do is make it better for our kids, if we have them. We can't perfectly time these things." A self-deprecating laugh. "I should know. Sometimes I think parenting is a combination of doing things the opposite of how you were raised, mixed with doing things exactly how you were raised and worrying that you're becoming your parents."

"Elodie clearly adores you," I say, and he softens at that. "And your dad joke game is A-plus."

"That's one part of parenthood that's come to me shockingly easily." He leans forward, dropping his hand to my knee. "I'm really glad you were here, though. I owe you one."

"Of course. I loved spending time with her."

That guarded expression falls back across his face. I can tell he wants to collapse, and I wish I didn't want to do it next to him so badly. I don't know what his room looks like, but I bet it's neat and organized, nothing out of place. I bet the bed is cozy. That's all I want in this moment—to go to sleep and wake up next to him.

Even though I know I can't.

"I should probably go call Liv. El told me she'd rather I do it, so she only has to tell one of us, though I told her there's no way her mom won't want to talk about it with her."

"And I should head out. Sorry for staying this long."

"Don't apologize. Thank you. For staying. For all of it." He leans in for a soft kiss, his nose bumping mine. When I reach up to drag a hand through his hair, he's already pulled away.

Suddenly I feel like I might cry. *Jesus*. I should be stronger than this. I shouldn't be wondering where I fit. They're already a family—they've been one for years, and while I don't want to think about my relationship with Russell ending, they'll be one long after I've left his life. "I'll see you at work on Monday?"

"Monday," he says, and kisses me again, smoothing some of my hair behind one ear.

When I close the door, I try not to think about how badly I want to be on the other side of it.

24

FORECAST:

Flood watch issued as new revelations burst forth

"I FEEL LIKE the cool quarterback just asked me out," I tell Russell Thursday evening. "And I'm the girl who no one notices until she takes her hair out of a ponytail, and then she's suddenly beautiful."

"I'm getting the feeling you're more nervous about this date with our bosses than you were on our first date," Russell says. "Which is fine, because I am, too."

We were surprised when Torrance and Seth asked us on this double date—her treat, as a way of expressing her gratitude for my staying at the hospital with her. A few weeks ago, we'd have meticulously engineered something like this. Now the Hales are doing it all on their own.

Russell stopped by to pick me up, and I may have had ulterior motives for inviting him upstairs. Namely, wanting to properly kiss him a few times before we meet up with Torrance and Seth. He waits on the couch while I rummage around my dresser for a few accessories, insisting I don't need any help. Miraculously, I was able to attach a jeweled tulip brooch to my black halter dress with one hand.

"It's a different kind of nervous." I extricate an earring from beneath my bed, a twist of wire coiled in the shape of a tornado. "And only because you're about twelve times less frightening than she is."

"Then I guess that's a good thing."

In the full-length mirror next to my dresser, I can see him watching me while I sift through one of several jewelry boxes, searching for the earring's match. Tonight's jacket is beautifully dapper, navy velvet with a white shirt unbuttoned at his throat.

Our schedules haven't lined up for us to do anything more than kiss since that perfect night of our first date, and having him back here reminds me how desperate I am to get him into bed again. Or into a desk chair. Or against the kitchen counter. As long as I can touch him while he falls apart, I'm not picky.

"I've always loved your jackets," I say, trying to refocus on the task at hand, pushing aside a handful of raindrop studs. It's possible I have too many. "Have I ever mentioned that? You have great taste."

"Thank you," he says earnestly. "Some shirts . . . they don't fit right, or they cling. It took me a while to figure out what I was most comfortable in, and now I love them, too."

When I find the earring, I hold it up to Russell with a questioning look. "Would you mind?" I'm out of the sling, but I still can't fully bend my arm, and it'll be a few more weeks until I have enough strength in my fingers to type for longer than twenty minutes without them aching.

"I've had some practice." He settles behind me, brushing some of my natural curls out of the way. His fingers graze the strap of my dress, thumb tickling my ear as I melt back against him. It would be so easy to drag him onto my bed that for a moment, I almost hate the Hales. "And I feel compelled to mention that it would be impossible not to notice you, no matter what your hair looks like."

"It's surreal, though, isn't it?"

"That you experienced Torrance and Seth becoming grandparents? Yes."

"No," I say with a laugh, pushing gently at his chest as he secures one earring. "That after everything, they're almost back together. The woman who threw her ex-husband's Emmy out a window is giving him another chance. Maybe we're done with all this scheming."

"Are you—" Russell pauses, letting my hair fall back over my other ear. "Are you sure it's real? That they've really changed?"

"I want to think anyone can. Sure, at the beginning, I wanted to do this for less than honorable reasons, but I truly want them to be happy. I want to believe they can change. Maybe I'm too naive, but . . ."

"You're not naive. You want to believe the best about people. You want to see the good."

I like the way he says it. That optimism, both false and genuine, has been weaponized against me before, but not now. And maybe this makes me doomed to be a sunshine person for the rest of my days, but so be it. I'll be seventy-eight and sunny, a cool breeze and a place in the shade.

Maybe it's that soft haze of contentment that draws out my next question. "So . . . I'm having Shabbat dinner with my mom and my brother's family next Friday. And I was wondering if you might want to go with me? To my childhood home?"

In the mirror, I watch his face light up. "I would love that," he says, and those four words do their best to diminish my anxiety about it.

He finishes the second earring, pressing a kiss to the back of my neck before shifting my hair back into place.

"How do I look?" I ask, meeting his eyes in the mirror.

His mouth tips into a sly smile. "If you want me to adequately answer that, then we're going to be late."

I turn, smoothing his slightly crooked collar as best I can. I used Torrance's trick; my mauve lipstick won't budge. "I don't mind being a little late." I hold my hand over the front of his suit pants, where he's growing hard, tugging a groan from his throat. I wonder if he knows how fucking irresistible that sound is. That I want to find a hundred new ways to make him groan like that. "I haven't been able to stop thinking about last weekend. That was . . . maybe the hottest experience of my life."

"I can't stop thinking about it, either. About you." He kisses the corner of my mouth, then my jaw, then nips on the earring he just helped me put on. His hand trails up my leg, past the hem of my dress, brushing the fabric of my panties. "You bring out this completely different side of me, and I love it." His voice drops another octave. "*Fuck*. Are you wet for me already?" he asks as he strokes back and forth.

What we did in my bed must have given both of us more confidence. Lowered our walls.

"Yes," I say on a heavy breath, adjusting to give him easier access.

He pushes aside that strip of silk and teases me with his finger, the lightest touch before he sinks into my tight, damp heat. I let out a whimper, rubbing my palm harder against him. As my legs start to sway, he brings his other hand under my dress, cupping my ass to hold me steady.

"What else have you been thinking about?" I ask.

He lets out a low hum. "Many, many things. All the places I want to kiss you. How I want to feel you on top of me." It's agony, the way he slides his finger everywhere but the place I need him most. Then he removes his hand completely and lifts it to his mouth, sucking gently at his slickened fingertip. "How badly I want to taste you when you come."

Jesus. This man will be the death of me. I'm certain of it.

"Tonight," I tell him, because if we keep going, I won't want to leave.

"Tonight," he confirms. "If we make it through this alive."

AT FIRST, I assume it's a jazz club. But the music is decidedly not jazz. It's . . . I'm not even sure what to call it, but there are three banjos and a glockenspiel. Maybe I shouldn't be surprised, given Torrance's favorite Christmas song was "Run Rudolph Run."

"These people will never cease to amaze me," Russell says so only I can hear as we slide into a booth across from Torrance and Seth.

The club is classy and expensive, two words I have never associated with the types of places I frequent. And if I say it's loud, that might officially make me Old, and the Hales are a good twenty years older than we are. So I will simply say nothing at all.

"We used to go here all the time when we first got married," Torrance says, needing to shout to be heard over the music. If she hadn't been wearing this silver dress that makes her look like a disco ball, I wouldn't have been able to spot them when we arrived. "The band is always something we've never heard of but fall helplessly in love with by the end of the night."

The guy playing the glockenspiel hits a sour note, and I find Torrance's declaration hard to believe.

"They even had to kick us out a couple times." Seth waggles his eyebrows at his ex-wife, who blushes.

When a server brings over a round of champagne because she's so thrilled to see them, Torrance lifts her glass in a toast. "To second chances," she says, looking right at Seth.

He spills half of it after he takes a sip. "Whoops," he says with a sloppy grin. "We did a little pregaming before we left."

"*You* did a little pregaming," she corrects.

"How could I not celebrate? I'm out with the most gorgeous woman in the world, the Kraken won last night, and we just had a grandkid." He throws an arm around Torrance and plants a kiss on her cheek. It's surreal, seeing him this cheery, like a grizzly bear offering up its head to be scratched behind the ears.

I turn, not used to the sight of them kissing in public—and that's when I spot someone familiar a few booths away. The champagne in my mouth instantly goes flat.

"I love this song," Torrance says, reaching for Seth's hand. "Dance with me."

"We'll get the next one," I say. When the Hales are safely out of earshot, I tug on Russell's sleeve, motioning in the mystery man's direction. "That guy over there. He's the one I saw Torrance with at brunch a few weeks ago." I told Russell about it, but especially after Torrance said she wasn't involved with anyone else, I stopped worrying.

"Are you sure?" he asks, and I nod. Same too-stylish hair, same single hoop in his left ear.

It's clear Torrance sees him, too, based on the way she stumbles over her feet. Seth says, "Careful there!" and holds her tighter. When they head back to the table at the end of the song, her face is flushed, and I'm not sure it's just from dancing.

"Everything okay?" I ask as she sips her ice water.

Russell's eyes go wide at something over my shoulder, and I barely have time to react before the guy approaches our table.

"Torrance," he says in a bright, friendly voice, the twinkling lights above our booth glinting off his earring. "Fancy seeing you here."

"If I recall, I'm the one who told you about it." She looks like she's trying her hardest to keep her cool. "What brings you out tonight?"

That false cheeriness hits too close to home. I've been that person trying to hold everything together, fixing cracks with Scotch Tape instead of superglue. I've held on, faking that smile long past its expiration date.

"I'm with a few friends from work." He motions to some people at his booth on the other side of the room.

"I'm sorry, I'm being rude," Torrance says. "Ryan, this is Ari and Russell. They're at KSEA, too. And this is Seth."

"Seth Hale, in the flesh." Ryan extends his hand, and Seth just stares, like he's never shaken someone's hand before.

"Hasegawa Hale," he finally says, correcting him.

"Ah, my apologies, man."

I clench my fist around my bag so hard, the sequins start stabbing my skin. This is going to be bad. All the toxicity Torrance talked about—if anyone could draw it out, it's got to be another man, even if it's one Torrance only went on a couple casual dates with.

But Seth flashes him a good-natured grin. "Torrance giving away our secrets?"

"It was too great not to share," she says. "The glockenspiel player is pretty spectacular, right?"

Ryan nods his agreement while I reassess everything I have ever known about music. Then he gives them a salute. "You two have a great night."

When he leaves, I wait for someone to yell. For fists to fly.

"So you can definitely do better than me," Seth says, but there's no edge to his voice. In fact, he's still smiling.

Torrance relaxes instantly. "I mean, I tried. But you make it so hard to stay away."

He slings an arm around her again, pulling her close, and she rests her head on his shoulder.

What . . . is happening?

Beneath the table, Russell's hand finds my knee, thumb rubbing a soft circle. Maybe it's reassurance that this is really happening. That maybe we really are done meddling.

"We should do this more often," Torrance says, reaching for an olive on the too-pricey appetizer plate she and Seth ordered. By my calculation, each of those olives cost $2.50. "It's been a while since we've been out with anyone from work."

Seth gestures between Russell and me, and I try to push away all my Hale-induced shock. "How long have the two of you been a thing?"

"About three weeks, I guess?" I say, looking to Russell for confirmation. He nods. We haven't talked about making this official, but I want to believe we're heading that direction.

"I've gotten to know Ari a little better lately," Torrance says. "But I'm afraid you remain something of a mystery, Russell."

"And your daughter." Seth spears an olive with a tiny appetizer fork. "Have you two met?"

"I sort of accidentally babysat her last week," I say, hoping Russell's okay with me mentioning this. "We were supposed to only do dinner, but we wound up spending the whole evening running lines for a musical she's in."

"Mixed families can be a lot of fun," Seth says. "Both my parents remarried, and I have . . . fifteen siblings now." He squints, as though mentally counting, needing to make sure he gets the number right.

"Sometimes just one is a lot for me," I say with a laugh.

It's only when Russell removes his hand from my knee that I realize he's been quiet during this entire exchange.

"You two do make a great couple." Torrance lifts her eyebrows in this suggestive way. "And if Ari and Elodie get along . . ."

A muscle in Russell's jaw twitches. The Hales are pushing a little too hard, and I'm not sure how to politely tell them to back off.

"This is still very new," Russell says, more to his glass of champagne than to any of us. He puts a half inch of space between us in the booth. It's slight, but it's enough to notice. "And . . . I'm not exactly in the market for a stepmom for my kid."

The sentence hits like a one-in-a-million bolts of lightning, straight to my chest.

I'm not exactly in the market for a stepmom.

Suddenly, I feel very, very small.

Seth launches into a story about his last family reunion, but I can't bring myself to do anything but smile and nod as the club around me blurs.

I think about the Russell I've gotten to know over the past few months. The man who got me vending machine junk food and watched a solar eclipse while holding his breath. He's protective of his kid, and I can't blame him for that, especially knowing his history. But if I'm being honest—and selfish, because god do I feel selfish for obsessing over it—my brain won't let it go.

It's not a role I'm actively seeking out, so I can't understand why it feels like I've taken a fist to the stomach.

It invades the most vulnerable parts of my mind the rest of the night, when we're dancing and when we're saying goodbye to the Hales and later, too, when Russell comes back to my apartment and we're too exhausted to do anything but sleep. Even then, I lie awake, wondering if this means he thinks I'd be a bad mother. If he somehow knows my history.

If he's already decided we're not meant to last.

25

FORECAST:
A tentative glimpse of early spring optimism

REDMOND IS NOTHING like the place I grew up.

Every time I come back, the suburb looks different than it did during my last visit. At first, those differences were small—*I didn't realize we had a MOD Pizza now* or *Was there always a CrossFit gym there*? Now the downtown core is almost unrecognizable, chains having replaced the shops and cafes I knew so well as a teen. There's no longer a forest two houses down from mine, and the hiking trail at the end of the road that once led to summers of blackberry picking—and my and Alex's sorry attempts at making blackberry jam—has been turned into condos. I can't remember exactly what went where in this strange suburban puzzle, only that I could have sworn some of my favorite spots were *right there*, and suddenly, they're not.

All this time Redmond's been changing, I've been just on the other side of the lake.

This is the first time I've seen this house in almost a year, and it's made me a knotted, tangled mess all week.

I try my usually foolproof method of pushing all those messy feelings away, but today the silver linings feel more out of reach than they've ever been. My shoulders are tense, my breath stalled in my lungs.

It's not working.

"No rush or anything," Russell says from the driver's seat. "But did you want to get out?"

"I'm getting there."

Depending on traffic, Redmond is twenty to fifty-five minutes east of Seattle, and this afternoon's drive was somewhere in the middle. We're parked next to Alex's Prius, early March sun streaming in through the windows. I let out a sigh and only fiddle with the seatbelt for a moment, then flex the fingers on my left hand a few times. Even without thinking about it, I've been slipping into physical therapy exercises to relax myself. They've been helping clear my mind when the silver linings won't. Like right now.

I'm not exactly in the market for a stepmom.

No wonder I can't find a silver lining.

Russell asks if I want him to carry the Whole Foods apple pie in the Subaru's backseat, but I shake my head, tell him I've got it, and together we head up the drive.

The porch is lined with geraniums and marigolds and begonias that look newly potted, and maybe there's my silver lining: my mother gardening again.

I knock, because even though I lived here for eighteen years and for a couple summers after that, it feels too intrusive to just let myself in.

When the door opens, Orion grins up at us, showing off another lost tooth. "Hi. Are you Aunt Ari's gentleman caller?"

"You're supposed to ask who it is before you open the door," Alex says, jogging up behind him. His face lights up when he spots Russell, and with a narrowing of my eyes, I will him not to embarrass me tonight. "Welcome! I'm Alex, Ari's brother. You must be Russell. And this is Orion"—he claps a hand on Orion's mop of curls—"who just learned an important lesson about opening the door to strangers."

"Sorry," Orion says, fidgeting to get out of his dad's grip. "I didn't think Aunt Ari would bring over anyone bad!"

"He called Russell my 'gentleman caller,'" I inform Alex.

"We may have been watching too much of that new period piece on Netflix," Alex says. "Guess he picked up a few things."

Maybe a precocious five-year-old is exactly what Russell and I needed to break the tension, because he starts cracking up. "Good to meet you," he says, shaking Alex's hand.

The house is tidy. That's the first thing I notice. Almost too tidy, as though my mother wanted to make sure we were seeing it at its best. No stray laundry, walls adorned with minimalist geometric artwork, the scent of a lemon air freshener stinging my nostrils. While it doesn't have much in common with my childhood home, at least aesthetically, all the memories are still here, trapped inside these walls. Getting home from school after staying late at a science club, throwing open the front door and hoping I'd find a mother who was happy to see me. Hoping there wouldn't be a stranger waiting to introduce himself to me and asking if it was okay if he stayed for dinner.

My mother rushes over, a light pink apron I've never seen before tied around her waist. Come to think of it, I'm not sure I've ever seen her in an apron. "Ari, hi. You look great. Traffic okay?"

I assess my unremarkable striped skirt and linen button-up. "Hey, Mom. Yeah, not too bad."

It's okay. Maybe we're talking about traffic, but that's not a bad omen. Besides, I'm sure Hannah would have as much to say about traffic as small talk as I do about weather. We continue the introductions as Javier walks in carrying Cassie, who buries her face in his chest, suddenly shy.

"You certainly look familiar," my mother says to Russell as Alex takes his coat. "I'm sure I've seen you on TV."

"Are you a meaty—meter—weatherperson, too?" Cassie asks, stumbling over the word, her face scrunching up with the effort of it all. Her curly hair is in two pigtails today.

"I'm not," he says, bending at the knees a bit so he can be eye level with her. "I cover sports. But I still get rained on a lot of the time."

Cassie gasps, like this is the greatest thing she's ever heard. She wiggles in Javier's arms until he sets her down. "I love sports! Daddy and Papa just signed me up for soccer." She shows off the ribbons on her pigtails which, sure enough, have little soccer balls dangling off them. "I'm going to be the goalie!"

Russell's jaw drops open. "Are you serious? I used to play goalie for my hockey team. It's the best position."

"He also gets to go to a lot of games for free," I say to Cassie, and she looks like she might explode.

"I want to do your job," she declares. No allegiance, this kid.

"She's wanted to be a meteorologist for the past year," I say to Russell as we head into the living room. "You've poisoned her."

"Nothing to poison. I just happen to have a very fun job."

Alex drops onto the couch with Cassie and Orion on each side of him, who've started squabbling about how much money the tooth fairy should leave them. It's not the same couch we found our mother on the day our dad left, but it's in the same spot.

"Do you need any help in the kitchen?" I ask my mother.

"I think Javier and I have it covered. It should be ready in ten."

She slides a loose strand of hair back into her bun. I can tell she's not used to the shorter length yet. "I know it's not quite sundown," she says to Russell. "But with the kids, we kind of fudge it. We did the same when Ari and Alex were little. It was impossible to get them to wait."

"Don't drag our good names through the mud like that," Alex says. "We were extremely good children!"

"I have several photo albums that prove otherwise." My mother brings a hand to her throat. "Ari . . . you still wear that necklace?"

It dawns on me that I wasn't wearing it at the hospital. Russell had taken it off that night in the hotel, and I wasn't able to do the clasp myself.

"It's my favorite necklace," I say, grazing the lightning bolt with my thumb, and the warmth in her deep brown eyes takes me back to the day I graduated. When she hugged me, pressed the jewelry box into my hand, and told me she couldn't wait to see me on TV. "Wherever you end up," she promised, "I'll eat breakfast or dinner with you every day." I was still an intern then, hadn't even locked down a job—but she knew I'd make it.

Somehow, I'd forgotten that.

While we're waiting, and in part so I can prove to my mother that I can be *very* patient when it comes to food, thank you very much, I take Russell on a brief tour of the house.

"Unfortunately, she converted it to a guest room a few years ago," I tell him as I open the door of what used to be my bedroom. "But just imagine some posters of Zac Efron, a star map, and a few more posters of Zac Efron, and you'll get the idea."

Meanwhile, Alex's old room has been turned into an exercise room, a Peloton in one corner and a rack of free weights in the other.

For a while, we squabble-joked about whose room got the better upgrade.

"I hope this isn't too awkward for you. Meeting everyone like this." I lean against the wall outside Alex's room. I want Russell to be here, I do, but I can't let go of what he said at the jazz club. "I just . . . don't want you to be uncomfortable."

He settles himself next to me, grazing my arm with a few fingertips. In a perfect world, that light touch would be enough to convince me everything is okay between us. "I'm not. Are you?"

I shrug, because the answer is yes but it's too complicated to explain all the ways in which I am uncomfortable in this house. "I was kind of hoping we could talk—"

"Dinner's ready!" my mother calls from downstairs.

"Or eat," I finish.

"We'll talk," he says, giving my hand a quick squeeze, and he must be able to sense my insecurity. "I promise."

Shabbat dinner wasn't a weekly tradition for us growing up, but every so often, we'd get out the candles and the good tablecloth. I've always loved the prayers over bread and wine, grape juice when we were kids, and as much as I'd have rolled my eyes about it when I was younger, the togetherness. The instant sense of community.

I take a seat between Russell and my mother, Alex and Javier and the twins squeezed onto the other side. There have never been this many people at our table.

As is the custom, my mother waves her hands and then covers her eyes after she lights the Shabbat candles. "*Baruch ata Adonai, Eloheinu Melech ha-olam, asher kidshanu b'mitzvotav vitzivanu l'hadlik ner shel Shabbat,*" she recites, and I'm struck with another memory. Alex and me as kids, trying to write out the transliterated

Hebrew words, our ridiculous spellings making my mother laugh until tears streamed down her cheeks.

All my memories of the holidays we observed—they were mostly good things. Even if these days, I only make it to temple during the High Holidays, Judaism is an integral part of my identity. My history.

My depression has warped so many of those memories.

"Where do you go to temple, Russell?" my mother asks between bites of lasagna.

"Technically, I don't," he admits. "Not regularly. But my daughter's bat mitzvah is at the end of next month. This is delicious, by the way."

Javier beams. "Thank you. I tried something new, adding the braised eggplant. We're always trying to sneak more veggies into the kids' food."

Cassie and Orion are oblivious, their mouths already painted red with marinara.

"Have you been to Honeybee Lounge?" Alex asks Russell. "In Capitol Hill? That's his restaurant."

"Are you kidding? I love that place."

Javier brushes this off, but I know he's pleased, and I can't deny that I am, too.

My mother assesses Russell with a furrowed brow. "Your daughter's preparing for her bat mitzvah? You're . . . very young."

I stare down at my plate, wincing.

"It doesn't always feel that way," he says with a good-natured laugh. He must be used to deflecting.

"No judgment," she says, and there has to be a limit to the number of times this evening can shock me.

Once I've relaxed enough to enjoy myself, something in the living room catches my eye. It's a woven piece of art hanging above the couch, natural colors with pops of turquoise, and it definitely wasn't there the last time I was. "Is that new?" I ask, motioning to it with my fork.

An odd flush covers my mother's cheeks. "I started playing around with a loom when I was . . ." Her eyes land on Russell, and I can tell she doesn't want to explain where, exactly, she was. "Away," she finishes. "And I loved it. I'm not very good or anything, but it's so calming."

"Mom, no. It's amazing."

"Really? I've always admired the way you do your jewelry, and I thought it would be fun to have a hobby like that. There's gardening, of course—did you see the flowers?" I tell her I did, and that they look great. "But the weather doesn't always cooperate, as you know. I could make you one, if you want. Once I get a little better. In fact, it's probably for the best if all of you take some off my hands so I don't end up living in a house made entirely out of yarn."

"I would love that."

I keep expecting her to purse her lips and start complaining, to make an offhand comment about my appearance or my past boyfriends, but none of that happens. In fact, it's a lovely meal, even when the twins' tooth fairy argument escalates to the point where Cassie flings a noodle at Orion.

Alex and I offer to clean up while my mother, Javier, and Russell keep the twins busy in the living room.

"Yarn art. Who knew," I say as I scrub at the lasagna pan Javier told us not to dare put in the dishwasher.

Alex is ready to dry it off with a towel. "We all contain multitudes."

In the living room, my mother lets out this unselfconscious laugh I haven't heard in ages. Russell's in the middle of a story, waving his arms for emphasis, and the kids are gazing at him, rapt. My heart twinges in the way it's been known to do around Russell.

"She just looks *happy*," I say. "It's the only way to describe it. I haven't seen her like this in so long."

I know that a few weeks in a facility weren't going to cure her depression. She wasn't going to check in as one type of person and check out as a completely different one. That's not how mental health works.

But for now, she's taking her medications as prescribed, or at least that's what she told Alex, and he told me. She and I have yet to discuss it, and while I want to, I have no idea how to begin that conversation.

So I'm choosing to be hopeful.

"She does." Alex throws the towel over one shoulder before leaning in, nudging me with his elbow. "And it's good to see *you* happy, too."

AFTER WARM SLICES of apple pie, Russell and I take a walk through the neighborhood. We're lucky my parents bought the house when they did because it would be laughably unaffordable now. Houses on this street are going for four times what they paid for it. But my mother doesn't want to move, despite the fact that she's one of the only people in this neighborhood living on her own.

"God, everything's so different," I say. "There used to be a forest there, and Alex and I would dare each other to go into it at night and see how long we could last before we ran out. I was convinced monsters lived in the trees, waiting to snatch children who were foolish enough to step inside." I wave a hand toward it. "But now it's just houses. And downtown, when we drove in . . . there was so much I didn't recognize."

"Paved paradise and put up a parking lot?"

"More like paved paradise and put up a Five Guys," I say. "Not quite as catchy. And maybe gentrification is the scariest thing of all."

We head toward what used to be the edge of my neighborhood but now leads into a newer development, boxy three-story homes in shades of beige and light brown.

"This is where I fell off my bike the moment after my training wheels came off," I say, pointing to a row of mailboxes. "And this is where I'd park with my boyfriends so no one could catch us making out. Now there aren't enough trees here—no good make-out spots. I really feel for today's teenagers."

"This is a very enlightening tour."

We stop at a playground, one with monkey bars and slides and a handful of equipment I've never seen before.

"What the hell," I say as Russell and I sit on a pair of swings. "This playground is ridiculous. Is that, like, an interactive climbing wall?"

"Yeah, we definitely didn't have that in Michigan, either."

"It may be a bougie playground, but at least there's no one here," I say, aware I'm talking a little too much. Avoiding the real issue. "We don't have to be the creepy adults on the swings."

Russell scuffs the bougie bark with his shoe. "So."

"So." No more stalling. I let out a long breath, working up to it. "I'm really glad you came. Thank you."

"Of course. We're . . ."

A strange laugh slips out. "Yeah. What *are* we, Russell?"

I hope he knows that having him here means I'm fully in this with him. And if he's not, well—then I need to know.

"I didn't miss how you acted last week with the Hales," he says quietly, still staring down at the bark. "After what I said about Elodie."

"About how you weren't exactly in the market for a stepmom?"

This draws his face into a grimace. "You, ah, remember the precise wording, huh."

"It was kind of hard to forget."

"That was . . . not the right thing to say. Especially in front of the Hales. I'm so sorry." He brings his eyes up to mine, and I can tell he means it. Until that night, he was so sure of me in a way I've always struggled to feel about myself. I want that back. "I can tell you I didn't intend for it to hurt you, but I know that doesn't make it more okay. This is all new for me. I'm not used to thinking about anyone but Elodie—not even myself, if I'm being honest."

"I can understand that," I say, because even if I can't relate, I can imagine.

"I don't know how to do this. I don't know how to be a boyfriend and a father at the same time."

My heart plummets. Maybe it's as simple as that: he can only be one, and he's made his choice. "Oh."

But Russell shakes his head, not finished yet. "I want to, Ari. Believe me, I do. But I haven't exactly had a lot of practice. I'm always worried someone will think Elodie is a burden, or baggage, or they won't want to get to know her at all."

I reach down, covering his hands with mine. I can do that now—hold him with both hands. "Elodie is *not* a burden. She's *amazing*, and a huge part of that is because of you, and because of Liv. You're a great dad."

"Don't give me too much credit there," he says, but he seems softer than he did ten minutes ago. There's pride in his expression, and I love the way it looks on him. "I don't want you to feel any pressure to spend time with her."

"Russ. I'd love to spend more time with Elodie."

He brightens even more. "Yeah? Because she's been asking about you since last weekend. You must have made quite the impression."

"It was the show tunes," I say. "Very few things tie people together like show tunes. And burritos." Then I turn serious again. "You don't have to choose—between fatherhood and a relationship. You deserve both. I mean, I know you're going to be a father regardless of whether I'm here, I'm just—" I break off, drawing in a breath. "This is coming out wrong. What I'm trying to say is, I want to try. We won't be perfect at it, at least not right away, but if you're ready, I want to try."

He links his fingers with mine. "I'm ready," he says, bringing his other hand to my face, his thumb stroking my cheekbone in this way that makes me feel safe. Cared for.

"I've been scared, too," I admit, our feet still planted in the bark as our swings sway. "I don't know if I have the best track record with relationships. I've never really been . . . myself."

Russell drops his hand to my shoulder and waits for me to continue. Listening, but not pushing me.

"For the longest time, everyone has gotten me at full brightness. Every light in the studio on. No darkness, no negativity. Every time I feel something like that coming on, I force myself to act the opposite. I give a compliment or an affirmation to restore the balance, I guess. Or tip it the other way completely. I thought I had to be this very specific kind of person for anyone to want to be with me. And it worked for a while, or at least I thought it did. I even thought I was going to get married."

The defense mechanism won't make sense without the explanation. I knew there was no way I could invite him here without unlocking that barricaded door of my past, and yet that knowledge doesn't make forming the words any easier.

"If I'm going to explain it—and I want to, I really do—I have to start back here," I continue. "In Redmond. My mom and I . . . it hasn't always been like this with us. Well, I'm not even sure what 'this' is, to be honest."

"I picked up on a little of that, I think."

"She was different when I was growing up. She'd have these dark days that made it tough for her to be the person I wanted her to be." I don't want to divulge too much of my mother's mental health yet. It doesn't feel wholly mine to tell, especially when she's only a couple blocks away. "And we . . . struggled in similar ways."

I grip the swing tighter, aware I'm about to throw the door wide open. Somehow, though, it doesn't feel as difficult as I thought it would be. There's no pressure in my chest, no flashing neon sign in my brain warning me to shut my mouth—only the desire to share something I haven't been able to articulate with anyone I've let come close.

If my mom can change, so can I.

"I have depression," I say. "I've had it for a long time, and I'll probably have it my whole life, since it's not something that tends to magically go away." I watch his face, the way he slowly nods, taking this in. "When I was a teen, every so often I'd have these days that blurred together. I'd go through school on autopilot, barely registering anything anyone was saying. I'd get home exhausted, though I hadn't done anything to exert myself. Everything *hurt*, even though there was nothing physically wrong with me. I felt weighed down . . . like some kind of terrible magnet was tugging me to the center of the earth, this heaviness that made it impossible to find joy in any of the things I used to love. I couldn't even make myself do my science homework—that was how I really knew it was bad."

I force a laugh at this, and he humors me with a small smile.

"It wasn't until college that I was diagnosed. I went to the health center on campus because I was so tired all the time, and everyone around me was having the time of their lives. I didn't know what was wrong with me that was making it impossible to do that. Making it impossible to make friends. Once I had that diagnosis and started learning more about it, started seeing someone, it started to get better. Not instantly, but by the end of my freshman year, I was finally starting to feel like myself again, this person who'd been a stranger for years.

"I still go to therapy," I continue, "and I'm on antidepressants. And most of the time, I'm okay. But I still have dark days, and I don't want to hide any of that from you."

He cups my knee with one hand, stilling my swing. I didn't realize I'd been twisting back and forth. "Why would you hide it?"

"I've never told anyone. Not anyone I was dating. Not anyone who—who mattered." I glance down at his hand, watching his fingers move back and forth in this calming, hypnotic motion. "My dad left because he couldn't handle my mother. So for someone to care about me, for someone to stay—I thought I had to be the overly cheerful person I am on TV. Or else I'd become my mother, and that's what I've been trying so hard to avoid. I told you that's what my ex thought, that I was too sunshine. And maybe I have been, but I don't want to do that anymore." *Not with you* is the implication. I hope he hears it, because I'm not sure if I have the courage to say it.

"Thank you for telling me," he says, bringing his free hand to my other knee, his eyes never drifting from mine. "I've been to therapy, too. When I first moved to Seattle. There was so much with Elodie I'd never properly dealt with, and I was going pretty consistently for a few years. I'm . . . really glad we can talk about that."

"Me too." I motion with my head back in the direction of the house as something glows inside my chest. "The way she was in there—that's not the mother I grew up with. Or maybe it was, some of the time, and the other times were so tough that it's hard to remember everything else. I want to forgive her. I want things to be different between us. I had this vision, when I was younger, that I'd have the kind of mother I could go to brunch with every Sunday, and we'd dish about everything going on in our lives. Maybe that sounds ridiculous. And then I imagined getting married, and having a mother who'd want to be part of the wedding planning, almost to the point where it got annoying. I would have *loved* to be annoyed by her because she was insisting on a sit-down meal over a buffet. But even when I was engaged, none of that happened. She didn't have an interest in any of it."

"It's the worst when family isn't there for you the way they're supposed to be," he says. "When Liv got pregnant, it felt like I'd shattered some unspoken bond of trust. *You will not knock someone up. You will not fuck up your future.*"

"But you didn't."

"It took a while for me to get there." He's quiet for a moment, scratching at his stubbled jaw. Pensive. "And I hope tonight is just the start for you and your mom. You don't deserve anything less than that."

"Thank you." If my words are a whisper, it's only because I'm trying not to cry. "What I'm realizing," I continue, "is that I like myself the most when I'm around you. And I think it's because I'm the most honest version of myself. I don't have to try as hard, and I don't have to hide. I can just . . . *be*."

He turns in his swing, bracketing my legs with his and reaching for my hands again. "I—I don't know what to say. I'm honored. Truly," he says. "Letting you get close is the best thing I've done in a long time, and it means the world that you brought me here. And none of what you said changes anything. It doesn't change how I feel about you."

"And how is it you feel about me, exactly?"

A wry grin. "I think you know, weather girl." Those six words might as well be composed of hearts instead of letters. It feels like it's been ages since I heard the nickname, and I'd forgotten how much I love it. What I love even more: the way he pulls me in for a slow, soft kiss as the sun sets over my not-quite-childhood playground.

26

FORECAST:
EXCESSIVE HEAT WARNING.
Be sure to stay hydrated

RUSSELL HAS THE house to himself tonight, a fact that makes me rest my hand on his leg during the drive back to Seattle, thumb skimming from hip to knee and back again.

At the playground, I wanted to bundle myself up in him and savor his wonderful Russell sweetness. Now that we're locked in a small space together, I'm greedier. Every time he exhales, I want to stretch it into a moan. When he coaxes the steering wheel into a turn, I imagine his fingers beneath my skirt.

And yet every ounce of desire is underscored with something else: a sense of comfort I've never known in a relationship. Safety. I've always been so afraid of pushing people away, afraid I'd reveal too much of myself, expose a piece that wasn't summer-bright, and they wouldn't like who I was underneath.

Except . . . Russell's seen those parts. And he's not running.

We start kissing the moment he parks the Subaru in his driveway, a desperate clash of tongues and teeth. I twist in my seat, pressing myself closer as his hands plunge into my hair. This sensible family vehicle wasn't meant for this, I'm certain of it.

"You have a lot of dexterity there," he says as I grip the lapels of his jacket.

"Oh, I can do a lot of things with this hand now." And just to prove I can, I palm the front of his jeans, where he's already hard for me.

"*Ari.*" He wraps my name in a fantastic groan that sends a pulse of need straight to my core. "We should get inside. I can't do nearly enough of what I want to do to you in this position."

"Funny. Because I kind of like you in this position."

He smirks before shifting me back to the passenger seat and opening his door. "Out with you."

"Ooh, I like it when you're bossy, too."

We trip inside—literally, I stumble over a carpet strip while my mouth is fused to his—and Russell wrestles with my sweater while I kick off my shoes. Outside his bedroom, he cages me against the wall, a hand braced above my head. "You want bossy?" he says into my ear, and I'm shocked by the thrill that simple question sparks through my body.

"Yes," I breathe.

His lashes lower to half-mast. "Get on the bed. And take off your clothes."

I can't oblige quickly enough, though I steal a moment to examine his room. Stylish mahogany furniture, striped comforter. Minimalist and organized, just like I imagined, with a biography of a hockey player on his nightstand. More graceful now, I slip off my skirt and impress myself with how deftly I can unbutton my linen shirt after all these weeks of physical therapy. I lower myself onto the bed in my bra and panties, and almost immediately, I'm overwhelmed by how much the sheets smell like *him*, even when he is right here next to me.

Russell walks inside, his shirt unbuttoned and his hair already a disaster. His facial hair has grown out a bit, a shadow along his jaw, and I want it to burn up my entire body.

"Come here to the edge," he says, patting the comforter, a tremor in his voice now. Heart in my throat, I do. "Show me where you want me to touch you."

"Everywhere."

He lifts his eyebrows, as though this answer isn't good enough. So I drape a hand behind one ear, dragging it down along my jawline. My collarbone. "Here."

When his lips meet my neck, all hunger and gorgeous heat, I let out a low hum. *God*. I'm not sure if my body has always been this sensitive or if it's just perfectly attuned to his mouth. His fingertips.

"Where else?" he says into my skin.

Already lightheaded, I slip my fingers inside the cup of my bra, pinching my left nipple. "Here."

He obeys, dipping his head to my chest, unhooking my bra before he sweeps his tongue over my breasts, drawing my nipples to tight, hard peaks. The torturous pressure of his teeth makes me close my eyes, losing my center of gravity as I fall back onto the bed. He sucks one nipple into his mouth and then the other, then removes his lips so he can blow cool air across them.

"God. So beautiful," he murmurs, kissing a line from my breasts down to my navel, pausing at the lace band of my panties. "What about . . . here. What do you want me to do to your pussy, weather girl?"

This wicked streak in him—I'm obsessed with it. "Lick me. Please."

"I would fucking love to."

He grins before lowering himself down my body. Slowly, he nudges my legs apart, lips burning a path from calf to knee to thigh, and I feel the earth simply dissolve beneath me, one great *swoosh* of air leaving my lungs. He kisses me through my underwear at first, because he is awful and terrible and so extremely cruel, and I love it. I love it all. I'm too desperate for his tongue, bucking my hips, fisting a hand in his hair. Begging for what I've asked him to do. When he finally slides down my panties, I'm on the verge of passing out.

Until he parts me with his middle and index fingers and buries his face between my thighs.

The first swipe of his tongue is fucking *lethal*, hot and slick and igniting anything in me that wasn't already wide, wide awake.

"Tell me what you like." Even Bossy Russell is polite, and I love that, too.

"More of this," I gasp out as his tongue feathers over where I'm most sensitive. "But a little slower. Softer. *Yes.*"

He slows down and takes his time, not eager to race to the finish. A finger joins his mouth, and then another.

"Now you can go faster," I say.

That feeling builds and builds and builds before plateauing, again and again, and I will myself not to get frustrated. I'm about to tell him as gently as I can that I'm not sure it's going to happen for me, but then something tightens at the base of my spine and suddenly I'm not so sure after all. He strokes my clit with his tongue, giving it all of his attention with these warm, insistent flicks. *Dear lord help me.* My legs start to shake, but he's gripping them, keeping me steady. Anchoring me to the earth.

I bite out his nickname as I ride that feeling, *Russ—Russ—Russ*—and then in one brilliant burst, I'm gone. Launched into the center of the sun.

He presses these grin-kisses into my thighs, clearly pleased with himself. "You are amazing," he says before he slides onto the bed next to me.

"And you're a very good listener."

I barely let myself recover, still glowing from my orgasm as I peel off his boxer briefs. The sound he makes when I close my mouth around him is even hotter than I imagined it would be.

"Ari. *Christ*. That's—that's really good. *Fuck*, that's good."

He throws his head back, exposing his lovely throat. Swallowing hard. Somewhere in the back of my mind, I'm wondering how long it's been since anyone touched him in this specific way, and it makes me want to make this even better for him. I take him deeper, swirling my tongue over the head of his cock, savoring the salty taste of him.

"Wait, wait," he says, gently tugging at my hair. "I don't want to—before we—"

I glance up, our eyes locking as we both realize what he means.

I straighten into a sitting position. "I have an IUD." It's not the sexiest of dirty talk, but at least it leaves no doubt as to what I want. "And I got tested last month. After our first date."

"Me too. I mean—not the IUD part. The other part. Can you tell I'm nervous?"

Nervous Russell is the most endearing version of him. "Seems to be a common theme with us."

"It's good, though," he assures me, giving my shoulder a squeeze. "Good nerves. The best kind."

"So I take it this means you want to?" I ask, and he kisses the grin right off my face. Still, I pull back for another moment. "There's one more thing I want to ask. This might sound presumptuous, but a few weeks ago, I put some lube in my purse. Just in case. Would you . . . be okay with that?"

"Why wouldn't I be? I can't say I've had a ton of experience with it, but if you want to use it, then I'm game."

"God, I like you." I hurry to retrieve it from my bag out in Russell's living room. When I get back to his bed, I tip a few drops into my palm, rubbing my hands together before I reach for him.

His head lolls back as I run my slickened hands up and down his shaft. "Well. I'm a big fan of lube, as it turns out."

"Good." I straddle him, my knees at his hips, kissing him long and deep.

"You're gonna ride me?" he asks, gripping my ass, fingers digging into my skin. I'm addicted to the sexy-sloppiness of his words.

"If that's okay." I lift my hips, letting his cock nudge my entrance. Teasing. I'm aching and empty and so fucking needy, but I hold myself back, waiting for his yes. "I just—really want to see you lose control."

A choked-sounding laugh. "Yes. Yes, it's more than okay."

When I reach down to guide him inside, he's so warm and hard and *right* that I have to close my eyes for a moment. With nothing separating us, what I'm feeling is purely *him*. I let out a gasp right away, more at the shock of the sensation than anything else. My brain short-circuits, unable to focus on anything but the feeling of being filled so completely, so perfectly. A pure and exquisite torture.

"You feel," I say, "so goddamn good. *God*, I like you like this."

"What, losing my mind because you're so fucking sexy?" He hisses out a breath as I lift up slightly, then sink back down, finding a new, frenzied pace. "Because you tasted so good that I nearly fell apart when I was fucking you with my mouth?"

I cry out, pushing my hips forward so I can take him deeper. "Am I horrible if I say yes?"

It's not just his surprisingly filthy mouth that I like. I like the way he asks me questions, the way he checks in with me. I like his soft kisses and his desperate ones. And I love watching him unravel, his eyes dark and pupils dilated, hair wild, his thumb rubbing dizzying circles just above where our bodies are joined.

And while he starts to shudder beneath me first, he makes he sure he takes me down with him.

"It isn't always like this, is it?" he asks once our breathing has slowed.

"No," I say, snuggling closer, draping an arm across his chest. "It isn't always like this."

"YOU HAVE A working wood fireplace," I say from the couch in his living room, a knitted throw draped across my legs. "I might just have to move in here."

I expect it to create some weirdness because we're nowhere near that stage in the relationship, but somehow it doesn't. Maybe we've put all that discomfort behind us, and these new versions of Ari and Russ are the most mature yet.

"That was one of the reasons I fell in love with this house." He reenters the room carrying two mismatched mugs of hot chocolate dotted with rainbow marshmallows. "Sorry about the marshmallows. You can guess who picked them out."

"I love them."

He slides onto the couch next to me, and I adjust the blanket to cover his legs, too. It's a chilly night, and the crackling fireplace is perfection. Russell's in a navy robe and I'm in one of his T-shirts, not caring that it's big on me. It all feels so domestic, a word I once thought would never be attached to a scene in my life.

It's good to see you *happy, too,* my brother said, and maybe I really am.

Russ nudges me with his knee. "You seem pensive."

"I'm peaceful, I think. There's a difference." I take a slow, sweet sip of hot chocolate before placing it on his coffee table. "I don't know. I'm just thinking about families, I guess."

"Ah. A not-at-all fraught or complex topic."

"I meant what I said about wanting to spend more time with Elodie. If you want me to."

"Absolutely," he says. "It's a wonder she turned out as well-adjusted as she is, or she's great at hiding it. Liv and I obviously didn't have a clue what we were doing." He sips from his mug. "She surprises me all the time, and she makes me laugh, and she's this whole person with fears and ambitions and likes and dislikes, all completely different from mine. She's so fucking funny, and she's smart, and it's just . . . kind of amazing."

That awe is written all over his face.

"It's obviously not without its challenges," he continues. "I had no clue what to do when she chipped her two front teeth a few years ago on vacation and it took us three hours to find an emergency dentist. Or how to help her with her math homework. And I had to see *The Emoji Movie.*"

"Was that the one with Patrick Stewart as the poop emoji?"

"You know, he did what he could with it." He glances down at the melting marshmallows in his hot chocolate. "I never had the time to decide whether I wanted kids. It just happened, and maybe it happened in a completely backward way, but . . . things are really good right now."

"I'm so, so glad," I say. "I used to worry whether everything with my mom would make me a bad parent. Around college, I started thinking it would be really great to have a family of my own someday. Obviously it would be different, and I'm sure it would be imperfect in its own way, but I want that. The imperfections. All of it."

"The imperfections can be pretty damn great."

We sip in silence for a few moments, until it occurs to me that we haven't talked about Torrance or Seth once all day, and it's a freeing thought. Maybe we found each other because of them, but what we have here—it's all our own.

"I think part of the reason I was scared to give a hundred percent in relationships was that it meant I could potentially get to that place where I might start a family," I say quietly. "I don't even know what that would look like, if I'm being honest. But with you . . . I think I could get close."

Whatever percentage of myself I was giving to those boyfriends, I realize now that wasn't nearly enough.

Or maybe it's that Russ is the first person who's felt worth it.

"Come here," he says, pulling me up against him. "I need you closer." When I rest my head on his belly, Russell pats it and says, "Is this what they mean by a dad bod?"

"I don't know," I say. "Whatever it's called—I like it. I like all of you."

"I like all of you, too. Every version." He brushes some of my hair out of the way, pressing a kiss to my temple. "I like you when you're talking about sun in the forecast." His mouth moves lower, lips fluttering over my eyelashes. "I like you when you're gleefully telling everyone to expect about a hundred more days of rain." A kiss at the corner of my mouth. "But I like the real version best. And I feel really fucking lucky that I get to see that Ari Abrams."

When our hot chocolate gets cold, we can't bring ourselves to care.

27

FORECAST:

The calm before the storm

"YOU TEND TO say 'right now' a lot," the talent coach says. Matter-of-fact, not an admonishment.

On a monitor in the weather center, I watch myself deliver last Tuesday's forecast. *Right now you can see showers moving in this evening. And we'll take a look at your seven-day forecast right now.*

I haven't had this kind of feedback since my college internship at one of KSEA's rival stations. Melissa, the talent coach, is exactly right. Now that it's been pointed out, it seems so obvious. But I'm not embarrassed—I'm learning.

"And you had a lot of slides too fast there." Melissa points to the screen. "You could slow those down a bit more."

"Absolutely, I can see that now. Thank you."

Across the studio, Torrance is chatting with one of the camera-men. She catches my eye and gives me a wink, and I bite back a smile.

For the past couple weeks, I've floated. My body forgets to be tired when I wake up at two in the morning, and even when Russ is sleeping over or I'm at his place, he never complains about my early starts, though he drags me back into bed on more than one occasion. He's always too warm and too attentive for me to decline.

We spend most nights together the weeks Elodie is at her mom's, sometimes at my place and sometimes at his, though I'm partial to his fireplace. When he has Elodie, we eat gelato in the park and help her with her homework and make plans to see *The Prom* when it comes to Seattle in the summer. I take my antidepressants and never worry whether he's watching me, never hiding.

Since the reorg, the station has been calmer than I could have hoped. Caroline Zielinski has been easy to work with, both understanding and decisive in all the ways a manager should be, always open to one-on-one meetings and eager to help me set professional goals. And as a mentor, Torrance is . . . well, she's still Torrance.

But she's also more available than she's ever been. We have regular lunch meetings, and she spends more time telling me about her career trajectory, even teaming up with me on a big air pollution story we'll debut on Halestorm once it's ready. It's a role she takes seriously, and I'm grateful for that. Even if sometimes I still have to sneak into her office to water her plants.

And I have a mentee of my own, a bright and eager junior from the University of Washington named Sophia who dreams of one day working for the National Weather Service.

Melissa and I go through more clips, and she pauses to replay a moment where I'm speaking too quickly and have to gasp for air. "It's a weird one to have to remind people to do, but don't forget to *breathe*," she says with a smile.

And I'm really trying.

• • •

ELODIE'S MUSICAL IS at the end of March, and she gives it her all, transforming into the wicked Queen of Hearts, complete with an evil cackle I didn't know this sweet twelve-year-old was capable of. We wait for her in the middle school lobby with a bouquet of red roses, to match the song, and after hugs and congratulations, she hands the flowers back to Russ and promptly asks if she can grab burgers with her friends. She's still in full makeup, red hearts painted around her eyes, face smudged with white.

"Thank you love you bye!" she calls as she practically flings herself out into the parking lot with the Cheshire Cat and Tweedle Dee.

"I'm not sure I've ever felt older than I do right now," Russ says with a laugh as we follow her outside.

I lean in and rub a hand along his stubble. "That would explain all the gray hairs."

"But they make me look distinguished, right?"

"Extremely." I drag his face down to mine, and it's in that spark of a moment that it happens. There's nothing grand or explosive about it—just Russ and me in a middle school parking lot on a Thursday night.

I think I love him. It's the softest starburst of a realization that turns my world blurry at the edges. We've barely been together a month, and yet there it is, golden-bright and impossible to ignore.

I keep it there in my heart, a little secret, but I imagine he can tell in the brush of my lips, the way I tuck my face into his neck and whisper jokes into his skin. Until I'm ready, that's how I'll let him know.

And then the blizzard hits.

28

FORECAST:

Ninety percent chance of absolutely everything going to hell

SNOW IN SEATTLE is a unique phenomenon. People tease us about not being able to handle a few inches of snow, or about the year our former mayor infamously botched the city's response to a major snowstorm, plowing only the streets in front of his house and other city officials'. The roads were sanded instead of salted, and for two weeks, Seattle essentially ground to a halt. I was thirteen and fascinated by all of it, even when I couldn't feel my hands after my mom, Alex, and I dug out our car.

Half the time, though, Seattle only gets an inch of snow or less each year, and it's those off years that are a little less predictable.

This year, the flurries start on a Sunday evening in early April, and I'm overcome with that maybe-school-will-be-canceled-tomorrow giddiness I knew so well as a kid, especially as I sip coffee from a KSEA mug at Russell's house, fireplace crackling next to me. When I wake up at two, it's dark and quiet and perfect, the entire street blanketed with white.

"Come back to bed, weather girl," Russ whispers. I'm on the afternoon shift today, a rare day we can go in together, and yet my internal clock forced me awake at my usual time.

I open his curtains wider and jab a finger at his backyard. "But . . . snow."

"It'll still be there in a few hours," he says, but he pushes himself into a sitting position, hair mussed and eyes half-closed, and we watch the weather for fifteen minutes before falling back asleep.

I've stopped fighting with the hair straightener and let my hair be wavy on camera, at first because it meant more time with Russell, and then because I realized I liked it better that way. It's a small change, but it surprised me to learn something new about myself in my late twenties: that I prefer my natural waves.

I will never not love a snow day, especially when I'm working. I only get a few more hours of sleep, waking up early to make breakfast for Russ and me, fumbling my way around his kitchen. It's worth it for the way his face lights up when I present my attempt at snowflake-shaped pancakes, dusted with powdered sugar.

At KSEA, we have a tradition during the first snow of the year, if we're lucky enough to get one. We call it the Winter Olympics, splitting into teams for a full day of office games and food, low-partition walls be damned. I don't recall ever seeing Torrance and Seth participate, yet there they are, Seth immersed in a game of paper clip relay in the middle of the newsroom while Torrance clutches a stopwatch and tracks points on a whiteboard below the bank of TVs. She got here early to set up and rearrange desks, and I have to wonder if she's making up for lost time.

"Really coming down out there." GM Fred Wilson has finally decided to emerge to impart this bit of wisdom. He helps himself to a brownie from a spread in one corner of the newsroom. "Don't go too wild," he calls to us, shoving a bite into his mouth as he disappears down the hall.

Russell appears by my side, shaking his head. "Like clockwork," he says before his gaze shifts to Torrance. "I've never seen her like this. I've never seen either of them like this."

"I think they're *happy*."

"Happy, or high on cheap grocery store cake?"

"Those two things aren't mutually exclusive."

Eventually, we'll have to do real work, and there's a *lot* of work waiting for me in the weather center this afternoon, but this is such a welcome shift in the station atmosphere that I can't tear myself away quite yet. I'm dreaming, too, of the sledding Russ and I have planned later today at the huge hill near his house.

I'm taking my turn in paper clip relay—a contest to see which group can straighten a paper clip the fastest, and you can only start after the person in front of you finishes—when Torrance approaches me, twirling a whiteboard marker between her thumb and index finger.

"Ari, do you have that press release from the city about their new snowplows? I think they sent it back in January. My inbox is a mess right now."

"Oh—yeah. Of course." My computer's on the other side of the room, so I tug my phone out of my pocket, search for the original email, and forward it to her. Then I turn back to the game, fingers poised on the wire of my paper clip. In front me, Hannah Stern is about to finish. Russell's on the other team, headed up by sports anchor Lauren Nguyen and undefeated, and I'm not about to let them win.

"What's this?" Torrance's voice has turned colder than the temperature outside.

"It should have all the info in it," I say. "Though we may have to make some calls to the city with everything going on today."

"No. Not that." She shows me her phone just as Hannah whirls around, signaling that it's my turn.

When I read what's on the screen, I drop my paperclip.

"Ari?" Hannah says. When I don't respond, she grabs my fallen paper clip and thrusts it into the hands of another player.

I didn't forward her the original email. Because the original email, I'd forwarded to Russell with a joke about how to scheme Torrance and Seth back together.

And that's the one currently in her inbox.

> Re: City of Seattle Snowplow
>
> Idea: trap T and S somewhere during a snowstorm. Reunite them through forced proximity + the beauty of Mother Nature.

Hannah's team lets out a collective groan. Lauren Nguyen remains undefeated. Or at least—I think so. I can't process anything except the words on Torrance's screen, and even those are starting to blur.

I stagger backward, away from the games and the sweets and my cheering coworkers, this scene I never thought Torrance and Seth would be part of. It's too much. Too loud. I squeeze my eyes shut, concentrating on my breathing. *No. No, no, no, no, no.* They were finally making progress. Finally *happy.* If she finds out what we did . . .

It's entirely possible I've never paused to consider the consequences, and now that they're chasing me out of the newsroom and down the hall, weighing down my legs and tightening my lungs, I'm deeply, thoroughly terrified of them.

When I open my eyes, I'm hunched against the wall across from the kitchen, right beneath a photo of a thirtysomething Torrance accepting an award for excellence in science reporting from the American Meteorological Society. I've walked by this photo hundreds of times, and it's an award I've always hoped I'd have a shot at one day. With a single click, I may have shattered that possibility.

The real Torrance, the mentor I've wanted so desperately to be proud of me, followed me out here, and I have never felt as insignificant in front of her as I do right now.

"It's not—it's not what it looks like," I stammer. "T and S, that's—" My unhelpful brain goes blank.

Torrance crosses her arms over her burnt-orange dress. "Really? That's all you have? You improv every day in front of thousands of people, and that's the best you can do?" When she holds out her palm, I realize I'm still clutching her phone. "Meet me in my office. And bring Russell."

I wait until the sound of her heels clicking across the linoleum fades, and then I do my best to compose myself. Deep inhales and shaky, strangled exhales. A hand to my heart, willing it to slow down.

There has to be a way to salvage this. I can't accept what might happen otherwise.

Back in the newsroom, Russell's immersed in a game of desk hockey with his sports colleagues. "Hey," I say, tapping his arm, the single word sounding unsteady. Now is the time for my star performance. Pretend everything is okay when it's on the verge of collapsing.

He grins at me, and for a moment, I feel a brief flash of annoyance toward him. Shouldn't he be able to tell that this isn't a real smile? "Hey. Do you want to play?"

"No, I—" I break off, unsure how to phrase it. "Torrance wants to see us in her office."

"O . . . kay?"

The collar of his blazer is wrinkled. I smoothed it out this morning before we left for work, but it's a stubborn slice of fabric. For some reason, focusing on this helps ground me.

"Russ." I take hold of his arm, towing him a few steps away from his friends, who are too distracted by the game to notice my imminent panic attack. "She *knows*."

His face goes pale, jaw slack. "Oh. Oh shit." His eyes flick to Torrance's office, as though he's imagining what kind of fate awaits us. "How did she—?" he asks, but I can't muster a response.

I keep my gaze trained on the space in front of me as we walk toward her office, a hand around the lightning bolt at my throat. It's a wonder I don't yank it right off my neck. There's no way anyone in the newsroom could guess what's going on, and yet I'm half convinced it's written all over my face. BETRAYED BOSS'S TRUST. WORST MENTEE EVER. DISGRACED METEOROLOGIST SEEKS NEW JOB.

Seth is already inside, leaning against Torrance's shelf of meteorology books with two succulents for bookends.

"Take a seat," Torrance says, gesturing to the two chairs on the opposite side of her desk. "And please. Feel free to start explaining yourselves at any time."

I'm grateful when Russell speaks first.

"It was originally my idea." He sounds solid. Sure of himself. "The night of the holiday party, both of us were feeling a little down about everything that had happened, and, well . . . I suggested trying getting the two of you back together as a joke. I don't think either of us were serious about it until a few days later."

"Did you even know each other back then?" Torrance asks. "I don't remember you spending much time together at the station."

"We'd always been friendly, but it wasn't anything more than that until the party," I say, my voice small and fragile. "We bonded because of you and Seth. Because—because you were so preoccupied with each other that KSEA became such a hostile place to work."

While she knows this about KSEA, I wish my words sounded less trivial. Less selfish. We may have begun that way, on a mission to make work better for ourselves, but that was before we really knew the Hales. Torrance has become more important to me than I ever imagined, and I don't want to have betrayed what little trust we had. If I can explain myself, clear my conscience, maybe she'll understand.

Because it's not just friendship, this bond between us. She's slid into something of a mother role for me, and it might have happened even before I started working for her. When my mom was unavailable, Torrance's show was where I sought comfort. When I was hired at KSEA, I craved her approval—I still do.

More than that, I want her to be happy.

"The reason we started spending time together," I continue, urging more confidence into my words, "is because at first, we wanted the station to be more peaceful. For everyone. And there were these moments that seemed like you two had unfinished business. That it wasn't really over. At the holiday party, you talked to me about Seth almost like you missed him. And when he asked you to dance before, well, you know, there was something there. We thought—we thought maybe it wouldn't be too big of a leap to try to get you back together."

"The swing dancing at Century Ballroom," Torrance says, as though it's starting to click for her. "Was that you?"

Russ nods, his elbows resting on his knees, fingers linked. "It wasn't anything nefarious. Most of the time, we were just trying to talk to you two. Get to know you better. So there was the swing dancing, the couple's massage, the yacht—"

"I did wonder how they knew the precise menu of our first date."

"And that succulent," I add. "The one that showed up without a card. We . . . wanted you to wonder if Seth sent it."

I glance over at Seth, who's still examining Torrance's books, silent and stoic. He'll explode any second, I'm sure of it. Or maybe we'll get another sign: **KINDLY REFRAIN FROM MATCHMAKING YOUR EMPLOYER. –SHH.**

Torrance purses her cherry-red lips. "I see." It's impossible to interpret her expression, and it hits me, then, that I don't know her well enough to know all her moods yet.

"I'm so sorry. You know I'm grateful for everything. For the mentorship. And I—I'm glad we've become friends, even if the way it started was . . ." I grasp for the right word. "Slightly dishonest."

"And you thought we'd never find out?" she says, a new fierceness in her tone. "You could interfere with our personal lives and get us to tell you deeply private things? Manipulate us like that and face zero consequences?"

Russ tugs at his wrinkled collar. "You'd already brought your personal lives into the office and made them everyone's business," he says calmly, and Torrance goes quiet.

I can't get over that word. *Manipulate.* In this moment, the wrongness is so clear that I can't believe we really did it.

Except—it worked, didn't it? There were times I was so sure it would fall apart, but it hasn't. They have their second chance, and they've been *together* for at least the past month, maybe longer. We helped mend something everyone assumed was broken. We interfered, but we didn't hurt anyone. That has to be a net positive, even if it means we're no longer welcome at this station.

Torrance's silence is worse than her icy questioning, Every time she's been furious at Seth, I've been all too aware of it. But I never considered what it would feel like to have that rage directed at *me*.

"I—I can start looking for work at other stations," I say. "If that's what you want me to do. There has to be a way for us to make this right. I know we crossed about a hundred lines, but you have to believe we were doing it for the right reasons."

Russ is nodding vigorously. "What Ari said. We just—" He finally meets my eyes, a soft, worried blue behind his glasses, and it's enough to reassure me. Whatever happens, he's in this with me. We'll get through it together. "We just want to make this right."

Seth still hasn't said anything. But his shoulders—they're *shaking*. Holy shit. He can't be *crying* . . . can he? If so, this is even worse than I thought. Maybe it won't be enough to leave KSEA. Maybe I'll have to find a job in another part of the state. Or switch careers completely.

When he finally turns around and catches Torrance's eye, the two of them burst out laughing.

Laughing.

Russ looks stricken, and my expression of horror must match his. Seth doubles over, clutching his stomach, and Torrance is laughing so hard she has to grip the edge of her desk.

"What's going on?" I ask, a little afraid of the answer. Surely, the two of us being fired isn't that comical?

When Torrance can finally breathe again, she brushes blond strands from her face, swiping away what might actually be a tear. "It's funny," she says, "because we've been doing the exact same thing to you."

29

FORECAST:
WINTER STORM WARNING.
Prepare your disaster kit

WE DON'T LAUGH. Not the way Torrance and Seth did. Technically, Seth is still laughing, body shaking from the sheer hilarity of it all, and now it's clear why he wasn't looking at us—because he didn't want to give anything away.

We were doing the exact same thing.

Russ is frozen in the chair next to me. When I open my mouth to speak, nothing comes out.

"I'm sorry," Torrance says. "I couldn't resist playing around with you two at first. It makes sense now, that you started spending time together because you were plotting to get us to spend time together. That was the only reason we noticed how well you got along, and that made us start pushing you together, too. It's rather amusing, when you think about it."

"*Push* is a bit of a stretch. Let's call them gentle nudges." Seth rolls up his sleeves, as though all that laughter was some athletic achievement. "Nothing big. When Ari fell down the stairs, Tor was ready to take her to the hospital, but with Russell there, and given the way you two had been acting at Century Ballroom . . . we saw an opportunity. So we encouraged him to go instead."

That night: when my feelings for him became impossible to ignore. When I let him in for the first time, guided him through a museum of my past.

"What else?" My voice trembles. "What else did you do?"

Torrance holds her palms up, this expression of guilt I'm also not used to seeing from her. "I may have disconnected your computer from the internet a couple months ago. I didn't know for certain that you'd go ask Russell if you could use his, but you two were friendly, so it seemed worth a shot." And I did. I did exactly what she'd wanted me to do. "Then when he started feeling seasick on the boat, I gently nudged you to go home with him. And we tried to bring the other person up in conversation as much as we could. That's it."

"Oh, and the storm-chaser story," Seth puts in. "With that tsunami guy."

"Typhoon," I say quietly.

"Right." Torrance snaps her fingers. "But you two were together by then, so that was just icing on the cake."

Gentle nudges—okay. Except . . . something significant happened each time they meddled. That night in the hotel, our first kiss, Russell asking me to watch Elodie.

None of that feels gentle to me.

"It was clear you two liked each other," Torrance continues. "You seemed like a good match. And what do you know, all that scheming brought *us* closer." Her mouth quirks upward. "You helped us without even realizing it."

"Just so we understand all of this," Russell says, "you're not upset with us?"

"I'm not." Torrance glances at her ex-husband and current boyfriend, and there's a real tenderness in the way she looks at him. "Seth?"

He shakes his head. "How can we be? You helped us realize we weren't over." He strides over to Torrance, draping an arm around her shoulders, and while it should be a casual, effortless move, I don't miss the way Torrance's eyes flutter, like she's still processing the adrenaline rush of his touch. I know that feeling. I love that feeling. "It was a hell of a way for us to get here, but . . . it worked."

"Our therapist is going to love this," Torrance says.

God. They're even going to therapy together.

This is surreal. They know the truth, and they're not furious. I have whiplash—my emotions have done multiple one-eighties in the past half hour.

"I guess it worked for both of us!" Seth gives Torrance's arm a quick squeeze before moving toward the door. "I'm going to see if they have any more of that champagne out there."

And with that, he hustles out of the office.

"I don't know what to say," I admit. It should be comforting, maybe, that we were all conspiring together. But something about this wild truth has melted away all the magic from this snow day. I want to be as eager for a champagne toast as Seth, and yet there's a hockey-puck-sized lump in my throat I'm not sure how to explain.

"I take it this means we're not out of a job?" Russell asks. It sounds as though he's across the room, maybe in a different office or different building, and not in the chair next to me.

"Definitely not," Torrance says. "And I'm no longer managing Ari directly, but I see no reason why HR would need to know any of this. What you two did . . . it doesn't change the kind of journalist or scientist you are." She lets out a sharp *ha*. "In fact, it was almost its own form of journalism. But I think we can agree on honesty from here on out?"

"Yes," I say emphatically, pushing my boots hard into the floor to keep myself present. "Of course."

"Then I'm going to get back to that party!" She springs to her feet, scrunching a hand through her curls to return them to their usual state of perky perfection. "Let's do another double date soon, okay?"

We're quiet after she leaves, reality settling over us like a too-thick blanket. I'm desperate to know what's going through Russell's head, and if it's anywhere near as chaotic as what's going through mine. And yet I have no idea where to start. Probably with getting out of this chair. Out of this office.

"I think I'm going to take a walk," Russell says. "Ari?"

He doesn't need to ask me twice. I zip my coat and follow him outside, my brain buzzing, buzzing, buzzing.

"I'm still trying to process this," Russell says when we're a couple blocks from the station, ducking out of the way to avoid being caught in a snowball fight. "How exactly did they find out, anyway?"

My boots crunch into seven inches of snow. This street is usually jammed with cars waiting in traffic; today, only a handful of drivers are braving the roads. "Torrance saw an email we sent months ago, where we joked about trapping them somewhere in a snowstorm. I fucked up when I was forwarding it to her. I'm sorry."

"It probably would have happened eventually," he says, and I can't tell if there's a hint of blame in his voice.

"It doesn't matter how they found out. What matters is that they've been doing the same thing. They've been manipulating us, the same way we were manipulating them."

"Gently nudging," Russell says, borrowing Seth's wording.

"Sure." The single syllable hangs in the air between us, shifting the temperature. Dragging it far below freezing.

It should make us equal. Two couples meddling in each other's romantic lives—logically, they should cancel each other out. A mathematical relationship equation. I'd love to laugh it off like Torrance and Seth did, but this revelation has shaken me in a way I wasn't expecting. We don't have the foundation Torrance and Seth did. We weren't building on something that was already established, albeit shattered. We were starting from scratch.

"We're both a little on edge right now," Russell says. He runs his fogged-up glasses along the hem of his jacket before putting them back on. "Let's calm down, maybe get coffee and talk?"

I can calm down over coffee.

But first, I want some answers.

"I need to know," I say as we pass the Thai restaurant where I had lunch with Torrance a few weeks ago. Across the street, some asshole kid swipes a carrot nose from a fresh snowman and chucks it into an alley. "That night on the retreat. If Torrance had gone with me to the hospital, would we have gotten as close as we did? If she was the one who took me back to my room afterward and helped me with everything?"

"Would we have—what?"

"I'm just trying to imagine what might have happened. If she hadn't *gently nudged* you to take me, would we have started dating?"

"It's not like the alternative was me letting you lie there in pain." Russell's voice is knife-edged now, his steps in the snow more deliberate. "She didn't track me down and beg me to take you. I was glad to do it—I cared about you, and I wanted to make sure you were okay. She also didn't ask me to go to your room or bring you vending machine candy. Or talk to you."

The memories of that night flood back, warming my face even out in the cold. "I understand that," I say softly, wanting to keep that memory untainted.

"Do the details really matter? We're together, and it took us a while to be able to express what we both wanted, but we're finally *here*. Can't that be enough?"

I want it to be, so desperately I can almost feel the desire thumping next to my heart like a brand-new organ. He looks so lovely out here in the snow, the pink tip of his nose and ice crystals caught in his hair. I want to say *okay* and live out our snow-day fantasy. We'll go sledding and build a lopsided snowman and drink cocoa in front of the fireplace. When we settle into bed, he'll sweep my hair away from my ear and tell me again how good it feels to be around me.

"And my feelings for you didn't suddenly materialize that night," he continues. "I didn't realize I cared about you after they disconnected your computer. And I didn't instantly want to kiss you after Torrance told you to go home with me when I faked being seasick. I'd liked you for a while, Ari. I want to think we'd have gotten together eventually, whether I went with you to the hospital or not."

Truthfully, I don't think he's wrong about that. But it's not that we wouldn't have found a way to each other. It's that there's been something keeping us together, preventing us from veering off course. And whether it's a gentle nudge or a firm shove, it doesn't change the fact that someone was pulling strings, making sure we never strayed too far from each other.

"This whole time, we've had a safety net," I say. "We don't know what we're like without that."

Russell brushes his arm against mine, and I want it to feel warmer than it does. "Then we'll figure it out. I meant what I said that night we were at your mom's—I'm ready to do this with you. That hasn't changed."

But.

There's that tiniest *but* at the back of my brain, the one I can keep quiet some of the time but now refuses to listen, the one hell-bent on self-preservation. The one that asks, *But what if he's wrong? What if that changes?*

What if he can't handle you on your dark days?

"But—you haven't seen me at my worst yet." It's only when I say it out loud that I realize it's a genuine fear of mine. "Because it's not pretty, Russell. It's sitting-in-a-Taco-Bell-parking-lot-and-trying-not-to-cry levels of not pretty. It's can't-even-do-basic-tasks levels of not pretty, and I rarely know when one of them is coming. Is that something you're ready for?"

He pauses, leaning against the side of a coffee shop with a sign that declares, **CLOSED FOR SNOW!** with a doodle of a heart-eyed snowman. "I—I think so," he says, stumbling over his words. That uncertainty—it'll turn into frustration. Anger. Dismissal. In my mother's relationships, it always did.

"That's when we'd need that safety net, but it won't be there. It's just going to be you and me and my fucking brain conspiring against me." That troublesome organ I've never been able to fully trust. The thing that distorts reality and cloaks it in the grayest fog.

If there isn't someone there to catch us, what happens if we fall?

When we fall?

"I think we should take a few steps back," he says again. "We'll have clearer heads if we come back to this in a few hours, or maybe even tomorrow."

No. Taking a few steps back would mean becoming the girl I know how to be: reassuring, quiet, pliable. The one I've always been, who puts other people's hurt above her own. He doesn't get it. He can't simply take a few steps back from my mental illness.

"That's what I'm trying to tell you," I say, digging my hands deeper into my coat pockets now that we've stopped walking. "I may not have a clearer head tomorrow. I can't control it. Not completely. It doesn't matter how many steps back we take—I'm still going to be this way. I'm still going to have depression, and sometimes it manifests in ugly ways. No matter how content I am at any given time, it always comes back. And I've learned to accept that."

The way he's seeing me now is the realest I've ever been with him. Uncensored, all the fear and negativity out in the open. I've been standing in the sun for so goddamn long that when I blink, I see painful, too-bright bursts of light.

We're too much, my mother says. It wasn't a singsong in real life, but that's how it sounds in my memory.

Russell's features are pinched, and I can't tell if it's because of the cold or because he doesn't like what I'm saying. There's no *I like all of you, every version* here.

"What?" I challenge, fully aware I'm pushing too hard but unable to stop myself. It's for the best—I'll know before we get any deeper that this won't work. We might be too deep already. I throw my arms wide, ignoring the snap of pain when my elbow bends too far. "You don't like me like this?"

"That wasn't what I was going to say." This puts him on the defensive, too, his arms tightly folded across his chest. Armor. "I really don't want to say the wrong thing here, okay? I want to tell you we'll get through it together because we care about each other, and because we want to make this work. But I've never done this before, either. I've been more open with you than I have with anyone in a long time. But this is—you're—" He breaks off, as though trying to hold himself back from saying it, but then goes for it anyway. "You're not acting like yourself right now. You can't blame me for being a little taken aback."

Not acting like myself.

If he only knew.

"And you know me so well after spending a couple months together?" I fire back. "This *is* me, Russell. And this is exactly why I don't show that person to anyone."

"That wasn't what I meant," he says, and there it is—a thread of irritation in his voice.

There's a limit to how far I can push him, because there always is. I'm already spiraling, my mind taking me down a familiar path.

He can't handle this.

Handle *me*.

"I don't think I can do this." The words claw up my throat, but it has to be done. I have to put them out there, save myself while there's still time.

"This conversation?"

"All of it."

The sentence lands across its face with all the sharp edges I've been so good at hiding. Russell's back slackens against wall, the tension leaving his face in one great exhale. And then all at once, it returns—his mouth turned down, a crease reappearing between his eyebrows. A hard swallow.

"Ari—" he starts, but I cut him off.

"We should get back to work."

He stares at me for a long moment, unblinking. His eyes, that brilliant blue I love, have none of the light they usually do. "If that's what you want," he finally says.

Even when I'm breaking his heart, he's good to me.

I force myself to want it, the way I've forced all those smiles and compliments and bullshit positivity. With any shards of optimism I have left, I try to straighten my posture and project sunshine, but my body isn't listening. It won't budge.

"Yes," I say, still fighting with my shoulders, with my mouth, with all the noise in my head. "Please."

I hate that I say it.

Worse, I hate the way I believe it.

He trudges back to the station first, leaving me alone and shivering in the snow.

30

FORECAST:
Near-apocalyptic darkness. Avoid leaving home at all costs

IT SHOULDN'T BE a shock that the next day is a Dark Day.

That's the thing about depression. You can know it's there, know it's part of you, but you can go ages without seeing it. It lives with you, an invisible roommate, up until the time you start sinking, and then it sprawls itself across your couch and kicks its feet up on your coffee table and uses up all the hot water. Never pays its half of the rent, either.

You can be okay for months, for years, before it creeps back in, telling you lies like *you will always feel this way* and *no one will love you because of it* and *why bother.* Once, you could tell they were lies, but now they weigh down your shoulders and take up space in your lungs. Sometimes they come out of nowhere. Other times, some grim event helps yank you back to that dark place.

And god, you are so fucking exhausted, so you let it happen.

I beg weekend meteorologist AJ Benavidez to cover for me and spend the rest of the day under my weighted blanket. Depression has made all my breakups rough, but there is no comparison to this one. I could wrap every ounce of heartache a man has made me feel into one devastating package, and it still wouldn't come close to the aftermath of Russell Barringer.

The snow has turned to rain, and for once, I'm not thrilled to see it. By Tuesday afternoon, when the snow has become piles of gray slush and the gutters are overflowing, I've watched a season and a half of *America's Next Top Model*, which I thought would be comfortably nostalgic but has only shocked me with how problematic it was. Still, damn it if I don't hold my breath for the photo reveal at the end of every episode, and it's nice to feel something.

I'm about to hit play on a go-see episode when an alert pops up on my phone, letting me know I have an appointment with Joanna in two hours. *Shit.* When I saw it there at the beginning of the week, I almost laughed to myself, assuming I wouldn't have much to talk to Joanna about. *Nothing to discuss! Everything's swell,* I imagined saying, because a few days ago, when everything was different, I could see myself becoming the kind of person who used the word *swell* in casual conversation.

I want to go to therapy even less than I want to be on camera wearing a dress made from human hair like the models did in Cycle 14, but I drag myself out of bed. And only partially because it costs $120 for a same-day cancellation.

Once I get there, wearing sweatpants that say GOOD VIBES ONLY on the ass that Alex got me as a joke gift years ago and a scarf so long it doubles as a blanket, I'm less chatty than usual. Joanna has to pry the breakup out of me, though I guess the pants probably gave it away.

"Do you think," she says between sips of tea, "that maybe you were looking for a reason to end it? And this realization about the way Torrance and Seth interfered in your relationship gave you an out? You could tell Russell that you were questioning whether he could handle you at your worst without a safety net, because they gave you a reason to do that?"

I burrow deeper into my scarf-blanket. Joanna is the only one who won't judge me for being a mess. "Why would I sabotage myself that way?" I ask. We're twenty minutes into our session, and I've only just begun speaking in complete sentences.

"You tell me."

"He said I wasn't acting like myself, like whoever I was in that moment wasn't someone he found particularly appealing."

"What do you think he meant when he said that?"

"That I'm a terrible, draining person to be around," I say. "That there are limits to the time he wants to spend with me, and he'd rather I be the happy-go-lucky person I am on TV."

"Even I know you don't believe that," she says, which makes me let out a low grumble because she's not wrong. "You haven't always been that person with him, have you? That happy-go-lucky person?"

"No. I guess not."

"I think," she continues, "that maybe he meant that both of you were surprised and stressed out. And that maybe you needed some time to decompress and sort through how you felt about Torrance and Seth having played a small role in the beginning of your relationship."

"That's what he kept saying. That he wanted to take a step back," I say. "And it felt like what he was really saying was that he couldn't deal with me, the way I was."

"Hmmm." Joanna draws out the syllable. "I wonder if that was his way of working out, in real time, how *he* felt about everything. He was telling you what he needed, which unfortunately happened to be the opposite of what you were telling him you needed."

"Which means there's no point in trying to make this work. We want different things. Opposite things."

"I actually think that ultimately, you wanted the same thing: reassurance from the other person that you two were going to be okay. And, well . . ."

"Neither of us got that."

"Right."

I sit with that for a moment, distantly annoyed by how comfortable these GOOD VIBES ONLY pants are. "So are you saying it *doesn't* make us incompatible, the fact that we wanted to approach that situation in different ways?"

"What it seems to me is that you were focused on trying to get a very specific reaction from him," she says. "That was the easiest out, the quickest way to justify how you feel about relationships—and justify why you've hidden your depression and your history with your mother. This was the validation you've been looking for, even if you weren't aware of it. And that made it okay to shut down this relationship, even after you were open with him."

"Isn't that what I got, though? That validation? He hasn't exactly been blowing up my phone, letting me know I misunderstood him, that he was wrong and that I can be as grumpy and bitter as I want to be around him."

"I can't pretend to know what he's thinking, but I imagine his reasons for not blowing up your phone might be pretty similar to the reasons you're not blowing up his. He has a past, too, Ari. Do you think it's possible he's also feeling vulnerable, having shared everything he shared with you?"

"I . . . hadn't considered that," I say, which makes me feel like a self-centered piece of garbage. She's not wrong. I was so focused on my depression in that moment that I had no space for any of what he was going through.

"So I think it's up to you," Joanna says. "Do you want that easy exit route? Or do you want to do the work, even when it's hard?"

Here is what I'm certain about, the belief that has guided me most of my life: I don't want to turn into the mother I grew up with.

The mother who can change, I remind myself.

"I'm not sure yet," I say honestly.

Joanna's question lingers in my mind the rest of the week.

31

FORECAST:

Clouds parting to reveal the earliest signs of an epiphany

"LET THE ARTIST focus on her vision," Cassie says as she drags a paintbrush along my face. "You need to respect the process."

My niece and nephew are constantly picking up random phrases slightly too sophisticated for five-year-olds—see: gentleman caller, although I'm trying not to think about a certain sports reporter—and it's the cutest thing. When I showed up at the house and asked where his parents were, Orion calmly informed me, "Having an existential crisis," and Javier hurried to the door, assuring me he was fine, that he was just anxious about hearing from the chef he was trying to poach.

Then the twins asked if they could "give Aunt Ari some tattoos," and Alex and Javier agreed as long as I was game for it and they used washable paints.

Now Orion's perched on the leafy green rug next to me in Cassie's jungle-themed bedroom, focused on the lightning bolt he's drawing on my arm. "Hold still, Aunt Ari."

"I promise you, I'm trying."

Alex appears in the doorway, leaning next to a wallpapered giraffe. "Things must really be bad, because Cassie is making you look like some kind of swamp creature."

"It's probably an improvement."

"Oh, it *is*," Cassie assures me, the brush tickling as it swipes across my nose.

Somehow, I made it to the weekend. A small blessing: my schedule hasn't overlapped much with Russell's. Torrance and Seth, on the other hand, seem to have given up any pretense of acting like they're not madly in love. Yesterday morning, there was a jug of oat milk in the fridge with a heart-shaped sticky note on it, and I spotted them cozied up in Torrance's office in the afternoon.

"Let's give her a break from tattoo parlor," Alex says. "Papa needs some help making *pastelitos de guayaba*, if you want to—"

They've already scampered out of the room.

"Nothing motivates them quite like sugar." Alex sits on the bed next to me. I scoot over to give him more room, catching my reflection in the elephant-shaped mirror. And . . . yeah. It's a good thing these are washable paints. "You looked like you needed rescuing." Then he takes another look at my face and doubles over laughing. "I'm sorry, I don't know if I can take you seriously when you look like this."

I shove him. "Swamp creatures need love, too!" I've told Alex everything, and while he didn't judge me as harshly as I thought he might, there was plenty of older sibling headshaking. "Just don't ask me how I'm doing. Because that's been my whole week, and I still don't have an answer."

"Well then, guess I'll—" He makes a move to stand up.

"I'm just trying to talk about myself less! This is *growth*."

"Who *are* you?"

"A complete and self-actualized human being," I say, even if it isn't wholly true. I'll get there. One day. I think. "How are *you* doing? With Mom?"

"That is a good question." He considers it, as though wanting to make sure I get the most honest answer. "I'm okay. Good, even. Trying to stay hopeful, with a dash of realism. I really want her to be part of Cass's and Orion's lives. Both of us do."

I nod my understanding, hoping he gets exactly that.

"I don't know if it's because I was older, but I think it hit you harder than it hit me," he says. "I've wanted to be there for you in all the ways I can."

"You have been," I tell him, because it's true. My whole life, Alex has been the constant. As much as I can count on cloudy days in Seattle, I can count on my brother.

"Even when I'm preoccupied by two little monsters who never stop begging us to feed them?"

"Especially then," I say, shifting my arm to try to smear blue paint on his face, but alas, it's already dried. "This might sound strange, but how did you know you were ready for this?"

"The twins? We were never ready. It's a myth. You can think you're ready, but then they show up and throw your life into chaos. A good kind of chaos, but still complete and utter chaos. You could read all the parenting manuals and take all the classes in the world and still have no idea what to do when it's three in the morning and they won't stop crying."

"I was actually thinking something else." With my head, I motion in the general direction of the kitchen. "Marriage. Love. All of that."

"*Oh.*" Alex scratches at his reddish beard. "That one, I knew I was ready for. One could even say I was ready the night we met."

Of course, I've heard the story a thousand times. Alex was with a group of friends at a swanky downtown restaurant, and it was Javier's first day on the job. When a steak arrived at the table nearly burnt to a crisp, Javier rushed out to apologize, and after his friends left, Alex kept ordering small plates off the menu. Each item emerged from the kitchen undercooked or overcooked or missing something or oddly formed, and each time, Alex asked to speak to the chef.

By the end of the night, Javier had grown frazzled almost to the point of hysteria—he always says it was a miracle he managed to keep that job—though he couldn't deny the spark he'd felt whenever he dropped by Alex's table. And Alex had started falling in love, too.

"I get that you were instantly drawn to him," I say, "but how did you know he was . . ."

"The one?" Alex fills in.

"I was trying to think of a non-corny way to put it, but yeah."

He smiles, and it occurs to me that he and our mother have the same one: wide and unabashed, slightly crooked on one side. I'd been used to my mother's forced smiles—maybe I even learned from them—and it wasn't until Shabbat that I realized how long it had been since I'd seen a real one.

"Somehow, it doesn't feel corny when you're in it. I want to say I knew that first night because how romantic is that, but it took a little more time." He goes quiet for a moment, lost in thought. "We could talk about anything—that was the first sign. I loved the person I was when I was with him, and we had the same values. Of course, that didn't mean there weren't things that annoyed me about him. No one's perfect, obviously. But those things didn't matter when I considered everything that made me love him.

"It's still scary as fuck, though," Alex continues. "Putting your heart out there and not knowing whether the other person will be careful with it."

"So what you're telling me is that you can be ready, that you can want it, but it still might make you so anxious you want to throw up?"

"Yep. Buckle up, baby sis."

I can't help wondering, though, if it's already happened. I felt certain I was falling in love with Russell. What would have happened if I'd told him? Could that have saved us from the fight, or would it have only made it worse?

Javier races up the stairs and bursts into the room, cream cheese streaked across his apron, brown eyes bright. "It's happening," he says, almost out of breath. "We got her."

Alex leaps to his feet. "You did? I knew you would!" And he pulls his husband in for a kiss.

It's a relief, really, to have this break from my issues, a celebration with guava pastries and sparkling cider and too many photos of my faux-tattooed face I hope my niece and nephew don't use as blackmail someday. I've lamented the loss of not just Russell, but Elodie, too, and that split-second dream of a family. I know it doesn't mean I won't ever have one. But for a moment, I could see myself fitting into theirs, and I've been reluctant to admit how much I loved the way it felt.

This is a reminder that there's hope out there.

A reminder that my family isn't just me, even when I've felt the loneliest.

I'M PULLING INTO my apartment's garage—I drive now, and it's glorious—when I catch someone waiting outside the building. At first I assume it's another tenant's guest because when do I have guests, but as I inch into my narrow spot—less than glorious—I realize it's Seth.

He holds up a hand as I get closer, weekend casual in khakis and a gray sweater, hair still meticulously styled.

"Seth?" I ask as I shut my car door. "What are you doing here?"

"Sorry to surprise—" His dark eyes widen, and he gestures to his own cheek. "Are you okay?"

I clap a hand over my face. I scrubbed at it as well as I could at Alex's, but some of the blue lingered, giving my face a sickly hue. "My niece and nephew had some fun with paint earlier."

"Ah." A glance between me and the apartment building. "Do you think we could talk for a moment?"

My stomach prepares to reject the pastelitos. "Did you and Torrance—? Is everything—?"

"We're fine," he says quickly. "We're great, actually. I just came here to talk to you because, well . . . I realized we've never talked that much."

Despite how surreal it is to see Seth Hasegawa Hale in my garage, I invite him upstairs, where I become intensely aware of the messes I haven't cleaned up: plates in the sink, blanket spilling onto the living room floor, snack wrappers poking out between the couch cushions.

"I'll just, uh, tidy this up a bit," I say, rushing around and grabbing as much junk as I can. "Do you want something to drink, or eat, or . . . ?" I'm relieved when he says no. "Sorry. I eat all my meals on the couch, pretty much." I slam the dishwasher shut, praying Seth doesn't report back to Torrance that I have the eating habits of a twenty-year-old stoner.

"Patrick does, too. Dining tables aren't really a thing for your generation, huh?"

"Guilty. What will millennials kill next?" It's a cheap joke, but it gets me the pity laugh I was hoping for.

I motion toward the couch, and the two of us sit down.

"So . . ." he says, drumming his fingers on one of my pillows, the drawn-out syllable underscoring the fact that we have never had a solo conversation. Even when we were at that hockey game, which now feels like it happened years ago, we were buffered by Russell and Walt. Plus, there was very clearly something going on around us, and here there isn't, unless you count the empty bag of chips I attempt to casually kick under the couch.

He closes his mouth, and for a moment, I think he might get up and leave. Forget what he came here to say because it's just too awkward.

"I wanted to check on you," he says finally. "How . . . are you doing?"

"Oh. I'm okay?" Despite telling my brother I didn't want to talk about it, the question doesn't feel nearly as panic-inducing, coming from Seth.

"I know you and Tor have become close, and I can't tell you how much it means to me that you and Russell helped us like that." He's been staring at his shoes, sleek suede slip-ons, but now he turns his attention to me. "Perhaps it wasn't the most professional thing to do for your bosses, but as you know, I'd never gotten over her. Maybe we'd have found our way back to each other on our own, but maybe not. I think we really needed this boost."

"It wasn't as noble a mission at the beginning as you're making it out to be." I feel compelled to remind him of this.

"However it happened," he says, more confidence in his voice now, and maybe I see a glimmer of the man who used to want to be on camera, too, "I'm glad it did. And I wanted to thank you."

"You're doing well, then?" I ask.

When he grins, his whole face lights up. "We're better than we've ever been," he says, smoothing out some stray threads on my pillow. "We've even talked about going on vacation together this summer. And you and Russell . . . ?"

There's something familiar in the way he says it. A feigned nonchalance I recognize all too well. After what happened in Torrance's office, I know that Seth is a terrible, terrible actor.

That's why he's here. To help Russell and me.

"We're . . . not together anymore," I say. "It's for the best. Really."

"I don't know about that." Seth places the pillow behind his back, and I want to tell him there's unfortunately no comfortable position on this couch. I've tried them all. "He's been different at work. Still professional, of course, because that's Russ, but there's something off about him. A spark that's missing."

"I doubt it's because of me."

Seth just raises his eyebrows, like we both know that's not true. "A wise person with questionable taste in snack foods once told me that if something's right, if it's meant to be, then it's worth bending a little. I don't know all the intricacies of your relationship, and I don't want to overstep—"

"A first for any of us," I put in, but he doesn't laugh.

"For five years—longer, really, since we weren't happy for a while before the divorce—I was too proud," he continues. "Too stuck in my ways. If I'd realized that earlier, maybe we would have gotten back together sooner."

"Or maybe you'd never have split up."

He considers that for a moment. "Maybe we needed to," he says, "to learn that it was possible to become whole again." A pause. "Maybe none of this is relevant. Maybe what you two are dealing with is quite different. But in case any of it means something to you, I wanted to let you know."

"Thank you. I—I appreciate that," I say, wanting so badly to view this as the glimmer of hope Seth intended it to be.

"Well. That's all I came here to say." He gets to his feet, dusting off his pants. "Oh, and I think you have a Funyun in your hair."

• • •

"IT'S LOOKING GREAT," the doctor says, gesturing to my X-ray on her computer. "I can't see any evidence of the fracture. I'd say you're healed."

"Completely?" I stretch out my left arm, flexing my fingers. "There's still a little pain when I type for long periods of time, and I don't have nearly as much strength as I do in my right arm."

"That might be the case for a bit longer," she says. "Let us know if it gets worse, but as far as we're concerned, the fracture has healed nicely. You're good as new."

It's strange, leaving the medical center without another appointment on the books. Even stranger: how badly I want to tell Russell. There's too much I want to share with him, both large and insignificant—that Javier got his chef, that somehow my GOOD VIBES ONLY sweatpants have become my favorite article of clothing, that Seth was *at my house* and I lived to tell the tale.

But I don't.

And after a while, even the dullest whisper of pain fades away, and then it's just a memory.

32

FORECAST:

Thick layers of existential fog beginning to clear toward the end of the week

AVOIDING RUSSELL BECOMES a game, and if we were keeping score, I like to think I'd make it to the championships. Aside from our mostly opposite schedules, I've become stealthy, coming to the station with a full face of makeup so I don't run into him in the dressing room, doing most of my work in the weather center, eating lunch at my desk or with Torrance.

Two weeks after the Winter Olympics, we collide in the kitchen. I'm washing out my mug and he's come in for a coffee refill, his own mug dangling from the crook of his index finger. BRING THEM BACK, the mug says, along with a logo for the Seattle Sonics. The mug is so Russell that it makes my heart ache.

"Oh—sorry." He backs away from the coffee maker, which is a full five feet from the sink. "Did you want—"

"No, you go—" I say, both of us stumbling over the other's words.

Forcing myself to take a deep breath, I shut off the water and turn around, letting my damp hands flap awkwardly to my sides. "Hey."

"Hi."

Even when we've passed each other in the newsroom, I've tried my best not to get a good look at him. He's been a blur, a sketch, a blueprint of a person. But here in front of me, all those details that make him Russell fill my senses to the point where my knees go weak.

He's in a forest-green blazer and blue button-up a shade lighter than his eyes, a shadow of scruff along his jaw. It doesn't look amazing. I don't want to grab the lapels and press myself against him and sniff his neck. That would mean I'm not over him, and I have to be over him. At the very least, I have to be on my way there.

Otherwise, it would mean that he could have my darkness and my sunshine, and despite everything Joanna said, everything Seth said, I want a guarantee he won't run when it gets hard. I want something I know he cannot give me: certainty.

"This doesn't have to be awkward," he says gently.

"I don't think I got that memo."

"It was on one of Seth's latest signs. Garamond, size twenty." Then he makes a face. "Too soon?"

I match his grimace even as I'm biting back a laugh. "Maybe a little."

"But . . . you're doing okay? I saw you on Halestorm on Friday. You were great."

I try not to think about what it means that he watched it. Probably just that he works here and it's difficult to ignore, not that he misses me.

"It was great," I say. He's jammed my neural pathways so thoroughly that in this moment, I can't even remember what Torrance and I talked about.

"Great." Apparently, neither of us knows another adjective. He turns to the coffee maker. "I'm just going to—"

"Right, of course," I say, and for a few blessed seconds, the sound of coffee grinder covers up our awkwardness. Once it goes silent again and he sips his coffee, I force a smile. "And you're doing okay?"

The sudden question must startle him because he misses his next sip entirely, sending liquid spilling down his shirt.

I snatch up a paper towel, running it under the faucet before approaching him with it. "I hope that wasn't too hot. You have to be on camera later, right?"

"It's fine, it's fine. This is why I always have spare shirts." He sucks in a breath as I dab the towel against his chest. "I can, uh—handle that."

"Right. Right." I pass him the paper towel, taking care not to let my fingertips graze his. I take a few steps back until I bump up against the counter. "Have a good show. I'm sorry about your shirt."

"Thanks." He's halfway to the door when he says, "Ari?"

I turn around. "Yeah?"

"I'm not angry with you," he says, and I hope I'm not imagining the softness in his expression. "Just wanted you to know that."

THAT EVENING, I brave rush-hour traffic to meet my mom at Redmond's outdoor mall.

If you think it's weird to have an outdoor mall in a place that's cloudy 80 percent of the year, so does everyone who lives in Redmond. I don't remember Redmond Town Center being built, but my mom does, and every time we went there as kids, she'd shake her head as we pulled into a parking spot, muttering, "I don't know what they were thinking."

My mother's already at the coffee shop where we agreed to meet, a place with cushy chairs and enormous pastries and folk music playing in the background. I order a blueberry muffin and take a seat next to her in a corner, beneath some watercolors of the Pacific Northwest on sale from a local artist.

"How was work?" she asks. She's dressed business casual, tapered black pants and a coral peplum blouse. Her hair is loose and wavy, and she hasn't dyed out the grays yet. I wonder if she will. "It's strange to ask that after having seen you on TV. I always thought I'd get used to it, but nope, it's still surreal to turn to channel six and see your face."

"You still watch me?"

"Almost every day," she says, and perhaps this shouldn't surprise me, but it does.

I tell her more about the recent reorg, Torrance, my mentee before asking her the same question. It'll never not feel a bit odd: my mother and me, two adults discussing our jobs.

"I'm actually looking at retiring within the next couple years," she says, "which is exciting. I didn't realize it would be a possibility this soon."

"Retiring? Wow." My mother is almost sixty, but somehow I can't picture her retired. Maybe because I've always viewed her through a certain lens retirement doesn't quite match up with.

Because now, of course, my mind swims with what she'll do with all that free time. If she'll have enough to keep her busy, or if she'll fall into one of her old patterns.

"There's this guy in my department who's been there about as long as I have, and we've been talking about it a lot lately."

If there will be another man to drag her down.

"Talking," I repeat, and her brow furrows as she gets my meaning.

"I think I want to take it slow. I'm not exactly eager to jump into anything serious. I haven't been single in a while," she muses. "It's kind of nice—nicer than I was expecting, if I'm being honest, only to have to worry about myself."

"That's good. I'm really glad." I pick at my muffin, still feeling as though we're only skimming the surface of what I want to be discussing. I have to just go for it—I'll regret it if I don't. "And you're . . . feeling okay? If that's all right to ask?"

She goes quiet as she excavates a chocolate chip. Apparently, it's easier for us to converse with baked goods than with each other. Because this is another thing my younger self wouldn't have believed I'd do as an adult: talk to my mother about our mental health.

"Some of the medications had harsh side effects at first," she says, not making eye contact. "That was something I was anxious about. I told the doctors I'd go to therapy the way they wanted me to, but no meds. I wanted to still feel like myself, you know?"

My heart sinks. "Oh."

But she shakes her head, and when her dark eyes meet mine, there's a conviction there I've never seen before. "The therapist I talked to—she was amazing. And I had the time to do some research, and, well . . . the meds on the market today are quite different from the ones I heard about growing up. I thought they would numb me completely. That I wouldn't feel anything at all. I always thought it was better to feel too much than to feel nothing. But I wanted to get better so badly, Ari. I was terrified, but I agreed to give medication a try."

"Mom. I—I'm proud of you." The words are fragile, delicate things. I'm not sure if I've uttered them aloud. If I'm allowed to be proud of her.

"That was why they kept me so long. They wanted to make sure they had the right meds, the right dosage. But now that my body's gotten used to them . . . I'm not sure I can even express how much they've helped. Not an instant fix, of course, but—well, you know." A bite of her muffin, and then: "It makes me wish I'd started them much sooner."

I let that hang between us, processing it. All the things I've never said bang against the inside of my brain. All the things I used to want from her.

"Yeah. I do, too."

"Ari," she says, but I'm not finished.

"I'm glad you've gotten help," I continue, touching the tiny lightning bolt around my neck for a shock of courage. "Truly. And I know it's an intensely personal thing. A personal journey. But I've been wondering lately . . . why now? What made this time *the* time, instead of when Alex and I were kids? Because sometimes it makes me feel like—like we weren't enough for you back then."

I watch her absorb this, the way her dark blond eyebrows draw together and her mouth parts before she closes it, as though carefully considering what she wants to say. Then she drapes her hand over mine, giving it a squeeze. "Arielle. Ari. I've wondered that every day since I left the hospital. I wish I could answer that question for you in a way that was even remotely satisfying." She runs her thumb along my knuckles. "I don't know why it took so long. Maybe it was having the right therapist—the one I'm still seeing. Maybe it was feeling like this whole group of people cared about me and wanted me to get well. I don't know why it took me getting to that awful place I was in before I was admitted to the hospital, and I am so, so sorry.

"Eventually, you deal with something for long enough that it becomes such an intrinsic part of you, and you can't imagine yourself without it. You accept it, maybe because you think you deserve it but also because you're scared that if you tried to change it, it wouldn't work. It feels easier to live in that somber place because you don't know who you are otherwise, and you're worried about putting in all that effort without a guaranteed outcome."

"You knew I got help. You knew it worked for me."

"I did," she says. "And I'm even happier now that you were able to realize it so much sooner than I was. I'm sorry . . . if I let you down, by not getting you help earlier." At that, her voice wavers and she pulls her hand away, seeming to almost fold in on herself. My mother has never looked as small as she does in this moment, and it is absolutely staggering. "I'm not trying to make you feel sorry for me. I'm trying to give you an explanation—not an excuse."

"Being a person is hard," I say simply.

"The hardest," she agrees. Then she looks back up at me, the full weight of her gaze pinning me to the chair. "You and Alex were enough. I think . . . I think the problem was that *I* was the one who wasn't."

I'm not sure how many times my heart can break during the course of a single conversation.

"Mom. *No*," I say, though there were moments I thought the same thing. Moments I now know were warped by my own depression. My own brain waging war against me.

"Somehow I got lucky that you and Alex turned into such incredible people. You both have jobs you love, jobs you're great at. Javier and the twins couldn't be sweeter. And maybe you and Russell? Is that becoming serious?"

"It's not really anything at the moment," I say quietly. "For a while, I've had these distorted ideas about relationships. Dad was never able to handle us, and—"

"I have to stop you there." Her voice is firm, firmer than I've heard it in ages. "Your father was a sorry excuse for a human. He couldn't deal with me, fine. But disappearing from your life and Alex's? In no world was that okay."

I pause to consider that. When I think about my dad's abandonment, I always frame it in terms of my mother. He discarded all three of us because *she* was too much. That's what I have always believed.

But this is the truth: he made the decision to leave us.

My mother is the one who chose to stay.

"It's just—it's been easier to blame you, I guess." The words are nearly impossible to shove past my lips, but I keep going. "Because you were the one who was there. And ever since then . . . I've never been honest with people I've dated. I sort of felt like I couldn't be my full self, like I had to hide the less attractive parts. Until now, and then I got worried I was too honest."

"Is that what happened? With Russell?"

"Not just Russell. With my engagement, too." *And pretty much everyone before then*, I think but don't say. It's not right, I'm realizing, to attribute my problems to her. Even if that's where they started, I am in control now. Sunshine and darkness and everything in between. That's the real reason my relationships didn't work: because I was only ever giving a fraction of myself. "But it's getting better. I'm still figuring it all out."

And I hope I'm right.

"I'm so sorry," she says again, her own heartbreak creased into the lines on her face. "I wish we could have had this conversation a while ago, but I'm going to go out on a limb here and say I don't think I would have been ready. But now that we're here, I want to be part of your life, Ari. I want us to be able to talk about these things, even when it's hard. Do you think we could start over?"

I shake my head. "I'm pretty sure that ship has sailed. But . . . we could have something new. We could do better, from this point forward."

Maybe this isn't the two of us gossiping over mimosas at brunch, but it's *real*.

She drops her hand to my knee, and I am learning that I'm someone who really, really enjoys being comforted by their mother. Even at age twenty-seven. "I'd like that, Ari. I'd like that a lot."

THERE'S AN INVITATION waiting for me at home. *You are cordially invited to Elodie Watson-Barringer's bat mitzvah* is spelled out on the front in marquee-style letters.

At first I assume Russell must have sent it before the breakup, but then I turn it over and find the confident, loopy cursive of a twelve-year-old instead.

Dear Ari,

As you know, I've been spending the past year preparing for my bat mitzvah. And while it's maybe not as thrilling as the opening night of a Broadway show, I'm excited, and only partially for the presents and party afterward.

I wanted to say thank you. Again. For . . . you know. And that I'd love for you to come watch me Become A Woman, if you can make it.

I'm not entirely sure what happened with you and my dad, but I've never seen him happier than when he's with you. He was SO STOKED to go to work in a way he never has been. Like, okay, he always loves sports, but he'd spend more time getting ready in the morning. Sometimes he'd even ask my opinion on his clothes. It was cute but also embarrassing, which I guess is my dad in a nutshell.

So even if he hasn't said anything to you about it, I think he'd really love it if you came, too.

Elodie

I read it a couple more times, letting the words sink in.

Since our breakup, I've worked hard to convince myself that Russell wasn't worth my secrets. It's been easier than allowing myself to consider the alternative: that it scares me, how much he was worth it.

He's had more of me than I've given anyone else, and he might be worth risking even more. Even if he cannot possibly give me a guarantee—because truthfully, no one can. Every time I've let him in, he's surprised me by being good and understanding and all those wonderful Russell qualities I've grown to love. And I can't deny how fucking *nice* it felt, how freeing, not to wear a mask.

I've assumed anyone getting that close would eventually find a reason to leave. That my issues and past would drive them away. But that's not what happened here—I forced him away by giving in to my own worst fears. Neither of us has an uncomplicated past, like Joanna said. It was never that I was too much for him.

In fact, he's gone out of his way to prove the opposite. *I like the real version best,* he said. How could I have let myself forget that so quickly?

I stick the invitation on my fridge with a Halestorm magnet, and then with a new sense of determination and a cartoon Torrance watching over me, I open up my jewelry box and get to work.

33

FORECAST:

Partly sunny, with a chance of extraordinary courage

THE SYNAGOGUE IS new to me, a gorgeous building in Seattle's upscale Madison Park neighborhood that I'm delighted to see has solar panels. I'm instantly reminded of what I love most about temple: the way everyone seems glad to see you, even if they've never met you.

"Shabbat shalom," the security guard at the door says brightly.

"Shabbat shalom." I straighten the raincloud brooch on my modest plum dress and deposit a small jewelry box on the table of gifts inside.

"Ari Abrams, channel six meteorologist? At my daughter's bat mitzvah?" a familiar voice calls, and Liv rushes over to me, looking sleek in a black skirt suit, her short hair pinned back. "It's great to see you!"

"I was so glad to get Elodie's invitation," I tell her as she hugs me, which I was not at all expecting. "How are you feeling?"

"Like I'm about to jump out of my skin." She holds out her hand so I can see it shaking. "Of course, El's cool as a cucumber. All that theater training."

"She's going to be spectacular," I say, trying to act as though it is perfectly normal to have this conversation with my ex-boyfriend's ex-girlfriend, the mother of the girl who invited me to her bat mitzvah.

"Yes, but will I?"

I laugh along with her, then greet her husband, Perry, who introduces me to Clementine, a chubby-cheeked nine-month-old with a full head of dark hair and tiny hands reaching toward the gift table.

"Clearly has her priorities straight," says Perry, before he and Liv excuse themselves to greet more of the guests.

I take a seat toward the back of the sanctuary, behind a group of preteen girls who I'm guessing are Elodie's friends from drama. Every time someone enters, I twist around, looking for Russell, though I don't exactly want to confront him this way. This is a big day for him, for Liv, for their daughter. It's not about the two of us.

Oh god—what if he thinks I'm intruding? Overstepping?

Just when I'm deep in a spiral of second-guessing, Russell appears in the doorway. He looks, well . . . he looks dashing and perfect, because the universe is unfair. Herringbone suit, polished oxfords, the softest wave to his light brown hair. I hold my breath as he makes his way up the aisle, catching my eye for a brief moment and giving me a quizzical look. I try my best to communicate *your daughter invited me* with a few lifts of my eyebrows, but I'm not sure he gets the message.

Fortunately, the service starts shortly afterward, and the rabbi introduces Elodie, today's sole bat mitzvah, to the congregation.

Up on the bimah, Elodie's in a lavender taffeta dress, her hair curling past her shoulders. There are some nerves at first, I can tell, but then she comes to life. I shouldn't be surprised, given her penchant for theatrics. She is *riveting*, the Hebrew words like music in her voice.

The part of bar and bat mitzvahs that always makes me emotional is when the parents give their speeches. It's rare they don't cry, which makes *me* cry. Sure, I loved the party and the gifts and the dancing at my own bat mitzvah, but more than that, it was special to hear my mother talk about my love for weather. How she'd be shocked if I didn't become the next Torrance Hale.

Once again, I'm struck by how my brain kept all those good memories from me when there were plenty to choose from.

Liv goes first, with a promise that she won't embarrass Elodie too much, then immediately starts sobbing before launching into a story about a one-woman show Elodie performed for their extended family.

"It was hilarious and heartwarming and full of much more wisdom than I thought a nine-year-old was capable of," she says. "That was when it hit me for the first time that Elodie was this whole, amazing person who is definitely going to be smarter than me one day. And maybe even already is."

When it's Russell's turn to stand in front of the congregation, he pulls a crumpled piece of paper from his jacket pocket. "I wrote down some notes," he says. "But I hope Elodie won't mind if I go off-book. That's a theater joke, just for her."

Elodie groans, but she's grinning, her eyes bright.

"This is going to make her groan even more, but El, being your father is the highlight of my life. I know you don't love the baby book—yes, you better believe as many keepsakes as I can collect from today are going in there—and part of me is grateful you haven't tossed it in the fireplace yet, but it's been the most astounding thing, to see you grow up." In one quick but shaky motion, he removes his glasses to run a hand over his face, and when he puts them back on, they're a bit crooked. Then he swallows, as though trying to keep the emotion at bay, but if I know anything about Russell, it's that he won't be able to trap it inside for long.

"And even though you become a bat mitzvah today," he says, voice thick, "that growing up doesn't end. I cannot wait for everything you're going to experience. I want you to sing on a stage bigger than you can imagine, to an audience full of people who adore you. And I want to be sitting in the front row, cheering the loudest."

I dig into my bag for a pack of tissues.

Russell Barringer is a gentle, impossibly kind man, and I don't know how I felt anything other than lucky to have him in my life.

Even if he remains past tense.

"MAZEL TOV!" I say, lassoing Elodie for a hug. "You were *phenomenal.* I haven't had this much fun at a bar or bat mitzvah since . . . well, ever."

"Perfect. Exactly what I wanted: to ruin all future bat mitzvahs."

The party, which is at the JCC next to the synagogue, is Broadway themed: red curtains, a marquee spelling out MAZEL TOV, "cast photos" of Elodie and her friends hung around the room. There's even a mock Tony Awards ballot near the buffet, where they can nominate the night's best dressers, dancers, and singers.

Russell approaches from one end of the buffet, where he's been chatting with some of Elodie's friends' parents.

This is it. I can do this.

"Hi." I must suddenly forget how to act like a human being, because whatever awkward motion I'm doing with my hand is decidedly *not* a wave. Maybe I can't do this. "Mazel tov!"

"Ari. I didn't know you'd be here. I mean—it's okay that you're here, it's just . . . a surprise."

Elodie flutters her fingers, painted the same lavender as her dress. "I may have had something to do with that."

"Ah." Shyly, Russell buries his hands in his pockets. Up-close Russell Barringer in formal wear might be too much for my brain to handle.

"What my dearest dad is trying to say is that he's glad you're here," she says, giving him the least subtle eyebrow raise in the history of eyebrow raises. "And I think he's a shoo-in for best speech. Oh—that's my song!" Elodie makes a show of holding a hand to her ear. "I'll just leave you two."

As she flounces away to dance with her friends, Russell shakes his head. "She set us up," he says, not quite making eye contact with me. "I can't believe it."

"Like father, like daughter?"

"Guess so. You'd think we'd have had enough of people meddling in relationships."

"Matchmaking is an ancient tradition. A Jewish tradition, even." As if I need it to hold me up, I grasp the edge of the red curtain draped behind me, fiddling with the fabric. "If you don't want me here, I completely understand. I can leave if—"

"No," he says, his voice gentle, his gaze finally catching mine. It warms me all the way down to my toes. "Stay. I want you to stay."

I try to fight the smile threatening to spread across my face. "Okay. I will."

"You didn't have to get her anything, by the way."

"I wanted to." I tell him about the charms I found on Etsy that made perfect earrings: one that says STAGE RIGHT and another that says STAGE LEFT.

"She's going to love that. Thank you," he says. "And—thank you for coming. I'm not sure I said that yet?" The room has very much turned into a party for preteens, the adults self-consciously bobbing their heads to music most of them don't recognize. "Maybe we could talk somewhere that isn't blasting 'My Shot'?"

"Is that not the ideal background music for all serious conversations?"

This gets a soft laugh out of him, which lifts my heart higher in my chest. *We have a chance.* I just hope I can be brave enough to tell him everything that's been swirling in my head for the past few weeks.

After Russell checks in with Liv, we slip out into the hall, away from the music, past the coat check and outside. It's dusk, and out in Lake Washington, boaters are taking advantage of a rare April day that felt a little like summer, with a high near seventy degrees. I didn't even groan about it when I delivered my forecasts this week. Now that the sun has set, though, I regret leaving my sweater in the car.

"She did great," I say as we round the JCC building, settling against the wall outside their gymnasium. "A natural."

"I didn't know I could be this proud of her. It's unreal." He's quiet for a moment, and then: "You cold?"

I shrug, not wanting to be so obvious about it. Nevertheless, I savor his heat, his scent, when he drapes his herringbone jacket over my shoulders, taking care not to muss my hair. "I haven't seen this one before. I like it."

"Thank you," he says. "Had to break out something special for the occasion."

As fond as I am of his jackets, we have to move past small talk.

"Something occurred to me recently," I say. "And it's that I've been a complete idiot."

The frankness of my declaration smooths some of the awkwardness between us, and Russell gives me a half smile. It's slight, but god, I've missed it. "Well. I wouldn't go that far. And if we're being fair, I've been a bit of an idiot, too."

I press my shoulders into the bricks. "I keep replaying what happened after Torrance and Seth found out, trying to figure out why it affected me that way. Why I felt it meant our relationship was doomed. And I think I was looking for a way out. A reason this wouldn't work." I'd asked Joanna why I sabotaged myself, and now it's clearer than the most cloudless day. "I was so convinced you'd eventually end it because I wasn't who you wanted me to be that I decided to do it before you could. Because I thought that would somehow make it hurt less."

"Did it work?"

"No. It was the most fucking painful breakup I've had in my life." I want to leave zero doubt that it was the wrong thing to do. "You know I'm not used to being so open. So vulnerable. I just . . . didn't know how to handle it when Torrance and Seth told us what they'd done," I say. "But that wasn't the issue, really. I do believe we'd have gotten together one way or another. They didn't do anything that manipulated our emotions. I was starting to have feelings for you long before they intervened." God, it seems like so long ago. "When we were swing dancing? That was torture. And before that, back at the bar after the holiday party . . . I kept thinking you were cute."

And even though we've slept together, even though he knows I find him adorable and hot and fucking fantastic, he blushes at this. It absolutely ruins me. "It must have been the jackets."

"Entirely."

He shifts, propping one shoulder against the wall so he can face me. "I've wanted to talk to you for a while—really talk to you, not like what happened in the kitchen. But I didn't want to push you if you weren't ready," he says. "I'm so sorry. Everything that happened on the snow day—I could have handled it better, too. I wish I hadn't told you that. That you weren't acting like yourself. I've replayed it over and over in my head and come up with a hundred better things to say. I can't believe I said something so wrong."

"I understand. And I forgive you, " I say. "I'm sorry, too. I'm sorry it took me this long to tell you I'm sorry, and I'm sorry I broke down when they found out."

"You don't have to apologize for that," he says, inching closer. "I was serious when I told you I wanted to figure this out together. I still do. And that might mean stumbling through it for a while, but that doesn't mean I'm going to stop trying."

"I can see that now." If I weren't already in love with him, his sincerity might send me over the edge. "Thank you. For giving me that time. And—and for letting me come back."

His eyes on me are warmth and sweetness and a thousand other good things. It's ridiculous that I ever wondered whether I was in love with him when I know now that I fell a long, long time ago.

"If I can't hug you right now," he says, voice shaky, "I might lose it."

That's all it takes for every stashed-away emotion to break the surface, and suddenly I'm fighting back tears. "Oh my god, please. Please hug me." And before he can, I throw my arms around his neck, inhaling his woodsy-citrus-Russell scent, standing on my toes to press a kiss to his ear.

He holds me tightly, steadily, because Russell is always sure of himself. Sure of *us*.

"The truth is," I say against his chest, his arms at my waist, "I love that I don't have to put on a show when I'm with you. I'm still a little closed down with other people, though I'm trying to get better at that, too. But when I'm with you, it's always been natural. You've seen all of me, and that's *terrifying*. But taking the risk—it's so fucking worth it."

He kisses my forehead, thumb coming up to swipe away a tear before it falls.

"For the longest time . . . I've thought I was unlovable." The word comes out in a whisper, because I'm not sure I knew I felt that way until I said it out loud. But Russ doesn't flinch. "I didn't think you would want me if I wasn't always the best version of Ari Abrams. I didn't think you'd want the person with issues. The person who wasn't always happy."

"Ari," he says, his voice a rumble against my throat, "I'm still trying to understand how you wanted *me*."

"Because you're the best," I say simply, and I love the way it makes his gaze burn brighter.

"I meant it when I told you before: I want every version of you." A fingertip lands in the center of my lower lip. "I love every version of you."

Then his mouth is on mine and my hands are in his hair and it's impossible to get as close as I want. With every touch and stroke and breath, I tell him how I feel about him until my words come back to me.

"I love you, too," I say when we move apart and he hugs me to his chest again. "God. It's annoying how much I've missed you."

"Thank you."

"For . . . missing you? Because you're welcome."

A laugh, a gentle nudge of my arm before he drops a kiss to my forehead. "For trusting me."

Epilogue

FORECAST:

A quintessential summer day, not a cloud in the sky

"HOW DO I look?" Torrance asks as she opens the door of the dressing room. "And don't lie to me."

I sat beside her while a makeup artist worked on her face, and I was with her when she bought her dress, but nothing could have prepared me for the full effect of Torrance Hale on her (second) wedding day.

She's radiant.

"Like a powerful, exquisite sun goddess," I say.

Her floor-length cream dress is accented with gold lace at the neckline and along the skirt, and instead of a veil, she had sunflowers woven into her hair. She swapped her usual red for a shimmery nude lipstick, the rest of her makeup soft and understated. When she turns, her necklace catches the light—a jeweled sun medallion I made for her last month.

I'm wearing a smaller version of that necklace with my maid of honor dress, a golden one-shoulder gown that stops just below my knees and that I love maybe more than any article of clothing I've ever owned.

Torrance and Seth have been officially reunited for almost a year and a half. All our double dates, which we've had plenty of, have been drama free, except for when Russ and I took them to play air hockey and they got so competitive, they scared off a group of kids waiting their turn. They didn't want to rush back into anything, and it wasn't until a few months ago that Torrance proposed during Halestorm. There wasn't a dry eye in the studio when Seth raced on camera, shouted out his answer, and kissed her with so much passion, we had to cut to commercial.

Most venues were booked for the season, but given Torrance's local celebrity status, they were able to snag their favorite park, Golden Gardens, for July 28. The anniversary of their first date. And so gold and white became the wedding colors, and I somehow became Torrance's maid of honor.

Torrance beckons me into her dressing room so I can adjust the one strand of hair that's not sitting the way she wants it to, and then she helps tuck a single sunflower in my own hair, which I've left loose and wavy.

"You think I'm making the right decision?" she asks, meeting my eyes in the mirror. It's true, she's more stunning than any human being should have the right to be, but looking at the two of us, I can't quite believe I used to want to be just like her.

Being her friend is so much better.

"Marrying your ex-husband?" I say. "Yes. I think it's about time you locked that down."

She laughs, shaking her head. "If myself from five years ago could see me now . . . she'd have some choice words, for sure."

"Ah, but that's the benefit of growth."

"Maybe you should mentor me."

Sometimes it's difficult to wrap my mind around how work has changed. There's a calm in the newsroom I have to force myself not to take for granted. I'm not used to it, and frankly, I don't ever want to be. I don't want to forget how hard it was to get to this place. Maybe one day I'll start looking for a role at a bigger station, but for now, I'm more content than I imagined I could be. No pretending, no forced silver linings—that's the honest truth.

While Torrance gets ready to walk down the aisle arranged on the beach, bracketed by rows of white chairs with gold ribbons, I adjust Russ's sunflower boutonniere, which pops against his light gray tux. It's criminal, the way his blue eyes match the summer sky.

"You look incredible," he says in my ear as I link my arm through his, and what's really incredible is that it still makes me shiver after all this time.

The guests are a small group of family and friends, including Seth's many siblings, his friend Walt, and a handful of our coworkers. Patrick is Seth's best man, and Roxanne helps their one-and-a-half-year-old, Penny, scatter pale yellow rose petals down the aisle. I'm stunned to realize I know most of these people. That we've become our own family in a way I thought we never would.

"You may now kiss each other," the officiant says, and we cheer as Seth lowers Torrance into a dramatic dip.

The reception takes place beneath a white tent only steps from the shore, sunflowers at every table. "As long as I'm not watering them," Torrance said to me when the wedding planner was setting up. It's full of both excellent food and bizarre music—I'd expect nothing less from the Hales.

When it's time for the toasts, Patrick and Roxanne tag-team a story about the night Penny was born. "That was when I realized my parents might just have big, sappy crushes on each other," Patrick says, which gets a lot of laughs. Seth's mom talks about the first time she met Torrance and knew instantly how smitten her son was, and I talk about growing up watching her on TV.

"We have one more toast," Seth says after I pass back the mic, looking pointedly at Russ.

I lift my eyebrows at Russ. He didn't tell me he was giving a toast, but there he is, accepting the microphone from Seth and heading toward the center of the tent.

"Good evening," he says into the mic, as solid as if he were reporting from inside a stadium. "I think I know most of you know that Seth and I have grown closer over the past year . . . but what you may not know is that it started out with some matchmaking."

Some of the guests trade confused murmurs, but across the table, Torrance and Seth look amused. Clearly, Russ asked permission for this.

"More specifically," he says, "it started with a drunken night in a hotel bar with my girlfriend, Ari." His eyes land on me. "We wanted to improve the atmosphere at the station, but she was convinced there was still a spark between our bosses. And so we started plotting."

"Did you have any idea?" Chris Torres asks Avery Mitchell at the table next to me, and she shakes her head. Even Kyla Sutherland, our top investigative reporter, seems shocked.

"There was a carrot cake we bought because they were the only ones who liked carrot cake. A succulent we sent to Torrance with no card, because we wanted her to think it was from Seth. An impromptu swing dancing setup, during which Ari and I learned to dance, and I sweated so much, I was positive she'd lose any interest she might have in me."

A few laughs.

"Then there was a couple's massage. And a dinner cruise. But somewhere in the middle of all that, while Torrance and Seth were falling back in love . . . I fell in love, too. With the brilliant, magnetic girl sitting right here."

I feel myself glow warmer than the Seattle sun.

"It's been a good year," Russ continues. "Right? It would be really awkward if you disagreed with me."

Yes, I mouth, beaming at him.

"Both of us were over the moon when Torrance proposed. She and Seth are great together, and only partially because it might be impossible to find someone else with the same taste in music." Torrance holds a hand to her heart, pretending to be wounded. "After a lot of thought, and after asking permission from the bride and groom, I figured out what I wanted to do with this toast." At that, he turns serious, striding toward my chair, eyes never drifting from mine. He readjusts his grip on the microphone, and this close, I can see his hands shaking.

My heart is in my throat. I got a little weepy during the ceremony and had to touch up my makeup before the reception. At this rate, there'll be none of it left on my face by the end of the night.

"And it felt kind of perfect, when I thought about it. Because our histories are pretty tightly intertwined at this point, wouldn't you say?"

Torrance lets out a whoop, reaching across the table to give my arm a squeeze. I barely register it.

Now Russ is only a couple feet from me. And maybe the microphone is still in his hands, but it feels like he's speaking only to me, like we are the only two people in this tent, on this beach.

"Ari Abrams," he says. "Weather girl. I am so deeply in love with you. Will you marry me?"

It's the easiest question I've ever been asked, one that requires zero second-guessing. "Yes," I say, blinking back tears. "I love you so much, Russ. *Yes.*"

He slips the ring on my finger, a thin gold band with a small raindrop-shaped diamond, and it's the most beautiful thing I've ever seen—until I look back into his face and his eyes are shining.

Even if we're going through darkness, I know we'll always find our way back to each other.

IT'S IMPOSSIBLE TO tear myself from his side the rest of the evening as we dance and drink and laugh, people clinking their glasses for Torrance and Seth to kiss and demanding we do the same. Because it's an infinite Seattle summer, the sun won't set for another couple hours. The whole day feels like a dream. The very best dream.

"I'm not sure I can dance anymore," I say when another jazzy slow song starts up and Russ holds out his hand. I've been working on my second slice of cake. "You might have to drag my limp body around the dance floor."

"Now, I don't think that would be a good look for any of us."

Russ bypasses the dance floor, leading me out of the tent and along the shore, toward a more secluded part of the beach. I slip off my shoes, letting my feet sink into the sand, and Russ rolls up both his pants and the sleeves of his shirt. Loosens his tie.

"I can't believe that just happened." I stare down at the ring, still awestruck. "Don't get me wrong, I can't imagine a better moment than the Hales' second wedding. I'm mostly shocked you kept it a secret that long."

"It's been torture," he admits, threading his fingers with mine. "I was so worried Elodie would tell you. She's going to be so excited you said yes."

I scoff at that. "Were you really worried? Because I'm kind of obsessed with you."

He tugs me against his chest, tipping my face upward, and kissing me while Puget Sound laps at our ankles. "A little stage fright, I guess. But mostly, I'm just so happy," he says. "So. Where should we go on our honeymoon?"

"Somewhere tropical, with summer rain. Or somewhere we can see a total eclipse. Any unique weather—I'm not picky," I say. "Ooh, or we could become storm chasers. I still have Tyler Typhoon's contact info."

"The most on-brand honeymoon."

"Don't knock the brand!"

"I would never."

Both of us fall quiet, basking in this world and this moment and the sheer magic of finding that person who gets you the way no one else does.

"When I first thought about proposing to you," Russ says after a few minutes, drawing a hand through my wind-wild hair, "I imagined doing it in the middle of a rainstorm. The sky would open up, and I'd get down on one knee in the mud, probably, and we'd both still look amazing despite being drenched."

"I'm not really that predictable, am I?"

"Maybe," he says. "But it's one of my favorite things about you.

That, and the face you make when it's just starting to snow." He glances out at the horizon before his lovely gaze meets mine again. "You wish it were raining?"

I shake my head. "Perfect weather," I say, and together we close our eyes and tilt our faces toward the sun.

Acknowledgments

Weather Girl is a deeply personal book in many ways, and I am beyond grateful to everyone who's treated it with love and care. Tremendous thanks to my editor, Kristine Swartz, for immediately understanding what I wanted to do with this book and seeing its potential. You helped grow Ari's story into something I'm incredibly proud of, and I couldn't be happier with the final product.

Thank you to my agent, Laura Bradford, for continuing to be a fantastic partner in all things publishing. The team at Berkley/Penguin Random House consistently floors me with their compassion and creativity: Jessica Brock, Jessica Plummer, Megha Jain, and Alison Cnockaert. Vi-An Nguyen, I feel so lucky to have two absolute beauties from you! This is my ultimate Pacific Northwest dream cover, and I love it to pieces.

This book would have been grayer than the gloomiest Seattle day without input from meteorologists Shannon O'Donnell and Claire

Anderson. I have all the admiration for what you do—thank you so much for your time and expertise! Thank you to my sister, Michelle, who helped a great deal with the hospital details. And to the therapists I've had over the years, especially LZ: thank you for helping me understand my brain a little better.

The authors who blurbed this book: Helen Hoang, Sophie Cousens, Sonia Hartl, Annette Christie, Chloe Liese, Jasmine Guillory, Tessa Bailey, Alison Cochrun, Olivia Dade, and Julia Whelan. Your generosity and kind words mean the world to me. I'm also sending much love to Kelsey Rodkey, Courtney Kae, Auriane Desombre, and Lillie Vale, my early readers whose enthusiasm for Ari and Russell made all the difference.

As always, thank you to Ivan. I'm so glad you prefer rainy days, too.

Weather Girl

RACHEL LYNN SOLOMON

Discussion Questions

1. Did you begin this book with any preconceived notions of a TV meteorologist's job? If so, how did that change over the course of the book?

2. Were Ari and Russell wrong to manipulate Torrance and Seth? Did they ever cross a line? Given the outcome of the book, was it worth it?

3. If you could read this book from Russell's point of view, what do you think his character arc would be?

4. Ari and Torrance spend some time discussing the sexism and misogyny in their industry. Why do you think people are able to get away with treating them this way? What would need to happen for this to change?

5. How does Ari's mental health journey compare to other depictions of mental health you've read in books or seen in TV and movies?

6. Later in the book, Ari remarks that her family "isn't just me, even when I've felt the loneliest." How might she have defined family at the beginning of the book, and how has that changed by the end?

7. While this book contains many lighthearted moments, it also explores some serious issues. Would you call it a romantic comedy? What is your definition of a romantic comedy, and how does this book either reflect or contest that definition?

8. What do you think the future holds for Ari and Russell?